MISSING PIECES

OTHER BOOKS AND AUDIO BOOKS
BY JENI GROSSMAN:

Beneath the Surface

Behind the Scenes

MISSING PIECES

A NOVEL

JENI GROSSMAN

Covenant Communications, Inc.

For J.J. and J.L.—welcome to the family!

Cover image: *THE GYPSY GIRL (GAIA) Ancient Mosaic* © 2009 Tulay Over/istock

Cover design copyrighted 2009 by Covenant Communications, Inc.

Published by Covenant Communications, Inc.
American Fork, Utah

Printed in Canada
First Printing: February 2009

14 13 12 11 10 09   10 9 8 7 6 5 4 3 2 1

ISBN 10: 1-59811-643-6
ISBN 13: 978-1-59811-643-4

Ideologies separate us.
Dreams and anguish
bring us together.
—Eugène Ionesco, dramatist (1909–94)

Acknowledgments

Although writers spend a large amount of time in isolation, no writer produces a book without the help and support of a great many people. I am blessed to have a large number of truly remarkable people in my life who have encouraged my writing by letting me borrow their houses or cabins, reading early manuscripts, feeding my dog, and keeping my life going in the United States while I lived in Turkey.

With a great deal of love and gratitude, I wish to mention them here and to dedicate this book to all of them:

To the fantastic women who explored Turkey with me in 2006: Kristy Benton, Doe Daughtrey, DeeAnna and Naomi DeGroff, Megan and Deb DeLaney, Sally DeSpain, Bobbi Fischer, Kay Gaisford, Jill Homer, Sue Jacobsen, Karen Monasch, Holly and Judy Naegle, Dianne Nissle, Sharron Owens, LinDee Rochelle, and Sue Werner

To the board members of Tiny Peaces for all their hard work and generosity on behalf of the women and girls of southeast Turkey: Jill and Brad Homer, Sue and Dean Werner, Jeanne Leavitt, Naomi DeGroff, and Dave and Kristy Benton. Go to www.tinypeaces.com to learn more about how anyone can create a "tiny peace" in the world.

To my friends who share with me their vision and spirit: Cheryl Cobern-Browne, Tanya Edmeier, Shae Daniels, Shauna Phelps, Lorelei Poulton, Deb Katz, and Margaret Starbird

To my friends at the Zeugma excavation: Dr. Mehmet Onal, Dr. Jennifer Coolidge, Dr. Hugh Elton, Mustafa Aydoğdu, and Kutalmış Görkay. And to Dr. Olcay Ünver—who introduced me to the wonders of Zeugma.

To Dusty Edwards for standing in for me with my mother while I was in Turkey—and for taking care of my dog for a year and a half.

To Maxine Neville and Jane Porter for their unconditional love.

To my family members, who are always there for me and have made my life a thrilling, five-star action movie: Donna Dowd, Carol and Lynn Crosby (and Chelsea and Mitch), Ken Grider, Marilyn Willis-Grider, Zach and J.J. and J.L. Grossman, Lindsey Grossman, Mary Grossman, and Larry and Mildred Spalla.

To my Turkish friends for their insights and mentoring—and for the use of many of their names throughout this novel. Zeynep and Edib Kırdar, Tanju and Zafer Yolcu, Ali and Zahide Yıldırım, Zeynep Kılıç, Filiz Hosukoğlu, Mehmet and Guzide Öner, and Adalet and Ibrahim Akbaş. And a special thanks to Taner Yenidoğan for smoothing out the rough spots. (To all of you—I hope my deep love for Turkey comes through in this novel.)

To my wonderful editor at Covenant, Noelle Perner. Thank you for making this novel the best it can be.

And most importantly, I want to thank my amazing husband, Gary, who is my co-adventurer, my staunchest ally, and the love of my life.

CHAPTER ONE

Dulcey Moore held her microphone up against the towering ebony door of the Iraqi National Museum. She heard a key turn and a steel bar scrape across the width of the door. One after another, six deadbolts snapped into place. She hoped the mic had picked up the sound of the curator's leather soles hurrying away over the mosaic-tiled floor. Dulcey turned and faced Frank Kerzi's camera. "The locks you heard sliding into place offer too little protection far too late. Some of the most precious artifacts of Mesopotamia were already stolen from this museum during the fall of Baghdad."

Dulcey walked down two of the eight steps leading to the museum and paused. CNN rookie Christofer Barrows, whom everyone called "Tofer," quickly held up the black side of the reflector screen so Dulcey would not have to squint into the searing sun.

She looked intently into the camera and followed Frank, who walked backward down the steps. "We have shown you the treasures that remain—the gold jewelry that once belonged to Babylonian queens, bronze soldiers' helmets that survived ancient battles, and exquisitely carved marble statues—all of which are similar to the treasures that have been looted from this museum. We have shown you photographs of the stolen art and statues that are now finding their way to the underground art market to be sold by sophisticated art mafias. You heard the curator, Mahmoud al-Imam, make a desperate plea for the return of his country's irreplaceable artifacts. Imagine how you would feel if you heard that the Louvre had been looted. Imagine the world's outrage if the Mona Lisa—or the lovely Venus de Milo—were for sale to the highest bidder on the black market."

Dulcey gestured downward. "The edges of these museum steps were broken when a four-thousand-year-old bronze statue of a Sumerian king weighing more than a ton was dragged out of the museum right through that front door after Baghdad fell to American forces."

Frank zoomed in on the chipped edges of the steps.

Dulcey continued, her bright green eyes flashing with passion. "The money from the sale of this art will finance fleeing war criminals, Iraqi exiles who are now in hiding, and Saddam Hussein's government officials, who will be on the run for the rest of their lives—or until they are caught. Museum officials, private collectors, and academic institutions *must* be on the lookout. If anyone has information about any of these stolen treasures, we urge you to contact Interpol or any law enforcement agency. The Interpol number will appear at the bottom of your screen several times during this report."

Dulcey signaled to Frank to pause, then tucked her shoulder-length dark hair back under the black silk head scarf that was making her sweat like a lawn sprinkler.

"Don't forget the segue, Dulcey," Frank reminded her as the red light on his camera flashed on again.

Dulcey nodded. "Next, we take you to southeast Turkey in upper Mesopotamia—the land between the Tigris and the Euphrates Rivers—to show you the stunning artifacts that are *still* being discovered here in the cradle of Western civilization. This is Dulcey Moore reporting for CNN from Baghdad."

"Got it," Frank said, flashing a thumbs-up. "Let's get back to the hotel. It's like a sauna out here."

"Where's Asena? She's got the keys to the van," Dulcey said, squinting into the sun, feeling rivulets of perspiration slide down her back and under her long-sleeved blouse and Kevlar vest. Her ankle-length khaki skirt, Nikes, and thick white socks were all wrong for the hot October weather. But this was Iraq, and all the women journalists had to wear several stifling layers of clothing every time they set foot outside the Green Zone.

Frank set his camcorder down on a step, furrowed his brow, and made a visor out of one of his big, meaty hands. "That's our van in the parking lot across the street. But our guards are gone—and so is Asena," he said, buttoning the high collar of his Kevlar. "Looks like that bus down there's causing problems. Maybe they went to help out."

A long city bus was angled awkwardly to the east of the museum, its back bumper wedged tightly against a leaning streetlight. A tow truck had backed up and then positioned itself next to the bus's front bumper, sealing off the entire street. The driver of the tow truck sat behind the wheel, apparently oblivious to the shouts from the bus passengers. He seemed to be waiting for something. The knot of cars stuck on the far side of the bus honked in protest.

Two Iraqi security guards from the museum stood on the side-walk nearby, murmuring to one other in Arabic and scanning the street through the scopes of their AK-47s.

Dulcey squinted, searching for Asena, the Turkish woman who was their guide and interpreter. "Okay, everyone, let's get some street footage until Asena shows up." She pointed at a thin boy of about fourteen. "Frank, why don't you film that kid standing on the cooler next to the bus."

Frank zoomed in on the kid swapping Cokes for cash through the bus windows. With his camera still rolling, Frank glanced over at Tofer. The tall young man wearing an Atlanta Braves ball cap was on his knees spreading a plastic tarp in the shade of one of the museum's cement blast barriers. "Tofer, where's your dad?"

"He's down the street getting stills," Tofer replied. He frowned, holding up his father's bulletproof vest. "I can't get him to wear this."

Now Dulcey could see John Barrows, Tofer's father, standing in the stalled traffic to the west, clicking off fifty-two frames a second with his Nikon D1X, focusing most of his shots on a man directing cars away from the street blocked by the broken-down bus. John had been embedded with an American battalion during the first three weeks of the Iraq war and had lived in Baghdad for months at a time during the occupation.

"Frank, get John back here. He has no protection out there," Dulcey said, gesturing down the street.

"Get your vest on, John!" Frank shouted to his coworker, who wore nothing but sandals, Levis, and a sweat-soaked shirt with rows of bulging pockets down the front. As John moved toward an empty spot in the middle of the street, a dust devil of yellow sand began to circle around his knees, kicking up a swirl of cigarette butts and dry leaves.

Tofer shook his head again and blew out a gusty sigh. He took off his lucky ball cap and scratched his scalp under a pile of dirty blond curls. "Dad won't wear his vest because it makes it hard to get to the lenses and filters he carries in his shirt pockets." Tofer laid out John's cameras and tripod, clucking his tongue like the mother of an incorrigible child. Dulcey shook her head, then looked back at John.

Suddenly, something felt very wrong.

Frank stopped filming; his eyes panned the street. Tofer rocked back on his heels and took off his cap again. Dulcey stood statue-still, listening to the booming of her heart. All her instincts seemed to peak, creating a sensation like an electrical field that prickled over her scalp and crawled down her arms. Adrenaline raced through her body, making her feel twitchy—making her notice everything in bright detail.

The tow-truck driver shouted something and put his truck in gear. The museum's security guards stood together, shouting in Arabic and aiming their guns at the truck.

Tofer yelled, "Dad!" to the oblivious photographer in the street.

What happened next would be forever emblazoned in the memory of everyone present. For Dulcey, the memories would come as if she were seeing an amateur movie filmed with a handheld camera, each scene juddering and dissolving into the next at bullet speed with no transitions, no explanations.

First, the tow-truck driver made a wide, deliberate circle until the vehicle was pointed toward the museum. The boy who had been selling Cokes scaled a wall near the bus and disappeared, abandoning his grimy cooler and the fleshy row of hands waving money through the bus windows. The man who had been directing traffic got into a car and drove away. One of the museum security guards herded Dulcey, Frank, and Tofer together and then pushed them onto their hands and knees behind the row of cement blast barriers.

Dulcey raised her head over the barrier and caught sight of the truck driver. She saw a look of intense determination on his face as he headed straight for them. The guard who had been kneeling next to her quickly stood and shouted something in Arabic. He fired a shot. The truck's windshield was suddenly a spiderweb of cracked crystal as the driver slumped against his side window. The tow truck continued forward, moving in a slow, eerie circle, then rammed ineffectually against the side of the bus. The passengers began shrieking and stampeding, exiting through the doors on the far side.

"Dulcey, stay down!" Still filming, Frank yanked her behind the barrier by her head scarf and tried to hold her down. Then he stuck his head up and shouted, "John, get behind something!"

Dulcey struggled out of Frank's grip and saw that John was now photographing the dead tow truck driver. Blood was blossoming on the car window. "John! *Get back here!*" she screamed. John waved her off, popped an attachment onto his Nikon, and moved in closer to the bloody window.

Suddenly, a tiny panel truck with hand-painted Arabic script on its side careened around the bus through the space where the tow truck had been, jerking to a stop in front of the crash barriers.

The guards from the museum aimed their guns toward the little truck, shouting in rapid Arabic. They seemed to be ordering the driver to step out. Then one of the guards leaned into the passenger-side window, spoke to the driver, then turned around and waved the other guard off.

At the wheel was a woman dressed in a black coat and a full head covering that extended below her shoulders, just like thousands of other women in Baghdad. The woman shouted at the CNN crew in English. "Get in, and don't ask why. *Move!*"

Frank moved cautiously closer to the vehicle. "Take off your head covering," he growled.

"Hurry, Frank," she pleaded, tearing the scarf off to reveal a woman in her late forties. Standing behind Frank, Dulcey saw that it was Asena, the CNN fixer whom they had only met the night before. It was Asena's job to do anything necessary to help them get the story—including filling them in on local customs and vital facts so that their news reporting would be as accurate as possible. Dulcey noticed the distinctive silver bracelet stamped with interlocking spiral shapes that Asena had worn both days.

Tofer shouted over the roof of the vehicle, "*Dad!* It's Asena. Get in!"

John remained where he was, photographing the fleeing pedestrians and commotion in the street. Camera equipment clanked together as Tofer gathered the four corners of the tarp and crowded into the cargo hold of the truck with Frank and Dulcey. Even before the sliding door had closed, Asena had stomped on the gas pedal and began driving the little truck between two blast barriers, then down the museum's sidewalk, away from the commotion.

"We can't just leave John here!"

"We have no choice. We have to go!" Asena replied.

A moment later, they heard the explosion. A hailstorm of shrapnel came at them and blew out the truck's back window. The percussion of the blast flung their little vehicle sideways and left the crew inside deafened and nauseated. Every organ and blood vessel in Dulcey's body responded to the change in air pressure. Buildings all down the block shook. Pieces of the tow truck rained down like missiles, stabbing into the hot asphalt. Gravel and debris clattered on the thin metal roof above the crew's heads, and a cloud of gritty dust billowed around them, but Frank kept his camera rolling.

Gasping for air, Asena turned the little panel truck around so everyone could see what was going on through the front windshield. People to the west were getting out of their cars and walking around in a daze, holding their ears and stomachs, staunching the flow of blood from shrapnel wounds. As the dust settled, the CNN crew could see one of the museum's security guards lying on the steps, covered with glass and pieces of cinder block. People were running from the museum. One man knelt next to the guard, removed his tie, and pressed it against a seeping wound on the guard's neck. Mahmoud al-Imam, the curator Dulcey had just interviewed, held his head with both hands, staring at the sight before him.

Coughing violently, Asena drove slowly onto the debris-strewn road, trying to find a hole in the traffic big enough to squeeze into.

Dulcey and Tofer looked through the fringe of broken glass that had been the truck's back window and saw John lying in the street. "Dad . . ." Tofer whispered, his eyes wide with shock.

Frank put his camera down, his face pale with worry. "John . . ."

Dulcey yelled, "Go back for John, Asena!" In the chaos, Dulcey caught sight of the thin teenager who had been selling Coca Cola on the street. She watched in disbelief as the dirt-covered boy bent over John, loosened the camera strap from the photographer's bloody hand,

and tucked the camera inside his shirt. "*No!*" screamed Dulcey through the jagged opening, her face contorted with outrage. The boy quickly disappeared into the fleeing crowd. "Go back, Asena!" she pleaded.

"We can't risk that crowd!" Asena yelled back, inching ahead into the traffic.

Dulcey crawled over Tofer and Frank, the camera equipment, and shards of glass toward the driver's seat. Her knee bumped against a wooden tool box. She reached into it and grabbed a rusty socket wrench. "Asena, you do what I say or you'll be sorry. John is *my* responsibility."

"It's too dangerous!" Asena yelled back. "Let the museum staff tend to him." She muttered something in Turkish, stared straight ahead, and continued on into the snarled, honking traffic. Dulcey hiked up her skirt and squeezed between the two tiny front seats. Then she pulled herself into the passenger seat and brandished the socket wrench in Asena's direction. "How do we know you're not one of them?"

Asena stomped on the brake and gave Dulcey a piercing look. "We go back." She slammed the car into reverse and backed all the way to where John lay in the street. An Iraqi woman dressed in a black hijab, face veil, and long coat knelt next to him, cradling his head, rocking him and wiping the blood off his face with the cuff of her sleeve. John stared at his hands. *He's wondering where his camera is,* thought Dulcey as she watched blood pumping rhythmically from a gaping wound in his upper chest. Frank and Tofer slid the side door open, jumped out, grabbed John by his shoulders and legs, and carried him to the little truck.

"We've got you, Dad," Tofer said to the rag doll of a man in his arms.

"Steady, pal. You're going to be fine. Stay with us, John," Frank soothed, using the authoritative tone he'd mastered as a television announcer. John shouted in pain as the men positioned him on the hot metal of the cargo hold.

"Dad," Tofer sobbed, stripping off his own vest and shirt and pressing the shirt hard against his father's bubbling wound. "Daddy!" he screamed, his voice pinched up high.

"We'll make it better for you," Frank whispered, tucking his and Tofer's Kevlars under John's body to cushion him for the zigzag ride through the chicane at Assassin's Gate. "Ten minutes to the hospital in the Green Zone, John. You can do this."

Tofer stared at Frank. "It'll be longer than that. This vehicle doesn't have the security pass. It's back in the van. *Why aren't we in the CNN van?*"

"It's not safe," Asena said, working the wipers, frantically clearing the windshield of dirt and debris.

"We have to have that security pass," Tofer muttered, trying to slide the door open. "Let me out. *I'll* get it."

"No!" Asena shouted back. "The CNN van may be dangerous—I think someone may have put an IED under it. That is why I got this vehicle for us."

"We'll never make it through security in this thing. Give me the keys to the van, Asena!" Tofer commanded shrilly.

"Hold on, Tofer," Frank said, grabbing the boy's arm.

Asena pulled Dulcey toward her by her sleeve. "*Please* believe me," she hissed.

Dulcey knew Tofer was right. No vehicle with Arabic writing would pass through the security chicane very easily. The delay could cost John his life. On the other hand, if the CNN van had been rigged with an explosive device, none of them would be going anywhere. She looked at Asena's face and made her decision. "Don't let him go, Frank. We have to go through security in this. Our van's not safe," she said, staring straight ahead.

Asena sighed and shot Dulcey a look of relief. She drove a few feet toward the tangled traffic, waiting to take her place.

While they waited, the Iraqi woman who had been comforting John tapped on Dulcey's window, pulled her veil away from her face, and moaned like a wounded animal. The woman closed her eyes, held her cupped hands at shoulder level, and chanted a woeful prayer.

Dulcey rolled down the passenger window, reached her hand out, and touched the woman's arm. The woman opened her eyes and, with one of her still-cupped hands, wet with John's blood, pounded her chest as though she were adding yet another handful of pain to the mountain of it already inside her.

Dulcey nodded in recognition of the gesture. She stared at the woman, whose kind face reminded her of Consuela Fuentes back home in the Plano Texas Fourth Ward. The woman was dressed in the same clothing that women had worn here for centuries—since the time of Abraham, a man who had fathered her own religion as well. *This woman, a daughter of Abraham, is my sister.* Dulcey squeezed the woman's hand and moaned with her. It was the sound women all over the world made in the face of mind-numbing horror and human agony.

Just as a driver slowed to let Asena into the line of traffic, another explosion rocked the vehicle. In the parking lot across the street, a black column of smoke shot into the air. Burning car parts pelted the street and parking lot. The abandoned CNN van was consumed by fire within seconds.

The Iraqi woman wailed again and held her cupped hands toward the heavens for the both of them.

CHAPTER TWO

John Barrows died at 4:07 the next morning. By seven, his body was on a C-31 military transport plane headed for Dover Air Force Base. Sharing the ride were thirty-six dead American soldiers in black, plastic body bags. The military pilot had sent word to Tofer that he could accompany his father's body back home, but Tofer refused to go.

"Your family needs you," Dulcey said to the young man, who looked much younger than his twenty-four years. "They won't take to the idea of you staying here."

"No. Something inside me is all wrong," Tofer said, his knees drawn up against his chest, the bill of his lucky cap turned backward, his powerful arms wrapped around his shins. Dulcey could tell that rage simmered beneath his skin. "I don't want my family to see me like this. Dad would've wanted me to carry on. We even talked about it—what I would do if something like this happened . . ." He stared straight ahead. "I'm taking his place on the crew."

It was not a request. Dulcey knew that. Tofer was claiming his father's place. After several minutes of watching his eyes and the new set of his mouth, she nodded her assent. *Who could turn him down?*

* * *

Later that morning, after being examined by the military doctors, Dulcey and Frank sat in shock on a gold brocade sofa at the Palestine Hotel in shock. Since the beginning of the war, the hotel had become a gathering point for foreign journalists and reporters. A Major Thurman had asked them to wait in the little alcove off the main lobby until he called them in for a debriefing. Asena was down the hall talking loudly in Turkish to her boss at CNN's Istanbul office. Tofer had fallen asleep on the Persian carpet in front of the couch, curled around John's equipment, his head on his father's backpack. He tossed and moaned in his sleep, the straps of his father's camera cases wound around his bandaged hands.

Dulcey had bandages around her knees and hands from crawling over glass. Her skirt was torn, and her face was still streaked with dirt. None of them had had time to wash up yet. She looked over at Frank. One of his eardrums had burst, and he had a cork of cotton sticking out of it. All the crew members' faces and arms and hands were war-painted with iodine where the medics had removed bits of glass from their skin.

Reporters milled about in the once-elegant lobby, glancing at their well-known colleagues from CNN, trying to give them more privacy than they normally gave victims of terror in Iraq. A coffee table shoved up against a wall overflowed with scraggly wildflowers sticking out of water bottles and soda cans. The wall above the table was petaled with messages of encouragement addressed to the CNN crew, to Tofer, and to John's family. Other walls at the Palestine were dedicated to other dead reporters.

Frank held his head, rubbing his temples. The man had been like a father to her for years, and she hated seeing him in such pain. Dulcey sat with her arm across his back, her head resting on his shoulder, murmuring comfort for the both of them.

"I should have taken John's vest to him," Frank said for the hundredth time.

"He never wore his vest. Tofer told you that," Dulcey repeated, also for the hundredth time. "John knew the risks better than we did."

"Tofer's sister Molly . . . she's at Northwestern—her senior year, I think. His kid brother Jason's still in high school. How will they . . ." he trailed off.

"How can we work when we're grieving like this?" Dulcey asked. "Maybe we should go home, Frank—just call off the trip to Turkey and get everyone home."

Frank looked tenderly at the sleeping figure on the floor. "Even when Tofer was a little bitty kid, he had his own camera. This was his dream. And John and Sharon . . . they had such a great marriage," Frank said, exhaling a painfully long sigh as he stood up.

Dulcey's head felt waterlogged from crying, and her body was numb, as though it belonged to someone else. She picked at the bandages on her hands, peeking at the lacerations underneath.

"John told me this was his last story in Iraq," Frank continued. "He said a story about looting would be safer than riding in a convoy of Bradley fighting vehicles. He never would have allowed Tofer to come if he'd thought . . ."

"He couldn't have known. I mean, all our families know the dangers, but . . ." The faces of Dulcey's husband, Matt; their nine-year-old daughter, Isabel; and their six-year-old son, Michael, flashed into her mind. She swallowed and pushed the images to the back of her consciousness. Though Dulcey had her own weekly syndicated news show that she taped in Dallas, she took one travel assignment each year for CNN. And this year, her assignment had taken her to the most volatile place on the planet. Dulcey reached for Frank's hand. "I know Tofer thinks he wants to press forward, but maybe we need to make it easier on him and cancel the rest of the assignment."

Frank looked at the throng of people milling a short distance away and rubbed his reddened eyes for a long time. He let out another sigh that seemed to come from the bottom of his soul. "No. No, we'll finish what we came to do. Turkey's just over the border. Let's finish the job. John lost a lot of buddies in Iraq, and he went on. Tofer can always go home if he changes his mind," Frank said, straightening his denim shirt, which still had a dark smear of his friend's blood across the front. "I need to call Sharon and offer my sympathies. Tofer talked to her for an hour last night. She wanted to know every detail. Now it's my turn." His wide face drained of its usual ruddy color. He stood, stretched, and walked a short distance away, but made no move to make the call.

Dulcey sighed and looked around at the ornate, marble-tiled lobby of the Palestine Hotel, which was littered with reporters' backpacks and water bottles, trays of dirty hotel dishes, and candy-bar wrappers. Three armed and helmeted soldiers hurried down the hall toward the briefing room. Dulcey was struck again by how young they were and how grim their faces looked. Their eyes were cold—sealed over—as though they'd seen things they could never talk about.

In a conference room just off the lobby, Dulcey could see a military spokesperson giving a press briefing. The speaker was pointing to a map of Iraq on the wall. Reporters scurried in and out of the room, jotting notes, talking on cell phones wedged between chins and collar bones. Little knots of broadcast journalists stood together, filing stories over the Internet or doing live broadcasts on their laptops, which were hooked up to cameras and satellite phones. When filming their stories, the reporters would often step outside the hotel or go to the roof to broadcast so viewers could see a bit of Baghdad or perhaps a distant curl of smoke from one of the dreaded IEDs, the soldiers' term for "improvised explosive devices."

Dulcey looked across the throng of people, easily differentiating the newspaper reporters from their television counterparts. The former were generally not as attractive. Not having to appear on camera, newspaper reporters generally dressed in oversized T-shirts and wore the same sweatpants day after day. She noticed that most of the reporters were younger than she was. At thirty-five, Dulcey was glad she had some years behind her. She remembered what it was like when she was paying her dues—proving daily to everyone and to herself that she could do the job. She shook her head and thought, *If I've already paid my dues, what am I doing in Iraq?* Dulcey knew the answer to that one. Matt would have been able to come up with a few reasons of his own. And he had. In fact, that's what had started the argument they'd had as she had packed her bags to go to Iraq. Dulcey squeezed her eyes shut and tried to remember every detail of the argument.

* * *

"Always proving you're the best. That's what's been driving you all these years. Give it a rest!" Matt said as she folded the Kevlar vest CNN had provided for each member of Dulcey's news crew. "Look what you're packing, will you? Not just a blouse or a pair of jeans—or one of those nice pantsuits you wear on television. No, my wife has to pack a bulletproof vest for where she's going."

"Would you rather I just wore the blouse, then?" Dulcey taunted, holding up a thin cotton blouse from her suitcase.

"You know what I mean. That vest should give you a clue. And that vest should give me a clue—about what you value most. And it's not your family," Matt said. *The look in his eyes—like that of a cornered animal—caught her off guard. She'd rarely seen her husband as angry as he was now.*

"Ever since I was a little girl, I never backed down from a dare," she said. *"I never walked away from a fight. And I never said no to a job I knew I could do." She said the words as softly as possible, but they only further enraged her husband.*

"No one is questioning whether you can do the job! Everyone knows you're good at what you do. Who is it you're trying to impress?"

"Mom?" Isabel said, keeping Michael behind her like she did when she felt protective of him. Dulcey saw the fear in her daughter's eyes and the way Michael had stuck his thumb into his mouth, hiding behind his big sister.

She greeted her children as pleasantly as she could, then checked her watch and glared at Matt. "It's only two o'clock. I didn't know the kids were home. I took them out for ice cream last night and said my good-byes at breakfast."

"I picked them up early from school," Matt said innocently.

"You picked up some ammunition to try to keep me from going on this assignment. You know I hate to say good-bye to them. You know how Isabel gets when I leave," Dulcey said quietly through clenched teeth. She turned and smiled broadly, kneeling next to the kids. Izzy inched away from her mother, still keeping Michael behind her.

"It's all right, kids. Mommy and I are just having a disagreement," Matt said, flashing them his expensive television smile.

Dulcey felt beaten. Matt was using the kids to break her will. She was on the verge of tears, so she changed the subject. "GramMaria and Poppie Joe are taking you to Galveston. Remember? You're getting to play hooky from school for a whole week. How great is that?"

Isabel refused to be placated. "But why're you and Daddy fighting?" There was a honk outside as Dulcey's driver pulled up to take her to the airport. She was going to have to leave her family with all these raw, unsettled emotions.

"We're not fighting. We're . . . discussing," Matt said, herding the children back into their rooms down the hall.

When he returned, Dulcey was already bumping her heavy suitcase down the stairs, trying hard not to cry. Matt followed her to the front door. "Izzy's in tears up there in her room. And Mikey's angry. He's kicking things."

"You know," she said as evenly as she could manage, "those kids up there have a father. I, for one, never had one of those. Mom hardly ever even talked about him. I always had to rely entirely on myself when I was a child. That's part of who I am. That's what made me strong. Who would I be if I let everyone else in my profession take the risks while I only show up for the glory?"

"But we need you so much," Matt said. There were tears in his eyes too, but she wasn't sure if they sprang from tenderness or anger.

It wasn't as though she and Matt never fought. There were often tears and accusations, but there was always a joyful reunion after one of their spats—until this one.

Dulcey looked away. "I'm not used to being . . . essential . . . to anyone," she whispered as she got into CNN's limousine.

* * *

This argument had not come to a close. It had been cut off. Truncated. And it had left a gaping hole in Dulcey's heart. She shuddered a little, remembering her last words to her husband—words so full of unexplored meaning. The word she'd used—*essential*—she repeated it over and over to herself as she had headed toward the airport. The word had run through her mind again as she had flown to Kuwait and while she was riding in the military convoy to Baghdad with Frank. As she had unpacked her suitcase at the Palestine Hotel two days ago, she had asked herself over and over, *Am I essential to anyone? To my children? To Matt? Wouldn't they just carry on without me if anything happened to me?* After all, the children did have a father. And they had two doting grandparents and loads of cousins and other relatives. A great looking, vital man like Matt would most likely marry again, she reasoned, so the children would have a new mother. *After all, our children are adopted. The kids made the adjustment once before. They could do it again . . . couldn't they?*

* * *

Dulcey was startled out of her reverie when Frank sat down next to her on the couch. "What did you say?" she asked. "Sorry, I was sort of off in my own—"

"I said I can't put off that phone call to John's wife any longer." For the past half hour, Frank had been stretching and pacing, talking to other journalists, staring at the paintings on the walls, examining the statues in the foyer—stalling. "Okay. Here I go," he whispered to Dulcey.

"I'll be here for you," she said, patting her heart. She watched Frank walk away from her through the crowd, his cell phone against his ear, his huge shoes slapping the marble tile, the sound going soft on the plush carpets.

As Frank walked away to make the call, Dulcey saw a familiar face in the crowd. Asena Özturk walked toward Dulcey down one of the long hotel corridors, her high heels clicking briskly on the polished floor. She wore her signature silver bracelet with its interlocking spirals, which caught the light as she walked. Without her head covering and overclothing, Asena was dressed like any professional woman in the West. Three stylish blond streaks highlighted the petite woman's chin-length, auburn hair and pale skin. Now that her face was newly washed and her makeup freshly applied, Asena was all business again. "They're still looking at Frank's video in there," she reported, nodding toward the east wing of the hotel. "And one of the museum guards found the boy who stole John's camera. They are developing John's photographs as well." Asena spoke flawless English and knew two other Middle Eastern languages besides her native Turkish. CNN had depended on her during Turkey's recent fifteen-year civil war with the Kurdish rebels in the southeast.

"Did you find us a ride to Turkey?" Dulcey asked.

"Do you still want to go?"

Dulcey frowned. "CNN's been promoting our live coverage of the goddess excavation for weeks. Schoolteachers all across the world are going to show it to their students. And as far as our appeal for the return of looted artifacts goes, we can't just keep showing photographs or the bare spots in museums where they were once on display. We have to make people care. We have to show the world what's still in the ground—and what's still in danger of being looted. We have to show how a country's cultural heritage can be lost during war."

"I could not agree with you more. If you have decided to continue, we can all be on a military transport plane to Gaziantep, Turkey, at eight tonight. It will be a short flight—less than six hundred miles from here. Dr. Nash will meet us at the airport and take us to the excavation camp at Zeugma about a half hour away."

Dulcey studied the woman's guarded, distant expression and knew that Asena was no longer the animated woman who only the night before had regaled them in the hotel restaurant with stories about life in southeast Turkey. "Threatening you with that wrench was not my finest contribution toward international relations, Asena. I apologize again for the misunderstanding. I'm so grateful for what you did. And I'm so glad you kept Tofer from going back to the CNN van."

"You have already explained yourself. You were panicked. You did not understand why I was driving that unfamiliar truck and why I had abandoned you and the CNN crew at the museum," Asena said. She handed Dulcey some forms that would allow the crew to be transported by the American military.

"I really am sorry," Dulcey said, signing the forms and handing them back. "I understand everything now. Except . . . how did you get that truck? And what happened to the other two security guards CNN hired for us?"

"The two guards were with the van in the parking lot while we were inside the museum. When I came out to tell them we were finished, they told me a boy had tried to sell them a Coke and then dropped his bag of coins. The boy had had to crawl around under the van to get all his money back. After the boy left, the guards became suspicious that he had put an IED under the van. They believed he could have hidden it in his cooler and then taken it out after he dropped the coins. The guards suggested that the three of us walk to the police station around the corner and get the police to transport our crew. The police had no patrol cars and no officers to spare, so they commandeered that little truck for me from a plumber who was working nearby. I paid the guards for the day and told them to go home."

"But why?"

"To be honest, I did not entirely trust those guards. I thought they might be setting us up."

"But they saved our lives."

"Yes, I know that *now*. But because of all the confusion with the stalled bus and the traffic jam, I could not tell what was really going on," Asena said.

"Hmm. So, Asena, in the confusion, *you* didn't know who to trust either, did you?" Dulcey waited for a few seconds until she saw a tiny smile of forgiveness flicker across Asena's face. She moved over on the couch, and Asena sat down next to her.

"None of us knows who we can trust, I suppose," Asena conceded. "But it is more than that. You questioned my *honor* today. And even though I paid the guards a full wage, I am sure they were deeply insulted as well. Honor is everything in this part of the world. Without our honor, many of us would have nothing left."

Honor. Asena's word choice struck her as interesting. "We don't use that word very often in the States," Dulcey said. "It's kind of an old fashioned word like *temperance* or *prudence*."

"Honor is everything here. If you understood that, you would understand why Americans will never be truly welcome in Iraq. To have Americans here on Iraqi soil, questioning centuries of tradition and religious ideas—to have people from the decadent West dictate how life should be here in a Muslim country—is *unthinkable* to the people here. A Muslim does not distinguish between his everyday public life and his religious life. With a very few exceptions, Iraq is a nation of Muslims ruled by other Muslims."

Dulcey squeezed her eyes shut. "I'm trying to imagine what that would be like."

"I will help you. Imagine how Catholics would feel if a powerful imam and a band of Muslims took over the Vatican. Or imagine the outrage if a gang of Hell's Angels occupied the Salt Lake Temple and declared themselves the rulers over all American Mormons."

Dulcey briefly pictured a row of huge Harley-Davidson motorcycles parked outside the Salt Lake Temple and rough-looking, leather-jacketed, tattooed men and women strolling around inside, setting up offices and smoking lounges in the elegant, pristine endowment rooms. She imagined the Hell's Angels ordering around the temple workers and hiring them to help set up their headquarters. "That would be awful . . . Mormons wouldn't stand for it," she said. "But . . . American soldiers aren't like Hell's Angels. American soldiers came to Iraq to rescue the people from an evil dictator and to keep him from starting World War III. Don't tell me Iraqis would still rather be under Saddam's rule."

"That is your perspective because they are *your* soldiers. At least Saddam paid lip service to the religious rulers, and you must admit— he did keep order. Your government is not influenced by any religious leaders, and there is no longer any order in Iraq. To most Iraqis, whose daily lives are in chaos, this makes the Americans worse than a band of thugs."

"But Americans aren't trying to take away the people's religion. They're only insisting that the people themselves be given power over their own lives."

"No true Muslim wants power over his or her own life. This goes against the Koran." Asena breathed a deep sigh as though Dulcey were a slow-witted high school student. "Look. Once land has been claimed for the religion of Allah, it is Allah who loses face when that land is occupied by unbelievers. Any Muslim would gladly die to save the honor of Allah."

"So the people don't want to choose a government made up of honest, fair leaders who are accountable to them?"

Asena shook her head and looked sadly at Dulcey. "If there were democratic elections in Iraq, most people would choose to follow a religious leader and Shariah law—right from the Koran. Your words *democracy* and *freedom* do not make sense to people here. Islam means *submission to the will of Allah*. To these people, there is no honor in following the will of mere mortals."

"Having a religious leader in such a position of political power is almost incomprehensible to me. And I couldn't imagine not having the freedoms I do," Dulcey said. "And what about women? Iraqi women are now free to take off their hot, bothersome head coverings and long coats and wear comfortable clothing instead. So, why don't they?" Dulcey said, getting frustrated.

"Honor. A woman's honor is paramount. A family's honor depends on the modesty and chastity of its women. *Honor,* Dulcey, is worth more than life itself in this part of the world."

"But the Middle East is so out of step with the rest of the world. People here seem like they're stuck in the Dark Ages."

"The people consider being out of step with the rest of the world the *proper* way to live. These people feel honorable only when they reject clothing that reveals women to the eyes of men who are not their husbands. This culture only *seems* like it is mired in the past to you, because you do not understand the Middle East," Asena said calmly.

Weary beyond belief, Dulcey rested her head against the back of the stiff antique couch and mulled over Asena's words. She admitted that what Asena had said about being out of step with the world had struck a chord with her. Members of her own religion were often criticized for the same reason—for being a peculiar people. Still, nothing else the woman said had made any sense to her. At their feet, Tofer had finally drifted into a deep sleep and was snoring softly. "How could the men who killed this young man's father be considered honorable?" Dulcey said softly.

"John's killers are considered to be honorable in a culture that values honor *above* human life," Asena said. "Islamic extremists simply have extreme rules about Islamic honor."

Dulcey closed her eyes. "Maybe I do understand what you mean. But no one in the West would ever accept that definition of honor."

Asena only shook her head and smiled.

CHAPTER THREE

A few minutes before noon, Major Thurman asked the CNN crew to step into his office at the Palestine Hotel. The four crew members shuffled in and stood glumly like schoolchildren called into the principal's office. Tofer rubbed sleep from his eyes; his hair had been smashed into the shape of his ball cap, which he held respectfully in his hands now. Frank seemed distracted; his hands were shoved into his pockets, jiggling coins against keys. Dulcey hooked her arm through Asena's as they waited for the major to speak.

"First of all, Mr. Barrows, on behalf of the United States military, I extend my deepest sympathies to you for the death of your father."

"Thank you, sir."

"Will you be going back to the States to see to your father's arrangements?"

Tofer looked at the others and cleared his throat. "No, sir. I will take my father's place."

Thurman pursed his lips and nodded his admiration. "I'll get right to the point then, since all of you seem determined to go on to Turkey this evening. However, what I have to tell you may change your minds about going there," Thurman said, pacing in front of them. "It turns out that recent events were not a case of your news crew being in the wrong place at the wrong time, as with most journalist fatalities. Our investigation suggests that everything from the stalled city bus to the civilian directing traffic was a carefully orchestrated plan to assassinate all of you while taking out a minimal number of local citizens. The tow truck, it seems, was the backup plan in case the bomb placed under the CNN van didn't wipe you out. Even though you lost John

Barrows, I believe you have some alert Iraqi guards and a courageous Turkish translator to thank for your lives."

"We all did what we had to do," Asena said quietly.

"How is the guard from the museum?" Dulcey asked, remembering the man who had pushed her and her crew behind the blast wall and fired on the tow truck driver.

"He's in critical condition at the American military hospital, but he's expected to live. He told my soldiers what tipped him off—he saw the tow-truck driver praying before he drove toward your crew. The guard had been watching the driver because, despite the honking traffic and all the hot, complaining passengers, the driver never looked at the bus's engine or attached his tow bar to its bumper."

"He was probably waiting for John to rejoin us so he could take us all out at once," Frank said.

"Yes, and we believe Mr. Barrows was targeted specifically because he had photographed the man who was directing traffic onto the side street," Major Thurman said.

"Who was he?" Asena asked.

"The man directing traffic was Ahmed al Aboud, a key member of a group called Victorious Islam, or V.I. for short. V.I. is one of the training arms of al Qaeda. The group is led by Saif bin Rabeh, who was an early organizer of al Qaeda. We believe bin Rabeh now runs a safe house on the Iraqi border somewhere. One way al Qaeda gets into Iraq is through that house. V.I. also has an al Qaeda training camp somewhere in Syria, where all their new recruits are trained."

Frank whistled through his teeth. "So these are pretty bad guys," he said.

"Aboud had never been photographed before, but we knew it was him because he has a distinctive characteristic. He is missing the little finger of his right hand—courtesy of Shariah law. The story goes that his own father cut off Aboud's finger with a pair of wire cutters after his son was caught stealing a melon. He did it right at the market Aboud had stolen from, in front of a crowd of neighborhood children."

"Restoring the family honor," Asena whispered.

"Our intelligence had already determined that Aboud was likely in Iraq, heading for Baghdad. We've been expecting him."

Dulcey leaned over the major's desk. "As you know, journalists are rarely targeted intentionally, Major. The new Iraqi government invited CNN to Baghdad to help retrieve valuable national treasures. John Barrows set the whole thing up for us."

"Aboud is not an Iraqi. He's from Riyadh, Saudi Arabia—he went to Afghanistan with bin Laden to fight the Russians."

"But why kill journalists?" Dulcey asked, sitting down hard in a big, wingback chair.

"Although we don't know exactly why yet, we think someone in al Qaeda doesn't want CNN to film while the golden goddess statue is being dug up at Zeugma. They would have tried to stop you before you got to the Iraqi National Museum yesterday if that had been the sore spot."

Frank shook his head, rubbing his temples. "Zeugma is a two-thousand-year-old city that was reburied by archeologists when they ran out of excavation funds. Why would a CNN story about Zeugma be a threat now?"

"We don't know for sure, but we're working on some possible explanations," Thurman said. "We would like to ask you to cooperate with us, but after what's happened to your colleague, all of us here at command would understand if you chose to go back home to America instead."

Asena spoke up. "Cooperate how, Major?"

"We would like to assign an undercover CIA team to your film crew. We would then ask you all to proceed with your story assignment as planned in order to draw out the al Qaeda operatives who would most likely follow you to Zeugma, since they were unable to stop you here. There must be something in Zeugma they don't want you to tell the whole world about." Thurman sat on the edge of a desk and ran his thumb along the crease of his trousers, testing its sharpness.

"I need to call my boss," Asena said and quickly exited the office. Dulcey got up and stood by the window. Tofer went to her and put his arm around her shoulder. She leaned into him and whispered, "I'm sorry we got you into this. You're just an intern. We had no right to bring you into this mess."

"It was my choice to come. Dad and I discussed the risks. I wanted to work with my father, and if I hadn't come, I'd never have gotten that chance."

"We should have made him put on his vest . . ."

"No one could ever get Dad to wear his vest."

Dulcey put her hands on each side of Tofer's face and bent his head down so she could kiss the top of it. "You're a wonderful son, Christofer Barrows. And none of us will ever forget your dad." She cleared her throat several times as she fought back a wave of emotion. "I never knew my father. I can't imagine what it would be like to have one and then lose him—especially a father like John Barrows." She stepped back and examined Tofer's face, settling on his sad eyes. "You can go home, Tofer. All of us can."

"No. I want to finish Dad's last assignment. It's important. Otherwise, the terrorists win . . ."

Dulcey turned to Major Thurman. "How much danger would we be in, Major, if we went on to Turkey? I mean, I know you can't answer that with any certainty, but . . . Let's put it this way—how would you hope someone in your own family would answer the question you just put to us?"

"I'd hope any family member of mine would tell me to go jump in a lake," Thurman said with a gruff snort. "But my wife's name is Donna Thurman, not Dulcey Moore. I saw the special you did when you went undercover in that women's prison. And that story you did where you wore a disguise and bought heroin from Senator Dale's daughter. You're no soccer mom."

Dulcey was not amused by his point. "Well, in fact, both of my children play soccer, Major Thurman, so I *am* a soccer mom. My work sometimes takes me to places that aren't safe, but I always calculate my risks—and I always have backup."

The major ducked his head in apology. "I only meant . . . you go where other women have never been. And about the backup, of course we would be protecting your crew with one of the best CIA teams we have. For two years, under General Manheim at the American military base in Incirlik, Turkey, the military has been working to capture Aboud—and they want him bad."

Dulcey shook her head. "I might have been satisfied with that explanation a few days ago, Major, but you're talking to a woman who's just lost a fellow crew member, a *journalist*. Killing a journalist is like killing a Red Cross worker. Those two jobs are supposed to be *above* the fray. We're not legitimate targets. With all due respect, sir, you really can't legally ask my team to do this."

Thurman was unfazed. "Terrorists don't play by the rules, Ms. Moore. Sometimes we have to bend them too if we're going to win this thing."

Dulcey's jaw twitched like a pulse. Frank looked at her for a few seconds, then said, "Major, could I speak to Dulcey alone, please?" They went out into the hall but were forced to move into an office off the corridor, because Asena was shouting into her cell phone in Turkish a short distance away, her free hand gesturing like a darting bird.

"Don't you dare feel pressured by that challenge," Frank said. "Don't get your pride all mixed up in this. You aren't a New York rookie anymore, jumping up and down to get attention—taking assignments no one else wants. You've been there, done that. You have young kids now, Dulcey, and you've got Matt. I know the two of you are having troubles right now over just this sort of thing. What would it do to him and to the kids if they were to lose you? Izzy and Michael have already lost their birth mothers. Think about what it would do to them if they lost you after all it took to get them to trust you."

At the mention of her family, Dulcey felt weak. She thought of the looks on her children's faces before she left them to come to this hellish place. Then she thought about what had happened on American soil on September 11. She thought about the towers collapsing and the way CNN had played the scene over and over, making everyone feel the buildings were collapsing again and again. She thought about her first trip to the grocery store the day after it had happened—how she had felt like an open wound. She remembered taking extra care with everyone she met at the market that day, meeting their eyes and really seeing them—and noticing their same tenderness toward her. She recalled her rising anger and the resolve she had felt as she had gone back to work the next day. Ever since that day she had looked—really looked—for ways she could use her job as a reporter to make things better in her world. "We don't have a good choice here. Al Qaeda is a threat to us either way—here or back home. Going home won't make us any safer."

"A journalist's job is to *document* the horrors and the casualties of war, not to fight the war itself," Frank reminded her.

"And that's exactly what we've been asked to do—to carry on with our assignment as though Baghdad never happened. I don't like it either, but the major has actually done us a favor. He could have had that undercover team follow us to Turkey without our ever knowing it. Instead, he gave us a choice."

"I just don't want you to make the wrong choice because someone dared you."

"I know. You've warned me a thousand times about falling into traps I set for myself," Dulcey said. "And I won't go to Turkey with anyone who needs to go back home. And that includes you." Dulcey knew Frank's wife, Lanie, had begged him to come home and to bring Tofer with him.

"No, Tofer and I are in. We already talked about it."

"I won't put either of you at risk unless you're sure you want to go. It's the honorable thing to do—to give you a choice." *Honorable.* She had rarely used the word before. And the definition she had heard from Asena was nothing she wanted any part of. Frank was silent, massaging his temples like he did when one of his headaches was coming on.

They both turned around as Asena snapped her cell phone closed and walked into the little office where they stood. "CNN is leaving it in your lap, Dulcey. They have been advertising the live goddess excavation for weeks, so they are under a great deal of pressure to produce the segment. Charles Litton at the London bureau sent you a message. He said to remind you that this whole war was based on faulty U.S. intelligence in the first place and that you may be in no danger at all if you choose to go on to Zeugma." Asena sat on a desk near the window and turned her back to Dulcey. She seemed agitated and edgy. There was barbed wire covering the grimy window, and the sun threw rust-colored stripes across her face.

Dulcey was quiet for several moments, then she went to stand in front of Asena to look her full in the face. "You've lived practically on top of Zeugma all your life. Tell us why al Qaeda would go to this much trouble over the golden goddess."

Asena looked as though she were struggling against competing instincts. Then she directed her gaze at Dulcey. "I will tell you. But you may not entirely understand this because of—"

"I know, I know—because of the huge blank spot in my brain where the Middle East is concerned."

"Yes. But I will tell you anyway, because I have strong suspicions about what all this might be about."

Tofer appeared at the doorway, and Frank signaled him to join the group to listen to Asena's theory. Asena shut the door to the little office and spoke quietly. "The ancient site of Zeugma is on the Euphrates River. And the Euphrates has a very prominent place in Islamic scripture, as it does in Jewish and Christian scripture. There are Islamic prophecies involving the river that you should know about."

"Prophecies in the Koran?" Frank asked.

"Not in the Koran but in the Hadith—the Sayings of the Prophet," Asena said. "There is one particular passage that makes trouble for us at Zeugma. I know it by heart—it is from the Bukhari Collection. The prophecy is in volume 9, book 88, saying 235. Every time one of the imams speculates about Mohammed's prophecies, people turn up at Zeugma to hurry fate along."

"What are they searching for?" Tofer asked.

Asena went to the window and looked out at the Tigris River, sister and traveling companion to the Euphrates. "They are searching for the mountain of gold in the Euphrates River."

"A mountain of gold in the Euphrates?" Frank asked. "But the Tigris and the Euphrates start in Turkey, then go through Syria and Iraq and empty into the Persian Gulf. So, how would people know where to look?" Frank had always been the geography whiz on the team.

"I know, the prophecy is vague—as are many prophecies. It could be interpreted many different ways. But the people who search for this mountain of gold are not only interested in the gold."

Frank came over and tried Dulcey's tactic of standing in front of Asena to get a direct answer. "What's supposed to happen when the mountain of gold is found in the Euphrates?"

Asena looked into Frank's eyes. Then she looked away and shook her head. "Something very terrible will happen once it is found. The person or persons who find the mountain of gold will be considered blessed—*chosen* you might say—by Allah. Mohammed warned that people will fight over it when the gold is found. He even suggested that no one should touch it . . . in order to avoid a terrible war."

"So if someone finds the mountain of gold . . ." Dulcey said. "What happens?"

"Whoever finds it will be in a position of absolute power in the Muslim world. This person or group of persons might even be seen as the restored Muslim caliphate. The old caliphate of the Ottoman Empire was disbanded by Atatürk in 1924 when he came to power in Turkey. He thought that weakening the hold of Islam over his people would help westernize them. So basically, the central leadership over all the world's Muslims was permanently removed right here in Turkey."

"So Turkey would be the natural place to restore the caliphate," Dulcey said.

Asena nodded. "A new caliphate could finally unite Muslims from all over the world. Whoever finds the mountain of gold would be the *legitimate* ruler over a billion and a third Muslims. And perhaps more importantly, he would have an army of followers at his disposal."

"Are we talking about Muslims? Or *radical* Muslims?" Dulcey asked. "My research says only about one percent of Muslims are radical."

"As you say in America—do the math. One percent is thirteen million radical believers, who would be happy to kill or be killed in the name of Allah. That's quite an army. An unstoppable army."

It was Dulcey's turn to pace. "But how can the golden goddess be considered a mountain of gold? The goddess is in Trench 25 on the hill *above* the Euphrates. Her gold wouldn't be found in the river itself."

"That's exactly right. However, if you wanted to be considered the rightful leader of the entire Islamic world, you could take the goddess with her two-thousand-year-old gold, melt her down, and fashion some sort of 'mountain' out of her. Most of the world would not be suspicious, because most people do not yet know of her existence. No one has ever said how big the mountain had to be or how it would look. It could be a gilded painting or a sculpture of a golden mountain. No one knows how it will look."

"And when the time was right, someone could pretend to 'discover' the mountain in the Euphrates River," Dulcey said.

"It sounds to me that you've been considering the possibility of something like this happening for a long time," Frank said to Asena.

"Considering it? No. I have lived in sheer dread of it. Even though I have known about the prophecy since I was a child, it has never been a conceivable event . . . until now. That is why CNN *must* excavate the golden goddess on live television so that the whole world will know about her."

"So Muslims will not be fooled," Dulcey said, putting a hand against her racing heart and feeling a shiver ripple over her arms.

"Why would Allah choose to give power to a group that most Muslims think is evil?" Frank asked.

It took Asena a few seconds to speak. Then she swallowed hard and said, "I hate to admit this . . . but that possibility is also covered in Islamic doctrine. Muslims are taught that Allah sometimes uses 'evildoers' to achieve the goals of Islam."

"No wonder the moderates aren't protesting against bin Laden," Frank said. He ran a hand through his thinning hair, making it stand straight up, "If al Qaeda can convince Muslims they are the *legitimate* rulers of the Muslim world . . ."

"That's when we need to worry," Dulcey said.

Asena looked at each of them in turn. "Just like Jews and Christians, Muslims are examining prophecies and looking for signs—"

"Of the end of the world . . ." Dulcey whispered.

CHAPTER FOUR

After a rocky takeoff in a dark cargo plane, Dulcey and her crew gradually relaxed. The pilots had taken off without running lights and wore night vision goggles to identify any rocket-propelled grenades that might be shot from the fields below. Besides the two pilots in the cockpit, there were only two soldiers on the plane. The transport plane would pick up humanitarian supplies from the Turkish Red Crescent's warehouse in Gaziantep, then return to Baghdad with the load.

When the plane crossed into Turkish airspace, everyone breathed a collective sigh of relief. Turkey was a member of NATO and a long-time American ally. Asena stood with one knee planted in her seat, leaning toward the window and pointing into the darkness of southeast Turkey. "Right now, we are flying over the Harran Plain, where Abraham lived with the two women who eventually gave birth to those rowdy sons of his, Ishmael and Isaac. The people who live on the plain still raise sheep and goats and even dress much the same way as Abraham's family did. And there are still mud-walled houses with cone-shaped roofs made of mud that have kept Harran houses cool even in the deadly hot summers."

Frank read from Dulcey's combination Turkish guidebook and dictionary. "It says here that Muslims consider themselves descendants of Abraham's son Ishmael."

"Right, and Jews and Christians are literal or adopted descendents of Abraham's son, Isaac," Dulcey said.

Dulcey took back her guidebook and flipped through the pages. "I didn't know Tarsus was in Turkey. That's where the Apostle Paul was born. And near Tarsus, there's Antioch, where the followers of Jesus Christ were first called Christians."

"Most Christians don't know that their religion was born right here in Turkey. Somehow they think everything happened in Israel," Asena said, sighing pointedly.

"I know, ignorant Westerners," Dulcey chanted, not looking up from the guidebook.

Asena said, "Zeugma had three Christian churches by the fourth century, and the bishop of Zeugma participated in the famous Council of Nicaea, which was held near what is now Istanbul."

"Are there Christians in Turkey now?" Dulcey asked. "Or is the whole country Muslim?"

"Turkey is about ninety-nine percent Muslim. But we just flew over Mardin, where there is a Syriac Christian monastery called the Deyrul Zafaran, named for the saffron crocuses used in its mortar. Aramaic—the language of Christ—is still written and spoken by the monks there. It is their job to keep the language of Christ alive."

"Mardin? Never heard of it," Dulcey said, catching a look from Asena. "Okay, now I have."

Asena continued her briefing. "Jesus, or 'Isa' as the Muslims call Him, is a key person in Islam. Allah appointed Him to be the judge of all people in the world during the Qiyama—or end times. When Jesus comes back, He will tell everyone in the world that Islam is the true religion. Forty years later, He will die and be buried next to Mohammed, peace be upon them both."

The three Americans looked at Asena in silence, their mouths open.

"You believe that?" Frank asked. "I mean, why would he die again while everyone else on earth was being resurrected?"

"I do not know everything about Islam, so I cannot answer that. But one thing we all agree on is that all the major religions of the world believe the Messiah will return," Asena said.

"And Muslims believe Jesus will tell the world that Islam is the one true religion?" Frank asked as though he'd been told Muslims would try to convince people the earth was flat after all.

"Yes, Muslims believe that," Asena said cheerfully. "Just as Mohammed is the world's last prophet, Islam is the world's final and most perfect religion."

The pilot's voice came over the PA. "We have just received clearance to land at Gaziantep Airport. Everyone, please sit down and belt up."

The landing was a well-executed three pointer, and Dulcey felt a rush of relief to be on friendly soil. As attendants wheeled portable steps to their plane, several white trucks with red crescent moons on their sides drove up. The tailgate of the plane opened, and a swarm of workers began loading the supplies that had been donated by the Turkish people to the people of Iraq.

"It just dawned on me that your Red Crescent is like our Red Cross," Dulcey said.

"Exactly." Asena smiled."You can hardly expect people in the Middle East to do good works under the sign of a cross."

"Why is the crescent your symbol?" Dulcey asked.

"Most people think it is the symbol for Islam, but the crescent was actually used thousands of years before Mohammed. It was the symbol of the goddess Diana. So when the Ottoman Empire chose the goddess symbol for its flag, the crescent became associated with Islam." Asena chuckled at the blank expression on Dulcey's face. "You did not know? Well, do not worry, most Muslims do not know that either. It is a well-kept secret."

* * *

As Dulcey searched the crowd at the airport for Zeugma's chief archeologist, Dr. Lee Edward Nash, the glint of gun barrels caught her eye. Outside of Iraq, Dulcey had never seen so many soldiers carrying machine guns.

"Wait up," Tofer called from behind her, loaded down with the camera bags he had refused to be helped with.

"It's so nice not to have to wear the scarf and long sleeves now," Dulcey said as they walked. "Thank heaven for President Atatürk."

Asena said, "Not so fast. As you'll soon find out, southeast Turkey is a world away from Istanbul and Ankara and the western part of Turkey. Even though many of the young women in the southeast dress like rock stars on MTV, most of the mature women still cover their heads and wear long dresses and coats just as they have always done for thousands of years. It is as though they have never heard of Atatürk's reforms."

"But Turkey's a Muslim country, right?" Frank asked.

"The fact that you are calling Turkey a *Muslim* country means that *you,* Frank, have never heard of Atatürk's reforms. Turkey is a secular state. But, it is true; nearly all of our people are Muslim, and many of our women cover themselves in order to be modest and to save men from being tempted by them."

"So, it's up to the women not to tempt the men," Dulcey said. "Have the men ever heard of self-control?"

"Many women in this area also choose to cover because of tradition. Cover or not, it is your choice in this country."

Dulcey, who had had enough tradition for a few days, chose to leave her head scarf in her bag. "So, where's Dr. Nash?"

Asena looked over the crowd. "He will be here soon. For some reason, cell phones cannot get a signal at Zeugma, so I called my contact at the Birecik Dam. He saw Dr. Nash leave Zeugma a little while ago. Nash is *famous* for being late though."

The airport terminal was the smallest Dulcey had ever seen. There was a newspaper kiosk and a tiny souvenir shop on one wall. Taxi drivers stood in a group, shouting at the passengers who might need a ride into town. An old man headed toward the airport café with a huge plastic bag of bread rolls on his back. A man and a woman took a big burlap bag of potatoes off the baggage conveyor belt, plopped it onto a luggage cart, and hailed a taxi. Two teenagers in blue jeans and wearing backpacks were met by an older woman in a head scarf. The woman screamed and kissed them over and over, sobbing and holding them as though she had thought they'd been lost forever. Dulcey saw a mother with an infant over her shoulder. On the collar of its sleeper, the baby's mother had safety-pinned a tiny blue bead that looked like an eye. A covered woman with tattoos on her chin and cheeks held the hand of a little girl in a ruffled red dress. A pilot and two stewardesses in shape-hugging uniforms walked past Dulcey going the other direction, rolling their suitcases behind them.

Then Dulcey caught sight of an attractive, sunburned man in his mid-fifties who towered over the crowd of Turks. Across his brawny chest, his faded red T-shirt proclaimed, "I survived the Luxor Excavation." His dirty beige chinos revealed about an inch of skin above two ragged high-top sneakers. Amused at the sight of the eccentric-looking archaeologist, Dulcey said to Asena, "You don't have to tell me—that's Dr. Nash."

* * *

Two trucks full of Turkish soldiers positioned themselves in front and in back of Nash's battered army surplus Humvee. As a soldier opened the back door of the Humvee for Dulcey, her least favorite smell in the world hit her in the face: the smell of cigarettes. As she sat down, she noticed that the ashtray under the radio was over-flowing with cigarette butts and that Nash was now working on filling an ashtray sitting precariously between the seats on a leaning stack of books and spiral notebooks. She suppressed a grimace and tried to focus her attention elsewhere. Lengths of duct tape had been slapped over what looked like bullet holes in the front window shield. Dulcey fervently hoped the holes had been there when Nash had bought the battered old war vehicle and were not souvenirs of daily life in Turkey. She was about to say something, but stopped herself and instead studied the man in front of her. Something about him that she could not place felt familiar to her. She shrugged, deciding it was just that he was an American.

Asena climbed into the passenger seat in the front of the vehicle. In Turkey, according to Dulcey's guidebook, the front seats were reserved for drivers, staff, and bodyguards. A soldier had seated Dulcey in the VIP seat behind Asena. Frank and Tofer had taken what was left.

As the Humvee left the airport parking lot, sandwiched between the two military trucks, Nash explained that the CNN crew would be staying in tents at the Zeugma excavation camp because of the heavy security available at the site.

"We'll be staying in tents?" Dulcey asked, shooting Frank a look of dismay.

"That's right, Ms. Moore. Our tents are not the most comfortable places you've ever bedded down, but no hotel in Nizip or Birecik or Gaziantep can be made as safe for the next three days. We've got Madame Euphrates on one side of us and a good-sized hill called Belkis Tepe on the other. In 323 B.C., a general under Alexander the

Great, and later the Romans, chose this spot for a town and fortress—for the very same reasons. Zeugma can be defended."

Dulcey looked at the bullet holes again. "Defended?" she asked in a small voice.

Frank nudged her as though she were a child asking rude questions. "We'll adjust, Dr. Nash. You know how to take precautions better than we do."

Nash looked at Dulcey in the rearview mirror. "The Turkish government is very concerned about the safety of one of America's most famous journalists. They can't afford an international incident during this television event."

After a half hour on an asphalt highway, Nash turned off into a vast pistachio grove and rattled down a potholed dirt road, continuing his commentary on the history of Mesopotamia and the wonders of Zeugma. Most of Nash's lecture went unheard, however. Tofer's head nodded toward his chest. Frank dispensed a string of halfhearted acknowledgments that made him sound like a bored psychiatrist. Dulcey rested her head against Frank's shoulder, not bothering to follow Nash's rambling monologue.

Dulcey glanced over at Asena. The woman's whole mood had changed since they'd gotten into Nash's vehicle. Asena sat in gloomy silence in the front seat, her cheek pressed against the window. Whenever they hit a rough patch on the road, she would turn and try to steady the stack of books and Nash's smoldering ashtray.

After a long ride on the dirt road, Nash's Humvee followed the leading truck as it turned and chugged to a stop on a circular driveway covered with gravel. Dulcey yawned and took in her surroundings. The bright moon revealed a dilapidated, flat-roofed house shoved up against the base of a sawed-off hill. A breeze rippled through the pistachio and olive trees that sheltered the house. Next to a large clearing where an old Land Rover was parked, Dulcey could see a small cemetery full of leaning headstones.

"This is my place," Asena said, exiting the vehicle. "Zeugma is just over there behind Belkis Tepe." She pointed to the flat-topped hill silhouetted in the moonlight.

A groggy security guard ambled out from a guard shack next to Asena's house, his gun held feebly in front of him. He peered into the

Humvee, and Nash flashed him a smile and a thumbs-up sign. The guard rolled Asena's bag toward the dark house, passing a baby goat that was tied to the fence near the guard shack and a baby bottle that stood upright in the dirt next to it. The front yard was barren except for three nearly leafless olive trees, their branches scraping against the closed window shutters.

As Asena got her purse from the front seat of the Humvee, Nash said, "I hope your grandmother's all right. I know you've been worried about her. Let me know if there's anything I can do."

"That will not be necessary. We will manage just fine," Asena said, never looking at Nash. She turned toward the rest of the group. "I will see you all tomorrow at breakfast. Sleep well."

As the group drove on toward Zeugma, Dulcey raised her eyebrows and nudged Frank. "Asena and Nash don't like each other much, do they?" she whispered.

A short distance farther down the dirt road, the entourage came upon a rickety wooden watchtower and a group of soldiers standing around a campfire. A metal gate extended over the road. A soldier up in the tower trained his searchlight on the vehicle. Nash allowed one of the Turkish soldiers to poke around among the suitcases and equipment bags in the Humvee until he was satisfied. This was followed by a short exchange in Turkish, and then the soldier waved all three vehicles onto the Zeugma compound.

Dulcey's first sight of Zeugma featured the moon and stars spangling the still water of the Euphrates. The water, flanked by a distant dam, looked more like a lake than a river. The camp was perfectly quiet. A half dozen dark, sleeping tents dotted the edge of the pistachio grove. A large woven tarpaulin covered an eating area with rows of picnic tables under it and three big camp stoves at the back. Near the canvas wall behind the camp stoves was a big bookshelf made of cinder blocks stacked between long boards, overflowing with shabby books and rumpled magazines. Beyond the dining tent, Dulcey saw two Turkish soldiers tending another campfire. Four more walked along the edge of the water. All of them carried M-16s. Dulcey felt strangely comforted by the presence of all that firepower.

"You're looking at a wide spot in the Euphrates River, Ms. Moore, just before it goes over the Birecik Dam three kilometers downstream,"

Dr. Nash said, standing by the open tailgate. Frank and Tofer picked up their bags and wandered off with one of the soldiers. Since some of Zeugma's ruins were under the Euphrates, Dulcey planned to shoot some underwater footage. Though she'd brought only a few clothes, her scuba equipment and weighted dive jacket made the bag nearly impossible for her to manage. She tugged and pulled it toward the tailgate of the Humvee and let gravity do the rest.

Nash didn't seem to notice her struggle. "This dry limestone soil you see all around here is the reason for the world's best pistachios. And seventy percent of the world's hazelnuts are grown here in Turkey too."

"I don't particularly care for nuts," Dulcey said, wrestling with her bag until it stood up on its wheels. "Were you able to order oxygen tanks for my underwater shoot?"

"They're behind the dining tent," Nash said, lighting another cigarette. Dulcey was sure he'd gone through a whole pack since they'd left the airport. "Someday Zeugma's splendor will rival the excavations of Pompeii, Italy. Tourists from all over the world will come to see the ancient city of Zeugma in all her splendor," Dr. Nash said with a grand gesture. His enthusiasm made Dulcey feel even more tired.

"That's great. Could you—"

"That dam has been good news and bad news. If the Turkish government hadn't built it, we never would have found Zeugma. The bad news is that the water that rose behind the dam covered a third of the Zeugma excavation before we could remove many priceless mosaics and artifacts. But we were able to save a good number before the water flooded them."

Dulcey eyed her loquacious host. Nash's ridiculous canvas slouch hat had obviously not offered much protection from the sun, because his nose had a pink and brown swath down the middle where the skin had flaked away. *He must be a walking glob of cancer cells,* Dulcey thought. "Would you mind giving me the grand tour *tomorrow,* Dr. Nash?" Dulcey grumbled, trying to roll her bag, too proud to ask for help from Nash. "I need sleep."

"We have a tent for the women. Your only roommate right now is Tanju. I was hoping she would be back from the dam by now—she calls her parents and her grandmother every night about this time.

Turkish people are devoted to their families, you know. You won't find a nursing home or a day-care center in the whole country."

Dulcey moaned dramatically. "Are you suggesting Americans *don't* love their families, Dr. Nash? Well, I never knew my father, and my mother is *dead,* so I hope you will forgive me for not calling my parents tonight."

Nash fell silent, then slowly said, "I'm sorry. How long ago did your mother die?"

"Five months ago. Breast cancer."

Nash nodded, but his face remained expressionless.

Dulcey inched away, but Nash spoke again.

"I received your autobiography—*An Accidental Life*—in the mail." Nash stood looking out over the water, his jaw twitching just below his ear. "I guess you know that I requested you . . . in particular . . . for this assignment. From reading your book, I knew you would be someone who would understand the importance of all this," Nash gestured over the Zeugma compound. "So many people *can't* understand . . ." he said slowly, then lapsed into an awkward silence.

"I guess you're referring to my mentioning how my grandfather was the foreman of a stone quarry in Missouri. And you're right, there was never anything more exciting to me as a kid than when his workers found something buried in the dirt."

"I believe you will be able to understand what is here, and you will appreciate—" Nash stopped mid-sentence, took a deep drag from his cigarette, and gazed out over the Euphrates.

Dulcey yawned pointedly, certain that Nash had gone into some sort of trance and was no longer aware of her presence. "Dr. Nash, in the past thirty-six hours I have witnessed a suicide bombing, the death of a friend, and hundreds of wounded people. I've just come from Iraq, for heaven's sake. Pardon my incivility, but I will drop from exhaustion right here on this limestone gravel if you don't show me to my quarters."

Dr. Nash was silent for a moment, one eye squinting. "Your tent is the last one down there, Ms. Moore. Kahvalti—that's breakfast—is served from seven to nine each morning in the big dining tent over there. The Yildirims, a nice Kurdish family, will be serving us. And they're roasting us a lamb for tomorrow's dinner." He flashed her a wide smile.

Dulcey decided she liked Dr. Nash when he smiled—or smoked—because it meant he wasn't talking while he was doing either one. She stood for a minute, hoping for some help with her enormous bag.

Nash turned his back and walked up the hill toward his tent. "Night, Ms. Moore."

"Good *night,* Dr. Nash," she said to his back. *Strange man. Not many social skills,* thought Dulcey as she trudged toward the women's tent over the stony path, wrestling her bag with its now-useless wheels.

Dulcey was asleep as soon as her body settled onto the narrow cot in the spacious tent. She didn't hear Tanju come in and slip under the blankets on her own cot. She didn't hear the soldiers singing a sad ballad near the campfire. She didn't hear Nash playing his Leonard Cohen songs on his MP3 player as he smoked a last cigarette. And she didn't hear the sounds of the three al Qaeda terrorists and a young teenaged boy who were leading a flock of bleating sheep to their camp directly on the other side of the Euphrates River.

CHAPTER FIVE

Maria Moore adjusted her stylish sunglasses and took a sip of bottled water with a sliver of ice still floating inside. She said into her cell phone, "Hold on a minute, Matt. I lost sight of the kids."

"Aren't they with Dad?" her son asked.

"Of course, but I keep my eye on them too."

"Mom, you worry as much about your grandkids on the beach as I do about my wife who's in the middle of a war zone," Matt said.

"Sweetheart, Dulcey told me you two had a fight about her going to dangerous places. Things will be better when she gets home."

"I'm going to call her again. I can't stop thinking about her."

"You can't call her now. She said her cell phone wouldn't be working while she was at Zeugma. And Turkey is *not* a war zone, dear."

"No, but Iraq is. After what happened to John Barrows, I just wish she'd come home," Matt said.

Down the beach, two energetic children caught Maria's eye. "There's Poppie with the kids, just past the lifeguard's station. They're so gorgeous. They are the diamond of my eye, Matt," Maria said dreamily. "Imagine how their lives would be now if you and Dulcey hadn't adopted them . . ."

"Apple of your eye," Matt corrected.

"Apples? No, no, Mattie. Apples are ninety-nine cents a pound at Kroger's this week. Izzy and Michael are more like diamonds," Maria said, waving her husband and the kids back for lunch. "I just know the angels are with our Dulcey."

"Yeah, yeah, the angels. I know," Matt said, his television voice made even deeper by his gloom.

"Who can blame you for trying to keep her from going? Any husband would have done the same thing to keep his wife safe," Maria said.

"Yeah, maybe back in Ecuador, Mama, but American men are supposed to keep their mouths shut when their wives decide to endanger their lives. Ever since her mother died, Dulcey's been so lost. We're not a team anymore."

"She's still grieving over her mama. She's an orphan now."

"Well, not really."

"It will be so, *so* much better between you two when she comes home. I've already sent the angels, so quit worrying. Go back to work. I have to feed the babies."

"They're not babies, Mama," Matt said. "I'll talk to you later."

* * *

"Gram, Michael isn't even afraid of the big waves this year," Izzy said, dumping a handful of sand-encrusted seashells on the blanket.

"Why should I be? I'm almost six now," boasted Michael, who had lost a second front tooth the night before. He rifled through both pockets of his Hawaiian swim trunks that snugged up under his belly and nearly reached his knees. "Oh, no! I lost my tooth."

"You took your tooth into the ocean?" Maria asked.

Michael stood up, frowned, and kicked up some sand with his chubby foot. "Now the tooth fairy will have to go scuba diving to get my tooth."

"Mom's a scuba diver," Izzy said, her dark eyes peering over the edge of her cheese sandwich. She swallowed hard, put her sandwich down on the paper plate, and busied herself with the straw of her juice box. Then, one by one, she put her shells into the pink Hello Kitty purse she always carried. "I'm saving these to show Mom," Izzy said, her voice taking on a sullen tone.

Everyone was silent for a few seconds. Maria stole a look at her husband and then said, "Your mama told me last night she's going to scuba dive in the Euphrates River. And Frank's going to use his new under-the-water camera. Isn't that neat? She is going to send us pictures of Turkey in her next computer letter."

"E-mail, Gram," Izzy corrected without enthusiasm.

"You sure can't tell we're on vacation," Maria's husband, Joe, said. "Why are you two so quiet?" "Poppie" Joe was a handsome man in his mid-fifties who had taken to grandfathering "like a duck to his family," as Maria often said.

Maria offered the distraction. "What do you say after we eat lunch and swim some more, we all go for a carriage ride on the Strand? And tonight we can ride the trolley to the Ocean Grill Restaurant. Mmm, shrimp scampi for me."

"Fried clams with ketchup for me," Michael said, rubbing his tummy.

"Nothing for me," Izzy said. "I'll sit on the pier and wait for all of you."

"You liked the shrimp cocktail last year," Joe coaxed.

"Mom was with us last year," Izzy said. "You eat. I'll sit on the pier and look at the stars."

Joe stood and swept Izzy off the blanket. She handed her juice box to Maria and nestled against her grandfather's chest. He whispered in her ear, "Your mother can see the very same stars. Do you remember what she told you? She will get them first, then she will pass them on to you. Then, when you're finished with them, you pass them back to her. Same stars going back and forth between you and your mama until she comes home." Then, as he had done so many times before, he gently put his big hand over her face. After a few seconds, her tense little body relaxed in his arms. Joe waited until he felt the curve of her smile against the palm of his hand.

CHAPTER SIX

A light rain was falling when Dulcey woke up. The rain had soaked the fibers of the tent, making it smell pungent and musty, like a wet dog. But even though the coarse fabric had sagged with the water, not a single drop had trickled into the tent. She slipped into jeans and a CNN T-shirt. Dulcey smiled. *A tempest in a T-shirt.* Her mother-in-law's malapropism came to her whenever she wore one. Thinking of Matt's mother made her think of her own. Having Latina mothers was one of the things that had drawn Matt and her together. Their mothers were so intense and so utterly full of love. *Mama, keep us safe,* Dulcey thought and then went out to find the others before the grief could come.

Dulcey made her way through a dense moat of yellow field daisies and lifted the frothy wall of mosquito netting attached to the edge of the dining tent. She stepped inside the huge, circular tent, which was made of the same thick, woven fabric as her own tent. In the exact middle of the tent, a sharpened telephone pole provided ample head-room. The enormous tent was anchored to nine sturdy pistachio trees that had been left standing when this part of the grove was cleared away for the excavation. Dr. Nash and the others were cradling mugs of Turkish chai and hot chocolate to keep warm.

"Good morning. What time is it here in Turkey?" Dulcey asked, pulling out the stem of her watch to set the new time.

"We're an hour ahead of Baghdad—almost nine A.M.," Dr. Nash said. "Tanju here says you were asleep by the time she got back from her phone call last night, so she hasn't met you yet. Dulcey, this is Dr. Tanju Boyraz."

A woman in her late twenties wearing baggy flowered pants and a scarf wound around her head came over to Dulcey, shook her hand, then quickly kissed her on both cheeks. "Welcome to Zeugma, Ms. Moore. I bought *An Accidental Life* in Ankara when I was home last week. You have had an amazing life. I hope it will be even more amazing now that you have come to Turkey."

Tanju's English was that of a careful student, and her grammar, like Asena's, would no doubt prove more precise than Dulcey's own. Her friendly handshake was a clue that she had lived in the West. The fact that she included the Turkish kisses in her greeting indicated she was proud to be Turkish and would insist on being herself. Dulcey liked her right away.

"You'll notice that Tanju is wearing those awful shalwar pants. She bought a whole trunk load last time she went to the bazaar in Urfa," Nash said, frowning at her.

Dulcey could barely keep from laughing—here was Mr. High-water Pants passing judgment. "I like them. They're perfect for digging." Tanju put one sandaled foot up on the bench of the picnic table so Dulcey could see how the billowy skirt was sewn in gathers that cuffed at each of her ankles. "They are a cross between a long skirt and pants. The crotch of the skirt is sewn here at the level of the knee. You see? Very loose and comfortable."

"Well, don't let Tanju's getup fool you," Nash said to Dulcey. "She's no rural farmer. She has a PhD in archeology from the University of West Virginia, and she's a deputy director at the Turkish Ministry of Culture and Tourism. She's kind of our Turkish watchdog here at the excavation site, you might say."

A young man with a medium build wearing Levi 501s and a tight polyester polo shirt stepped up to meet Dulcey.

Dr. Nash said, "And this is Mehmet Demirel, an archeology assistant on this dig. He's a PhD candidate from Istanbul University and is doing his dissertation on the statues of Zeugma."

"Nice to meet you," Dulcey said, sticking out her hand toward Mehmet, trying to remember the Turkish words of greeting from her guidebook.

Mehmet didn't seem to notice her hand. He gave her a shy smile and stepped back quickly. "I am most happy to greet you. Welcome, or *hosh geldiniz,* as we say in Turkish."

"*Hosh* . . . uh . . . *bulduk,*" Dulcey answered, relieved to have remembered at least one of the greetings.

"We just got word from the dam that the CNN satellite trucks will be here tomorrow," Frank said. There were dark circles under his eyes.

"That gives us a day to decide exactly where to put the cameras around Trench 25," Tofer said, whose face also evidenced a sleepless night. "The rain is going to be a problem for the equipment right now, so we should wait. If it doesn't stop, we'll need to put up tents around the dig." Tofer's words and movements were robotic.

"Whatever you think, Tofer." Dulcey caught his eye, smiled at him, and wondered what would happen when his numbness wore off.

"We did this sort of live excavation program in Egypt a few years back," Nash said as he brushed a lock of dark hair back under his hat. "Dug up a pharaoh's tomb and opened it right on the Discovery Channel. All our experts were sure there'd be gold and rare jewels in that casket, but there was nothing but dust and a few bones. It made for very disappointing television. But that won't happen this time, *inshallah*—that's 'God willing'—since we pretty much know what we've got under that dirt."

"We've discussed the uncertainty factor with our producers," Dulcey said, blowing on her hot chocolate to cool it. "Some of them want you to dig up the trench beforehand to make sure there's something worth seeing, then bury the statue again and pretend to be surprised when you dig it up on live TV."

"And I hope you persuaded them to do it the correct way?" Nash said. "I'm an archeologist, Ms. Moore, not an actor."

"Bringing three CNN television trucks and three crews from Ankara is not cheap, Doctor. Neither is a half-hour of prime television time using a live satellite feed, plus our own traveling security guards and the salaries of about fifteen professionals. How sure are you that Trench 25 is everything you hope it will be?" Dulcey asked as though she were conducting an interview with Nash and had just shoved her microphone under the man's chin.

Dr. Nash stood and stretched his six-foot-three-inch frame, bending slightly at the waist to keep from hitting his head on the slope of the sagging tarp. His T-shirt du jour featured a dolphin under a Greenpeace logo. And today, a pair of socks covered the space between his high-tops and chinos. He sipped his chai and stared over the expanse of wet limestone and dirt to the Euphrates beyond. "Let's put it this way. Back in the spring, in Trench 24, we found a carved granite pedestal on its side. Attached to that were two solid gold feet and the bottom of a solid gold robe."

"Since it's near the temple dedicated to her, we have speculated that the statue is the goddess Tyche, who was later called Fortuna by the Romans," Tanju added. "Even the coins minted at Zeugma show the goddess standing there in front of her temple."

"How do you know she's solid gold?" Frank asked.

"You are right to ask this. Usually only small statues can be made of solid gold," Mehmet answered. "Large statues are usually made by 'lost wax' process. A wax figure is carved, then covered with bronze— or, in this case, the gold—and then the wax figure is heated to allow the wax to run out of hole in bottom of the statue."

Nash chimed in. "But Zeugma was such a wealthy city, they sometimes flaunted their wealth by pouring melted gold into the hollow cores of their statues. No one would see the gold, but everyone knew it was there. And it guaranteed that the statue would be too heavy to carry away easily."

Mehmet said, "The gold inside was not wasted—it served as a . . . uh . . . in English . . . Dr. Nash?"

"A savings account for the city," finished Nash.

Tanju set her chai on the table and explained more of the story. "We believe the statue was so heavy it had to be left behind by the residents of Zeugma as they were fleeing the Parthians. The Parthians, however, were also unable to lift it and take it back to their strong-hold. So that is why we have it today."

"Heavy statues, huge floor mosaics, frescoes on walls—nothing could be taken when the people fled for their lives. And it's all still here," Nash said reverently.

Dulcey probed the archeology crew. "How do you know you have a whole statue there? Maybe only the feet and the bottom of the robe and the pedestal are there."

"We used satellite photos and ground-penetrating radar to make sure we had complete statue," Mehmet said, dragging out a notebook of drawings and black-and-white photos. He showed them a murky image of a reclining figure under the dirt.

"Why didn't you just go ahead and dig 'er up?" Frank asked.

"I found the goddess back in April, but I left her under three meters of dirt to protect her from looters and because I knew a CNN story might bring in enough money to develop a world-class open-air museum here at Zeugma," Nash said. "For years, I've begged my American colleagues and archeology foundations all over the world to excavate this area. But during the Kurdish rebellion, thirty-seven thousand people died around these parts. Of course, no one wanted to come here then."

"But I thought the Randower Humanities Institute gave five million dollars for the Zeugma excavation," Dulcey said, checking a notebook of research she had brought with her to Turkey.

"Yes, when the dam was built, RHI gave five million dollars so we could rescue as many mosaics and artifacts as possible before the river covered the lowest part of the excavation site. But now that the emergency is over, so is the motivation to excavate the rest of Zeugma. So we're out of funds."

"It must be excruciating to wait," Tofer said, with an air of being very familiar with anything that felt excruciating.

"I've been sitting on this find for half a year," Nash said. "You can't imagine how badly I've wanted to see the goddess."

Tanju stood and poured herself some more chai. Unlike most Turkish women, who were small-boned, she was a tall, solid woman who did not seem inclined to smile easily. Dulcey watched Tofer's reaction to her. His eyes followed her, but she seemed not to notice. He moved over to invite her to sit next to him, but she sat on Dulcey's bench instead. "Dr. Nash convinced the ministry that there was a very important find about to come to light and that CNN should show it to the world," Tanju said. "Whatever is found at Zeugma represents the early history of Western civilization—not just Turkish history. This place belongs to the world."

Dulcey felt that familiar racing of blood in her veins as she stared at the pockmarked earth on the hill where twenty-five trenches had been dug up and then reburied. "The place I grew up looked a lot like this . . . a big old rock quarry."

Nash said, "Right now, Zeugma looks like a bare hill at the edge of a pistachio grove instead of one of the world's richest archeological discoveries. But someday, we'll expose it completely so people can see the entire city all at once."

Dulcey repeated her concern. "CNN wants to help. But the last thing I want to do is to narrate a total disaster."

"I guarantee you, excavation of the Goddess Fortuna is very worthy of your time, Dulcey Hanim," Mehmet said, nodding curtly and closing his eyes tightly for a brief moment.

Dulcey had learned that *Hanim* was equivalent to "lady" or "madam" and was a gesture of courtesy, just as using *Bey* after a man's name was comparable to saying "mister." She had also learned that the way Mehmet had closed his eyes was a Turkish promise. She had seen Asena use her eyes like that and had found it charmingly sincere. She smiled back at Mehmet. "I believe you."

A white, battle-scarred Land Rover crunched to a stop on the gravel near the dining tent. Asena jumped out. "*Gunayden,* everyone. That's Turkish for 'good morning,'" she said cheerfully. "I have brought you some *kiymali borek* from the *pastahane*—minced lamb rolled in flaky pastry—and some fresh fruit from the market." She added it to a table already laden with a traditional Turkish breakfast buffet. "And here is a *Turkish Daily News* for each of you—it is the only English language daily in Turkey."

Dr. Nash motioned for his guests to fill their plates. Despite her world travels, Dulcey found it hard to face sliced cucumbers, tomatoes, and ripe olives first thing in the morning. For her, they just weren't breakfast foods. She settled instead for a hard-boiled egg and one of the rolled pastries Asena had called *borek*.

Except for Mehmet and Nash, Asena kissed everyone on both cheeks. Then she straightened and inhaled the damp air. "Hah. Nothing quite like the smell of goat hair after a rainy night."

"So that's what that smell is coming from the tents," mumbled Tofer around a bite of feta cheese.

Dr. Nash flipped through the newspaper and lit a cigarette. "The dam just sent word that the CNN trucks will be here in Zeugma by tomorrow evening. Asena, perhaps you could just come back when they get here."

Asena ignored Nash's rebuff. "After six months of waiting, are you looking forward to finally seeing your golden goddess, Dr. Nash?"

"As you well know, I'm a patient man," Nash said, eyeing Asena crossly over his cigarette and moving to the far side of the tent.

Dulcey noticed how Asena avoided looking directly at Dr. Nash and how Nash seemed to prickle at the sight of her. It had been the same at the airport the night before. The two of them had acted like strangers—each of them trying to be more polite than the other. But Asena had lived behind the hill called Belkis Tepe, just a stone's throw from the excavation, for the entire twelve years Nash had been digging. Was it a personality clash or were they real enemies?

"I say we spend this rainy day in trenches fifteen through twenty. They have canvas tents over them, and it will give Dulcey and the crew an idea of the mosaics and frescoes that are being found at Zeugma. What do you say?" Asena asked.

Nash stubbed out his cigarette with more force than was needed. "Could I have a word with you, Asena Hanim?"

Despite the drizzling rain, the two of them stepped outside the dining tent and walked along the riverbank. The crew ate their breakfast and discussed preparations for the shoot, trying not to notice the heated Turkish conversation taking place by the river. At a signal from Mehmet, the Kurdish family cleared the breakfast dishes.

"They're not very fond of one another, are they," Dulcey said.

"They used to be," Tanju said. "They were engaged to be married until about a year ago. But Asena has secrets. She has a history here in Zeugma that she is trying to protect. And that disturbs Dr. Nash very much. She is a very . . . closed . . . uh . . . *private* person about certain things."

"And they have disputations about who is boss of the Zeugma," added Mehmet. "Asena lives on other side of the Belkis Tepe all her lifelong, and she thinks herself maybe queen of the Zeugma."

"And Dr. Nash is an uppity foreigner who wants to call the shots on the excavation?" Dulcey asked, digging out a pen from her backpack and scribbling "uppity foreigner" in her notebook.

"Uh," Mehmet said, looking confused. "Turkish people are very proud of their land, and they enjoy not at all when foreigners tell them what to do with treasures of Turkey."

Dulcey, ever watchful for the human side of her story, jotted more notes. Mehmet peered over her shoulder to see what she had written. "Oh, *lutfen*," he gasped, his eyes wide. "*Please* do not say I called Dr. Nash *uppity foreigner*. I do not know 'uppity,' but it sounds . . . un-respecting."

"I apologize. I will change it right away," Dulcey said, making a big show of crossing out the word *uppity* and writing the milder words Mehmet had actually said. Across the room, Ali Yildirim poured soap into a big tub and filled it with water he had heated over the campfire. Then he lit the propane stove to make more chai in a double kettle. He put tea leaves and water in the smaller kettle on top and plain water in the bottom one.

His wife, Fatma, was a short, stocky woman with tattoos on her face like some of the women Dulcey had seen at the airport. She wore a lilac head scarf made of loosely woven cotton and a long traditional dress made of navy velveteen embroidered with gold trim.

Tanju caught Dulcey looking at Fatma. "Facial tattoos were popular among Kurdish women of about her age. When she was young, the women in this area preferred the tattoos to jewelry."

Fatma's pretty teenaged daughter Aysha began to put the breakfast foods into plastic containers. She wore a shapeless vest made of blue velveteen over a cotton blouse and flowered shalwars similar to Tanju's. Her head scarf was also made of lilac gauze but with a pretty trim of crocheted violets across her forehead. Dulcey was relieved to see that the girl had not tattooed her face. Dulcey rose and began to help her. Aysha looked startled and worked more quickly.

Tanju came up behind Dulcey and whispered, "You should not help her."

"Why not?" Dulcey said, dumping sliced cucumbers into Aysha's container.

"It is not proper for a person as important as you are to do this work. I know that in America it is polite to help. But you will embarrass the Yildirim family. They may worry they are not doing their jobs properly."

"Tell the girl I apologize," Dulcey said quickly. Tanju translated.

Aysha looked relieved. She glanced back at her mother, then hurried to put the food containers into the ice chests.

By the time breakfast was finished, the rain had slowed to a drizzle. Dulcey put on a light jacket and wandered on the riverbank, looking over Zeugma's misty landscape. Did Nash know about the danger that may have followed them from Baghdad? Did he know about the undercover operatives? Thurman had told the CNN crew not to say anything that might give the agents away. Dulcey scanned the perimeter of the camp. Indeed, Turkish soldiers were every-where—by the river, in a watchtower near the gate, and walking along the crosscut road halfway up Belkis Tepe. But where were the Americans?

* * *

Across the Euphrates, a fourteen-year-old boy named Nayif also made chai on a small campfire. He felt relieved to be given jobs again. After what he had failed to do in Baghdad, he knew that even being trusted to make chai was a sign in his favor.

As Nayif poured the steaming liquid into the men's cups, he tried not to spill a drop.

"Look at the infidel woman, walking without an escort over the holy banks of the Euphrates. She is taunting us." The man rested his hand on the pistol protruding from his belt.

"Brother, be calm," another man said. "She has no idea anyone is watching her. You, Nayif, help me move the microphones into place. And be ready. You will be delivering your first message soon."

Nayif followed the man into the tent, carried out two wooden boxes containing the parabolic microphones, and positioned them toward the Zeugma camp. They placed a small pillow on top of each microphone and set a round table between them. Nayif watched as the men tucked tiny receivers into their ears, sat on the boxes, and spread their legs wide apart so as not to interfere with the sound.

One of the men wrote something on a piece of paper and gave it to Nayif. "Take this to our friends in Birecik. They should be at the Firat Pansyon by now. Let them know everything is in place."

Nayif pocketed the message, straddled a muddy motorbike, and rode over the dam toward Birecik.

* * *

High on Belkis Tepe, behind the ruin of a Roman military fortress, three American operatives snapped photographs of the shepherds and radioed a message to their agent in Birecik, describing the boy on the motorbike.

CHAPTER SEVEN

The single minaret of the little mosque in Bloomsbury Square seemed to have pinned a cloud of chilly mist against itself. Nala al Aboud shuddered in the unheated women's section as she bowed her head to the worn rug. She rose again, cupping her hands toward heaven, and murmuring in concert with a long row of head-scarved women. A few minutes later, she was out of the mosque looking for her shoes among the hundreds of pairs lined up on the low shelves.

Another woman sidled up next to her. "Any word yet?" the woman whispered, lacing up her Adidas underneath her shapeless coat.

Nala looked up. "Khadija," she said and then sighed. "I think he and his father are being trained in Syria. They may be going to Turkey for an assignment. My sister got a call from Damascus asking for a money transfer to a Turkish bank."

"Is there a way to get a message to your son without your husband finding out?" Khadija asked. "You could fly to meet him. Then you could bring him back here to London. Or go somewhere where no one knows you."

Nala's eyes grew wide, and her lower lip trembled. "You expect my son to blithely meet his mother who he believes martyred herself in Riyadh and is in paradise awaiting her family . . . and not tell his father?"

"I see what you mean. He is too young to understand that you actually are as good as dead since you have disobeyed your husband. Or that you would be as good as dead if Ahmed found out what you've done. And if he . . ."

"Shh. I get the idea," Nala said, putting her finger against Khadija's lips.

"But you are alive. And so is Nayif."

Nala closed her eyes. "You have no idea what it's like to be cut off . . . from everyone I have ever known except my sister in Riyadh. To live a life of solitude. To live for the hope of saving my only child from the fate his father has planned for him. I never understood how painful . . ."

Khadija encircled Nala's sagging shoulders with her arms and squeezed hard. "Stay strong. Once you have your son, you can start over again. Nayif is young and is not a programmed machine. He can still learn new ways."

The women left the mosque and hurried along Great Russell Street. Nala glanced at her watch. "Walk faster or we'll be late. Once you have worked at the museum a few more weeks, they will not be so strict about the lunch hour. But you are new, and you need to make a good impression."

"I don't know how to repay you for getting me this job. My scholarship left me half starved all the time. On Saturday, I bought a book that wasn't even required for my classes, and I had lunch with a friend."

"Don't forget, the British Museum is lucky to have you as well. There aren't many ancient studies graduate students who speak Arabic and English as well as you do," Nala said, appreciating the flush of pleasure in her young friend's face.

"I love working with the old Arabic inscriptions and talking to the scholars who are preserving history. Our history. *Ours.* The new exhibition shows how Islam saved the knowledge of the world during the Christian dark ages. People will see we're not such backward—"

Nala abruptly took Khadija's elbow and steered her toward the employee's entrance at the back of the museum. "Don't show so much pride. You will offend the British. They suspect all Muslims right now, and we mustn't draw attention to ourselves."

"How can I keep my eyes from shining? How can I keep from smiling as these scientists of the West show respect for Islam in this terrible time of fear and mistrust?"

Nala hissed in Khadija's ear. "Don't be so naive. Do you think this was the museum's idea? The museum is only doing it because some Saudi prince with a guilty conscience gave them a million Euros and a boatload of artifacts to put on display."

"They could have refused it if they were not interested," Khadija whispered back, looking offended.

Nala swiped her identification card across the scanner by the door, and Khadija did the same with hers. "Just be calm. I want to come and go to my job without anyone noticing me. So please, stop waving red flags while we work together."

"But who will tell them how wonderful Islam is if we do not tell them?" Khadija followed Nala into the women's restroom.

"Once I'm gone from the museum, you can hold seminars in your silly head scarf and your tattered old coat three sizes too big and exclaim how enlightened we Muslims are." Nala bunched the front of her coat up into her hands so it would be tight against her figure, then she sucked in her cheeks and pranced in front of the row of mirrors as though she were modeling in a fashion show. "Ladies of the West!" she announced to her imaginary audience on the other side of the mirrors. "You too can wear one of these gorgeous costumes that hide your figure so that no man but your husband will ever want to look at you. And, after a few months of marriage, even your own husband will forget to notice you." She held her hands out as though to stop a stampede of women. "Now, ladies, now, now—not all at once. Take turns please. No pushing! There are coats and scarves for everyone." Nala swept her hands across the bank of sinks as though they were tables piled high with Muslim clothing. "You there, Miss, don't bother trying to match them up. A pink flowered scarf and a brown and green plaid coat—yes!—that's even better." She turned to another imaginary customer. "Stripes and polka dots together, dear? Divine! Now even other *women* won't look at you."

Khadija giggled behind her hand, glancing nervously toward the door, hoping no one would come in and see Nala in one of her crazy moods. "You've lived in London too long. How bold you are!"

Nala wasn't finished. "But you insist on showing your figure, ma'am? Well . . . I have the answer. This lovely beige vest will fit you more snugly. Yes, tie it tightly at your waist. Never mind those wires protruding . . ." Her expression became pained. "No one will notice . . ." Nala clapped her hand over her mouth and doubled over. Even her own sense of humor could not save her. She held her stomach tightly, retching, panting—trying to push the horrific memories away.

"Don't think about it. Don't think about it," Khadija whispered, holding Nala tightly in her arms, patting her friend's heaving back.

"Ahhh. I will never forget how it felt to wear that vest," Nala whispered back, wiping hot tears away with her fists. "I must try to find him. Nayif will be lost forever—I will be lost forever as well—if I don't find him."

"You will. You *will* find him," Khadija said emphatically. She twisted her pinched fingers in front of her lips as though she were locking a safe. "And I promise I will stay quiet."

"Thank you for understanding," Nala said, straightening her clothing and composing herself as best she could. "Let's get back to work."

The two women returned to a large room full of artifacts and dusty documents. Khadija took up the Arabic text she had been deciphering and began typing the English translation.

Nala loaded a brass plate into the engraving machine and breathed a sigh of relief that she had finally made Khadija understand. As she pressed the lever that held the brass plate in place and stomped on the pedal that brought down the heavy stamp, she thought of Nayif—how would she find him and rescue him from his father? It had been Nayif's sweet face that had stopped her from detonating her vest full of explosives that day. With a rush of sorrow, she thought of the innocent family from Alabama who had all died in the blast—though not by her hand.

She remembered every moment of that day. It was never far from her mind. As she had walked past the security guards, it had been her sudden vision of Nayif's large, dark, innocent eyes that had caused her to keep walking without pulling her wires. She had allowed the others to think her vest had malfunctioned. They had carried on dutifully with the backup plan. All witnesses to her betrayal had instantly died as their own bombs had successfully detonated.

Nala had hidden in the bombed-out buildings until it was safe to leave. It had been the thought of saving her only child that had emboldened her to carefully remove each of the wires connected to the explosives and then remove the deadly garment.

Once the vest was away from her body, Nala al Aboud could clearly see that it had been designed and sewn with the tightly-woven fabric of ignorance and hatred.

CHAPTER EIGHT

Asena drew back the canvas tarp that served as a door to the covered trenches. Dr. Nash turned on a high-watt klieg light attached to a tripod, and the mosaic under their feet lit up.

Dulcey gasped. The mosaic was the size of an entire room. And it was perfectly intact. The face of a Greek god with a curly, white beard peered out from the inner frame of the mosaic. He was riding a dolphin through the waves of a stylized ocean.

"That's Oceanus, the god of water. People who lived on the Euphrates were very keen on the water gods," Dr. Nash explained. He sat back on his heels and watched Dulcey's reaction, clearly relishing her surprise and appreciation. "Know anything about Greek myths, Ms. Moore?"

"My mother taught them to me as a child—she'd make up songs about them. And I studied them in college—so much of the world's art and literature is based on mythology," Dulcey said. She dropped her backpack and knelt down on her hands and knees. Frank removed the lens cap of his camcorder and filmed Dulcey's reaction. Tofer snapped pictures of the mosaic with his father's Nikon.

"It's—I had no idea . . . It's stunning," Dulcey said, running her hands over the tiny stones that had been laid down in exquisite shapes and figures two thousand years before. "Is it okay to touch it?"

"Absolutely," Nash said, kneeling next to her, talking in a hushed tone. "That's the beauty of mosaics. You can walk on them, use them at the bottom of fountains, drive horse carts over them. Sun doesn't fade them. Water doesn't hurt them. Even if the rocks get worn down, the color is the same all the way through. Frescoes and oil paintings will fade with time and exposure to light, but mosaics last forever."

"I used to find spearheads and pots in the quarry when I was a child. Bones sometimes. But nothing like this."

"Yes, I remember that from your book," Dr. Nash said. "That's why I wanted you here to cover the goddess."

Dulcey bit her lip in confusion. *An Accidental Life* had arrived in bookstores in late June. But she'd been assigned to cover the Zeugma excavation in early May. *How could Nash have read my book before requesting that CNN send me to cover the excavation?* The first time he'd mentioned this, she'd been too exhausted to notice the oddity, and now was hardly the time to pursue it. Making a mental note to ask about this later, Dulcey shook her head and watched as Nash took a stick and counted the borders around the mosaic of the Greek god. "Seven borders. Five geometric borders and two florals. You see how the widest one here is full of deep-throated lilies and lush, ripe fruits that repeat all the way around the central figures?"

Dulcey signaled Frank and went into interview mode. "How did the mosaicists get these colored stones?"

"Most of them came right out of the Euphrates. Or they used colored glass for the bright blues and colors that didn't occur in nature. Some mosaicists used real gold nuggets in their work—but we haven't found any of those at Zeugma."

Dulcey looked into the lens of Frank's camera. "The mosaicists created these figures with tiny stones instead of paint. And yet the picture is perfectly symmetrical and includes even the tiniest details. It's absolutely breathtaking."

"Tesserae—those stones that make up a mosaic are called tesserae," said Nash, smiling broadly.

After another few minutes of silent staring, Dulcey raised her head and looked at Nash. "I'm truly overwhelmed by the beauty of this."

"There are sixty-six more of these mosaic floors that we've already unearthed. Most of those are at the Gaziantep Museum. And there are hundreds more still buried here at Zeugma. The people who lived here got very rich from the customs fees they charged the traders who wanted to cross their bridge over the Euphrates. This was the old Silk Road, you know, between the Roman Empire and the Orient. The Roman military was stationed here too—to protect the eastern edge of the Empire and the trade routes."

Asena, who had been watching Dulcey's reaction to the mosaic, spoke up. "Turkey has always been a bridge between the East and the West. Because Zeugma is very close to the Mediterranean Sea, the traders would also bring their products by ship. They would land at Alexandretta and carry their goods by camel to this spot on the Euphrates. This was a good-sized city at one time—maybe seventy thousand citizens."

"Alexandretta—I didn't see that on the map," said Frank, who had been filming each of them as they spoke. Tofer too was kneeling now, taking close-ups of the tiny tesserae placed in exact formations according to their hues and shapes.

Dr. Nash stood and drew a map of Turkey's Mediterranean coast with the toe of his high-top tennis shoe. "I'll give you a ten-second geography lesson. That funny looking tail on the island of Cyprus points right to Alexandretta on the coast of Turkey. Zeugma is farther inland. Alexandretta was named, of course, after Alexander the Great—who conquered this area three hundred years before Christ. Zeugma was built by Seleukid the First, one of Alexander's generals. Alexandretta is called Iskenderun now—that's the Turkish name. It's still a big seaport."

After a few minutes, the five of them moved to the next trench, and Dulcey examined another mosaic that had just been cleaned of its dirt. This mosaic portrayed a male angel looking lovingly at a mortal woman. "Psyche and Eros?" she guessed.

"Correct," Asena said. "In this mosaic, look how Psyche's robe is nearly transparent. Look how the artist shows the outline of her body underneath the thin, silk fabric."

"You can see the curve of her breasts and even the indentation of her navel," Dulcey said in amazement. "A master. An absolute master. To achieve that effect using stones from the Euphrates is amazing," she said, pressing a hand against her chest.

Dr. Nash watched her for a long time, chuckling at her pleasure.

Tofer let out a whoop from the next covered trench. "Come look at this fresco!"

Dulcey was soon standing in front of a long wall with an entire Greek myth told in a single painting. "Ariadne and Theseus. And here is her father, King Minos, with the minotaur held captive in the labyrinth. There's the ball of thread Ariadne used to help Theseus find his way out of the labyrinth."

"Right again," Nash said. "You'll notice that the entire border is itself an intricate labyrinth."

"What is a fresco exactly?" Dulcey asked, notebook in hand as the archeologist answered.

"A painting done on fresh plaster. As the plaster dries, it captures and embeds the paint. It's much more stable than painting on a dry wall—and that's lucky for all of us who come along thousands of years later."

Dulcey walked over to the next mosaic, telling herself the story of Achilles, whose mother had hidden him in women's clothing to keep him safe from war. Achilles' mother and the other women in the mosaic wore scarves over their heads. "This mosaic was done hundreds of years before Islam—why are these women's heads covered?"

Nash gazed lovingly at the mosaic. "That's the irony of this whole head-covering thing—you put your finger right on it. It was Jewish and Christian women who had a strong tradition of head covering. And chaste or married women of many cultures did so as well. Mohammed asked Muslim women to follow the example of those modest women. Then Jewish and Christian women stopped being so modest, and Muslim women carried on the tradition. Look in your New Testament. First Corinthians, chapter eleven, if I remember correctly, starting at about verse five. The Apostle Paul insisted that Christian women cover their heads when they prayed or prophesied. Some Catholic nuns carry on the tradition—but not many. And think of Mary—she was a Jew and the mother of Christ. You can't even think of her without her head covering."

Dulcey wrote the scripture reference down in her notes. "You know the Bible pretty well then?"

"Use it all the time in my work. It's one way we archeologists date things and find historical references. Great little reference tool."

"Uh-huh . . . *reference* tool," she wrote. "Did anything from the Bible happen here in Zeugma?"

Nash stood and continued the lesson. "Not from the Bible itself. But we know that one of the later apostles—man named Rufus—was murdered here in Zeugma. Two of the earliest Christian churches are underwater now. And there is another one—we think—on the hill near the temple."

"Temple? A Jewish temple?" Frank asked.

"No . . . a pagan temple. It was built to honor the Goddess Fortuna, who is the goddess of destiny."

"Goddess of destiny," Dulcey murmured, jotting notes. "That's the golden statue you're digging up tomorrow for our cameras."

Asena, who had been hanging back from the group, spoke up. "Turkey was full of goddess religions—Cybele, Diana, Artemis, the Mother Goddess."

Nash broke in. "You've heard Turkey referred to as Anatolia? Turks call their land *Anadolu,* which means 'full of mothers.'"

"Full of mothers . . . how lovely," Dulcey repeated, lost in thought, her pen hovering briefly above her pad before she began writing quickly again. Now that she'd had a night of sleep, she was mesmerized rather than irritated by Nash's passion for his work.

Frank appeared, camera at his side. "Got some great footage. You should see the mosaics at the other end."

Tofer joined the group as well, panting a little from climbing all over the trenches to get the best shots. "These things are stunning. People are not going to believe what's been under the dirt of this place. Dad would have *loved* this . . ." Tofer fell silent and sat down hard on a low stone wall.

Dulcey noticed the glazed look in his eyes. She reached out and squeezed his arm. "You okay? Do you need anything?"

"So where is Trench 25?" Tofer asked, swallowing hard and ignoring her offer. "Frank and I need to plan this shoot before the CNN trucks get here tomorrow."

"Sure, you two go on. I'll start writing the scripts," Dulcey said, mentally kicking herself for treating Tofer like a kid. John Barrows had become the elephant in the room that none of them could afford to talk about until their work was finished. Maybe she'd made a mistake allowing Tofer to come with them to Zeugma. When her mother had died, Dulcey had found that each suppressed emotion was like a low-hanging tree branch obstructing her path. The farther and longer she'd held one of them back, the harder and more painfully it would eventually hit her. *I'll talk to Frank—maybe we should send Tofer home.*

Nash pushed a canvas flap to the side and pointed across Belkis Tepe, toward Trench 25. Goose bumps skittered up and down Dulcey's arms as she watched the three men set off sideways across the steep hill where a sleeping goddess lay.

* * *

That evening, Hikmet Budak, the owner of the Arkadash Pansyon, was about to retire for the night when a man entered and inquired about a room. They chatted a bit and drank a cup of chai together in the hotel lobby, as was the custom with all introductions in Turkey. Then Budak went to his desk and laid out the registration book. As the man signed his name, Budak noticed his guest was missing the little finger on his right hand.

The guest looked up from the book and motioned toward the boy lying on a cot behind the registration desk. "Your son?"

The boy looked up at the guest and offered a crooked smile.

"Yes, my eldest," Budak replied. "He was delivering newspapers during the troubles. Soldiers accused him of being a messenger for the Kurdish PKK terrorists. They shot him twice as he ran from them. His brain is damaged, and there is still a bullet in his lower spine—so he does not walk."

The guest shook his head; his eyes filled with sadness. "My sympathies, brother."

"Thank you." Budak coughed, turned the registry around, and said, "And how long will you be staying?"

"Two nights, perhaps three . . . full board please." The man spoke to him in a mixture of very proper English with a few Turkish words thrown in. He signed his name, *Abdullah Kabul,* using the Roman alphabet. *A well educated man,* Budak surmised.

"Your meals will be served in the restaurant owned by my friend Fikret Bey next door. We have an arrangement with him since we are such a small hotel." Budak handed the man some meal vouchers. "Do you have a vehicle? The police require a license plate number."

"Yes, the big truck across the street is mine. License number 43 YTT 03. I need to rest before I go on. I am not feeling well."

"I am sorry to hear that, sir," Budak said.

"Of course, I always feel well enough to do business. Would you be interested in seeing one of our furniture brochures? We sell our

Moda furniture line all over Turkey and Syria. Very reasonable prices. And I am the man to see for an extra discount."

"Times are very bad here in Nizip. Until the war in Iraq is over and the borders open up again, we will have to make do with the furniture my father bought for this hotel."

"Very well. Will I have a television in my room? I like to watch CNN."

"Yes, sir. You can get CNN International and CNN Turk on your television—we have satellite here," Budak said proudly. "On Friday evening, there will be a program about Zeugma. They have reportedly discovered another great treasure there, and the whole world will be watching."

"I am not much interested in such things, but thank you anyway. One more thing; an American man may call for me on some furniture business. But I would like no one else to enter my room—not even to clean. It is my policy while I travel." He smoothed his neatly trimmed mustache and smiled at Budak.

"An American? Not a military man, I hope. I do not want trouble here. People in this town have relatives in Iraq. And we are all poor because we have not been able to do business there since the war began."

"My American friend is not in the military. He will look like any other tourist."

"Very well. Here is your key. Your room is on the floor above, near the stairs."

The hotel guest stroked his mustache again and laid a small tip on the open registration book. "That is for you." Then he dug into his pocket and peeled off several large Turkish bills. "And that is for your son. Tell him he did a good day's work."

CHAPTER NINE

Sometime past four in the morning, Lee Nash sat on the riverbank with his back resting on a pillow made of two small Turkish carpets sewn together with loose cotton inside. Smoke spiraled up from the dying campfire. As he sipped a steaming cup of salep, he looked up at the dome of stars above him. Then he gazed across the Euphrates, where the vaulted ceiling of stars reversed itself in its reflection. The sluices of the dam must have been closed, because the water before him was as still as a slab of black marble. Nash never tired of the amazing place where he lived and worked.

At the perimeter of the camp, he could see the soldiers' faces illuminated by the glowing ends of cigarettes. The low talk of the soldiers on night watch comforted him. He poured himself more salep and turned his attention back to the manuscript that lay across his lap.

For about the twentieth time since he had received it, Nash reread the letter that had been written in purple ink on the back of the title page of Dulcey's autobiography, *An Accidental Life*.

Dear Lee,

I am very ill. The doctors don't give me much time. But I wanted you to know that you and I shared something more than a brief relationship in Griggsberg, Missouri, thirty-five years ago. We have a daughter.

Dulcinea never asked questions about her father until she wrote this book about her own life. I think she was being loyal to me by never trying in earnest to find out who you were. I was afraid she would never find you if I didn't help her a little.

I read about you in Newsweek *when you first discovered what you were certain would prove to be a solid gold goddess. It said in the article that you wanted CNN to provide live coverage during the excavation, so I asked Dulcey's agent to contact you. If Dulcey is selected as the reporter who will cover the excavation, please don't reveal who you are until after her work is finished. Dulcey is a professional and will not appreciate having her emotions in play when she is trying to do a good job for CNN.*

In chapter two of her book, Dulcey talks about the quarry near the house where she grew up. You remember that my father was the foreman there. That's where you had your first job as an archeology intern while you were still in college. That's where we met, where I fell in love with you, and where I became pregnant with our child. When my father's backhoe uncovered those wonderful Osage pots in the quarry, you packed them up and went back to your university—and you never looked back. At first I didn't even know how to find you to tell you about our child. Later, I stopped trying because I was afraid you or your family would take her from me.

Please find the right way to tell Dulcey you are her father. I am leaving it up to you to break the news. I've had a wonderful life, Lee. No regrets. And, as you get to know Dulcey, I am sure you will see why I couldn't bear to share her with anyone in case I would lose her. Forgive my selfishness. I needed her so badly. She was a godsend in my life.

Sincerely,
Rosa Martinez

Nash shut the book carefully as he thought back to how excited he'd been about the twelve perfectly preserved pots in that Missouri stone quarry. There had been a beautiful etching on each one that reflected the life of the Osage Indians when they'd lived in the area two hundred years earlier. The pots had been his first find, and he had rushed back to the university to make a name for himself, oblivious to what he was leaving behind.

A few moments later, as the sky turned a royal blue with the approach of dawn, Nash watched a figure step out of the darkened women's tent. It was Dulcey. It was as though his reflections had wakened her from her sleep. He watched her pick her way carefully over the smooth river stones until she stood by the edge of the water. She folded her arms and hugged herself against the slight morning chill. His heart began to race a bit, and he willed himself to breathe normally. *Everything is falling into place. Go slowly. Things will work out if you go slowly. Yavash, yavash . . .*

As Dulcey came closer to his campfire, Nash was again struck by how much she looked like Rosa. He closed the manuscript and hid it under a stack of books.

This woman is my daughter—flesh of my flesh, bone of my bone. The wonder of it! Besides his archaeology papers and academic work, he'd had no idea that anything of himself would be left behind once his own life was over.

Dulcey continued to move toward him. Should he use this moment to tell her? No. In her letter, Rosa had insisted he not breathe a word of his secret until after the work was finished. Rosa was right—Dulcey would be shocked by the news, and it might interfere with her assignment. He would respect Rosa's wishes and tell Dulcey only after the goddess had been excavated.

As Dulcey drew nearer, Nash fumbled with his thoughts. *Say something. Anything.* "It all comes down to how big your tribe is, Dulcey," he said as she approached, trying his best to sound as though she'd caught him in deep philosophical thought.

Obviously startled, Dulcey called into the dark, "Dr. Nash?"

Nash saluted her with his tin mug of salep as she came toward him. "Come join me."

"I couldn't sleep. I guess you couldn't either," Dulcey said, perching herself on a smooth, flat boulder near his campfire. She gave him a quizzical look. "So you're out here thinking about tribes?"

"My thoughts were keeping me awake—wanted to mull them over. What you said at breakfast yesterday morning got me thinking." He set his mug down, took another drag on his cigarette, and blew a smoke ring into the night sky.

"What did I say at breakfast?"

"You were reading the *Turkish Daily News*," Nash said.

"About the plane crash in Egypt?"

"You said, 'I wonder how many Americans were on board,'" Nash said, digging out another tin mug from his rucksack. "Would you like to try a cup of salep? It's kind of like hot eggnog. One of the best drinks in Turkey."

"Any alcohol in it?" Dulcey asked, wrinkling her nose.

"Never touch the stuff," Nash said.

"All right. I'll try it. But what did the plane crash have to do with tribes?"

Nash poured her a mug of warm liquid from the brass pot that had been sitting on the fire grate. "After you read about the plane crash, you looked at the story about Iraq and said, 'Twelve more Americans died in Baghdad yesterday.'"

"Uh-huh. So America is my tribe," Dulcey said. "Oh, I see. I didn't wonder about how many *people* died yesterday—only the Americans . . ." Nash watched a look of concern cloud her face—so much like the beautiful face that had charmed him when he was a boy of nineteen.

"We all have tribes. People think of the Arabs as being a tribal people. People say they are *fiercely loyal* to their tribes—to these large extended families that have lived in one area for centuries. But Westerners have tribes too. Your tribe seems to be all of America. But your tribe could have been even smaller. You could have said, 'How many Texans were on that plane?' Or 'How many journalists?'—as if only those people were worth grieving over."

"Well, I can't worry about *everyone* in the world," Dulcey said, taking a sip of salep and smacking her lips. "Very nice. Could use a little nutmeg."

"Got it right here," Nash said, passing her a tiny, covered bowl with a wooden spoon sticking out of it. "Aysha ground it fresh this morning."

"I feel like I should be apologizing for the fact that I have a tribe," Dulcey said, spooning the nutmeg onto the surface of her drink.

"No. We all protect and worry about the well-being of our own tribe members. But we're responding to very primitive animal instincts when we worry *only* about our own tribe—those connected to us by DNA. When we become more fully conscious—more fully human—we tend to worry about the well-being of people in other tribes as well."

"Who do you worry about?" Dulcey asked, squinting suspiciously.

"I was just thinking about that. I have no family. Have never taken a wife—although I came close once. I belong to no religious group—although I study them all as part of my work. I guess I've kept myself pretty much apart from all tribes. I think it suits my profession. Archeologists tend to be loners, internal people—thinkers, curious about how everything fits together—not too worried about where they themselves fit. I feel very loyal to the people who lived at Zeugma, even though they're all dead. It's their story I'm concerned about preserving—not my own."

"Sounds lonely," Dulcey said. "And can *you* honestly say you're just as interested in the number of Iraqis who died yesterday as the number of Americans?"

"Yes, I can," Nash said quietly. "I've been gone from America for twelve years. Except for an occasional guest lecture or a paper at a professional conference, I have not lived in America for over a decade. And so yes, I think I can honestly say I want to know how many Iraqis died yesterday and how many are likely to die tomorrow. And it bothers me that it's so hard to find out that number from the Western press when we know to the *person* how many Americans are dead."

Dulcey shook her head, sipping her drink. "Dr. Nash, you don't sound very patriotic . . ."

"What does that word mean?"

"Patriotic? It means you're loyal to your country."

"It also means you're concerned only with your own DNA . . . and no one else's," Nash said.

"Nonsense. I'm simply protective of my homeland—which has been attacked. I want the terrorists to be stopped before they have a chance to hurt us again."

"Why don't you want to know how many *people* were on that plane that went down in Egypt? We're not at war with Egypt . . . it was an equipment malfunction. No terrorists were involved in that plane crash."

Dulcey looked flustered as she finished off her salep and wiped her mouth with the back of her hand. "You make me sound like some kind of villain."

"No, you just sound like an American. You've lived in isolation between two big oceans all your life. And *that's* what I've gotten out of living here—concern for a lot of tribes besides my own," Nash said. "They live all around me—dead ones and living ones."

"Well, you're more broad-minded than most people," Dulcey said, handing him her empty cup. She stood up and stretched her arms, holding her face to the stars. "I've always contended that what we need to unite the world is a good threat from outer space. Nothing like being attacked by aliens to remind us earthlings that we're all—ultimately—on the same side."

"In the same tribe . . . ultimately . . ." Nash laughed softly and poured some hot water into their mugs, rinsed them out, then threw the water on the stones. "Good idea. Know any aliens who have a bone to pick with planet Earth?"

"Wish I did."

They were silent for a moment, and then Dulcey spoke again. "Dr. Nash, my book wasn't released until June. How did you read it before you asked for me in May?"

Again Nash considered telling her. But Rosa's request had been the only thing she had ever asked of him. No, he would tell Dulcey in the most careful way possible—and only after her work for CNN was finished.

"Maybe your agent contacted me before I read your book. I can't remember now," he said finally, lighting up another cigarette. Before she could respond, he added, "We should get some sleep. Big day tomorrow."

Dulcey nodded her head slowly and studied him for a moment. "You've heard that smoking cigarettes causes cancer, haven't you?" she asked. "Or hasn't the news reached you yet . . ."

Nash laughed. "Yes, Ms. Moore, we get that kind of news here, too." He sent another smoke ring wafting into the air and held his cigarette vertically until the ashes stacked up on top of it. "I guess the Middle Eastern idea of fate has sort of rubbed off on me. People around here figure they will die when Allah decrees it and not a second sooner. Most people don't even wear seat belts in this part of the world."

"Convenient way to think if you don't feel like you have much control over your life, I guess." Dulcey yawned and turned to go. "I think I'm going to make another attempt to sleep now."

"I'd like to talk to you again . . . before you leave. We might have more in common than you think."

"Sure. We'll talk again," Dulcey said, walking into the darkness. "Good night."

Nash stood and poured a pot of water over his campfire. "Rosa, Rosa . . . what did you unleash upon me . . ."

Dulcey stopped walking and called back to him. "What did you say?"

Nash, who was used to talking to himself in his largely solitary profession, was not used to being caught at it. "I said, *iyi akshamlar*. It means 'good night . . .'" Dulcey waved, and Nash watched until she disappeared inside the tent.

As the archeologist stuffed Dulcey's manuscript and his books into his rucksack, the morning calls to prayer from two different mosques sounded out from the little village across the river. In the distance, he could hear the warbling tones from the mosques in Nizip as well, a medley of male voices calling the faithful out of their warm beds to dip their heads to the ground for morning prayers. "No one around here has gotten a whole night's sleep for fourteen hundred years . . ." Nash muttered, trudging up the dark hill to the tent he shared with no one.

CHAPTER TEN

High atop Belkis Tepe, CIA On-Scene Commander Steve Cantwell positioned his forty-inch M40A1 sniper rifle through a gap in the ancient fortress wall. Now that it was almost noon, his garrison of Roman ruins no longer cast cooling shadows. Dressed in wool Turkish soldiers' uniforms, he and his men were already sweating profusely. Cantwell hoped the bank of thunderclouds to the east would soon bring rain.

Through his Schmidt and Bender scope, he could clearly see the shepherds across the river. He moved behind a tripod that held a pair of high-powered binoculars outfitted with a laser range-finder and calculated the distance to the shepherd's tent.

In the village, beyond the field of grazing goats and sheep, Cantwell could see the old mosque where one of his agents was stationed this morning. A skeleton of scaffolding identified the new mosque that was being built on the other side of the village. Cantwell wondered idly why a tiny village like Tilmusa needed two mosques.

Behind him, two American agents were looking the other way, scanning the roof and outbuildings of Asena Özturk's home. They could see directly into the mosaic-floored courtyard where Asena patiently fed an elderly white-haired woman, stopping often to dab a napkin to the woman's chin.

A fourth agent, positioned in a broiling toolshed full of shovels, photographed the shepherds' movements. The boy on the motorbike had returned from Birecik and was taking a turn watching the sheep near the water. The satellite picture on the commander's LCD monitor showed the movements of the shepherds as they busied themselves near their tent. A Turkish soldier working with Cantwell's team had stopped the boy on the way back from Birecik, asked him a question, and had attached a transponder locater under the boy's bike seat. They would soon be led to all the members of al Qaeda who were using the boy to run messages. Although cell phone signals were strong on the far side of the river, the terrorists were too smart to use cell phones.

Cantwell himself had had to bring a special military-issue satellite phone to avoid being caught without communication in the rural areas where cellular signals were spotty. Just then, his satellite phone vibrated against his shoulder, and he answered the call of an agent below who was keeping an eye on the CNN crew. "Is the crew planning a trip into town anytime soon or are they here for the duration?" Cantwell asked the agent.

"I encouraged Hat Man to keep 'em close. He says the crew may want to film at the museum."

"Discourage that. Destination too obvious—too insecure," Cantwell answered. "In fact, let's close the museum to the public until the crew is out of here. No sense in endangering civvies."

"Kid and Big Guy roamed last night again. Kid lost his father in Bag Town, I hear. We follow when they walk. And Star was up talking to Hat Man before the first call to prayer."

"Keep the crew sighted. Have a Turkish soldier do a check on the tents every hour. And move the women's shelter closer to the water— it's too close to the edge of camp for my taste. Copy?"

"Copy. What about the help? Nice Kurdish family—been with Hat Man for years. Their four sons dig trenches for him—the youngest girl works with Mom and Pop at the camp. They live in Tilmusa—come and go in a boat. We get antsy about that."

"Give them shelter on this side. Tell Hat Man we'll triple their pay if they'll stay on site until the crew leaves. Stop anyone who approaches the camp by boat."

"Copy. Over."

CHAPTER ELEVEN

While Frank and Tofer tested camera and light placements around Trench 25, Dulcey and Asena roamed the front slope of Belkis Tepe, pausing to talk with the various excavators toiling in the trenches.

Dulcey was amazed by the number of artifacts lying on the ground. She could not move without stepping on one. "Why are there so many pieces of pottery and bits of statues lying all over the ground?"

"You have to remember that the people of Zeugma fled from invaders. They had no time to pack their belongings. Everyone left their dishes and their tools and all their possessions behind. The excavators even found a plate with someone's dinner still on it. They found lamps, glass, window grills, jewelry, stone and metal furniture, and medical tools. When the customs house was exposed, there was money and a hundred thousand bullae still in it."

"Bullae?"

"Little personalized clay seals with figures on them that were used like stamps and customs seals to indicate who sent them. So every time the excavators dig with a shovel or a backhoe, these artifacts get scattered all over the excavation site."

Dulcey bent and picked up a piece of a pot with the handle still attached, then gently dropped it back on the ground. Each time she touched something made by another human being centuries ago or possibly millennia ago, she felt electricity dance up her arm. "It's like getting messages from the people who once lived here—clues about how they lived, what they thought was beautiful, what they cared about." She kicked what she thought was a red rock and heard a hollow thump. Stooping, she turned over a headless female torso, part of a terra cotta statue. Dulcey looked across Belkis Tepe and realized the entire hill was covered with bits of history. Like broken toys in a refuse dump, treasures from the past lay everywhere in the intensifying afternoon sun.

Asena took a wallet from her jacket pocket and picked out an old coin. "Look at this. It was minted right here at Zeugma. I have found six of these this year. I have to turn them over to the Ministry, but I love looking at them."

Dulcey held the coin up to compare the tiny imprinted image of Belkis Tepe to their current surroundings. "So, I'm looking at an image of what was once on this hill." The figures and some Latin words on the coin were worn but still clear. "Two thousand years ago, there was a temple with six columns and a goddess in front."

"No, there is *still* a temple with six columns and a goddess in front. You see the flat part of the hill? That is the top of the temple, but it is covered with dirt. And the statue in front of it is the statue we will dig up tomorrow. Can you imagine her?" Asena turned toward the Euphrates and raised her arms over her head. "I am the golden Goddess Fortuna in my flowing robes, welcoming all you people who are searching for your destiny. Every boat coming down the Euphrates can see me glinting in the sun with my magnificent temple behind me."

Dulcey sat on the side of the hill. "You live in a world most people can't even imagine. Goddesses buried in the soil, warriors' swords hidden under the dirt . . . priceless objects lying on the ground like fallen leaves waiting to be raked up."

Asena sat next to her, handing her a long piece of limestone with a vine of ivy carved down its length. "People in Turkey do not care much about old things. I think because these things are so easy to find. But I care. And Lee Nash cares. The poor man looked for Zeugma for eight years on the wrong side of the Euphrates. When the dam was built, he finally realized where it was."

"You knew him then. Why didn't you help him find it?"

Asena sighed. "I have so much to lose. When Lee finally began excavating on this side, near my house, I was afraid I would lose everything. I never planned on falling in love with him. I knew that if I did, it would be that much harder to keep my secrets."

Asena shook her head and then continued. "I was afraid my inheritance would be taken from me. There are many treasures in my house—treasures that have been passed down through many generations. There are cultural heritage laws you know. If Nash found out about my inheritance, I would be questioned, and if I could not prove the house and its contents were handed down to me, everything would be taken from me."

"You haven't told any of the excavators either?"

"I have confided in Tanju, because I have begun to trust her. She gives me very good advice. I wish I could show you and Tanju what's in my house. But I am not ready. Not now at least."

"So Nash has no idea about the things your family has passed down to you."

"He has his suspicions, because I know so much about Zeugma, but I have never shown them to him because I am afraid he would report me. He is very strict about the rules." She crossed her arms as the wind ruffled her hair. "My biggest problem is that one of my family's most precious possessions has been lost. The older and sicker my grandmother becomes, the more she begs me to find it."

"How old is it?"

"Very old. One, maybe two thousand years old—maybe as old as Zeugma. It has been in my family all these years. My grandmother always called it our *paha bichilmez mozaic*, which means our 'very precious mosaic.' When the Kurdish troubles started, she asked my husband, Guven, to bury it to keep it safe from the rebels, who were always looking for money. We were afraid our house would be taken over because it is in such an isolated area and would make a perfect hideout."

"And you have no idea where your husband buried the mosaic?"

"No, Guven died on the same night that he buried it. The outlaws from the PKK had been camping in the orchards near our house. I believe they asked my husband to feed or harbor them or perhaps give them something of value that they could sell. He must have refused them. We found his body the next day near the place they had made their camp—but the PKK themselves had vanished." Asena threw a pottery shard as far as she could. "I hate to think about what happened to him. Selene was just fifteen then. She was one reason why Guven was so protective of us. Can you imagine?"

"Horrible . . ." A rocket of guilt shot down Dulcey's spine. Back home, most of her worries were about finding a good parking place at the market or getting the kids to their soccer games and piano lessons on time. Usually the worst things that happened were having to fill airtime when a guest on her talk show cancelled at the last minute, or when Isabel had a terrible nightmare that kept the family up all night. *How would I have handled desperate terrorists camping in my pistachio grove?*

"Yildiz and I spent days searching for the precious mosaic, trying to imagine how Guven would have marked it so we could find it again. But then we realized that he may not have gotten a chance to mark it."

"That's awful. I'm so sorry about your husband," Dulcey said, thinking of her own kind-hearted husband and the fight they'd had before she left for Iraq.

Asena reached into her jacket pocket and took out a faded photograph. "I was just five when this photograph was taken. I carry it with me in case I ever come across the mosaic. You see it there on the wall behind me?"

"This one here?" Dulcey pointed to the mosaic above the little girl's head.

"Yes. It seemed so large to me when I was a child. But it is less than a meter wide and a meter long."

Dulcey was silent, thinking about how it must have been for Asena's family to know that desperate Kurdish separatists were roaming the countryside near their home. Asena's husband might have even died trying to keep this mosaic from falling into their hands. "How have you been able to hide your search from Dr. Nash?"

"I only look for it when he is not around. Can you imagine what he would do if I found a mosaic in the dirt of Zeugma and claimed it had always been in my family? No, I cannot risk that. I only wish I had found it before he began excavating here."

"So why don't you and Nash—"

"I loved him once. Sometimes I still think I love him. But he is an infuriating man. I came to believe his interest in me was really curiosity about the secrets I knew and the things I had in my house."

"But did he love you?"

"I am not sure Lee Nash is capable of genuine love. He once told me the emotion of love is simply the urge of a species to perpetuate itself. He told me when a parent loves his child, it is nothing more than the animal instinct to preserve the parent's DNA."

"How romantic." Dulcey looked up and saw a young man with two shovels over his shoulder approaching from the crosscut road.

"*Merhaba, Rifat Bey,*" Asena said in greeting. The young man glared at the two women, then hurried down the hill toward the dining tent. "Pay no attention," she said to Dulcey. "He was probably trying to get a closer look at the new girl in town."

"Who is he?"

"Rifat is one of Ali Yildirim's sons. Nash hires Ali's sons to dig for him. They're not very sociable. All the Yildirims resent the fact that I do not cover. They are not fond of Selene either. She's a very modern woman."

Dulcey bent over and picked up a piece of a clay bowl with a row of human figures painted along its rim. "Tell me more about your daughter."

"Selene is grown now. She studied in America and teaches at Ankara University. Like most Turkish young people, this place and anything having to do with antiquities bores her. She wants me to move to Ankara, but I do not dare leave the house." Asena stood and helped Dulcey up. "All that is my personal story. You and I have to write the story of Zeugma. We should talk about that instead."

"But you're the only person who actually lives in Zeugma— besides Dr. Nash—so your life is part of Zeugma's story."

"Please do not mention me in your story, Dulcey. I have too much to hide. It will only bring me trouble."

Dulcey picked up a broken pot with pale stripes on its handle. "Americans go crazy over antiquities because we only have four hundred years of history in our country. Turkey has things from *thousands* of years ago."

Asena shook her head and bit her lip. "So little history in your country? I wonder if your Native Americans think your history started four hundred years ago."

"No, I suppose you're right," Dulcey said sheepishly, remembering what Nash had said about tribes. "Tanju told me Cleopatra had a baby here. Is that true?"

"Perhaps. It is said that she went into labor while she was passing Zeugma after visiting the emperor of the region in Samasota—upstream. She docked her boat—or her barge maybe—and had her baby. Many historical records refer to Zeugma. Lawrence of Arabia lived near here for three years in the early 1900s."

"He did?" Dulcey asked, picturing Peter O'Toole in his flowing robes leading the Arab revolt against the Ottomans.

"T.E. Lawrence lived twenty miles downstream at Carchemish. Of course, the reason Lawrence was here was to spy on the Turks for England. He was a looter too. He kept writing his friends back home, telling them he could bring treasures—if they would send him money so he could hire diggers or buy artifacts from the locals. The old Ottoman Empire lost a lot of her valuable artifacts to men like him."

"But after the dam was built and part of Zeugma was excavated a few years ago, why did the digging stop? Why didn't your government fully excavate it?"

Asena dug her wallet out of her jacket pocket again and took out a pink-colored bill featuring a picture of Atatürk. "See this? This is worth about seven U.S. dollars today. Just ten years ago, it was worth about seven *thousand* dollars. For a country with that kind of economy, digging up old ruins is pure luxury. When the economy began to wane, only foreigners had enough money to dig all this up. And once the foreigners lost interest, it all went back under the dirt."

"But *why* have foreigners lost interest? There are still two-thirds of this city yet to be excavated. The temple on the hill, three churches under the water, a hippodrome, a theatre, Roman baths, tombs—and more of those wonderful mosaics and frescoes. How can we just leave all that to the looters?"

"Yavash, yavash," Asena said, motioning with her palms held downward. "Slowly, slowly. Your story on CNN will help. When people see what there is here, maybe they will want to study it themselves or send money to keep the excavation going."

"It seems to me that Lee Nash is one person you would consider a true friend in all this."

Asena sighed, shook her head, and started walking quickly down the hill. "I am weary of speaking about Dr. Nash."

Dulcey stumbled after her, catching up and stopping Asena's downward flight. "Asena! Please, stop and talk to me. It's your job to tell me these things."

Asena bent over, put her hands on her knees, and took ragged breaths until she had calmed herself. "The things in my house . . . would make Dr. Nash's work . . . much *easier*. But . . . they are my inheritance. I do not want to sell these things or give them to the state. They are all I have left of my family." She waved her hand, ending the conversation and taking off down the hill again.

The curiosity meter in Dulcey's brain spiked, and she hurried after the woman, stumbling on pottery shards and loose rocks. "Hold on."

"I am only trying to help you understand why Dr. Nash and I do not get along. He thinks I *owe* the world any knowledge I might have. He feels it is his duty to expose it to the world. And once he does, my life and my possessions will no longer be my own. Lee Nash cares only about history. He does not care about the needs of living, breathing human beings."

Dulcey scrambled after Asena all the way down the hill. "You asked me to tell the world about Zeugma—that's why all of us are here. You're supposed to *help* me get this story—not hide it from me. What if I ask CNN to pay you extra for your part of the story?"

"You argue exactly like Dr. Nash does. If you cannot get what you want with words, you try to offer money." Asena's eyes blazed.

"But CNN *is* paying you. This is your job."

"Then I will send my paycheck back to CNN and quit this assignment right now."

Panting, Dulcey sat down on a fallen tree to catch her breath and rub her sore ankles. "We could do it on your terms. *You* could call the shots. I could tell your story without disclosing my source—or source materials. How can I tell the story of Zeugma unless I understand what continues to be hidden here?"

"Do you remember what I told you about honor and trust?"

"Yes, I remember. They're the only things you have left in this part of the world."

"Ahhh, you do remember. My honor *depends* on keeping my secrets." Asena turned and looked at Dulcey for several seconds, seeming to weigh something in her mind. She clenched and relaxed her fists at her sides.

Dulcey looked at her carefully. "All right. I won't push you. But I think you *want* to tell me. I think it must be a burden to take care of . . . whatever it is."

Like the volatile weather in southeast Turkey, Asena too had a wide range of emotions—and they came and went without much warning. She stood there, looking over the Euphrates, watching the clouds roll toward Zeugma. "My grandmother is dying. Yildiz raised me since I was eight, after my parents died in a flu epidemic. She is passing things on to me as they were passed to her by generations of women before her. And yes, they are a great, great burden." Asena touched Dulcey's arm, and a smile that seemed as ancient as the ground on which they were standing crept across her face. "Thank you for sharing my burden for a moment. But please do not ask about my secrets. Can you do that?"

A wind that had traveled over the Asian plateau whipped Dulcey's hair. Dust from the kingdoms of the Bible and the Koran swirled over the limestone hill. The little place above Dulcey's jaw pulsed. She suddenly remembered a gesture from her childhood, which was always accompanied by a very old-fashioned phrase. "On my honor," Dulcey whispered, making the sign of a cross over her heart.

CHAPTER TWELVE

The usually quiet excavation camp bustled with activity now as it prepared to receive more television crews from CNN. Workers from the nearby villages were setting up additional sleeping tents and accommodations, and the Yildirims were shouting back and forth, preparing a huge meal for the hungry travelers who would soon arrive. Turkish soldiers patrolled the banks of the river, two by two, and kept watch from Belkis Tepe. Military vehicles came and went. The heady aroma of roasting lamb hung over the camp, making Dulcey's mouth water in anticipation of the evening's feast.

Midway through the day, Asena excused herself to go check on her grandmother. Dulcey watched as the Land Rover drove way, and then she meandered over to the women's tent. It had been moved nearly to the edge of the water. When she entered the dark tent, she found Tanju braiding Aysha's hair by the light of a kerosene lamp.

"Aysha is going to stay with us in our tent," Tanju said, weaving four silky ropes of hair into a complicated plait. "Nash asked the Yildirims to stay in camp until the CNN crew leaves, so Ali and Fatma have a little tent near the cooking area."

Aysha giggled behind her hand and whispered something to Tanju in Turkish. Both of her cheeks dimpled deeply. Then she blushed and looked away.

"I showed her your book just now," Tanju said. "Now she knows you are famous in America. I think she is feeling shy around you."

Dulcey reached out and took Aysha's face in her hands. "She's such a sweetheart. Tell her I'm just like everyone else. I don't bite."

Tanju translated, and Aysha giggled again. Then the girl tied her violet-edged scarf over her hair, kissed Tanju and Dulcey on both cheeks, and hurried out of the tent.

"I hope you do not mind that I let her stay with us," Tanju said. "Her parents are so strict, and everyone treats her like a slave around here."

"I'm happy to have her with us. But, it's October—why isn't she in school?"

"Her parents took her out six years ago, when she was ten, to help them with their work." Tanju groaned and flopped on one of the cots. "You have no idea what it is like for girls like her. Soon, she will be forced to marry a cousin or the son of someone her family knows, and she will never have the opportunity to educate herself." Tanju closed her eyes and a pained expression crossed her face. "Aysha is very intelligent. There is a teacher named Turkan from Tilmusa who brings her books. Turkan has pleaded with Fatma and Ali to let their daughter come back to school. Selene has tried talking to them too. But they refuse. She will bring a very high bride price because she is so beautiful. I believe they are holding out for the best offer . . ."

"Is that legal?" Dulcey asked, horrified.

"In this part of the country, tradition is more important than the law. It has always been like that."

Dulcey and Tanju walked to the dining tent. Ali was kneeling by a deep pit, peeling back layers of tin foil, testing the lamb with a long skewer. Fatma was busy spooning dollops of a rice mixture onto grape leaves, rolling them tightly, and wedging them into a pan slick with olive oil.

After a few moments, Dr. Nash came over a nearby hill, followed by Tofer and Frank. "We saw the CNN trucks coming down the road," Tofer said. "The weather is a problem, Dulcey. The clouds and the wind are picking up. We can put up tarps tomorrow if it's raining, but tarps are no good in a high wind—they create too much sound. If it's too windy, we'll have to forget the live show and go to tape."

She wanted to give in to him—to let him call the shots for a while like Frank seemed to be allowing. Tofer was being so diligent and serious in John Barrow's big shoes. *What if John had suggested we abandon the live story?* Dulcey knew the answer. He wouldn't have.

"No way, Tofer," Dulcey said. "The story's not worth doing if we don't do it live. We didn't come all this way just to do a taped documentary. We could have had someone else shoot the footage, and we could have narrated the voice-overs from the comfort of the studio back home."

"We'll do what we can, but we can't control the weather," Frank said. "Don't you think digging up a golden goddess will be impressive no matter whether it's live or taped?"

Dulcey folded her arms and dug in. "No. The weather is part of reality. I don't care if there's a tornado *and* an earthquake tomorrow afternoon—we're doing this thing live."

"Okay. We're doing it live," Frank said, shaking his head, giving Tofer a look that told him not to push it.

* * *

Soon a convoy of three CNN trucks accompanied by military vehicles clambered over the rocks into the camp. An hour later, more than twenty additional CNN employees and security guards were seated around the picnic tables eating succulent chunks of Ali's lamb wrapped in hunks of pita bread. Fatma's rolled dolma, mounds of rice pilaf, heaps of salad, and roasted vegetables of all kinds brought expressions of delight from the famished travelers.

Her stomach full, Dulcey sat back and enjoyed watching the people whose passion in life was communication. Modern-day storytellers. All around her they gestured and took turns acting out various incidents that had occurred on their nearly five-hundred-mile journey from Ankara.

Dulcey knew some of the people from CNN International, as well as a man named Cole Marburn, who had flown to Ankara from the main office in Atlanta. He had been quiet all evening after learning the details about the death of his good friend John Barrows. Cole and Tofer sat at the farthest picnic table, speaking in low tones. Dulcey watched Cole pour himself another glass of Turkish Raki, and then she watched him pour one for Tofer. As soon as the glasses were empty, he refilled them.

A short distance away, talking to Mehmet and Tanju, was Sophie DeNiro—the ace satellite techie from the Rome bureau she'd heard about. Another table was filled with photographers who didn't seem very interested in the rest of the group. They demonstrated their camera equipment to each other, showing off their latest toys and gadgets, and explaining how everything worked in a language all their own. *Are some of these photographers the undercover security team Major Thurman promised us?* Dulcey got up and casually walked by the photographers, searching the faces of each person, trying to determine if they were CNN or CIA. She heard phrases like "No way, man, eight million point *two* megapixels" and "a shutter lag of only fifty-five milliseconds," as well as an argument that started with "But Canon has the EOS 1DS. It *is* the fastest." *No CIA here,* Dulcey thought, smiling slightly. She moved to the other side of the table, nodding at the people she knew and continuing to listen to the photographers vying with each other.

She recognized the handsome Devrim Yolju, who was in charge of the team from CNN Turk. He stood near the photographers' table and shook his head. "Dulcey Hanim, I have already listened to them argue about who has the best equipment for five hundred miles. Now I know the answer to why there is no peace on earth."

Dulcey laughed and nodded in agreement. After a few moments of conversation, Devrim left and Tanju came over, stirring her glass of chai. "Why are television people so tiny?" she asked. "So many good looking men—and the best looking ones are all shorter than Napoleon."

"You ever see a miniature horse?" Dulcey asked. "I don't mean Shetland ponies—they're stocky and thick. Miniature horses are perfectly proportioned, smaller versions of normal-sized horses. That's how I think of television folk."

"But *why* are they small?" Tanju asked, swinging her own long legs over the bench and then under the picnic table, looking morosely at the sea of beautiful little men eating and drinking in the yellow light of the kerosene lamps.

"Well, with the weight and girth added by the television cameras, they all look average-sized on television. If you had average-sized people, they would look big."

"And what's wrong with being big?" Tanju asked, plopping her usual six sugar cubes into her chai.

"Good question. It's an American thing, I guess . . ." Dulcey said.

"Sounds stupid," Tanju said, wrinkling her brow.

"It *is* stupid," Dulcey agreed. "Better go for the cameramen—they have to be big to carry those hefty television cameras. Like Tofer, if he's not too young for you."

Tanju smiled but didn't comment on Tofer. "World is crazy, huh? A beautiful, intelligent woman like me worrying about whether someone will ever fall in love with her."

"You could just wait until someone offers your father a good bride price for you," Dulcey said. Her smile faded when she saw Tanju's expression grow dark.

"You should not make fun. This is a serious problem in southeast Turkey." Tanju checked behind her to make sure no one could hear. "I am considering taking Aysha back to Ankara with me after the goddess is in the museum. There are organizations that will help her go back to school."

"But would her parents let her go?"

"I doubt it, but I have been—how do you call it—laying the groundwork. I am miserable for her every time I see her hiding from her parents so she can read her books. The girl is starved for ideas and knowledge. And she is of age now. She should make her own choices."

After dinner, Fatma Hanim and Aysha walked between the rows of picnic tables serving chai and Turkish coffee from big silver trays. Then Ali came around with plates of some kind of toasted crust filled with a mild sweet cheese and topped with mounds of fresh whipped cream. Dulcey watched Aysha lower her eyes as she served the cups from her tray.

As the Yildirims served dessert, the CNN people, especially the Americans, raved about the great Turkish meal. Tanju translated their lavish compliments for the Yildirim family. Aysha blushed, and Fatma Hanim smiled for the first time, showing a gap on the side of her mouth where three teeth should have been. Ali went to the little tent he shared with his wife and came back with a long-necked stringed instrument he called a *saz*. He perched on a table and began to play.

The men pulled all the tables out of the tent to clear the cement floor for dancing. One of the diggers came in with a drum tied to his waist and began to pound to the beat of Ali's song. An archeologist brought out a reed instrument and joined in. An off-duty soldier began to sing a Turkish ballad.

"Basri is singing an old song from Urfa about a man named Pala Rimze who had a mustache shaped like a knife," Tanju explained to Dulcey. She curled her index finger above her lip as the others were doing. "That is the shape of his mustache." Other Turks sang along and clapped to its rhythm. Soon the foreigners were alternately clapping and holding their fingers over their lips whenever the mustache was mentioned. The song seemed to have at least twenty verses.

"Let's dance!" yelled a Turkish photographer. He ran to the middle of the floor and motioned for the other men to join him. The men linked their arms over each other's shoulders.

Tanju jumped up. "Come, ladies," she said to two women from the Istanbul bureau as she grabbed their hands. "We will show the Americans how to dance." The three of them linked their fingers and began a simple repeating grapevine step. Mehmet, Devrim Yolju, and several of the Turkish photographers joined the male line, their shoulders shaking in time to the music, taunting the women into more and more complicated steps.

The Americans leaned closer, eager to be invited into the dance. Tanju grabbed Dulcey and slowed the line so she could learn the steps. Cole and Doug joined in with the men. Tanju and Dulcey danced the line toward Aysha, sweeping her into their formation. The women wove in and out of the nine trees that anchored the edges of the dining tent and danced around the big telephone pole in the middle. The men made a circle around Devrim, spurring him on in his dance. Devrim let out a yell as he swooped up and down, kicking his legs out in front of him and slapping his heels like a Russian folk dancer. Two Turkish photographers tried to outdo him, leaping and cavorting in time to the music. Then the line of men took off around the dining tent again, making warrior sounds like the barbarians who had once invaded Zeugma.

Sophie, from the Roman bureau, let out a wild whoop and forced the women's line to join the men's. She grabbed an attractive off-duty soldier and added him to the women's line. A CNN security guard broke in between Tanju and a reporter from Istanbul. Now the whole line of men and women was connected by a chain of interlocking hands. Aysha danced and danced, her head thrown back, braids bouncing under her gauzy head scarf, her enchanting laugh mingling with the music. Dulcey noticed how the girl avoided her father's eyes. And how she refused to look at her mother.

"Tofer! Frank!" Tanju called. "Come join us."

Frank pushed Tofer into the line next to Tanju. Stumbling from having too much to drink, Tofer tried to keep up with the others. His steps were awkward, but the serpentine line of dancers kept him upright, moving to the rhythm, his confused but happy face lighting up as he passed each kerosene lamp.

As Dulcey danced near the outer edge of the tent, she noticed a young Turkish soldier on guard duty following the dancing Aysha with only his eyes. Aysha likewise continued to glance at the soldier. The two of them seemed mesmerized by one another. Every time the line passed the soldier, Dulcey could feel the attraction between them.

The dancers whirled around and around in time to the seemingly endless Turkish song. But Dulcey's high spirits broke in midflight when she caught sight of Fatma Hanim watching her daughter from the far side of the tent as she worked. The woman's obvious rage made the curling tattoos on her face come alive as she washed the tables, scrubbing them furiously with soapy water. Her mouth trembled and her eyes narrowed, never leaving her daughter's swirling, dancing figure. Dulcey watched Fatma throw the soapy water from her bucket out on the gravel as Aysha danced on and on, smiling at the soldier each time she danced by his guard post.

As the song came to an end, Fatma stepped into the dining tent and whispered into her daughter's ear. Dulcey watched the girl's face fall. Aysha wrapped her arms around herself as though she were suddenly cold. Without a word to anyone and avoiding the soldier's gaze, she walked to the women's tent. She was absent for the rest of the party.

CHAPTER THIRTEEN

Exhausted from dancing, the revelers found chairs or sat on the cement floor. Fatma and Ali served Turkish coffee again. As the tired dancers finished their tiny cups of the strong brew, Tanju showed the foreigners how to turn their cups upside down on their saucers and wait until the grounds dripped into interesting shapes. Then she asked each person to put a coin on the base of each of their upturned cups. "It absorbs the heat and helps me read your future better," she said with a wink. "The teller of fortunes, of course, keeps the coin."

"Can you tell me whether I should sell my Time Warner stock?" someone shouted.

"I must look at your cup, sir," Tanju said with the flair of a prophetess. "Those of you who want their fortunes read in the old Turkish way, please come see me at this table over here."

Doug Rickman was first in line. Dulcey watched Tanju pocket the coin and take his cup into her hand. She turned it around and around, holding it this way and that way in the light, muttering and looking pleased.

"Well, what do you see?" Doug said.

"I see a star here. And three dots in a triangle shape here . . . that must be holly," she told Doug with absolute gravity in her voice. "This means you will be a Hollywood star someday. I am sure of it."

Doug, who had an ego the size of New York City, leaned in closer, "I do have some acting experience. I even had an agent at one time. When would you suggest I make a career change like that?"

Tanju consulted the cup, then turned it toward Doug. "You see these three stripes? Those are years. Do you see how the last stripe is a bit shorter than the others? That means three years from now in the fall."

"Next!" she called as Doug went away looking happy, scribbling something on his notepad.

Dulcey, who didn't drink coffee, borrowed someone's cup and saucer from the dish bin and handed it over. Tanju took the coin and squinted into the cup. "You are looking for something you lost."

Dulcey thought of Matt and the fight they'd had before she left. "Go on . . ."

"You have become aware recently that you want it back."

Dulcey leaned in so she could see the inside of the cup. "Show me what you're looking at."

Tanju pointed to an empty space in the smudges of thick coffee grounds. "You see there? A perfectly clean place there—when the rest of the cup is covered with stories. And you see this shape here? A map of Turkey as plain as I have ever seen it. You will find what you have lost—in Turkey."

Dulcey nodded, amused, and relinquished her place to the next person in line.

"Ahhh, Sophie," Tanju said, pocketing the coin and examining Sophie's cup. "Are there *two* men in your life now?"

"Shh," Sophie whispered, leaning in closer. "Keep your voice down. One of them is here . . ." She scooted next to Tanju. "So what does it say?"

Tanju looked solemn. "To find true love, you must choose between them. The taller one is not true. The shorter adores you, but he is not ready for commitment."

"Where do you see that?" Sophie asked, clearly worried now. She peered into the cup, and Tanju pointed to two rivulets of coffee grounds. "Hmph. They both look like big *drips* to me."

The line for Tanju's prophecies grew longer. Someone let Tofer take a place near the front, and Tanju turned his cup around and around in her hand. "This is a very sad time in your life. But soon you will raise your head again," she said, showing him a round spot in the cup. "When you raise your head, you will see that a beautiful, tall, *very* intelligent woman admires you very much."

Tofer looked up and gave Tanju a crooked grin. "I do admire you," he said, slurring his words. "From the minute I saw you—" Suddenly he hooked his hand behind Tanju's neck, drew her toward him, and kissed her full on the lips. Tanju looked startled and drew back from him, setting his cup on the table. As though a spotlight were suddenly thrown on the picnic table, everyone in the dining tent stopped talking and looked at Tanju and Tofer.

Mehmet stormed toward the table, his fists clenched at his sides. "Tofer Bey, I ask you not to be uppity with Tanju Hanim—"

"Uppity?" Tofer's mocking laugh quickly dissolved into a sputtering, high-pitched choking fit.

"Disrespecting," Mehmet spat back. "Tanju is honorable Turkish woman. You do not do such things in our country."

Tofer stood, towering over Mehmet. "If I kiss a woman because I like her, is that disrespectful?"

Frank pushed through the crowd to get to Tofer. "Settle down, pal. This is just a clash of cultures. Let's keep our heads." He guided Tofer away from the Turkish archeologist.

Mehmet followed them, puffing his chest out. "She is Turkish woman, not *Sex in the City* woman. Not *Ally McBeal* woman. Not *Buffy*, harlot vampire slayer. Not rock star! Not prostitute *American* woman!"

Frank turned toward Mehmet, clearly battling down his own emotions and holding Tofer off with his other hand. "I apologize to Tanju on behalf of Tofer. He has had too much raki. I am sure he will ask for her forgiveness tomorrow when he is himself again."

Tofer shoved Frank away. "Apologize? To these people who live in the Stone Age? *No!* I will *not* apologize to these people who killed my father in the name of their *god*."

The Turks and the CNN crew fell silent. Frank put his hand on Tofer's shoulder once more. "Son, you've had too much to drink. These people did not kill your father. These people are our friends—"

"They're Muslims." Tofer turned to face the group. "You know who you are. Which ones of you are radical Osama bin Laden lovers?" Tofer yelled, throwing Frank's hand off his shoulder. "*You* people are the ones who need to lighten up. Not us. Americans are free. *Free!* Do you hear me, Tanju? You could have kissed me in America, and no one would have said a thing to you."

Dr. Nash, who had been conspicuously absent during the music and dancing, now hurried into the tent. "This will stop right now."

Frank pushed Tofer out of the dining tent into the darkness.

A Turkish excavator and two of the photographers from Istanbul encircled Mehmet, talking softly to him, soothing him. One of the photographers put his arms around Mehmet and held him until Mehmet's breathing slowed. The men took Mehmet out of the tent, murmuring in Turkish. Fatma cleared tables, angrily scraping garbage into a tub.

Dr. Nash clinked a spoon against a glass and announced, "Emotions are running high tonight. In Tofer's case, fatigue and grief and alcohol perhaps made him say things he would not ordinarily say. Please remember Tofer has just lost his father. By tomorrow, everything will be better. By tomorrow, we will all remember our manners. Tanju, are you all right?"

Tanju looked embarrassed. "It was nothing. Really. Mehmet over-reacted, and I apologize for him as well."

Nash nodded. "Listen, everyone, we have a job to do tomorrow, and we need to do it well. I'd suggest all of you refrain from drinking any more this evening."

The CNN crew gathered around Nash, looking grateful for his intervention. "Welcome to your first night in Zeugma," Nash said. "I know you're tired, and you're wondering where you will be sleeping tonight. While you were all cavorting like a bunch of Bacchanalians, I arranged all of your sleeping areas. Now, all the women will bunk with Dulcey and Tanju in that big tent near the water. We have an extra tent for the women if it gets too crowded in there."

A Turkish soldier brought Nash a big piece of paper with markings on it. Another soldier dragged a picnic table back into the tent.

Nash spread out the paper on the table, and the men crowded around it. "The men can look on this diagram to see which of the tents we have assigned you to. We've set up six big tents with a cot, a pillow, and a blanket for each one of you. You'll find a porta-pottie between every other tent. Now, people, this is important. Commander Steve Cantwell here has been assigned to keep track of your whereabouts. We didn't want him to stand out too much, so we put him in a Turkish military uniform. I'll let him explain the procedure."

An American wearing Turkish army fatigues stood in front of the group. His blond crew cut was just visible under a cocked beret with a brass star and crescent pin fastened to it. He yelled out the procedures as though he were drilling new army recruits. "Listen up, everyone. Your guards need to know exactly where you are at all times. No one is to take a walk or leave the premises without checking in with me right here in the dining tent."

"What about Trench 25?" someone shouted.

"The area between the tents and the excavation trenches will be considered internal. Anything past that requires a check-in. And by that I mean no hikes in the pistachio grove or a walk along the river bank without checking in with me. Most of you are guests in this country. You need to make yourselves easy to live with and easy to protect. If you go off by yourself, you may be mistaken for a hostile and find a bullet winging its way toward you."

"Won't they shout something at us before they shoot?" asked an American camera techie with a Southern accent.

"The Turkish soldiers, for the most part, speak very little English, but the soldiers will radio each other and identify friendlies. You make their jobs easier if you're predictable and stay in your assigned sleeping areas," Cantwell said.

"*Mannaggia*," Sophie cursed in Italian, rolling her eyes at Devrim, her mouth gathered in a pout of disappointment.

Dulcey felt relieved. Cantwell had to be part of a CIA team. The others must be somewhere nearby.

Doug Rickman, who had just flown in from Jordan, called out in his rich television voice, "Commander Cantwell, how do people around here feel about Americans? I mean about *real* Americans—not the cast of *Ally McBeal* and *Sex in the City* and . . . *Buffy*."

"Americans are not too popular anywhere in the world these days, sir. We have Syria just twelve miles across the nearest border and Iraq and Iran up the way. Most Turks like Americans, but none of them are happy about the war in Iraq."

"Yeah, well, maybe the Turks should remind themselves whose allies y'all are." The photographer from Atlanta stopped talking when he realized he'd created the second horrified silence of the evening. "Well, dang. I thought y'all had free speech here," he said, seemingly unrepentant of his gaff.

Dr. Nash shot the photographer a look and rejoined the conversation. "The Turks don't need a reminder, but you Americans need to know there has been a recent, very bloody civil war in this area of Turkey. Seven thousand Turkish soldiers and thirty thousand civilians were killed over the last decade and a half. Even though it's over, things are still sore around here, and we still need to watch ourselves."

Out of the corner of her eye, Dulcey saw well-mannered Cole Marburn put up his hand as though he were in school. "Can we travel to the Gaziantep Museum tomorrow morning? We have to shoot a certain amount of footage to fill in the dead parts of the story." Dulcey gave him a look, pretending to be insulted by the idea that there would be any dead space to worry about. "No offense, Dulcey. It's just that during a live shoot, if a shovel breaks or there's a problem with sound, we have to be able to show relevant footage to keep the viewers occupied."

"That's a negative, Mr. Marburn," Cantwell said. "You can shoot film at the museum after the goddess is transported there directly after the dig. Until then, the museum's closed to everyone."

Nash spoke up. "We'll all stay right here on site, and your viewers will sweat this out with the rest of us. What happens in real time is what your viewers will see."

Cole stepped back and bowed dramatically to Nash. "We'll do it your way, good doctor. It's your dig."

Dulcey stood up, notebook in hand. "By tomorrow at six P.M., I will be up to speed on Zeugma. And . . . I will be prepared to ad lib in case a *shovel* breaks." She flashed what she hoped was a dazzling smile at Cole.

"Who's going to give an overview?" Cole asked.

"Maybe we can have Dr. Nash point out the features of the Zeugma site before CNN Turk does their intro. Doug, can we have Cole standing at those mosaics in the covered trenches?" Dulcey asked.

Doug was producing both the live excavation at Zeugma as well as "The Pillaging of Mesopotamia" documentary with its opening scenes in Baghdad. He nodded and wrote some notes on his clipboard.

"Talk to Tanju, Cole," Dulcey said. "She'll tell you about the mosaics in the covered trenches in case we need to go to you."

"I'm on it," Cole said.

"Dr. Nash, you will need to explain exactly what you are doing as you go along during the excavation of the goddess. Try not to use difficult technical terms—if you do, I may stop you and ask for definitions so we don't lose our viewers."

One of the photographers asked, "What about rain—do we have cover?"

Dulcey paused a moment and scanned the crowd to make sure her decision would sink in. "We are doing this thing live no matter what. Have you got that? Doing this live means doing it with live weather. But, having said that, let's all pray for calm weather, shall we?" *Calm weather,* thought Dulcey as she sat down. *Like no al Qaeda waiting to steal the goddess. Like knowing who and where the U.S. security team is. Like not having people from two different cultures end up in an ugly brawl. Like not having this story end up costing anyone their life.*

"Why are we shooting so late in the day?" called another photographer, breaking into Dulcey's thoughts.

"Going live at six o'clock guarantees we're on for California school children during their morning classes. American schoolkids in the East will see it in the early afternoon. European viewers will see it in the evening, and viewers in the Middle East and Asia will catch it before bedtime. We all set then?" Everyone murmured agreement. Dulcey nodded at Cantwell and Nash to indicate that she was finished.

"Okay, if that's it, then you're all free to go to your tents," Dr. Nash said. "See you at breakfast."

"Which way to the showers?" Sophie asked, an impish look on her face. "I read in one of Dr. Nash's articles that the original residents of Zeugma had Roman baths, running water, *fountains* even—and an underground sewer system. So where are *our* showers?"

Dr. Nash sniffed and shook his head. "I'm afraid Zeugma's a little less posh than it was in the first century. You'll have to make do with a bath in the Euphrates tomorrow. Men, you can use the inlet next to the agora—where the market used to be. And the women can use the cove beyond the covered trenches—there are a lot of trees over that way. Please remember that you're in Turkey, so try to observe the strict codes of modesty so as not to offend the locals. You've already seen tonight that our cultures clash in some regards. The American television programs the people here see make our women look pretty loose.

So please be on your best behavior. Do your part for world peace while you're here. Okay? Good night, everyone."

Dulcey stood at Dr. Nash's side for a moment, watching his jaw. She hadn't noticed before how it twitched when he was determined. Just like hers did.

Nash caught her staring at him. "Good *night,* Ms. Moore. Make your friends go to bed before they manage to start a riot," he said and marched off.

She looked out through the grove beyond the camp and saw that even more soldiers had arrived while everyone was dining and dancing. The new troops had set up their tents and were cooking their dinners over campfires.

After most everyone had gone inside their tents for the night, Dulcey waited for the Yildirims and some of the local workers to move all the picnic tables back into the dining tent for tomorrow's breakfast. Then she sat at one of the tables and wrote in her notebook:

As everyone got ready for bed, Zeugma hummed with the sounds of a new community creating itself. Pecking orders were established. Leaders had been identified and challenged. New ones were already planning strategies. Rules had been broken; new ones made. Truces were called over disputed territories. The tasks of daily living had been divided up among us. One more civilization on top of the last one. And that one on top of another, which rests on top of another. Layers and layers of humanity, deep down underneath my feet. All of them with their warriors. None of them ever having found the way of peace . . .

When Dulcey finally entered her tent, most of the women were asleep, arms flung over faces, soft snores coming from under the blankets. There had been no running water for nighttime beauty rituals. The kerosene lamps, now dark, had not been strong enough to read by. Cell phones did not work here. There was nothing to do but sleep.

Dulcey saw that only Aysha was still awake. She sat on the girl's cot next to the tent opening. In the moonlight, she could see that Aysha had been crying. Having no words the girl could understand, she patted the girl's back, drew the blanket up over her thin shoulders, and kissed her wet cheek. She thought of her daughter, Isabel, and hoped Matt would remember to put his big hand over Izzy's eyes so she could let the world go—so she could trust enough to fall asleep. Then she went to her own cot and got under the covers.

As Dulcey pulled the blanket up to her chin, she thought of the fierce look on Mehmet's face as he had stood up for Tanju's honor. She thought about how American women were portrayed on the sitcoms that were sold to Turkish television stations. If that was all he knew, it was no wonder Mehmet and the other Turks had such an unfavorable view of American women. She wondered if Mehmet truly hated Tofer and the culture that had encouraged the kiss. And if he did have hatred in his heart for the West and its people, she wondered whether Mehmet would follow the man who was likely the most hate-filled Muslim in the world—that tall, turbaned man who lived in a cave.

CHAPTER FOURTEEN

At breakfast the next morning, Dulcey could tell no one had slept very well. The usually dashing Cole Marburn looked like he had bedded down in a cotton field. Bits of blanket lint stuck to his stylishly coiffed hair, and there was a smear of dirt on his cheek. "I'm craving a Hilton right now," he grumbled as he forked a cucumber over to his plate.

"Hey, Marburn, if we look a little rugged, so much the better. This ain't Disneyland," Dulcey teased, chasing olives around a serving bowl with a spoon. *Olives . . . for breakfast,* she thought again.

Doug was on his third Turkish coffee by the time Dulcey sat down with her breakfast. Aysha looked weary—Dulcey knew the girl had been up for hours preparing the day's food and stoking the campfire. A yawning Tanju wandered around with her clipboard, getting the names of everyone on the dig for the Ministry of Culture records.

"So, the big day has arrived," said a cheerful Dr. Nash as he straddled the picnic bench next to Dulcey and set down a plate heaped with food. It was clear that he was no longer bothered by uncomfortable mattresses and strange noises in the night. "The Yildirim boys got here early this morning, and they've already exposed the top half of Trench 25." He gestured toward the shovels flying above the trench on the hill. "Those boys have been digging with me since the youngest was twelve years old. Now they're all married, and they're raising my next excavation crew."

"Have you seen Tofer and Frank?" Dulcey asked, peeling a hard-boiled egg.

"They're up there at the trench with a big roll of canvas. Weather could go either way, it looks like."

"Where's Asena? She's supposed to help me with the script," Dulcey said, popping bits of the egg into her mouth, followed by several olives. "She wasn't at the party last night. I wonder if her grandmother's all right. Let me take a soldier and go knock on her door."

Nash turned and spoke to a Turkish soldier. After checking in with Cantwell, Dulcey found herself in a military jeep on her way to Asena's house on the other side of the hill. She heard a siren in the distance.

As they approached Asena's home, Dulcey saw a battered ambulance pulling into the circular drive. Two men carrying medical equipment rushed toward the house. Dulcey hurried in through the door the paramedics had left ajar. The soldier that had accompanied Dulcey stationed himself by the door as she disappeared inside Asena's house.

Once inside, Dulcey glanced around her and was surprised at the size of Asena's house. One spacious room led to another through a series of arches and enormous carved doors. In the front rooms, hand-woven kilims—decorative rugs—covered the walls; faded Turkish carpets covered every inch of floor space. "Asena!" she called, walking through room after room until she came to a courtyard, its floor a handsome mosaic of lush fruits and twining vines and flowers.

"Over here, Dulcey." On the far side of a fountain, Asena stood watching paramedics tend to a frail woman lying on a chaise lounge. Dulcey gave Asena a hug.

"My grandmother had a bad night and may have had a stroke this morning. She has had several in the past few months."

Dulcey made some quick decisions about the Zeugma shoot. "Listen, don't worry about the work—we have until the evening to put this together. You go with your grandmother to the hospital. Be with her. She needs you. I'll get Tanju to interpret for the Turkish crew and help me with the script."

"Thank you. I feel so badly that this has happened when I'm supposed to be working, but I need to be with her now." Asena turned to the paramedics and spoke harshly to them. They slowed their movements and lifted the woman more gently onto the rolling stretcher. Then they fastened a series of straps over the old woman's tiny body.

Dulcey gave Asena another quick hug. "Be with your grand-mother—that's the important thing now."

"Thank you. Tell everyone I wish them luck. I hope it goes well," Asena said. Dulcey waited as Asena gave orders to one of her house-keepers and her security guard. Then Asena gazed lovingly at the woman on the stretcher, tucking the blanket around her body and stroking her wispy white hair.

"I hope it goes well for you too," Dulcey said, remembering how her own laughing, vibrant mother had looked so small and quiet in her final days.

Asena gathered a tapestry bag and a small suitcase, and the two women followed the paramedics through the warren of corridors and rooms until they reached the front door.

"Your house is bigger than it looks from the outside. I was surprised," Dulcey said.

"Yes, it is meant to be . . . deceptive." Asena set her bags down near the door and took Dulcey's hand. "There are so many strangers in Zeugma right now. I am worried about the . . . things . . . in my house." Suddenly, Asena's eyes lit up. "You could stay here. Dr. Nash would have to assign extra guards for you. Could you do that for me?"

"But don't you have two housekeepers and a guard already?"

"They are all in awe of Dr. Nash. I am afraid he could talk his way in on some pretext or another." She looked at Dulcey with the same expression she had in Baghdad when she had pleaded with Dulcey to trust her judgment. "I need a *friend* right now—one that will not ask a lot of questions. Please stay in one of the front bedrooms until I get back, and *do not let anyone come into the house.* Especially Dr. Nash. Only you, Dulcey."

"Are you sure you want me here?"

"Just promise me you will let no one enter my home." The siren on the ambulance wailed as it sped away.

"Okay, okay. I promise. Just go—your grandmother needs you."

"Hasan?" Asena called to her guard. "Dulcey, this is Hasan. He's been with my family for thirty years."

The old man bowed slightly, then snapped to attention, his hand on an old-fashioned pistol belt. "*Memnun oldham.*"

"Hasan will take care of keeping the doors locked. Feyza, who cooks for me, lives here at the back of the house. Meltem, the other woman who helps me with the house, goes to her own home around eleven thirty at night when her son comes to pick her up. There is her coat and scarf hanging on the back of the door. Counting coats is how I keep track of who is here and who is out." Asena's gaze swept across the room, lingering on the long corridor that led to the rest of the house. "I would prefer that you wait until I return to see the rest of the house. Some doors have security alarms on them."

"Sure. Whatever you say."

"Now I must go be with my grandmother." Asena blew her a kiss, climbed into her Land Rover, and sped down the dirt road after the ambulance.

Dulcey stood in the doorway until she could no longer hear the siren of the ambulance in the distance. Then she wandered through Asena's house, taking care not to open any of the closed doors. Every room at the front of the house was full of heavy Ottoman-style furniture. She decided to sleep in the third bedroom because the small room nearest the foyer looked occupied, probably by Hasan. The one she chose had a high, wide bed with a faded, tasseled canopy hovering above it. As she walked down the long, echoing halls held up by arches—the signature of Roman architects—she was astonished at the immensity of Asena's home.

Above the large stone fireplace in the library, there was a framed photograph of Asena's beautiful daughter, Selene, dressed in graduation robes. The banner behind her read "Princeton University, 2001." The young woman looked a lot like her mother. It seemed ironic to Dulcey that these two thoroughly modern women had both grown up in what must have once been a royal palace, amidst rooms and rooms full of ancient history.

Dulcey saw a glint of color peeking out from behind the corner of a kilim tacked on the wall next to Selene's photograph. Curious, she pulled the rug back and saw that it covered a faded fresco like the ones she had seen in the covered trenches. It appeared that Asena had tried to hide the frescos so as not to call attention to the age of her home.

Dulcey kicked back a corner of a huge Turkish carpet and exposed another exquisite mosaic embedded in the floor. From the outside, Asena's one-story, ramshackle house had looked like a small, unassuming twentieth-century home with cracked adobe walls surrounding a courtyard. However, Dulcey now realized that the bulk of the house had been covered by centuries of hill wash that had gradually slid down the sides of Belkis Tepe. She ran her hands along the marble walls and realized they were as old as Zeugma was.

She stepped out into the mosaic-floored courtyard and examined the statues and fountains. Like Zeugma itself, Asena's house was one mysterious room after another. Had Asena's ancestors lived here since the Greek and Roman times? Or had they come more recently and made their home out of the ruins they had found there? A palace such as this implied a ruler or leader of some sort. It would not have been built in an isolated place. The fact that Asena and her family lived here meant that they were well aware of the huge buried city of Zeugma and, like the locals and the looters who had benefited from it, had kept it a secret from the rest of the world.

After her brief, self-guided tour through the areas of Asena's house that were not rigged with security alarms, it was clear to Dulcey why the woman needed to hide her family's treasures from Lee Nash. She was certain he would want to claim them as part of his excavation and leave Asena with nothing but a finder's fee.

As Dulcey returned to the entryway of the house, she saw Hasan snoozing in a comfortable-looking chair by the door. Dulcey cleared her throat, and he jumped to attention and held the front door open for her. *It's just me and this one old man who stand between Nash and the treasures and secrets of Asena's life.*

Asena had saved Dulcey's life once. Now Dulcey needed to save Asena. It was a simple matter of honor.

CHAPTER FIFTEEN

Dr. Selene Özturk stood in front of her American studies class, waiting for her students to finish their exam. One by one, they put their papers on her desk and took their seats again. "Is there anyone who has not finished yet?" She glanced around the room. "Good, then let's get back to our discussion of the American constitution."

A pretty girl on the front row raised her hand and waited until Selene noticed her. "Did you think it was difficult to be a Muslim when you were living in America?"

Selene's hands dropped to her sides. *Freshmen.* Fresh from their mother's kitchens. It was difficult for them to understand how long ago and far away Islam was from her thinking. Selene pretended to give the question a great deal of thought as she grew silent. She folded her hands together, then separated them, examining the rosy polish on her nails. She walked across the room, her stylish high heels making a confident clicking sound across the tile floor. "Let me turn the question back on you, Ms. Giray. In what way would you imagine being a Muslim might be difficult in America?"

The student shrugged, embarrassed at having to venture an opinion when she'd only requested a simple answer. "My father says it is impossible to live a true Muslim life in any infidel country."

Selene turned her back on the student and gazed steadily at the marker board, counting her breaths to calm herself. America had given her a PhD in sociology from a top Ivy League university. It was where she had made lifelong friends and learned to speak her mind—never worrying whether her religious affiliation would keep her from getting ahead.

Shortly after September 11, 2001, Selene had returned home to Turkey to take her current teaching position. Although she had been offered six times her current Turkish salary to teach at Rutgers, Selene had longed to go home. She loved her country. She saw its potential and how it stood right now on the very threshold of becoming a major world player. She saw how it constantly struggled between the ideals and principles of the East and of the West, between its Islamist leanings and its strong secular and democratic foundation. She wanted to be in the thick of things as her country took its rightful place in world politics.

But she had been shocked when she came home. So many changes had taken place that she hardly knew her country. More middle and upper class women than ever before covered their heads. Before she left, aside from the poor people who had come from rural areas, she had rarely seen a covered head in the Turkish cities. Now, wealthy, politically conservative women wore expensive Vakko scarves with their matching Versace suits. Billboards and commercials featured more covered women. And she noticed that more people than ever used the word *infidel* to mean anyone they considered less pious than themselves. The government was now being run by strict religious conservatives who knew how to appear secular to keep the military from using Atatürk's constitution to boot them out of office. It was all too much. She had had quite enough of religious extremists trying to run countries. She didn't want Turkey to end up like Iran. She was here in Turkey to speak her mind and to make sure her country stayed true to Atatürk's ideals.

"Ms. Giray. I am your teacher. You are here at Ankara University to get an education—not to carry on your father's prejudices. Do you understand?"

The student slid down into her seat a bit, looking hurt. "I only—"

"What do you suppose might have happened to me in America if I had entered a mosque or worn a head scarf or otherwise indicated I was a Muslim? What have we been learning about freedom of religion and freedom *from* religion in America, Ms. Giray?"

A second-year male student stood up at the back of the room. "I believe you are being unfair to Ms. Giray. She only asked you what it was like to be a Muslim living in America. How is she supposed to know?" There was a subtle murmur of agreement along the back row, but most of the students kept their faces blank, unwilling to take sides.

"I'm referring to the use of the very offensive word *infidel*," Selene said. She let the pause fill up with protests and a wave of indignant whispering. "The word *infidel* implies that you yourself are in a position to judge your fellow human beings as to whether Allah is pleased or displeased with their religious beliefs."

The young man stood up again. "But in the Koran it says that anyone who is not a Muslim is an infidel," he protested.

"Mr. Aslan, sit down please." Selene fixed him with a stare as he reluctantly sat down. "If infidels are non-Muslims, why do Sunni Muslims declare Shiite Muslims to be infidels? Does the Koran suggest a fair way to make this judgment against people who are also Muslims?"

"Shiites are infidels. Everyone just knows that," someone said quietly.

"Why? Because most Turks are Sunni? Or because Sunnis make up eighty-five to ninety percent of all Muslims in the world, so the majority gets to say who is an infidel? You know that the Shiites of Iran and Iraq and Lebanon call all of us Sunni folks 'infidels,' don't you?" She walked among the desks of her students, looking each of them in the eye. "Is an infidel a Muslim who has the wrong idea about who can become a caliph? Because that is the basic difference between a Sunni and a Shiite—their ideas about who can become a caliph."

A girl on the front row wearing tight Levis and a Tommy Hilfiger sweatshirt raised her hand. "But Muslims have no caliphate. Atatürk abolished it eighty years ago. So, if we are ever going to have a caliph again, is it not important to know the correct way to select a successor?"

Selene smiled broadly. "So! Our revered founder Atatürk abolished the caliphate, established a secular republic, and declared that Turkey would one day be part of the West—and many of you are worried about how best to restore the caliphate?"

Her students were silent. Selene let them think for a bit, then wrote the words *caliph* and *infidel* on the marker board in large red letters. "I want each of you to write a paper about what these words mean and how you use them in daily life. I want you to interview your family members and your neighbors. Then I want you to look in the Koran and on the Internet and in the library to learn more about these words. You have until Friday to do this assignment." Groans erupted from her students.

"But this is an American studies class," someone protested.

"Well? Didn't you just inform me that Americans are infidels? If they're infidels, we should ask ourselves why we're bothering to study them. And if you think the Muslim world needs to restore the caliphate, this will certainly affect your thinking about living in a country that elects its own leaders as people do in the West. And, by the way, why do we study America anyway?"

"I know why we study America," said a young woman with a baseball cap turned to the side and a smirk on her face. Selene knew the girl had spent the previous summer visiting her aunt in Minnesota and that she had returned to Turkey full of disdain for the ways of her own country. "Because while we Muslims are sitting here talking about the definition of the words *infidel* and *caliph* or whether or not women should cover their hair when they go shopping at the mall, the Americans are landing spaceships on the moon and trying to cure cancer."

Selene suppressed a grin. "Good point. The assignment stands. You may spend the rest of the class interviewing each other about the definition of these very volatile words."

The students immediately fell on each other as Selene knew they would. It was one thing to get them motivated, but she wondered if there were one or two of them who would take their displeasure a step further. Would one of her students use Law 301 to report her to the rector for insulting Turkishness?

At that moment, one of Selene's favorite former students, who often delivered messages for the front office, walked into her classroom. "Hello, Meral," Selene greeted the girl. Then she stepped closer and said quietly, "Someone told me this was your last day at school. What's going on?"

"Hello, Dr. Özturk." Meral dropped her gaze to the floor. "My father is pulling me out of college because his imam spoke to him about me. They both want me to start covering. Zafer, my fiancé—you met him at the party the other night—well . . . his boss told him he will get promoted at work if his new wife covers."

"Oh, dear. I imagine you feel a little like a pawn in someone else's chess game."

"A bit," Meral said softly, avoiding Selene's eyes and wiping her own with the cuff of her shirt sleeve. She handed Selene a slip of paper. "This phone message came in for you about five minutes ago."

"Listen, call me and let's talk about your leaving school, Meral. I can't belive this is what you want, is it?"

Meral turned quickly and hurried from the room.

With a heavy heart, Selene watched her student leave, then unfolded the message in her hand. She began to tremble as she realized how ill her grandmother had become. Then she turned to her students. "I'm canceling class on Friday. Please work on your papers over the weekend. I've been called home for a family emergency."

When the bell rang, the students gathered their belongings and surged out of the classroom. Selene headed for her office in the basement of the old building where she taught her classes. She hated old things. She craved new materials, uncluttered spaces, clean lines, and contemporary design.

As she descended the cracked, chipped concrete stairs, she located the tiny key on her key ring that would open the padlock on her office door. Her office was next to the building's boiler room, so it was always overheated, and the network of radiator pipes hissed so loudly that she often had to go to her apartment to get any work done.

Selene set her briefcase down near the door and fumbled with the tiny key and rusty padlock. Years ago, whatever rookie professor had been assigned to her office had accidentally locked his keys inside just before his class was to begin. He was to give a final exam in a few minutes, so he broke open his office door with a crowbar to get the exams—and ruined the doorframe in the process, making it forever impossible to install a normal lock.

The door finally swung open, but rather than enter the room, Selene stayed where she was. She stared at the key in her hand, wondering why it triggered a dim, niggling thought that had been resting in a dusty corner of her mind. *Must have something to do with Grandmother Yildiz, since I'm so worried about her,* Selene thought. However, unable to fully grasp the thought, she shook her head to dislodge it, then picked up the telephone sitting atop her shabby desk to reserve a seat on the next flight to Gaziantep.

An hour later, as Selene settled into a comfortable seat on the airport shuttle, she decided it was a good thing she'd be taking a break from her work. She'd been overdoing her professional responsibilities ever since she had come to the university. Selene longed to see her infuriating, stubborn, eccentric—and wonderful—mother and to kiss and hold her precious great-grandmother who would soon take leave of this tortured world.

CHAPTER SIXTEEN

Dulcey left the mysterious house and returned to the Zeugma camp to prepare for the live shoot, eager to return later that evening. By now, the sun had hidden itself behind bulging rain clouds. A damp breeze rippled the tarps and made the Euphrates lap the shore like a thirsty dog. She listened to the shouts of her coworkers and the buzz of the camp making itself ready for television. It was the kind of excitement Dulcey lived for.

She climbed the hill toward Trench 25 and saw that the men with shovels had leveled the area around the trench for the camera equipment and trucks. A crane towered above them with a hundred-and-thirty-foot arm. A cable dangled from it attached to a long, metal stretcher, as though it were waiting to rescue a very tall mountain climber. The crane, a satellite truck, and three identical Mack trucks marked with the Birecik Dam logo were parked around the trench. Frank and Tofer had attached hundreds of feet of white canvas sheeting to the fronts of the five trucks so that they now looked like a circle of covered wagons. Because the shoot was after sundown, the white canvas would reflect the lighting and fill in the shadows. It would also protect the site from the wind and blowing dust that could interfere with the equipment.

Sticking up above the canvas-covered trucks was the telescoping arm of Sophie DeNiro's satellite truck, its big dish holding its face toward the heavens. Inside the truck, Sophie shouted orders to her crew.

Photographers readied their lenses and checked their battery packs. Marburn and Rickman paced the hill, practicing monologues. Tanju lectured the Turkish crew members.

Cole Marburn's face was a mask of concentration as he wrote his script, reciting parts of it out loud as he went. "A golden sleeping beauty is about to awaken from a very long nap—one that has lasted nearly two millennia," intoned Cole. Then he paused, looked disgusted, and scratched something out.

"Are you feeling like the prince who is about to bestow the magical kiss?" Dulcey asked as she watched him.

"Where have you been? I thought I might have to narrate the whole show by myself. We've all taken our baths in the Euphrates, and we're writing our scripts. Where's Asena?"

"Asena had a family emergency. Tanju will be filling in for her," Dulcey said. "Where's Dr. Nash?"

"Said he had to go into Nizip to get some supplies. We could have used him here to help with this information, though. We're not the experts here, you know, and Mehmet is a little frosty toward the Americans this morning."

"Yavash, yavash, Cole," Dulcey said, turning her palms downward.

"I already know—Turkish for *slowly, slowly*. I've already heard it several times today, and it's driving me crazy," he grumbled. "This is television—not a Sufi monastery."

The makeup artist from CNN Turk walked over to Dulcey, glancing at the schedule attached to her clipboard. "Your hair and makeup are scheduled for four, Ms. Moore. Aysha will show you where the women bathe. Try to scrub that iodine off your skin. If it won't come off, I've got some foundation that will cover it." She looked at her watch and then her clipboard. "I'm in that camper near the dining tent."

Dulcey strolled toward the women's tent to get herself ready for the shoot. As she walked, she had the strange sensation that Zeugma was becoming more than just a story to her. Something very personal was calling to her from these ruins. It was as though they held keys that would unlock some mysteries of her own. She felt it every time she touched a mosaic or handled a sword that had belonged to a Roman soldier. She felt it when she handled one of the hundreds of goddess figurines that littered the site. Were they children's toys or were they sacred objects? Why did they touch her so deeply? This story was not just a half hour of prime-time reality TV. Something told her this story was going to change her life. This story was her destiny.

CHAPTER SEVENTEEN

Dulcey frowned as she imagined how cold her bath in the Euphrates was going to be. She wore her swimsuit under her clothes and carried a towel, soap, shampoo, and her Turkish guidebook/dictionary combo. Aysha carried Dulcey's cream blouse and gray Chanel pantsuit in a hanging travel bag. She led Dulcey past the covered trenches, down the hill, to an inlet shielded by leafy olive trees.

"*So-uk su,*" Aysha said, pointing to the water, pretending to shiver.

Dulcey thumbed through the dictionary, "Yes. Cold. Uh, will you . . . will you wait?"

Aysha looked confused.

"Here it is—*Bekle. Bekle, lutfen?* Please?"

Aysha's eyes lit up, and her dimples deepened at the sound of her own language. "*Evet.* Okay. *Bekliyorum.*" She planted her feet firmly on the smooth stones to let Dulcey know she would stand guard. Three soldiers appeared on the hill above, watching her, their stiff postures communicating their authority to be there. Aysha giggled as Dulcey shook her fist at them playfully, then went in search of a denser patch of trees.

Dulcey shed her outer clothing, then gasped as she lowered her body into the chilly water. Thankfully, after a minute or two, the water didn't seem so cold. Then she dove to the bottom and came up again. When she surfaced, something below the water caught her eye, so she dove again.

A portion of a mosaic glinted in the clear water from underneath two submerged Roman columns. Silt covered most of the mosaic so it was hard to see it very well. Dulcey dove again, brushed the silt away with her hand, and saw a mosaic of a woman's face. Dulcey's lungs were about to burst, so she sprang back to the surface.

"Dulcey Hanim? Dulcey Hanim!" Aysha cried.

Dulcey came face-to-face with a very worried Aysha, who had splashed fully clothed into the river to find out if she was all right. "Oh, sweetie, I'm okay."

"Okay?" Aysha said, breathing hard.

Dulcey was touched that the young girl had taken her watch duty so seriously. She had no words to explain that diving was second nature to her and that she had taught herself to hold her breath for more than a minute. She patted Aysha's shoulder to soothe her. Then Dulcey grabbed the floating shampoo bottle and handed it to the girl. Maybe the girl would relax if she had something to do.

After a short pantomimed instruction, Aysha was giggling again, washing Dulcey's hair. They splashed in the chilly water, shrieking and laughing until their lips were blue.

Tanju came down to the water's edge and called to Dulcey, "Frank wonders if you are decent. He wants to do the underwater shoot now. He's bringing your dive equipment and the oxygen tanks. He says you need to do it now because everyone thinks a storm is coming tonight."

"Okay. I left my swimsuit on to avoid offending anyone, so he can come now," Dulcey said. "Tanju, are you aware of all the ruins under the water?"

"Yes. Unfortunately, we had to leave many of them down there because the river rose so quickly behind the new dam. We only had a few months to excavate before the water flooded this whole lower area."

"Did you know that there's a mosaic of a woman's face over here? It's about three feet by three feet."

"We had to concentrate on the big ones. We knew we could recover the little ones later. But sometimes the river uncovers things that we did not find in the dirt. Ask Dr. Nash about it."

Aysha looked from woman to woman to see if she was in trouble. Her soaking blouse clung to her skin, and her shalwar pants were heavy with water. Her headcovering had slipped to her shoulders, and a mass of dark, wet hair streamed down her back. She spoke in Turkish to Tanju.

"She's worried her mother will scold her for getting wet," Tanju translated.

"I asked Aysha to help me wash my hair. Would you make sure her mother knows this was my idea? Poor girl. She got enough scolding last night at the party."

"Of course. I'll go with Aysha to explain things. And I'll send Frank down if you are ready."

"Send him down. And check in with Cole Marburn to see if he has what he needs. Dr. Nash seems to be AWOL today—just when we need him the most."

* * *

An hour later, Dulcey and Frank had finished filming the ruins that were underwater. Frank's bright yellow SeaLife Reefmaster DC300 had captured several hundred meters of columns and partial mosaics under the crystal clear water. Dulcey had pointed at interesting items, cleared silt away and moved a few rocks, all the while making mental notes about what she would say on her voice-over narration.

"Help me move this little mosaic of a woman's face to the shore," Dulcey said to Frank when they had finished filming. "It's so beautiful— I'm sure someone is going to want to see it."

"Are you sure we should move it?" Frank asked, shaking his finger inside his ear to clear the water from it.

"At this point, it's easier to ask forgiveness than to ask for permission. Nash is in town getting supplies. Tanju is doing her job and Asena's at the same time. Come on, Frank. We may forget where she is later, and she might get lost again."

"Okay. But remember this was your idea. I just work here," grumbled Frank, putting his camera on the shore and swimming back to where Dulcey stood in the water. She and Frank dove down, and together they removed the rock and the column that trapped the mosaic. They were about to dive again when Dulcey caught sight of a young woman on the other side of the inlet. She was holding a bulky bag over one shoulder and had a baby in her arms.

"Hello," the woman called. "I am Turkan, Aysha's schoolteacher." She picked her way down to the riverbank. "I understood that Aysha was here, so I came to give her some books. I guess she went back to the camp."

"Yes, we're all very busy getting ready to film the excavation," Dulcey replied.

"Would you take these books to her? And please do not let the girl's parents see them. They are opposed to the girl's reading."

"Sure," Dulcey said, surprised at the local woman's excellent English.

"We found a mosaic down here—a woman's face," Frank called to Turkan. "Do you think we should bring it up on shore or leave it in the water?"

"You should leave it in the water and tell Asena about it first. For many years, she has been looking for a mosaic that belongs to her family. That mosaic may be hers." Turkan set the bag of books on the shore and turned to go back the way she had come. "Tell Asena about it," she reminded them.

Dulcey said to Frank, "Asena told me about a mosaic that belonged to her family. They had to hide it during the Kurdish troubles. Her family calls it their 'precious mosaic.'"

"I think we should tell Dr. Nash about it," Frank said as he and Dulcey got out of the water, packed their equipment away, and toweled off.

"No, not Dr. Nash. I have my reasons why we should tell Asena about it." She looked over the water, trying to memorize the location of the submerged mosaic. "This is a big inlet. How will we find the mosaic again?"

"Let's mark the spot with this big rock. Across the inlet, do you see that flowering bush? The mosaic is in the water directly between that bush and this big rock."

Dulcey picked up the bag of books Turkan had left for Aysha. "Imagine not being allowed to read. Imagine Aysha's intelligent mind with nothing to help it grow."

Frank looked at the books Dulcey was plucking from the bag. There was a math book and an English dictionary, a history book with a globe on the front, and a picture book about the animals of Africa. "It's dangerous to take these to Aysha. You're sticking your nose into someone else's cultural rules. I think you're playing with fire here."

"I don't mind getting burned for a good cause. And Aysha is a good cause."

Dulcey felt her jaw twitching. Frank heaved a sigh, picked up his dive equipment, and trudged up the hill.

CHAPTER EIGHTEEN

Two minutes before the CNN cameras were to spring into life, a strong breeze stirred the lake, making the canvas sheeting around the excavation snap and ripple. A red sun had already been squashed like a bug across the horizon. Huge halogen lights lit up the excavation area as though it were still midday. Raindrops began to fall, hissing as they fell on the hot metal helmets covering the lights. Frank shook his head and signaled to the others that it was too late to spread a rain tarp, so the photographers near the trench attached spatter shields above their cameras. Techies wrapped the television monitors in clear plastic bags. Doug Rickman gave the "all quiet on the set" signal. Only the wind and rain failed to obey him.

Next to Trench 25, Dulcey held an umbrella over her head, practicing her opening lines and surveying the superbly organized chaos around her. Today she was the queen of this buzzing hive of activity. Without a sound, her windbreaker-hooded helpers scurried, eager to do her bidding, stepping carefully over wires and around tripods, filming, cueing, and signaling. Dulcey felt her face flush with delicious anticipation. She shot her thumb into the air and grinned at Doug Rickman. Doug yelled out the countdown. "Six, five, four . . ." He continued his count, silently now, with three fingers, then two. With his index finger high in the air, all the cameras sprang to life.

Inside the satellite truck, Sophie gave the final cue for the uplink. The monitors crackled as the satellite dish became a cupped hand throwing voices and images toward the heavens to be scooped up by an orbiting communication satellite and then scattered again all over the earth.

Reporters from CNN Turk took the first turn to describe the scene for their viewers. Zeugma was already well-known in Turkey after the vast trove of mosaics and frescoes had been uncovered a few years earlier during the digging of the dam. Devrim Yolju spoke into his microphone, gesturing and setting the stage for the unveiling of the goddess.

The four diggers who had been using small trowels to remove the final half meter of dirt yelled something in Turkish and traded places with Nash and his team. Moments later, the cameras panned over a reclining, larger-than-life female form covered with only an inch of wet limestone silt. As the archeologists used brushes to remove the final grains of dirt, CNN viewers got a front-row view of the goddess slowly appearing before them.

Devrim asked Nash questions for the Turkish public, and Nash responded in Turkish. Dulcey knew she would have to catch the interest of the English-speaking world quickly as Devrim tossed the dialogue her way. As she took a step toward the trench to say her opening line, a loose rock rolled out from under her right foot. Dulcey's umbrella cartwheeled into the trench, and she threw her weight backward to keep from falling into the deep hole in front of her. As she sat down hard on the wet dirt, she felt the soggy mud seep through the seat of her pantsuit.

At the very moment Dulcey lost her footing, Sophie pushed a cut button on her console and said casually into the microphone on her headset, "Go to Cole. We're okay, folks. The ten second delay covered that."

Doug gave a hand signal to the crew stationed near the covered trenches. Cole Marburn pointed to the mosaics and gave a one-minute spiel about all the fantastic mosaics that had already been found at Zeugma.

Nash stood up quickly and yelled over the berm of the trench, "For the love of everything holy, Dulcey, keep away from the edge so you don't fall on the goddess."

"Oh, please don't worry about me, Nash. I'm *fine*," Dulcey stage-whispered, giving him a scathing look and feeling the heat in her face as the makeup artist and her assistant pulled her to standing and swiped at the seat of her pants with some dry towels.

Dulcey knew it was all right for things to be a little jumbled during a live shoot, but falling on her behind was not acceptable. But neither was slapping Dr. Nash across the face, so Dulcey calmed herself. She refused the muddy umbrella Nash handed up to her. Instead, she held her face to the rain for a moment, breathed deeply, and turned back to the camera. The feel of the gentle raindrops had helped calm her, but she hoped the heavy pancake foundation wasn't oozing down her face and dripping onto her clean, cream-colored blouse.

Frank signaled for the three cameras on the satellite hookup to go back to Dulcey. He used a hand signal to tell her that Cole had already introduced her.

"Thanks, Cole," Dulcey said, looking toward the covered trenches as though she could see him. "And so here we stand above Trench 25. This is a *very* exciting moment. As we speak, Dr. Lee Edward Nash is there in the trench directing his team in removing the final layer of dirt. He told me earlier he likes to remove the final layer himself."

She leaned over the trench and pointed at the muddy goddess. "Dr. Nash tells me that sculptures of the Goddess Fortuna have been found in various places all over ancient Greece and Turkey. She is often sculpted with a wheel—which is where the phrase *wheel of fortune* comes from. Sometimes she holds a ship's rudder, indicating that she guides the direction of fate. And sometimes she holds a ball that symbolizes her power to roll fate in any direction she pleases. The phrase *lady luck* also originated with this goddess."

The cameras trained on Nash as he worked on the arms of the goddess. He used a small paintbrush to remove the last layer of dirt, then poured a cleaning solvent from a plastic jug. Two golden hands clasping a ball appeared. "This goddess is . . . holding a ball above her head," he announced, grinning into the camera lens.

"She's holding her golden ball like a basketball player—just like Michael Jordan would," Dulcey said, remembering the school kids in her audience.

Camera one went in for a close-up of Nash's weather-beaten face, showing his green eyes lighting up like traffic lights. Camera two went in tight on Dulcey. She smiled at the camera, pressing one hand to her chest to contain her excitement. "Now we are going to see the

Goddess Fortuna's face for the first time. A face no one has seen in nearly *two thousand* years!" she whispered.

Nash placed a pair of goggles on his face and a surgical mask over his mouth. Then he unraveled a small air hose and switched on an air compressor. As he blew away a final layer of limestone silt, everyone around the trench gasped as the face of the goddess came into view. "A very dramatic face," Nash whispered. He poured the solvent, and the goddess's beautiful golden features emerged, gleaming in the hot lights. "Quite a striking face. Imagine believing the Goddess Fortuna had your fate in her hands as you stared straight up into her face from below. Imagine imploring her to roll her ball in your favor."

As the archeologists dusted off the rest of the statue, Dulcey crouched well away from the edge of the berm and looked directly into camera two. "This golden goddess once stood on the hill behind me, a glorious presence in the ancient city of Zeugma when it was a bustling city of seventy thousand people on the Silk Road. Her supplicants would offer sacrifices and pray for her favor."

"Here she is!" Nash shouted, stepping back so the cameras could get the full view.

Dulcey pointed to the reclining goddess, whose body was becoming more golden every moment. "The cameras will now show you her full form. As you can see, she is perfect in every detail." Dulcey watched the monitor to see what the viewers were seeing. "You see there, her golden fingers curving around the ball she is holding—you can even see her fingernails. Now Dr. Nash is working on the sleeves of her robe—they have fallen back toward her shoulders because her arms are raised. You can see more and more of her upper body as Dr. Nash uses an air hose to blow away the dirt."

"My assistants will help with this part," Nash said. "This is Mehmet Demirel from Istanbul University." Mehmet ducked his head shyly and unraveled an air hose. "And this is Dr. Tanju Boyraz from the Ministry of Culture." Tanju gave a little wave and switched on the air compressor.

Nash blew the dirt away, and the others followed with the solvent. Within moments, most of the dirt was gone. "As we predicted from satellite photos and GPR—that's ground-penetrating radar—the goddess is complete and very tall, especially when she is standing on this large pedestal."

"Dr. Boyraz is examining the head of the goddess now," Dulcey said. "She told me earlier that a great deal of information can be gathered from the hairstyles and clothing of a statue."

"Amazing. She is simply beautiful." Tanju could barely contain herself. "Her face is twice the size of a real person's face. She is lovely."

"Not a ding or a dent in that golden face," Dulcey added. "I wonder what Cleopatra would have thought of this rival beauty standing on the banks of the Euphrates."

Standing next to Dulcey, Devrim Yolju spoke in Turkish punctuated by the international sounds of human amazement. He and Dulcey took turns narrating the events. Then Dulcey signaled for Mehmet to speak in Turkish and Tanju to speak in English concurrently so the pace could be maintained for both the local and international audiences.

"Look at her hair," Tanju said. "Ms. Moore, can you climb down the ladder there? Come see this."

Nash shot the women an irritated look as Dulcey climbed down the ladder. By now it had stopped raining, but there was a layer of gray ooze at the bottom of the trench. Nash had asked Dulcey to limit the number of people squishing around in it, but Dulcey was too excited to stay out of the trench. "Give me a second here," Dulcey said, squeezing past the men and joining Tanju near the head of the goddess. A techie lowered a pole-mounted light toward the head of the goddess.

Tanju pointed to the hair of the statue with the tip of the air hose. "The goddess's hair tells us a lot about *when* she was sculpted. Cleopatra would *not* have seen this particular goddess while she was empress of Egypt. From Fortuna's hairstyle, we can see the goddess was sculpted in the early part of the first century, long after Cleopatra's death."

"Now, explain to me how you can tell that from her hair," Dulcey asked.

"Everyone mimicked the hairstyle of the current Roman empress. The women of the realm would see the empress's hairstyle depicted on coins and immediately style their own hair in the fashion of their empress. The artists did the same when portraying the deities of the day."

"And the date on any given coin tells archeologists when a particular hairstyle was popular?" Dulcey guessed.

"Exactly. This is the Agrippina style, which places this goddess sculpture in the Roman period—between the years of thirty-seven to forty-one of the Common Era," said Tanju, pointing to the ropes of golden hair.

By now Dulcey had completely forgotten herself. As she knelt in the trench, describing what she was seeing to her viewers, her own hair hung limp around her face, and she was soaked to the bone. "Under her crown, Fortuna's wavy hair is tied back in a large bun at the nape of her neck," she said.

One of the cameramen held a fiber-optic attachment under the neck of the goddess. Tanju brushed some dirt away and pointed. "Her hair is held back with a hairpin called a *nodus*—do you see it there at the nape of her neck? Very nice little detail there."

The women knelt next to Fortuna's head. "Tell me about that unusual crown the goddess is wearing. It seems to be shaped like a city wall," Dulcey said and pointed as a photographer traced the details of the crown with the fiber-optic attachment. The monitors showed the enlarged image of the crown in such detail that the viewers must have thought they were standing on the Great Wall of China.

"Her crown is called a diadem," Tanju said. "Fortuna is nearly always portrayed wearing a crown shaped like a city wall, including a gate, because she is a city goddess rather than a nature goddess. You can see the turrets of a city wall there, complete with arched windows. Over here, above her left ear, is the gate to the city."

Dr. Nash and Mehmet descended the ladder and came over to examine the detail on the diadem. Nash said, "From the position of the gate above her ear, we might guess that Zeugma's main city gate would be on the east side of Zeugma. We have been wondering where to look for it, and now Fortuna may well have given us a clue where it is."

Mehmet reported into a camera, "The goddess, with her arms raised, is nearly twelve feet tall. Add another five for her pedestal, and statue is nearly seventeen feet tall." Mehmet scribbled in his notebook. A camera went in close on his page full of sketches and numbers.

Tanju explained. "Mehmet is recording Fortuna's measurements and assigning a context number that indicates where she was found. The exact location of a find is always very important to know." The camera hovered above Tanju's shoulder as she unfolded her excavation map, marked the exact position of the find with symbols, and recorded a context number.

"Look at the dress she's wearing!" Dulcey exclaimed, imagining how boring context numbers would seem to viewers when compared with a view of the actual goddess.

"This is a *chiton*," Tanju said. "A typical Roman dress of the early first century. This confirms what we guessed from the hairstyle. You see the empire waist?"

Dulcey turned to the cameras. "Even today, women wear dresses with empire waistlines."

Tanju smiled at her. "Now you know where that term comes from."

Mehmet stepped back to allow Tanju to dust off more of the goddess's torso. Tanju squirted solvent and spoke into the camera. "It was considered very feminine to have lots of gathers just under the bust along a high bodice. Look how the artist took great pains to sculpt each of the gathers of Fortuna's chiton."

"What is the name of the robe she has draped over her left arm there?" Dulcey asked.

Dr. Nash moved away so the viewers could see. "That robe is called the *himation,* which is always worn over the more form-fitting chiton. This one is very luxurious with fold after fold, all in gold of course."

Dulcey pointed to the feet of the goddess resting on the pedestal. "What perfect feet. And we can see the toenails and the details of each toe, because she is wearing an open shoe that is part sandal, part shoe. You see there how it laces up the ankle?"

Tanju scrubbed the feet of the goddess with a toothbrush soaked in solvent. "Ahh, Fortuna is wearing the fashionable shoe-sandals called *krepis,* which were invented by the Greeks in the fourth century B.C.E. Later the Romans called them *crepida*. Many of the Roman deities were pictured wearing them."

Dulcey turned to Nash, who had glanced at his watch twice in the past two minutes. "Do you know yet if this statue is *solid* gold, Dr. Nash?" Dulcey asked, standing back against the muddy trench wall so the cameras could get a full view of the goddess.

"Well, the outside is obviously gold. Anyone familiar with the sheen of real gold can see that. Naturally, we're not going to cut the goddess open to find out if she's solid all the way through." Nash signaled his team to begin digging the wet dirt out from under the goddess. "We will determine whether she's solid by her weight computed against her height, minus the approximate weight of the pedestal. Once she's in that sling up there, we should know if she's solid gold."

Mehmet stood by the stretcher, which was dangling from a crane positioned above the trench. He pointed to the heavy slings and harnesses that hung down from it and spoke in Turkish to the viewers. Tanju interpreted almost simultaneously. "This digital weight scale attached to the cable will tell us if she is solid gold."

Nash said, "You have to remember that Zeugma was a very wealthy city. We have already seen that no expense was ever spared in crafting the mosaics on the nearly seventy residential floors we have found so far. We have no reason to doubt that the goddess would be pure gold as a way to honor the deity and as a way to add monetary value to the statue."

The stretcher came lower and lower until it rested on the edge of the trench. Nash and Mehmet, accompanied by the Yildirim boys, who had joined them in the trench, unfastened the slings and let them fall into the trench. "Now for the difficult part," Nash said, his voice louder now. "The goddess is likely to weigh more than a ton if she's solid. We're going to treat her just like a very sick patient at this point. I'm going to ask everyone to climb out of the trench so we can get the hydraulic lift under our goddess here. Then we will slip these slings and harnesses under her and raise her very slowly and with extreme care."

The crowd around the trench buzzed, and Dulcey continued narrating as she scrambled up the ladder. Climbing out of the muddy trench was made more difficult by the microphone she was holding and the long cord attached to Sophie's satellite truck. "This trench has got to—ugh—be at least six feet deep. Whew! My shoes are very muddy. Can someone help me? Thanks."

The microphone took a beating as Dulcey slid over the lip of the trench, assisted by an off-camera hand. Sophie cut the sound down as the mic rumbled and popped.

"Hydraulics are in place!" Nash yelled. "Let's have it quiet so everyone can hear the instructions." The four Yildirim boys got back into the trench to help Nash and Mehmet. Tanju took the air compressor and tools out of the way.

Dulcey stage-whispered into her microphone. "These instructions will be in Turkish, and we all need to be quiet now so that everyone—"

Nash's face flushed with annoyance as he bellowed up at her. "Ms. Moore? Could you pipe down? This is the toughest part here, and I won't throw away this piece of two-thousand-year-old art because you're jabbering away!"

Dulcey made a face into the camera, drew her mouth into a dramatic frown, and pushed her lower lip out like a child who'd been scolded. *How dare he,* she thought to herself, though she maintained an outward calm. Knowing there was a ten-second delay, she glanced at Frank and surreptitiously made the cut sign to see if he could get Sophie to cut the bit. He shook his head and patted his heart. *It's live TV,* he was signaling. *Go with what's happening.*

Dulcey intensified her look of attention as the long steel and canvas stretcher went past her face. Inwardly, she seethed at Nash for speaking to her like he had, *on international television no less.*

Ten minutes later, the statue was swinging above them to a wildly cheering audience. Mehmet climbed out of the trench and checked the numbers on the digital weight scale. There was a hush as the goddess dangled, silhouetted against the deep red sunset. Mehmet peered at the gauge and then calculated her weight and length in his notebook. Briefly, a squawking pair of seagulls circled the goddess, the light from the kliegs glinting off their white wings. When the birds flew off, the only sound was the creaking of the metal crane cables as the golden goddess rocked in the slight breeze.

"Solid gold," Mehmet announced, then repeated the words in Turkish. The chant was relayed from person to person, from the techies to the cameramen, from the grips to the makeup artists, from the four Yildirim boys to their parents and to their sister, Aysha. A camera zoomed in on the girl's lovely face, shining with excitement. The chant echoed over the hill, from the crane operator in the cab to Sophie in the satellite truck, from archeologists to television reporters. And from Commander Steve Cantwell on his satellite phone to the other American CIA agents in their fortress above the dig.

* * *

Across the Euphrates, the parabolic microphones picked up the chant. Nayif took a note from one of the men dressed as shepherds, got on his motorbike, and sped toward the dam.

* * *

Dr. Nash looked up and over the trench, gazing across the Euphrates, sweat beading on his face as he rested his arms on the high berm. He pushed his goggles up on his forehead and removed his surgical mask, leaving a clean swath across his filthy face. He patted his empty shirt pocket, where his cigarettes were usually kept.

Dulcey stopped celebrating for a moment and followed Nash's gaze. Shielding her eyes, she caught sight of the boy on the motorbike racing along the river road toward the dam. She could have sworn it was the same kid who'd been selling cans of Coca-Cola in front of the museum in Baghdad. The boy who'd dropped his coins next to the CNN van. The boy who'd stolen John's camera as he lay dying in the street. She watched Nash's lips curl into a smile and noticed his jaw twitching rhythmically just above the collar of his shirt.

CHAPTER NINETEEN

At the end of their shifts, the employees of the British Museum gathered around the television set in the lunchroom watching the much-anticipated Turkish excavation on CNN. Nala and Khadija gasped as the crane lifted the golden goddess from the hole where she had been buried and then held her suspended in the air for several moments as a hushed silence fell over the crowd surrounding the trench.

"Solid gold!" the archeologist announced to a cheering crowd at Zeugma and to the appreciative group of British Museum employees, who well understood the rarity and importance of such a find.

Several CNN staffers quickly removed the canvas sheeting that had been fastened to a row of big trucks. The pretty American reporter's dirt-smudged face appeared again, and she pointed to the scene. "And now you see the excavators loading the goddess into the truck that will take her to the Gaziantep Museum."

"Did she say 'Gaziantep'?" Nala whispered to Khadija.

"Something like that," Khadija said. "Why?"

"That's the city in Turkey where my sister wired Ahmed that money. I even wrote it down." Nala searched through her handbag and found the note she'd written to herself. "See? FinansBank in Gaziantep, Turkey. I wonder if Ahmed's assignment has something to do with the goddess . . ."

"Let's hope not. Look at the number of soldiers guarding her. Unless Ahmed has an army, he would have a hard time getting near that goddess."

"Who says he doesn't have an army?" Nala whispered in Khadija's ear.

* * *

When the shoot was over, the crew members from the various television networks slapped backs and joked with each other as the adrenaline of the dig ebbed away. Dulcey's misstep was left tactfully unmentioned. Most journalists knew when to make down payments on their own future reprieves.

Dulcey went to the women's tent and shed her muddy clothes. She changed into her one remaining pair of blue jeans and a clean CNN sweatshirt. She had just smeared on gobs of cold cream to remove her makeup when Frank appeared at the entrance to the tent.

"That went rather well," Frank said, cleaning a camera lens with a soft cloth. "You okay?"

"My rear end's sore. My ego's sore. But I'm okay." Dulcey pulled her damp hair into a ponytail. "At least no one shot at us."

"Not a peep from the bad guys. Do you think U.S. intelligence called this one wrong?"

"Possibly." Dulcey thought of the kid on the motorbike. There was a better chance that her nerves were jumpy than that the kid she saw was the same one she'd seen in Baghdad. Had it not been for the expression on Nash's face, she would have dismissed the boy on the motorbike entirely.

Frank sat down on one of the cots. "It doesn't make sense. Why would terrorists try to kill us in Baghdad and then allow the live report to go on without a hitch? Now the whole world knows that the goddess exists, what she looks like, and exactly how much gold she's made of."

"Asena could have been wrong about why al Qaeda needed the gold. Maybe they need untraceable funds. If they intend to melt down the gold, why would they care if everyone knew about the goddess?"

Frank nodded and put his camera lens into its case. "Al Qaeda's got to be hurting for money now that the U.S. has shut down so many of its financial pipelines all over the world."

Dulcey hadn't told Frank of her suspicions about the boy on the motorbike, but she could tell he was worried. She leaned toward him and made him look her in the eye. "You and I are going to pass on the trip to Gaziantep, okay? You should go talk Tofer out of it too— there's still time for al Qaeda to make their move."

Frank shook his head. "Tofer insists on going. He's riding with Mehmet. I think he's trying to make amends for his behavior last night."

The tent flap opened and Tanju entered, carrying a big box of books and magazines topped with a bouquet of yellow field daisies like the ones that grew all around the dining tent. She looked outside to make sure no one was within earshot, then closed the tent flap. "Right now, everyone is making a big fuss about loading the goddess into one of the Birecik Dam trucks. The CNN trucks will film the goddess going to the museum, and the military will be escorting the truck convoy—front, back, and middle. They have roadblocks set up all along the road, and every store and all the side streets are closed all the way to Gaziantep while the goddess is being transported to the museum."

"Do you think we should go?" Dulcey asked, using cotton balls to remove the cold cream from her face. "I agreed to watch Asena's house tonight, and there's no point in Frank filming the convoy since CNN is covering it."

"No. Nash just told me that the goddess in that convoy is just a decoy."

"What?" Dulcey and Frank asked in unison.

"Dr. Nash just now told me the goddess in the convoy headed for the museum in Gaziantep is just a twenty-foot ladder stuck in a barrel of plaster, wrapped up in a big tarp. He said he will take the real goddess to Gaziantep later tonight. An armed guard will travel with him. Then it will be up to the Ministry to protect her and decide when it is safe to put her on display."

"Isn't Nash taking a big risk transporting the goddess himself?" Dulcey asked.

"He says it is safer this way. And, according to his contract, it is completely up to him to determine how to transport all artifacts to the museum."

"So the CNN crew and the soldiers have no idea they're transporting a fake?" Dulcey hung her muddy clothing on the clothesline the women had strung through the tent.

"That is correct. Dr. Nash told me that the real goddess was loaded into a different truck behind the canvas sheeting."

Dulcey thought of the boy on the motorbike. No boy of that age would be working alone. "But what if a thief or an infiltrator were watching? What if they know the goddess is still in the camp?"

"Dr. Nash said he took every precaution. The trucks are identical down to their license plates," Tanju said. "You are to tell no one what you know. But I felt you and Frank were owed an explanation."

"Thanks for telling us. What's with the box and the flowers?" Frank asked.

"Grandmother Yildiz is in a coma. Asena sent word from the hospital that she will not be leaving her grandmother's hospital room until . . . well . . . for as long as it takes. She asked me to bring her some books from the dining tent. And I am bringing these flowers to brighten the room."

"I'm so sorry," Dulcey said. "Should I come with you?"

"No. Please stay here. Asena is so worried about her house; she would like you to stay there for as long as you can. Were you able to get the extra guards?"

"Yes. It was no problem."

"While you are in the camp, keep your eyes open. I think Dr. Nash is acting very strangely. Lately, his decisions have made no sense to me. And he was gone all day—on the busiest day of the excavation—when we really needed him here."

Dulcey nodded. "He sure snapped at me during the filming. That seemed sort of out of character too."

"You are right. He is not himself." Tanju blew her a kiss and headed out of the tent. "See what you can find out. I will not be back this evening. Everyone is staying at the Tujan Hotel in Gaziantep tonight. They are all anxious to sleep in a comfortable bed, and I think there will be a big party after the so-called goddess is delivered to the museum. After Mehmet and Tofer's argument, I think we all need to become friends again."

"Yes, you go on. Tell Asena not to concern herself with anything but her grandmother. I'll take care of her house." As Tanju walked away, Dulcey muddled over all the ways Nash could be up to no good.

CHAPTER TWENTY

Now that the shoot was over and most of the crew was in Gaziantep for the night, the Zeugma excavation camp seemed to breathe a sigh of relief. The Yildirims set out a small supper and went to bed early. Nash, Frank, and Dulcey sat in the nearly empty dining tent eating a late meal. The few soldiers who had not accompanied the convoy to Gaziantep sat by a campfire near the water. Several others patrolled the grounds near the trenches. Cantwell sat in his military jeep, talking on his satellite phone.

Nash seemed nervous and had hardly said a word to anyone all night. Suddenly, he stood, threw his half-eaten dinner in the garbage, and excused himself from the table. Then he stalked off into the darkness toward his tent.

"I guess I don't blame Nash for being nervous about tonight if he's still got to transport the goddess," Frank said after the archeologist had gone. "He's a strange man."

Absently, Dulcey broke off pieces of pita bread and spooned thick lentil soup into her mouth. "All I can think of is getting home now. I miss my kids . . . and Matt. Izzy'll talk a mile a minute and tell me every little thing that's happened in her life since the second I left her. I usually get annoyed when she does that, but it seems charming at the moment. Michael will want to show me something new he's learned to do while I was gone. Or he'll want me to put my finger in the hole where his tooth fell out. They're so obnoxious and . . . so adorable. I just want to breathe them in."

At that moment, Cantwell approached them and said, "Just got word that Tofer will be on his way to the military base in Incirlik first thing in the morning. He's catching a ride home on a troop transport plane. Tanju convinced him to phone his family, and they begged him to get himself home the fastest way he could."

"What a relief," Dulcey said.

"Yeah, the kid cried his eyes out when he found out his family had delayed his father's funeral until he could get home." Cantwell nodded his head, remembering a conversation with one of his agents. "And do you know why Tofer went to Gaziantep in the first place? He wanted to buy Mehmet and Tanju dinner so he could apologize for his behavior last night."

"Tofer's a good kid. He'll do all right," Frank said, nearly shedding a tear himself at the news.

Cantwell nodded and turned to Dulcey. "Ms. Moore, let me know when you're ready to head on over to Asena's and I'll have a few Turkish soldiers go with you to stand guard over there."

After Cantwell went back to his jeep, Dulcey bit her lip and pushed her food around her plate. "I sure wish Matt and I hadn't fought before I left. The longer I wait, the harder it is to call him. And as long as I'm stuck here in Zeugma, I can't call him even if I want to."

"Hey, kiddo. You and Matt'll patch things up when you get home," Frank said.

Dulcey nodded slowly and then said, "With this awful weather, I wish I could ask you to stay at Asena's house too, Frank. But she was adamant about me not letting anyone come in while she was gone. I hope you don't mind one more night in the tent."

"Think of me while you're taking your hot shower tonight," Frank said teasingly.

"I'm sorry she didn't include you in her invitation. I hate to think of you tossing and turning another night, especially in this rain."

"Nah, I'll be all right. I need to pack anyway and get the equipment ready to survive the baggage handlers."

"Okay, then. I'm going." Dulcey got her rolling bag from the women's tent, and Cantwell gave the signal for two of the soldiers to accompany her to Asena's house.

* * *

It was raining hard by the time Dulcey had settled herself into the ornate bedroom at Asena's house, and she worried about Frank being cold and uncomfortable. Dulcey looked out the bedroom window and saw a military truck parked down the way. Two soldiers in dark rain ponchos and helmets got out and walked up and down the road, checking the trees and bushes. Then she heard footsteps overhead and knew more soldiers had been stationed on Asena's rooftop terrace. Feyza, the housekeeper who lived at the back of the house, brought Dulcey some warm milk and spread her wet windbreaker to dry on the radiator near the front door. It was pleasantly warm inside the house.

The old windowpanes rattled as the rain and wind blew against them. Despite her fatigue, it was hard to resist the temptation to snoop around and look at the treasures in Asena's amazing, labyrinthine house. At ten o'clock, Dulcey was still wide awake and could no longer resist her curiosity. She slipped into a robe and slippers and wandered through the house, trying to figure out how the rooms were laid out. A room off the long hallway caught her eye. The old wooden door had been removed, and a large aluminum one had been installed in its place. Dulcey could hear the whir of a generator inside the room. Her gaze traced a wire that went around the door and disappeared inside. A sign in Turkish probably warned that opening the door would set off an alarm. Dulcey sighed. Maybe someday Asena would show her what was inside that room. Whatever it was, she knew it was one reason her hostess had broken off her relationship with Nash.

From the large window in the library, Dulcey looked out at the courtyard. Rain bounced off the mosaic floor. The fountain had been turned off in favor of the one from the sky. As she watched the rain splash down, she found herself wishing she'd gone to Gaziantep with the rest of the crew. No doubt there would be a great celebration party after the fake goddess was delivered to the museum.

Dulcey went back into her bedroom and lay on the big bed, looking up at the faded, embroidered canopy, tracing the elaborate designs with her eyes. She thumbed through her Turkish guidebook, vowing to return to Turkey someday to explore its mysteries. She looked at the photographs of the hotels in Cappadocia that were inside hollowed-out mountains of soft tufa stone. She promised herself that someday she would stay there, inside the same mountains where thousands of early Christians had once taken refuge from their Roman tormenters. At Pamukkale, she wanted to bathe in mineral water warmed by the sun in one of the hundreds of calcified rock pools that cascaded down the mountain. The word *pamuk-kale* meant "cotton castle," and just from the name of the mountain, she could tell it was a remarkable natural wonder.

She flipped the pages of the tour book and gazed at the Hagia Sophia. The domed building, originally a magnificent cathedral in the fifth-century Holy Roman Empire, became a mosque in the fifteenth century under the Muslim conquerors and was now a museum. Why hadn't she known of these wonders? She knew about all the famous sites in Europe and had seen most of them during her life. But why had she never heard of any of the astounding sights of Turkey or in the Middle East? *Except for Jerusalem and Israel, this part of the world has been a big blank spot in my brain—even though my own civilization was born right here. Asena was right to be insulted by my ignorance.*

Just after eleven o'clock, Hasan knocked on Dulcey's door and motioned for her to follow him. There on the doorstep stood Frank. He was drenched and clutching a plastic trash bag around his head. Dulcey hesitated a half beat, thinking of Asena's instructions not to allow anyone into the house, and then pulled her wet friend into the foyer. Hasan crossed his arms and stood his ground. Dulcey motioned that he should return to his room. Reluctantly, Hasan left them alone.

"What's the matter?" she asked.

"Someone from the dam sent a message to us by way of the soldiers. Asena wants to see you at the Gaziantep Hastanesi right away. That's the hospital on Atatürk Boulevard. She says it's urgent."

"Did her grandmother die?"

"I don't think so. All she said was that she couldn't leave the hospital. She said it's important—and it has to be you. I asked Cantwell to get you an escort, but he refused—said it was too dangerous. So I walked through the pistachio grove to the dam and found a guy named Taner just getting off work. He speaks a little English, and he knows Asena. He's outside, waiting to drive us into town."

"I hope Cantwell doesn't catch us. Can he throw civilians in the brig?" Dulcey asked, grinning at her longtime co-conspirator. She grabbed her windbreaker off the radiator. Then she put it back, went to the door, and chose a long, shabby coat and head scarf belonging to Meltem, the housekeeper.

"What're you doing?"

"Meltem's son usually takes his mother home about this time," she said, tying Meltem's scarf over her head, then putting on a broad-brimmed rain hat that had also been hanging on the door.

"Oh, boy. Here we go," Frank said, stomping the water off his shoes on the doormat.

Dulcey took Frank's arm and leaned close. "Okay, so I'm Meltem, the housekeeper, and you're my son who has come to drive me home. Do you know if Dr. Nash has left Zeugma yet?"

"Yep. I saw him leave in one of the Birecik Dam trucks—about an hour ago."

"Good, then we don't have to worry about him." Dulcey tugged the rain hat down over her face and handed Frank an umbrella from the stand near the door. "Let's go. And remember, I'm old—so take my arm and let me hobble a bit."

"Do you think this is safe? Not telling anyone?" Frank whispered.

"We don't have anything the terrorists want. I think we'll be fine." Dulcey said, stepping out into the rain.

Frank opened the umbrella over the two of them, and they shuffled out toward the little white Toyota waiting by the gate. The soldiers, stationed well down the road, merely gave the old woman and her son a wave.

* * *

Even before they reached the highway, Frank spotted Nash's big Mack truck off to the side of the dirt road. It was parked in a big clearing beyond a row of trees. "What's Nash doing parked in all this mud?" Frank asked. He turned to the man, Taner, who was driving them. "Taner Bey, my friend . . . *arkadash, lutfen,* please turn around. Dr. Nash may be having engine trouble."

They were headlight to headlight with Nash's truck before they could see there was another truck behind Nash's. A long yellow truck with the word *MODA* emblazoned across its side was parked behind Nash's vehicle.

"What's going on?" Dulcey saw Nash standing between the two trucks, wearing his canvas slouch hat. His military escort was nowhere in sight. They heard the rolling tailgates of both trucks slam shut.

"Maybe they switched the statue to the other truck as one more step in the subterfuge," offered Frank.

"Well, he may need our help," Dulcey said, "Taner Bey, can you drive up closer to the trucks?"

When Nash saw the white Toyota, he ran over to the little car. Frank rolled down the passenger window. "Need some help, Dr. Nash?"

"What are you doing here? Where'd you get a car?" Nash barked.

"We were on our way to the hospital to see Asena," Dulcey said from the back seat. "She said it was urgent."

"Who let you out of the camp? I left strict orders that no one was to leave," he whispered in a vehement hiss. A stranger approached the Toyota, but Nash waved him away. "I'm coming!" he yelled at the man. Then Nash stuck his head all the way into the window, a crazed look on his wet, reddening face. "Get moving and don't stop. Do you understand? *Don't* go to the hospital; *don't* go back to the camp. Get to the airport and get out of here!"

Frank spoke in a low voice. "Are you in trouble, Dr. Nash? Should we send someone?"

"No, but you two are—get moving and don't look back. Don't worry about your stuff—your cameras and all of that. I'll have someone bring it all to the airport. Or we'll ship it to you. Just get on a plane—*any* plane."

The stranger, wearing a leather hat and gloves and a black leather coat came up behind Nash, bent down, and peered into the car. A slow smile spread under his neatly trimmed mustache. A prickle of alarm shot up and down Dulcey's spine. The hairs on her neck stood up.

"These people are leaving now," Nash said, leading the man back to the trucks.

Frank said to Dulcey, "Let's go. Something's not right."

"Nash was angry with us, but he was afraid too," Dulcey said as Taner backed up his Toyota and drove onto the dirt road again.

"*Arkadash*, let's park near the main highway," Frank said to Taner.

"Go to hospital now?" Taner asked, heading down the muddy road. "We will go later, after we make sure Dr. Nash is okay."

* * *

Taner parked behind a grain silo where the dirt road from Zeugma met the single-lane highway that ran between Gaziantep and Birecik. He turned off the Toyota's lights and the three of them sat in silence, listening to the rain pound the car's metal roof. Ten minutes later, a yellow truck with the word *MODA* on its side whizzed by them and turned left, heading toward Birecik. Nash's truck was nowhere in sight.

"If that truck has the goddess in it, why did it turn toward Birijek instead of Gaziantep?" Frank asked. "We need to find Nash. He should be heading back to camp if someone else has the goddess now. Maybe he'll tell us what's going on now that he's alone." Frank looked worried.

Dulcey said, "This isn't making sense. Nash acted so strangely back there." Then she turned to the driver. "Please . . . *Lutfen* . . . Taner Bey, go back—*shimdi*—now," Dulcey was glad she'd studied a few Turkish expressions at Asena's house. "We need to find Dr. Nash."

"You go hospital, now? See Asena Hanim?" Taner asked.

"No. We need to make sure Dr. Nash is all right. He was very frightened. Take us to find Dr. Nash, Taner Bey . . . *lutfen*."

The three of them headed back down the dirt road to the spot where they'd seen Dr. Nash.

"Nash's truck hasn't moved," Frank said, pointing to a path that led to the clearing. "Taner Bey, please pull up next to the truck and leave your headlights on. Our friend may be in trouble."

Nash's truck stood alone in the clearing. Frank and Dulcey got out and peered into its cab. Empty. Keys in the ignition. They walked around the truck and saw a man lying on the wet ground.

"Dr. Nash?" Dulcey knelt next to him, shaking him. Nash's canvas hat was lying upside down next to his head, slowly filling with rainwater. From a wound across his forehead, a swath of blood mixed with rain dripped down the side of his face.

Dulcey put her ear to his heart. "He's alive, but he's been knocked out. We need to get him to the hospital before he goes into shock."

Frank pressed a button on the back of the truck and the tailgate rolled up. He called out, "The goddess is gone."

"Where are the soldiers who were supposed to be with Nash?" Dulcey muttered, buttoning Nash's jacket and emptying the water from his hat.

Frank and Taner picked Dr. Nash up off the ground and gently placed him in the back of the big Mack truck. Nash was still unconscious, but he moaned as the two men lifted him. Dulcey got inside the truck and sat with her back against a side wall. She held Nash's head in her lap. Taner brought two blankets from his car and wrapped them around the soaking wet man.

Frank pressed some money toward Taner. "Thank you, *arkadash.* Now, please go back to the Zeugma camp and tell the soldiers what you saw. They will know what to do. Take this money for your trouble and for the blankets." The bills in Frank's hand were worth about fourteen U.S. dollars—two days wages for most Turks in the southeast. But Taner refused the money. Frank insisted again, but Taner still refused. Then he got into his car, waved, and headed back toward Zeugma to alert the soldiers.

Honor, Dulcey thought. She repositioned Nash's head on her lap so he'd be more comfortable for the ride.

"You think you'll be all right back here until we get to the hospital?" Frank asked, preparing to roll down the tailgate.

"Sure—just hurry." Dulcey looked into Nash's face and whispered, "Mean old man . . . I should be furious at you for being so rude." But as the gash on Nash's head continued to ooze bright blood, which dripped onto the truck's floor, all Dulcey felt was growing concern.

* * *

At Gaziantep Hastanesi, the orderlies rushed out with a rolling gurney and wheeled Nash into the emergency room. Frank stayed with the wounded man while Dulcey went in search of Asena.

In the front foyer of the hospital, Asena emerged from a little waiting lounge, a wad of wet tissues in one hand. Her eyes were red and her face drawn. "You came. Thank you," she said, going limp in Dulcey's embrace. "I just called everyone I know from the phone in there to tell them about my grandmother. She will not live much longer."

"I'm so sorry. I know you must be heartsick. Is Selene here?" Dulcey asked, leading Asena to an orange vinyl couch in the small waiting lounge.

"She is with Grandmother now while I was phoning everyone."

"You're doing all you can." The rain continued to come down outside, and thunder rattled the windows. Dulcey drew the heavy curtains of the waiting lounge, shut the door, and sat next to Asena on the uncomfortable vinyl sofa.

"She's getting good care, and she's not in pain," Asena said, fingering the wadded tissues. "The doctors do not ever expect her to wake up."

"That's so hard," Dulcey said, thinking of the final days with her own mother just a few months before. She plucked out four fresh tissues from a box on the table and handed them to Asena, keeping one for herself. "Nash is being treated at the hospital too. We found him lying on the ground next to his truck—unconscious. We think someone stole the goddess."

"This is what I feared—and why I sent for you." Asena dabbed at her eyes and wiped her nose. "Al Qaeda is here."

"How do you know?" Dulcey asked, a wave of horror washing through her as she recalled the man with the leather coat and gloves.

"Earlier this evening, I called my friend Fikret who owns a restaurant in Nizip. I was calling him to tell him about Grandmother Yildiz, who is an old friend of his. Everyone in Nizip loved my grandmother, you know. Anyway, Fikret told me that, at about noon today, Dr. Nash came to visit a man who is staying at the little hotel next door to his restaurant. He knows Lee because the excavators often eat at Fikret's restaurant. Lee and the stranger looked at the man's truck for a while—a big yellow truck from the Moda furniture company. Then they went into the hotel together."

"Yes, Nash was gone earlier this afternoon. Someone at the camp mentioned that he had gone into Nizip for supplies," Dulcey said. "And that's the exact description of the truck we saw parked next to Nash's tonight."

"Fikret said the stranger Lee met with spoke very little Turkish, but very good English, and . . . he is missing the little finger on his right hand."

CHAPTER TWENTY-ONE

"Aboud is here . . ." Dulcey eyes widened and her hands flew to her face as she quickly stood. "Come with me. This is starting to make sense."

Asena grabbed her bag and allowed Dulcey to guide her to the big Mack truck that was parked at the back of the hospital parking lot. Dulcey got into the cab and tore through the glove compartment. She checked under the front seat. Then she climbed over the seat and felt under the narrow bunk truckers use to sleep on during rest stops. *Nothing.*

"What are you looking for?" Asena asked.

"Something I hope I don't find. Over here," Dulcey said, leading Asena to the rear of the truck. She pushed the switch to raise its tailgate. The two women climbed into the back of the truck, and Dulcey turned on the ceiling light. "Who owns this truck?" Dulcey asked, patting the wooden walls.

"It belongs to the dam. When the dam is not using their trucks, Lee uses them to haul mosaics and artifacts from Zeugma to the museum. See how this conveyor belt down the center has teeth like a tank tread? It is perfect for loading concrete slab and dam machinery—or big mosaics and statues."

Dulcey stomped through the wooden bed of the truck on both sides of the conveyor belt, pausing to tap her shoe on the floor of the truck. Then she ran her hands along the wooden walls of the truck, rapping them with her knuckles as she went.

"Tell me what you are looking for, and I will help you," Asena said.

"Nash was acting so strangely tonight when Frank and I saw him. If Ahmed al Aboud, one of the most dangerous members of al Qaeda, were in the process of robbing you of a priceless possession, wouldn't you send your friends to get some help? Especially when they stopped and *offered* their help?"

"Lee Nash was with Aboud when you saw him?"

"Yes. Aboud was the driver of the Moda truck. Nash basically told us to run for our lives."

"He was trying to protect you." Asena took Dulcey's hands and looked into her eyes. "I found out something else today—by accident—and that is another reason why I needed to see you face-to-face."

Dulcey tried to resume her examination of the truck walls, but Asena held her hands in a tight grip. "Later. I'm trying to find something," Dulcey said.

"No, this is important. I should not be the one to tell you, but now that Lee Nash has been hurt . . ." Asena dug into her big tapestry bag and handed Dulcey a dog-eared manuscript.

"How'd you get my manuscript?" Dulcey asked incredulously as she flipped through the tattered pages she herself had typed for her autobiography. She could tell it was the copy she had given to her mother by the notes in the margins made with the distinctive purple ink her mother always used.

Asena explained. "I asked Tanju to bring me some books for my time in the hospital. She must have picked up the manuscript from the bookshelf the excavators share in the dining tent. I saw Dr. Nash with it once."

"Why would my mother have sent him this?" Dulcey flipped through it. The purple ink made her heart ache with longing for her mother.

"We all borrow books from each other because English language books are so scarce here. Nash leaves his books all over the camp. There are always stacks of them in the dining tent. He may not be aware that Tanju borrowed this with everything that has been happening at the camp."

"What are you trying to tell me?"

Asena took the manuscript and opened it to the back of the title page. She pointed to a note written in purple ink and said gently, "Read it for yourself."

Dulcey's heart began to race as she read her mother's letter.

Though her eyes had gone blurry and her mind felt numb, Dulcey glanced through the passages in chapter two and read some of the margin notes written by her mother. She also read a few of the notes written in black ink that must have been made by Nash. She closed the manuscript and held her breath, letting the idea sink into her pounding brain. "Dr. Lee Edward Nash is my father," she whispered.

"That's right," Asena said softly.

"Lee Nash is . . . my father," Dulcey said again in a tiny voice, staring past Asena. Nash's odd comments, the feeling that she somehow knew him, all made sense now. She sat down hard on the top of the wheel well inside the truck. She pictured Rosa as a reckless, teenaged girl falling in love with the young archeology student at the quarry— giving herself, without a second thought to her future, to the boy from out of town. She thought about how her mother's pregnancy at the age of sixteen had set the course for both of their lives. Rosa had eventually owned a café in town and had worked twelve-hour days, leaving Dulcey alone most of the time or sweeping floors and washing dishes from the age of seven. Rosa had died at the age of fifty-one. Dulcey shuddered and stood up again; the manuscript fell to the floor. Her jaw twitched madly. "Well, that doesn't change a thing."

"How can it *not* change a thing?" Asena demanded, hands on her hips.

With extra fervor, Dulcey examined the wood paneling all down the length of the truck, knocking against the wood, testing the walls with her fingertips. Toward the cab end of the truck, an inch or two under the ceiling, she saw a hemp rope that had been looped through two holes drilled in the wood. The panel, not as recessed as the others, was hinged near the floor. "Help me with this."

"What are we doing?" Asena asked, helping Dulcey tug on the loop of rope.

"Just because he might be my father doesn't change who else Dr. Lee Edward Nash might be." Dulcey pulled down hard, but the panel didn't budge. The two women stood on the conveyer belt to get better leverage and pulled with all their strength. Suddenly, the top of the panel gave way and jawed open toward them. Several clear plastic bags full of American twenty dollar bills fell out from the space behind the panel.

Dulcey's eyes burned like embers. "You were about to say Lee Nash may have been protecting me from al Qaeda? What do you say now?"

It was Asena's turn to sit down hard. "Are you suggesting that Nash *sold* the goddess to Aboud? And that he just wanted you out of the way?"

"He told me something the other night that got me thinking," Dulcey said, her eyes narrowing. "I thought about it all the way here to the hospital as I was holding his bleeding head in my lap. He said it all came down to which tribe you identified with. And he said he identified with many tribes and was proud of that. What if al Qaeda is one of those tribes he identifies with?"

Asena shook her head. "Lee Nash and I do not see eye to eye on many things, but I cannot believe he would sell an artifact. I certainly cannot believe he would sell an artifact to terrorists. It is not possible."

"We know he needs money to finish the excavation and build his open-air museum. How desperate is he?"

"It is true he is desperate, Dulcey. After the RHI funds ran out, he begged the Americans to help him excavate the rest of Zeugma and build the museum. But no one was interested. Turkey is so far away. And with the Kurdish unrest and the war in Iraq, Americans are hesitant to come here or even send their money here."

Dulcey struggled against a tide of emotions and thoughts, contradictory and violent, and tender as well, like sunlight on crashing waves. Her pulse raced as she leafed through the pages of the manuscript she had written herself, reading notations in the margins written by both her mother . . . and her father.

CHAPTER TWENTY-TWO

Behind a small hotel in Birecik, Ahmed al Aboud and his son waited in the dark truck for the two armed men who would accompany them and provide security as they delivered the goddess to the training camp in Syria. Aboud glanced at his watch. "More than an hour late. You know for certain they got the message?"

"I delivered the message to them at the Firat Pansyon. To the clerk at the front desk."

"You left the message at the front desk? You did not take it to their room as I asked you to?"

"The clerk refused to give me their room number. He said it was against security rules."

"Perhaps you should have waited until you saw them."

"But I have never seen them before. How could I?" Nayif protested.

"Yes, yes. I guess it cannot be helped now," Aboud muttered to himself, then got out of the truck and gruffly steered his son up the steps into the foyer of the Firat Pansyon. Aboud asked the front desk clerk to summon the two guests to the front desk.

"The police escorted your friends away this afternoon," the desk clerk said, spreading a pile of room keys on the desk and hanging each of them on their respective hooks. "The police would not tell me what your friends had done."

Aboud immediately changed tactics at the news. "Good! Those two were crooks. They took a shipment of my candy products and failed to pay me for them," Aboud said. "It was I who called the police. I dropped by to make sure they had been picked up. Thank you, my friend." Although he offered the clerk his best smile, Aboud's instincts had already been ratcheted up to battle mode. He stroked his mustache and tried to appear as though nothing were wrong.

Before they had entered the town, Aboud and Nayif had stopped by the side of the road and torn off all the plastic siding from the truck. The truck was no longer a bright yellow Moda furniture truck with the license plate 43 YTT 03. It had a new license plate, and its panels were now navy blue and brown with a large colorful advertisement for Ülker chocolate candy. Aboud had even bought a bag of the chocolate bars at a roadside market. He and Nayif planned to give the candy to people along the way, just as the Ülker drivers did.

"Have a candy bar, sir. Compliments of our company," Nayif said, handing over a *Çokonat* candy bar.

The hotel clerk smiled at the boy. "These are my favorite . . . thank you."

Aboud and Nayif left the hotel and stepped into a shadowed alley between the hotel and a store that had been closed and shuttered for the night. Aboud removed his leather gloves and dialed a number on his cell phone. Nayif, whose Arabic was nearly as good as his English, listened as his father spoke to someone on the other end.

"So you have already heard the bad news. No, I do not know where they were taken . . . Saif, please. I know they were your nephews. We will get them out. But that comes later."

Nayif's stomach rumbled. When his father was doing his warrior business, he often completely forgot about food for either one of them. After a moment, Nayif sat on a chair with a broken back that someone had set out with the trash. He dug into his bag of candy bars and ate two of them in quick succession. He knew the arrest of the two men at the hotel could be a very bad turn of events—especially if one of them talked.

Aboud turned toward him. Nayif smiled, wiping chocolate from his mouth, but his father frowned, shook his head, and turned his back on him.

Nayif hoped fervently that his father did not blame him for the arrest of the two brothers who were members of Victorious Islam. Aboud was a loving, concerned father much of the time—except when he believed his son had behaved in an incompetent manner. *Incompetence.* It was the one thing Nayif feared in himself above all other weaknesses. It was the personal, internal enemy of all jihadi warriors.

"Is our contact in place at the border so I can get the statue across? Good. Good . . . You say I should cross at gate three? Now, about your nephews, Saif. Perhaps we can find a well-known American, or perhaps even two high-value Americans . . .Yes, that's what I mean, to trade for them. As long as it stays out of the media, the United States may be willing to trade our hostages for their prisoners. Allah willing. Good night, brother Saif."

Aboud closed his cell phone. Then he and Nayif got into the truck with the candy advertisements on the outside—and a solid gold goddess on the inside.

CHAPTER TWENTY-THREE

Dulcey shoved the plastic bags of U.S. twenty-dollar bills back into the hollow of the truck wall and replaced the wood panel. "This is a crime scene now."

"What are you going to do?" Asena asked, carefully watching Dulcey's face. The women huddled together as a lightning bolt unzipped the sky. Rain pummeled the truck so heavily that the women now had to shout to be heard above its roar.

"How could an American—how could *anyone* make a deal with those monsters?" Dulcey paced back and forth in the long truck bed, folding her arms close to her body, a low keening sound bubbling up from deep inside her.

"Maybe it isn't what it seems," Asena said, raising her voice over the sound of the storm. "I have known your . . . Dr. Nash for twelve years. I almost married him. He may be stubborn and single-minded and a workaholic—and he would have made a terrible husband—but there is much good in him. He is no terrorist." Asena sat on the conveyor belt, staring out at the pounding rain and the open field beyond the hospital parking lot.

"He doesn't have to *be* a terrorist. He just had to be desperate enough to take their money," Dulcey said.

"Why would he do it now when CNN is helping him publicize Zeugma? If he had waited, I am sure someone would have stepped in with the funding he needs to complete his work."

Dulcey paced and gestured and shouted. "I don't know—greed? Impatience? Fear that the crass Americans won't come through for him? He's such an arrogant, selfish—"

"Maybe there is another explanation," Asena said.

"Maybe Nash is in debt, and he can't use grant money to bail himself out."

"Or maybe he was forced into giving up the goddess," Asena offered.

"But if he was forced to give Fortuna to them, why would al Qaeda give him *money?*" Dulcey asked, shaking her finger at the incriminating panel full of cash.

"Dulcey?" Asena stood up and put her hands on Dulcey's shoulders. "You have not said anything about the fact that Dr. Nash is . . . your father."

Dulcey jerked away from Asena's hands. "I never imagined that the first emotion I would feel after finding my father would be revulsion."

"Come. We will take a walk in the rain. You need to scream. I need to scream. My grandmother lies dying in that little room up there. My world is falling apart—and so is yours."

The two women walked out into the grassy field. When the thunder came again, Asena howled up into it. Dulcey faced the watery torrents and raised her hands to embrace the sky, her face golden in the flickering lightning. She closed her eyes and let the rain beat her face.

"In this country, we know grief. It is like *gübre.* Oh, what is your word . . . *manure.* Not a pleasant thing—but good things grow in it. Go on, woman. No one can hear you out here."

Dulcey looked hesitantly at the howling Asena. She thought of the old woman in Baghdad who had mourned John's death and had pounded her chest and wailed her heartache—and who had generously shared grief with her. A rumble of thunder came again, and Dulcey made a tiny noise in her throat, her tears undetectable in the wash of rain on her face.

Asena smiled at her and yelled above the rumble. "Learn from the East, Dulcey! Learn from women who have mourned for thousands of years."

Another thunderbolt shook the sky. Asena let out a scream, and Dulcey's voice rose until it hit the same otherworldly note. As Dulcey screamed, she imagined being surrounded by the raw elements. Fire. Water. Air. Earth. *Here I am in Anadolu—the land full of mothers—learning how to grieve.*

Dulcey and Asena screamed through the thunder and through the silence that followed it. They screamed when a lightning bolt hit a generator on the hospital roof and sparks shot up like fireworks. They screamed until their voices were hoarse, and they screamed again as rain sluiced down their sore throats, soothing them so they could scream some more.

Asena kept her eyes on the third floor window with the vase of yellow field daisies in it. Dulcey glared at the truck where she had found her father, along with his treacheries, and where she had found the root of what had created the fierce, stubborn side of herself.

* * *

Drenched, exhausted, and exhilarated, Dulcey and Asena returned to the hospital. They found Frank standing in the front lobby. He watched suspiciously as they dried each other's faces with tissues. Both Dulcey's and Asena's hair lay like soggy seaweed, and their shoes were large with mud. But Dulcey felt strangely calm as she led Frank into the little waiting room with the orange vinyl couches.

"And how is Dr. Nash?" she asked Frank in a hoarse voice.

"He's still asleep. They put him in a room on the second floor for observation," Frank said, bewildered. "Why are you so wet?"

"You mean he's still unconscious?" Dulcey asked, looking into the mirror of her compact, wiping away the mascara from under her eyes.

"Well, no. It's odd—after they determined that the wound on his head wasn't serious, they tested his blood. His system contained a large dose of a very strong sleep medication."

Dulcey shot a look at Asena. "I'm not surprised."

"You're not?" Frank said.

Asena took the manuscript from her bag and handed it to Frank. She pointed to the letter written in purple ink. "Dulcey has just found out some important information. I think you had better hear it too."

Bewildered, Frank read Rosa's letter. He whistled between his teeth and said, "I don't believe this. Dr. Nash is . . . your father?"

"Yes. I couldn't have thought up a more shocking introduction to my father if I had planned it for years," Dulcey said.

Frank rubbed his temples. "I wonder why your mother didn't tell you herself."

"We never talked about him. Never. He wasn't part of us. But I think my mother could tell from my writing that I finally wanted to know who he was—to make the pieces of my life fit together better. I think as she was dying, she wanted to make sure I found him."

"Does Nash know that you know?" Frank asked.

"Not yet. It gets more complicated," Dulcey said. She unbuttoned the housekeeper's oversized raincoat and held it open by the pockets, swaggering around the waiting room. "It seems that dear old Dad sold the goddess to Ahmed al Aboud—the man we saw with Nash. And Nash has hidden thousands of dollars in that truck out there."

"Nash wants people to think Aboud stole the goddess, right?" Frank said. "That's why he faked the assault."

"Right. We need to get Cantwell in here. He needs to know what Nash is up to," Dulcey said.

A few minutes later, Cantwell was listening to Dulcey's story. His face told her he didn't believe a word of it. Dulcey's face was a mask of outrage. "Why aren't you out looking for the goddess? Why aren't you making sure Aboud doesn't get past the border? I've just told you Nash has sold a priceless artifact, and you're just sitting there!"

Dulcey could tell that Cantwell was trying to stay calm, but he seemed frustrated with her more than anything. "I have my men looking for Aboud right now. But this doesn't involve you, Ms. Moore. You don't understand what you're getting yourself into. And you need to leave this to us."

"I am a witness to this treachery. I saw Nash selling the goddess!" Dulcey stormed at him. "Let me show you the money he took from Aboud. It's right out there in the truck."

Cantwell's satellite phone buzzed. "Copy. Stay on it." He turned to the small group in front of him, seeming to weigh whether or not to keep them in the dark. "The Birecik police just found a license plate and the yellow siding from a large truck with the word *Moda* on it. That means Aboud is no longer driving a yellow truck. It could be any color now." Cantwell looked at Dulcey as though she were the leader of a group of insurgents. "I want you and Frank back at Zeugma right now. I don't want you out here coming up with some way to help. We can't afford that."

"What is this—some kind of martial law or something?" Dulcey asked.

Frank gave her a look and moved in front of her. "We'll go. We know we've made things hard on you."

Dulcey wasn't having any of it. "Dr. Nash is no victim here. At least let me show you the money in the truck."

"Yes, of course. But after that, I need you and Frank to return to Zeugma so we can keep an eye on you. Agreed?" Cantwell said, following Dulcey and Frank out of the waiting room and into the hospital parking lot. Two of his agents followed them.

It was still raining as Dulcey marched the men toward the Mack truck. "What you're going to see will convince you that Dr. Nash is *not* on our side."

Cantwell coughed. "Ma'am, Dr. Nash is an American patriot. Same as you and me."

Dulcey opened the tailgate and climbed up into the truck bed. Frank and Cantwell followed her. "Help me pull this panel down so I can show you."

The men helped her tug on the rope handle attached to the panel until it swung toward them.

Dulcey gasped. The bags of money were gone.

* * *

Two of Cantwell's agents drove Frank and Dulcey back to Asena's house. Frank had a note from Asena in his pocket so that Hasan would permit him stay at the house.

Dulcey leaned against the window, nursing a sense of doom. Her whole life had been turned upside down. She was no longer an orphan—now she had a terrorist sympathizer for a father. And no one would believe her. She looked at her watch and calculated the time in Dallas. Since Turkey was nine hours ahead of Texas, dawn was the one time of day she couldn't call Matt. He did both the six o'clock and the nine o'clock evening news programs. Between his two news segments, he was always in a rush to rewrite copy and stay on top of breaking stories. Dulcey had called Marie from the Gaziantep Airport to check on the kids, but she had not yet spoken to Matt. She longed to hear his voice—and to begin to break down the barriers between them. *Now is not the time to tell him all that's been happening. I'll have to wait.*

The air felt cleansed by the rain, and the clouds had departed, revealing a deep blue sky. The morning calls to prayer wafted through the villages as they drove down the still-wet highway. A man hauling cotton stopped his truck on the shoulder of the road, and Dulcey watched through the back window as he spread a prayer rug in the glare of his headlights. Then he bowed his forehead until it touched the ground.

As a sliver of sunlight edged above the horizon, Frank snored softly, his head lolling against the back of his seat. Dulcey knew he had slept very little since John had been killed. She scooted next to him and curled the crook of her elbow around his head to steady him as he slept. As his head nodded toward hers, she kissed the bald spot on its very top. It's what Izzy always did whenever she saw her big buddy Frank.

Although she didn't have Matt right now, she was grateful to have Frank with her. The two of them had worked together ever since her first big job in New York—even before she and Matt had met. Frank had been there when she'd fallen in love with the two motherless children who were now like her own flesh and blood. He had guided and coached her like the father she'd never had. *Father. Now I have one of those. But who is he?*

She tried to pray, but her prayer came out like a string of indignant commands.

As the morning sun rose, Dulcey watched the stars wink out one by one. *I will pass them on to you, Izzy. When you see the stars, remember they were just with me—then you can send them back when you're finished with them.* Dulcey held one hand toward the sky like an empty cup, as she'd seen the Muslims do.

Then her hand curled into a fist.

CHAPTER TWENTY-FOUR

Selene held her great grandmother's hand and sang softly into her ear. She had already cried her tears and had turned her attention to comforting the old woman. She hoped her love would strengthen and then release Yildiz for her journey to the other side.

Asena too had drawn up her chair next to the hospital bed and was massaging her grandmother's feet to let her know she was not alone.

As Selene watched her mother, a wave of loneliness swept over her. Her mother would have no one now. But Selene's vicarious loneliness took on a tinge of frustration as she contemplated the number of times Asena had shut people out of her life. Her mother had never invited people from Nizip into her home, even though she and Yildiz were popular figures in the nearby town. The two women had shared tea with all the shopkeepers and half the women in town. But not once in Selene's memory had her mother reciprocated and brought those lovely people into her home.

And then there was Lee Nash. Selene knew the man was still in love with her mother. He'd told her so a few months before. It was her mother who had shut Lee out of her life—all because of her mother's need to protect their house from Nash's prying eyes.

Selene had known Lee Nash since she was fourteen years old. She had adored him as a teenager. His stories about America were the main reason for her love of all things red, white, and blue. When she was fifteen, Lee Nash had comforted her when her father had been murdered and had served as a sort of substitute father during her last few years of high school. It had been Nash's powerful recommendation letter and his relentless campaign with his well-placed colleagues that had helped her get into Princeton—on a full scholarship.

When he and her mother had fallen in love, Selene could not have been happier. During endless long-distance phone calls while Selene was away at college, Asena had regaled her daughter with hilarious Lee Nash stories. It had been the house that had finally come between them. That dark, miserable, mysterious house of theirs—what good was it to them when it kept her mother from finding happiness?

"Mother," Selene whispered, "I worry about you. Please move to Ankara and live with me. My apartment is big enough for both of us."

Asena gazed at her daughter. "Again, you ask me this. You know I cannot leave our home. What would happen to it if—"

"It's not our home, Mother," Selene whispered through clenched teeth. "It's been your prison all these years. It's time you open the doors that you yourself have locked."

Asena cocked her head and sighed. "You are young. Someday you will understand how important it is to keep your ties to your family. Our home is all I have left of them now."

Selene swallowed hard, then said what had been in her heart for months. "Then let Lee Nash back into your life. You still love him. I know you do by the way you talk about him. The two of you were so happy when you were together. And you've barely smiled since the two of you broke up."

Asena turned her head away from Selene and continued to caress the feet of her dying grandmother. "Please. Not now," Asena pleaded.

Yildiz had moved her legs a time or two since she had lapsed into her coma, and she had opened her eyes briefly at the sound of Selene's voice. But she had not moved for the last few hours. The old woman's breathing was shallow, and now there was a rattling sound deep inside her chest. Selene knew that she and her mother were about to lose their last connection to the glorious line of Özturk women from the lost city of Zeugma, Turkey.

* * *

Through an interpreter, Cantwell spoke to the Turkish soldiers guarding Asena's house and then turned to Dulcey and Frank. "At some point, you'll both be allowed to return to the camp under armed guard to pack your belongings and your equipment. Then, tomorrow at ten, we'll escort you to the airport to catch the noon flight. We would've taken you today, but there are no more flights to Ankara. You're to go nowhere without guards. Do you understand?"

Reluctantly, both Dulcey and Frank agreed. Frank showed Hasan the note from Asena. Hasan blinked and dipped his head to the side in the Turkish way and pointed Dulcey and Frank toward the table in the dining room. Meltem the housekeeper hovered nearby, gesturing to the food she and Feyza had prepared.

"I'm not hungry," Dulcey said, shaking her head at Hasan.

"Neither am I," Frank agreed. "I could use some more sleep though."

Dulcey began pacing. "I can't just sit here with my mind spinning like this. I'm going to the dam to find a cell phone signal."

Frank nodded. "I know. You need to talk to Matt and the kids. A lot has happened to you." He looked out the window at the military jeeps and the four soldiers standing guard in front of Asena's house. "Tell the guards you need to get your things from the women's tent. Then you can tell the soldier you need to get to the dam to make a call."

"I just want to hear Matt's voice. And maybe the kids are home from their vacation. It won't take long—you get some rest."

At Asena's front gate, the soldiers stopped Dulcey. Asena's little goat nuzzled her legs while she tried to explain to them why she needed to get to the excavation camp right away.

"I need my things, *lutfen.*" Dulcey pantomimed packing, then carrying a heavy suitcase. The soldier nodded and shouted to another soldier who drove his vehicle up to the gate. Dulcey climbed in. The soldier seemed to be waiting for Frank. "Frank will come later. Frank no *shimdi.*" She pointed to herself. "Dulcey now—*shimdi.*"

The soldier smiled at Dulcey's terrible Turkish and sped to the camp. Once there, she saw Fatma briskly washing breakfast dishes in the dining tent. A short distance away, she saw Aysha walking near the pistachio grove gathering kindling in her arms. The girl looked up when she saw Dulcey but quickly turned away. Behind the dining tent, Ali chopped wood, raising his ax high above his head, splitting the logs in one stroke. The rest of the camp looked deserted. Because the funds had run out, even the excavators had left. Each of their trenches was now filled with dirt to prevent looting. The CNN trucks were already gone, and most of the soldiers were gone as well. Without the golden goddess and the swarms of foreign reporters, the Turkish military must have considered the danger at Zeugma to be over.

The soldier who had driven her to camp dogged her wherever she went. Dulcey approached Fatma and asked, "Tanju? Mehmet?" She glanced around as though looking for them.

Fatma shook her head. "Gaziantep," she said sullenly and went back to her dishes.

"Nash?" Dulcey asked.

"Gaziantep Hastanesi," Fatma said without turning around.

"Americans?" she asked.

Fatma pointed toward the dam. "Birecik Baraji."

Dulcey realized there was no longer anyone at the camp who could help her. Two Turkish soldiers had been on guard near the gate, and she saw two more making their way up the mist-covered hill. She was certain that none of them spoke English and that all of them had been instructed to keep her from leaving the camp.

The dam was several kilometers away, and she was sure the soldiers wouldn't drive her there. Then she knew the answer. The little village of Tilmusa was only a few hundred meters across the Euphrates, shrouded in the morning fog. Remembering the word for "wait," Dulcey said to the soldier, "Bekle, lutfen." Then she pointed to the front of the women's tent. She flashed the soldier a quick smile and disappeared inside. She was confident that no Muslim man would dare follow her inside a place where women slept and changed their clothing.

When she stepped into the tent, Dulcey saw her dirty Chanel jacket and slacks hanging on the rope that was strung through the tent. Aysha's lilac head scarf and clothes were hanging next to them. Dulcey threw her CNN sweatshirt on the floor and slipped into Aysha's handmade embroidered blouse and shapeless velveteen vest. She traded her blue jeans for Aysha's flowered shalwars and stuck her cell phone into one of the deep pockets of the baggy trousers. Then she grabbed Aysha's scarf with the row of crocheted violets and tied it under her chin, making sure it covered all of her hair and extended an inch or two past her face.

Then Dulcey got down on her hands and knees, lifted the back of the tent, and crawled out on the side toward the river.

Quietly, she slid the Yildirim's wooden rowboat into the water and climbed inside. She'd had her own little rowboat as a child, and the handling of the oars came back to her immediately. As she rowed, she almost thought she could turn and see her grandfather with his fishing line dangling in the water, waiting for supper to chomp down on his hook.

As she pulled on the oars and put some distance between herself and Zeugma, her craving to hear the voice of her husband and children became almost overwhelming. It was all she needed to set her jumbled world back in order. Though the fog hid her destination across the river, it also offered a veil of protection. In Tilmusa, she knew she could reach the people she loved the most. With every dip of the oars, another layer of her infamous pride sloughed off into the chilly water of the Euphrates River.

CHAPTER TWENTY-FIVE

In his hospital bed, Nash wrestled with demons all night long. Cantwell had informed him that Dulcey had found Aboud's payoff for the goddess. His agents had removed the bags of cash, so she'd been left with nothing to prove her case against him. But the men had decided the less she knew about the CIA's sting operation, the safer she would be. The operation was not over yet. And until it was, no one was to know about it—or know Nash had sold a gold-leafed replica of the goddess to Aboud.

Nash had found and lost his only daughter—as well as two grandchildren. And the only woman he had ever truly loved now believed he was a criminal, or worse—a traitor in league with terrorists. The secrets he kept were costing him too much.

He had to get out of this hospital.

Nash dressed and slipped past the nurse's station. He took the stairs to the third floor and asked a nurse to direct him to the room where Yildiz Özturk lay in a coma. He stood quietly at the open door and looked in on Selene and Asena. Selene was bending toward her great grandmother, singing softly. Asena was draped across the foot of the bed, her hands holding tightly onto her grandmother's feet.

"Asena?" he whispered.

When Asena looked up, her face told him that he had already been sentenced and found guilty. "I do not want to see you," she whispered. "Please leave now."

"I know this is a terrible time for you. But please, I must speak to you for a moment."

Asena stepped out of the room, closing the door softly behind her. Nash hesitantly reached out to touch her. She flinched; her hand shot up as a defense against him. "Please be brief."

"You believe I sold the goddess, don't you?" Nash asked.

She folded her arms and whispered, "What else can I believe? I saw the bags of money you took from Aboud."

"You have to believe me. There are things you don't understand."

"What explanation could you possibly have for the money Dulcey and I found in that truck?"

"I'm not supposed to talk about this, because if too many people know, the plan might fail," Nash said, his gaze darting over the people passing in the hall.

"Could your plan have failed any worse than it has? The goddess is gone. Al Qaeda has what they need to gain even more power. Dulcey loathes the sight of you. And you have become someone completely different from the man I thought I knew."

"Look. This deal with Aboud was planned months ago, right after I found the golden goddess."

Asena looked aghast, as though his explanation had only made things worse. "But why? Someone who saw the CNN story would have given you the funds you need for Zeugma. Why did you have to sell the goddess?"

Lee Nash smiled wearily. "That's not what I meant." He was silent for a moment, weighing the cost of putting Asena in danger against the need for her support. He exhaled slowly and then said, "The CIA approached me after I found the goddess and asked me to participate in a sting operation in order to find an al Qaeda training compound in Syria run by Victorious Islam." Nash put his hand on the wall above Asena. He rubbed his eyes with his other hand. "Do you understand what a 'sting' is?"

"I watch American movies. I know what a sting is. You are saying the CIA asked you to sell the goddess so they could catch these terrorists?"

"They arranged the whole thing. The agents asked John Barrows to deliver the offer to Saif bin Rabeh, because Barrows knew how to contact him."

"How would Barrows know how to reach bin Rabeh?" Asena asked.

"Last year, Barrows filmed an interview with him. Do you remember that? Al Qaeda wanted the world to know exactly what they wanted and what they were willing to do to expel Westerners from Muslim lands. During the summer, John sent bin Rabeh word that he knew a crooked archeologist who would be willing to sell a solid gold goddess for five hundred thousand U.S. dollars. Bin Rabeh knew the gold alone was worth millions."

"Why should I believe you?" Asena shot back, her eyes wide with mistrust.

Nash saw that she was trembling. "Because I'm telling you the truth. And you know it—because you know *me* . . ." He reached out with both arms and tried to pull her toward him. She resisted but took one of his hands in hers briefly before letting it fall to his side. He relaxed for a moment, remembering how it had felt to be in love with her. How it still felt. "Look at me." With his index finger, he tilted her chin up so she would face him. "How could you believe I'd sell the goddess?"

Asena looked up at him and dabbed at her eyes, "But you *did* sell the goddess. They have her now."

Nash knew he could not involve Asena any further. Telling her that the real golden statue was still in Zeugma could endanger her life. There was also the risk that she might tell the wrong person and imperil the goddess. The only protection the goddess had was the fact that only he and Mehmet knew where she was hidden. Not even the CIA knew that the real solid gold goddess was still in the Zeugma camp. "You're right, I *did* sell her—but only so we could draw out al Qaeda and find their training camp in Syria."

"It sounds like a good story to me, but I am not convinced," Asena said, her eyes wet and bright. "Why did you take the sleeping pills?"

"My Turkish friends and colleagues—and you—would never have forgiven me if they thought I'd sold an artifact, especially to al Qaeda. After I hid Aboud's money in the truck, I cut my own forehead to make it look like a robbery. I knew I had to lie there bleeding in the rain until someone found me—maybe even all night. I took enough pills to knock myself out so I could pull it off," Nash said, begging her to believe him.

"Is al Qaeda trying to force the Mountain of Gold prophecy to come true?"

"That's my biggest fear. That's why I insisted we go ahead with the CNN story—I wanted the world to know that the goddess exists and to see what she looks like in case she is sold. But if they melt her down and fashion some sort of golden mountain out of her, nothing can stop them."

"I too fear this possibility more than anything." Asena leaned against the wall, her expression pained, defeated.

"If radical Muslims come to believe that al Qaeda is the legitimate restored caliphate, they will become an unstoppable force," Nash said.

"There will still be reasonable Muslims," Asena chided. "Like me, for instance. And Selene. And most of the rest of the Muslims in the world."

"You're right. Not many Muslims would be swayed, but if al Qaeda could gain the support of even a small part of the Muslim population—maybe a million believers—all at once, there would be no stopping a force like that."

Asena looked into his eyes. "Lee, tell me the rest of your story. I need to know."

Nash hesitated, feeling the weight of the risk but knowing this was the only way she would trust him again. "Okay, listen carefully. The goddess I sold is a fake—a decoy."

Asena looked at him in disbelief. "Fake?"

"The CIA gave Mehmet and me two GPS tracking devices. We were to place one inside the replica statue and one in the pedestal, since these pieces could be separated at some point. This way, the CIA would be able to follow the decoy goddess all the way to the training camp in Syria." Nash looked both ways and waited for a group of nurses to pass by them. "When they locate the training camp, they're going to take it out. Destroy it."

"Lee, I had no idea . . ."

He thought a minute, then slapped the wall above Asena's head, startling her. "That Dulcey—so headstrong. I tried to take precautions. No one was supposed to go anywhere without checking in with Commander Cantwell. No one was supposed to leave Zeugma."

Asena covered her mouth with a hand and drew in a sharp breath. "That part was my fault. I asked Dulcey to come to the hospital. I found out that Aboud was in Nizip, and I was trying to warn her. If you and I had been talking to each other, none of this would have happened." Asena paced the hall, then came back and said, "I must confess something else. I asked Tanju to bring me some books and magazines from the dining tent, and Dulcey's manuscript of *An Accidental Life* was in the pile she brought me."

"So she knows. You told her."

"I could not have guessed how all this would turn out. It has been one disaster after another." Asena stared up at him, her face pale. "You must . . . hate me . . . for interfering."

"No. You didn't know. I know that Major Thurman told you and Dulcey's crew not mention anything about the CIA to me. We couldn't have people discussing the operation in front of the other CNN crews."

"You know Major Thurman too?"

"He and General Manheim are the ones who came up with the plan. Everyone figured the risk to the Americans was low. That's why John Barrows invited his son on the assignment. And, after Rosa sent me Dulcey's manuscript, it's why I requested that CNN send Dulcey to Zeugma. I didn't believe any of us were in danger." Nash heaved a long sigh and took Asena's hand again, surprised at how good it felt to touch another human being when the whole world seemed about to crumble around them. "It wasn't meant to turn out this way."

"I feel so responsible."

"No, none of this can be blamed on innocent people." Nash was surprised at the way his chest felt—sore, as though he'd been punched hard. He watched his own hands shake.

"Why didn't you explain all this to Dulcey instead of letting her think the worst about you?" Asena asked, taking both of his trembling hands and squeezing them firmly between her own.

"I couldn't risk compromising the sting. When I saw her drive up in that car and Aboud was standing right there, all I could think of was getting her on a plane and making her safe." Nash swallowed. "I was afraid she and Frank would try to help me if I told them who Aboud was. You know how she is."

"Lee?" Asena said in a small, tired voice. "I believe . . . you were trying to do the right thing." She stepped toward him and let him engulf her in his arms.

Grateful, Nash held her tightly for several moments as though she were a life raft in a roiling, windblown sea.

* * *

The door to Yildiz's room opened, and Selene stepped out into the hallway and motioned to Asena. "Mother, you won't believe this."

"Selene, my sincere sympathies," Nash said. "Asena, go be with them. I'll talk to you later."

Asena went back into the hospital room with her daughter and her dying grandmother. "What is it?"

"Grandmother opened her eyes just now. She looked right at me and said, 'Selene, *paha bichelmez mozaic.*'"

CHAPTER TWENTY-SIX

Dulcey glanced over her shoulder several times in the Yildirim's green wooden boat to make sure she was rowing toward the shore of Tilmusa. The fog prevented her from seeing the other side until she had traveled well past the center of the river. Finally she saw an inlet with a fuzz of trees and rowed toward that.

As soon as the boat scraped over the rocks on the shore, Dulcey grabbed her cell phone from the pocket of Aysha's shalwar pants. *If I can get a signal from here, I can be back to the camp in ten minutes.* She punched in Matt's number, her heart beating in her throat. As the phone rang, Dulcey whispered, "Pick up. Pick up."

Five rings. The fog held the muggy scent of freshly caught fish. The cold water lapped against the side of the boat, and she rubbed her arms to keep warm. "Come on. Answer, Matt," Dulcey whispered into the phone.

"Dulcey?" came Matt's voice.

"Matt—" Dulcey's breath was cut short by a thick arm around her throat. Her cell phone hinged shut and clattered to the bottom of the boat. The man's other arm encircled her waist, and she felt herself being dragged out of the boat. Dulcey smelled the man's sweat and the grime in his corduroy jacket. Her heels scraped against the rocks as he hauled her behind a hedge of scrubby bushes. Her arms flailed in front of her as she kicked and writhed, the back of her head smashing again and again against the man's heaving chest.

There was a metallic click, and she saw the glint of a blade out of the corner of her eye. She stared at the dirt under the man's fingernails as he reached across her face with the knife. As the edge of the blade sliced into her throat, she thought of Matt and the children. A sense of excruciating injustice welled up inside Dulcey, giving her an explosion of strength equal to the searing pain. She jammed both feet into the ground, lurched forward, and twisted her body around—breaking the man's grasp. He backed away and stood staring at her, the knife still clenched in his left fist. She fell to her knees, gasping for air. Her hands flew to her throat and came away wet with her own bright blood.

The man said something to her in his own language as he backed away from her.

Dulcey tried to scream, but no sound came from her bruised throat. As blood rushed from the wound, she tried to staunch its flow with both hands. Aysha's lilac head scarf lay on the ground between her and her attacker. The man looked at it for a moment, then picked it up and handed it to her. He spoke softly to her, his palms held out like a shield, as though she might lunge at him.

Dulcey pressed Aysha's head scarf against her wound. But the blood was coming furiously now, making her head feel as though clouds were passing through it. An electric pain shot through her brain and down her arms and legs. She felt overcome by a desire to sleep, and so she stumbled toward a little patch of grass and lay down on it. Everything seemed too close up and too loud. A high-pitched sound whined in her ears. Her forehead hit the moist ground, and she watched in fascination as her blood ran down the blades of grass. The last thing she heard was the man's footsteps as he fled over the smooth stones washed ashore by the Euphrates River.

* * *

Asena's grandmother died at eight o'clock on Saturday morning. Islamic law required that she be buried within twenty-four hours, so two hours after her death, Asena and Selene brought her body back home in a quiet ambulance. They took Yildiz into a back bedroom and lovingly washed her and wrapped her in clean white linen. Then they placed her body in a wooden casket supplied by the hospital and made arrangements with the local imam to say the prayers. Yildiz was to be buried in the family cemetery early on Sunday morning.

* * *

Frank tapped his foot as he sat in the courtyard, his concern mounting with every passing minute that Dulcey did not return. Because Asena's house was so large, he was unaware that Asena and Selene had come home and had been tending to Yildiz.

Asena walked out into the courtyard. "There you are, Frank. Where is Dulcey?"

"She went to find a cellular signal—a long time ago. I woke up just a few minutes ago and realized that she still hadn't gotten back," Frank said uneasily. His eyes were bloodshot, his hair aimed in all directions, and his face was shadowed by a heavy growth of beard.

"How long has she been gone?" Asena asked. "Did a soldier go with her?"

"Yes, the soldiers won't let her out of their sight. She's been gone almost two hours now—she should have been back by now."

"We must find her," Asena said, heading for the door.

Just then, Selene walked into the courtyard. She walked toward Frank with her hand out. "Hello, you must be Frank. I'm Asena's daughter, Selene."

Frank's brow creased, and he said softly, "Oh. There's only one reason the two of you would be home at the same time. Grandmother Yildiz has died, hasn't she?"

Asena smiled and wiped her eyes. "Yildiz is waiting in the other room for her burial. And her soul has gone to a place much kinder than this earth."

Frank said, "I'm so sorry. I know how close you both were to Yildiz."

"It is very hard, but we will manage, won't we, Selene?" Asena grabbed her bag again and said, "Right now, we have to find Dulcey."

Selene gave her mother a kiss. "You two go. I'll stay here with Grandmother. And will you leave me your keys to the doors in the house, Mama? I need to look for something."

Asena handed her daughter a big brass ring that held everything from large skeleton keys to shiny modern keys to tiny rusted ones. Frank had seen Hasan use one of the keys to open the door of the guest bedroom he was using.

"Come on, we have to find her," Asena said. "I have some things to tell you and Dulcey that will put your encounter with Lee Nash into perspective."

* * *

By the time the soldiers had escorted Frank and Asena to Zeugma, the sun was out in full force and had burned off the layer of fog that had been resting on the Euphrates and the surrounding hills.

Their small entourage found Cantwell who, along with several agents, was poring over a map of the Zeugma area.

"Where's Dulcey?" asked Frank.

"She's gone again," Cantwell informed him. "I've got two of my men out searching for her. She's better than Houdini when she tries to get away from us.

"Dulcey was trying to find a cell signal. Did you check the dam?" Asena asked.

"Yes, we looked there. She slipped away from one of the Turkish soldiers who thought she was in her tent packing. By the time he figured out she wasn't in the tent, Dulcey had been gone nearly an hour," Cantwell said, a note of exasperation in his voice.

Asena leaned over the map. "The Yildirims live in Tilmusa. Maybe they can ask the villagers to help us search." She turned and spoke to Fatma Hanim.

Fatma shook her head and replied angrily to Asena. As she poured water into the double kettle for chai, she mumbled to herself and made a high-pitched sound in the back of her throat as she worked. Ali chopped logs as though he were slicing butter, splitting each down the center with one blow. He grunted as he piled the wood up near the back of the dining tent.

Asena said, "Fatma and Ali are acting strangely. I have never known Fatma to speak like that to anyone. I wonder what is going on."

"Ali seems out of sorts too," Frank said. "Look at him. He's chopped enough wood to last through the winter—and next winter too. Where's Aysha? Maybe she knows where Dulcey is."

There was no sign of Aysha. Exasperated, Asena asked Frank, "Why didn't Dulcey ask someone for help?"

Frank huffed. "You know Dulcey. She's a one-woman show— thinks she can do it all by herself. And besides, with all her suspicions about Dr. Nash and the way no one would believe her, who can blame her for feeling a little like an outlaw? She thinks no one's on her side."

Asena said, "I know Dr. Nash very well. No matter what Dulcey suspects, he is no traitor. I'm convinced of that."

Frank looked torn. "You're a lot more forgiving of Dr. Nash these days, I see."

"Forgiving an innocent man is not difficult," Asena said, holding his gaze.

* * *

A short time later, Dr. Nash arrived at Zeugma in a military jeep and jumped out. Frank eyed him warily. Nash avoided him. "I heard Dulcey's missing," Nash said. "How could she go off like that without telling—"

"She was trying to find a cell phone signal, Lee," Asena said. "She wanted to talk to Matt and the children."

Cantwell had just begun showing Nash the map of the area, telling him about the search, when his satellite phone buzzed. "They found the Yildirim's boat in Tilmusa."

"And?" Nash asked anxiously.

"Step over here, sir," Cantwell said, leading Nash away so Frank and Asena would be out of earshot.

After a few moments, Frank followed. "Cantwell, you know something. What is it?" He looked from man to man as if trying to read their faces. "C'mon. Dulcey's like a daughter to me."

Nash shot him a pained look and then told him what Cantwell's agents had discovered. "The men found blood near the boat, Frank. Lots of it. But there's no sign of Dulcey."

CHAPTER TWENTY-SEVEN

Nash took Asena with him up Belkis Tepe to get the binoculars from his tent. Then they stood together near the crosscut road taking turns searching for Dulcey through the powerful lenses. "If we can get higher on the hill, maybe we can see her over there," Nash said.

Asena followed him, pausing when they got near the covered trenches to gaze back over the water. "Dulcey, show us where you are," she murmured.

Nash turned and scanned the inlet below. Something near the riverbank caught his eye. There, amidst the olive trees, where the women liked to swim, a bright swath of flowered fabric lay at the edge of the water. Nash felt his heart bounce up into his throat.

Asena's eyes followed Nash's pointing finger. "Please, Allah, no!" she said.

The two hurried down the hill, stumbling on rocks and bits of pottery from the past, nearly falling several times in their rush to the cove.

"Dulcey?" cried Asena in a choked, disbelieving voice, as she and Nash splashed into the water and stared at the flowered shalwar pants and the pale white feet undulating in the water, barely touching the shore. A large rock pinned her neck and upper body against the river bottom. Blood colored the clear water above her head. Like strands of seaweed, her arms floated lazily above her.

Nash and Asena bent down to roll the huge rock away. As the body rose up toward the surface, Asena slid her arm under the thin shoulders. Together, she and Nash carried the body out of the water and laid it on the shore. Nash moaned. Asena let out a cry as she looked into the face of death for the second time that day.

"It can't be," Nash said, his fists raised in front of his face to ward off the sight.

Asena sobbed, gathering the limp, wet body to her and rocking back and forth on the riverbank. "My poor lovely girl. My poor lovely girl," she repeated over and over.

When Nash finally pried the body away from Asena, he could see the neck wound more clearly. "A clean cut, just under her chin, from ear to ear. The same cut used for the sacrificial lamb during the holy feasts."

"*Aysha!*" Asena screamed, weeping over the still form. "Who did this to you?"

* * *

Dulcey awoke in a stark white room, its walls towering above her. The room had been freshly painted. Leaning against the endless wall was a shovel and several paint-splattered boards. A wheelbarrow full of dirt and chipped cement stood in the middle of the room. Half of the wooden subfloor was plastered over, and the other half was bare wood. *A mosque,* she thought. *Tilmusa has a new mosque . . .*

Dulcey fingered the wound high on her neck and felt a row of waxy stitches protruding from her flesh. Her throat was sore, but she swallowed a few times and tried to make a sound. The faint whisper that emerged from her throat triggered a coughing fit.

Matt, she thought. *Where are you? Where are my babies?* With great effort, she tried to sit up. The three blankets over her body were too heavy to move. The one under her body was lumpy and wrinkled.

Her mind swam with confusion, and she felt sick to her stomach. She moaned. Her head felt as though it had been filled to bursting with a hot liquid. Through her feverish senses, she grasped at explanations for why she would be lying in a circular room with a ceiling that came to a point fifty feet above her head. She lay on her back and wondered why there were wires running up the wall, attached to four boxes of some sort poking through openings near the top of the towerlike room.

Then the memories of her struggle in the boat came back to her. She remembered being completely abandoned on the shore, wondering if the musk-scented grass beneath her face would be her last earthly sight and smell. She remembered being fascinated by the coppery taste in her mouth and by the sight of her own blood making its way down the sharp green blades of grass.

She fingered the stitches in her neck again. She was alive, and someone had stitched her wound. *But why? Why am I not in a hospital if someone wants me to live?* She could tell she had lost a lot of blood by the weakness of her body and the fuzziness in her brain. *Maybe I'm not being helped at all—just kept alive.*

Am I a hostage? Dulcey questioned, shuddering as she vaguely recalled the face of her attacker.

Just as she had concluded that this was the best explanation given the fact that al Qaeda was most definitely in the area, there was a sound of a key in the door. An elderly bearded man came into the room and stood over her, his arms folded over his chest. He wore a long, snow-white tunic over white pants and a white crocheted skullcap. Dulcey's heart raced. He said something to her in Turkish.

"Can you . . . do you speak English?" Dulcey asked in a hoarse whisper that the man seemed either not to hear or not to understand.

The old man shrugged and looked at his watch, then he shuffled over to a tall set of closed shutters and inserted a key into a padlock. He swung the shutters toward himself, revealing a little alcove behind them. After he switched on a dangling light bulb, Dulcey could see a chair and a small table covered with books and an electronic console. The man sat down, selected a worn leather-bound book from the top of the stack, and opened it where a ribbon had held his place. Then he cleared his throat, flipped a switch on the console, and leaned toward a reverberating microphone. At that moment, another male voice echoed through the high windows of the circular room. The old man's voice started as a scratchy bass rumble, then soared into a sweet tenor, mingling with the other voice in the air outside.

A minaret. This is a minaret. She had heard these calls to prayer five times a day in both Iraq and Turkey. By the patch of deep blue sky visible through the high windows, Dulcey guessed it was the evening call to prayer. She lay there spellbound as the voices of the muezzins danced and wove together like two boxers—not in harmony it seemed, but more in competition with one another. The other voice was younger, and its vocal tones more sure. The old man held his own against the younger voice as his crooked finger traced the words of his holy book. His voice resonated as it slithered up the wires and out over the four speakers high in the tower. The call to prayer seemed to go on and on. Then the other voice stopped, and the old man closed his book and intoned his final few words with his eyes closed. He remained silent, his eyes still closed, his head bowed for several seconds.

Now Dulcey heard people outside the minaret. She could hear the sound of shoes clattering onto metal shelves, water splashing, and deep voices murmuring companionably in Turkish to each other. There were no women's voices.

The old man rose, nodded to her, locked the shutters of the alcove, and left the room. She heard a key turning in the lock on the other side of the door. There was no doubt about it: she was locked inside the minaret. *A hostage? Was this Aboud's plan or someone else's?* A second attempt to rise off the bed left Dulcey swooning with weakness and nausea. As she flopped back onto the palette of blankets, a bolt of pain pierced her neck.

As she lay there, Dulcey scolded herself: *There are people at the mosque now. If I wait much longer, no one will find me here.*

Dulcey gathered her strength, kicked off the blankets, and got herself into a sitting position. *My family needs me.* On the strength of that thought, Dulcey stood, wavering for a moment. Then blackness rushed through her brain, and she collapsed onto the wooden floorboards.

CHAPTER TWENTY-EIGHT

Frank sat in the dining tent watching Fatma and Ali Yildirim arguing loudly near the camp stoves. He watched Fatma point out toward the Euphrates so that Ali's eyes would follow her gaze over the water. Then, to Frank's horror, she lifted the double teapot off the stove and poured the steaming water over her own head, shrieking at the searing pain. She threw the pot against the stove and, with incredible strength, upended one of the long, heavy picnic tables. Sobbing, she ran past the guards at the front gate. Ali ran after her.

Bewildered, Frank turned and saw a group of people coming from the shore toward the dining tent. Fatma must have seen them too. A soldier carried someone, half covered by his soldier's coat. He laid the body gently on the ground, and the group closed in around it. Frank's heart hammered against the wall of his chest, and he felt as though his breath had been knocked out of him. *Dulcey? Dulcey?* his mind screamed as he raced toward them.

Frank shoved Nash out of the way, knelt down, and drew back the edge of the soldier's coat. It took him a moment to realize it wasn't Dulcey. "Aysha? Why is her throat—"

"Honor killing," Nash explained. "It's usually done with a cut to the throat like that."

"Honor killing? What—she was sixteen!" Frank shouted. "*Whose* honor?"

"Aysha must have done something to dishonor her family," Asena said, looking at Frank through swollen eyes. "Do not even try to understand. The Western mind cannot grasp it."

"What could she have done?" Frank whispered, feeling a mixture of disbelief and revulsion. He also felt a guilty relief—*It's not Dulcey.* He glanced up to see the CIA agents and soldiers who had stayed in Gaziantep the night before returning to the camp in several vehicles.

Mehmet joined the circle around Aysha's body, and Frank watched his face fall as he stared at the dead girl. He shook his head. "I know what happened," he said in a choked voice. "The night we were all dancing, after excavation of goddess, Ali caught Aysha talking to one of the soldiers after everyone thought she was in bed."

A car door slammed, and Tanju ran toward the group. She stopped a few feet away from them. "Is it Aysha?"

Frank wondered how she knew. He stood up and motioned her over. "Yes, Tanju. It's Aysha. Someone killed her."

Tanju screamed and fell to her knees. "She held his hand. She told me all she did was hold his hand." Tanju pounded the rocky ground with her fists. Mehmet went to her and tried to stop her from hurting herself, speaking softly in Turkish. Tanju answered him in English. "When will this end, Mehmet? When will we save life—instead of saving face? When will *love* be more important than *honor* in this wretched place?"

CHAPTER TWENTY-NINE

Covered in a blue-and-white checked tablecloth, Aysha's body lay on one of the picnic tables in the dining tent. Nash had gone to find Ali and Fatma, but none of the Yildirim family could be found. Standing protectively near the girl's body, Nash and the others had given their statements to the local police.

Asena had given the police a stern lecture about how honor killings were a crime here and everywhere else in Turkey. Mehmet had sat quietly with Tanju as she had wept inconsolably and railed against the culture that had taken the girl's life. Now she seemed jaded and resigned that there would never be justice for Aysha's murder.

Frank, his face a mask of outrage and worry, seemed to hardly be able to sit still and paced endlessly. Asena walked with him around and around the dining tent, trying to explain why girls died when they intentionally—or even accidentally—broke their family's code of honor. "Will they catch who did this?" Frank asked. "You said it was probably a family member who murdered her."

Asena sighed, knowing that the answer was grim. "It used to be that the courts would sentence the killer to only an eighth of the sentence any other murderer would receive. However, the punishment is much harsher now. He may never be caught, as the villagers will try to hide the murderer and his identity. Honor killings are considered a family's private business in this part of the world. The Turkish government is trying to change all this, but it takes time, and there is a lot of resistance."

A short time later, Selene arrived with Hasan to take Ashya's body to the house to be washed and prepared for burial. A soldier went into town to buy a wooden casket.

As Selene mourned over Aysha, Asena knew in her heart that her daughter was severing the last of her ties to Zeugma. She knew then that Selene would never live in their ancestral home again. Only Asena herself could keep the Özturk family home and all its precious legacies intact.

* * *

That evening, Meltem, Feyza, and Selene prepared Aysha's body for burial. Selene stayed at the house to keep vigil over both bodies while Asena and the others stayed at the camp to keep vigil for Dulcey. All of them were quiet, lost in their own thoughts. Because Dulcey was still missing, everyone, including Mehmet and Tanju, had been ordered to stay at the camp rather than help look for her.

Nash was as low as Asena had ever seen him. His face was contorted with anguish at the senseless waste of life, and Asena knew that he feared greatly for Dulcey's safety. "What good is this police search?" he grumbled. If someone over there has Dulcey, no one will tell the police or the soldiers where she is. If they ask them to identify Aysha's murderer, the same thing will happen. The people of Tilmusa have closed ranks on us. They've shut us all out."

* * *

Dulcey awakened in the darkness of the minaret. She could see a few stars through one of the high windows and immediately thought of Izzy. It was always Isabel she worried about the most when she left on a news assignment. It was Isabel's nightmares that woke them all in the night. Her terrible dreams came less frequently now that she was older, but they could still frighten the child wide awake and fill the house with her terrified screams. Whenever the nightmares came, Dulcey and Matt would rush to her bed, and Matt would put his big hand over her eyes until the monstrous, unbidden images finally left her mind. Dulcey had come to dread the shadowy dream place the little girl could inhabit for days on end when her memories came back. Of her two children, it was Izzy who needed her most.

Michael had been a baby when Dulcey had adopted him. His sunny personality was due in part to the fact that he didn't remember living in a compound of houses deep in the woods of Connecticut where crack cocaine was manufactured. He didn't remember the panic Theresa, his mother, felt each time she collected money from her drug sales or how she slept in a crack house overnight when she was too tired to drive back to the compound.

The little boy's former life had stopped short when the police had raided the abandoned house where he and his mother and a bunch of drug-addled junkies were sleeping. Determined to keep him out of state custody, Theresa had buried the little boy under a pile of dirty clothes in an upstairs closet moments before she was handcuffed and taken away to jail. As the police were putting her into a squad car, Theresa had turned to the news reporter who shared her ethnic roots—Dulcey—and pleaded with her to take care of her son. When Dulcey found the little boy in the upstairs closet, he had given her a big, sleepy grin and held his arms out to her—and Dulcey had loved him instantly. Later, after another raid, Michael's cousin Isabel had been discovered in a child crisis center in New York—left there by her jailed mother. Shortly after Isabel was found, the two little cousins became orphans when the drug boss who had employed their mothers murdered the two women after they were arrested. He had known that the women would have easily traded information about his criminal activities rather than lose their children. He was right—and now they were dead.

The raids Dulcey had covered for her news job in New York had resulted in the deaths of the two sisters who had sold drugs to make a living. Dulcey had somehow felt she owed them something to make up for the horrible consequences of the raid. And so she had taken the women's innocent children, whom she had loved at first sight, to raise by herself. Matt, too, had loved the children immediately—and had married them all as a package deal when he came into their lives.

* * *

Dulcey once again fingered the stitches in her neck and grimaced at the pain. While she had been unconscious, someone had moved her back onto the palette of blankets. The way the blankets were tucked around her made her think her kidnapper was a woman or someone who wished her no harm.

Every bone in Dulcey's body was rigid with discomfort, and her throat was as dry as Baghdad. She looked around her and saw that there was a tall bottle of water on the floor beside her bed. She opened a foil packet next to the bottle of water and found slices of bread and pieces of cold lamb. Dulcey drank half of the water, relishing its soothing effect on her throat. Despite her weakness, she was not ready to force food through her bruised esophagus.

Dulcey remembered vaguely another call to prayer vibrating through the towering walls of the minaret as she had slept. It had roused her slightly, but she had preferred to sleep.

She propped herself on one elbow and listened to the utter quiet of the mosque. Perhaps someone was guarding her on the other side of the door. "Hello?" she croaked in a deep, phlegm-coated voice that sounded like someone who had smoked all her life. "Anyone there?"

Not a sound.

Dulcey remembered screaming into the cell phone just as Matt had answered and her attacker had snatched her breath away. *I have to talk to him.* She crawled over to the door and turned the doorknob. Locked. Using the doorknob to support her body, she inched her way up until she was fully upright, then she turned and stood with her back flat against the wall. Tottering forward a step, she tested her strength.

If I can get back to the boat, my cell phone might still be there. She remembered Asena telling her that stealing was almost unheard of in these parts. Turks went to great lengths to return things that were dropped or left behind. *Memories of severe tribal punishments?* she wondered. Dulcey thought of Aboud's missing finger—courtesy of his very honorable father. These people were such a strange mix of character traits. Asena had told her you could wish for no greater friend and fellow citizen than a Turk. But most of the rural Turks here in the southeast were still blindly obedient to monstrous, outdated rules. And it was the women who suffered the most.

Dulcey thought about Aboud. She had no doubt that he would kill or offer his own life without a second thought. After all, he'd been taught that his radical plots were part of Allah's plan for the world and that his own death would earn him a place in paradise. The thought of Aboud spurred Dulcey's anger. The thought of her family made her take a step forward.

Despite feeling light-headed from losing so much blood, Dulcey swung her arms to loosen them, then bent forward to massage her aching leg muscles. She breathed deeply to invigorate her body with oxygen. This was not the first time Dulcey's limits had been tested. And although she didn't know how much blood was still left in her body, the willpower inside of her was a known quantity. She knew her mind was strong enough to overcome this.

With a tremendous rush of adrenaline, Dulcey forced herself to walk around and around her circular prison cell. Eighteen steps on the new plaster, eighteen steps on the exposed wooden subfloor; eighteen on plaster, eighteen on wood. She stumbled round and round the minaret several more times, holding onto the wall for support, until she finally had her balance back.

She surveyed her resources: a wheelbarrow full of dirt that was too heavy to move, a shovel, several pieces of wood—and the locked and shuttered alcove. Dulcey selected the shovel and used its handle to steady herself. Then she gripped it with both hands like a baseball bat, testing her strength. She stood in front of the alcove and mentally practiced smashing the shutters. Then she swung at them hard with the edge of the shovel. A few slats broke, but the shutters remained largely intact.

She swung the shovel again, and a few more slats of one shutter splintered to the floor. Dulcey leaned on the shovel again, drained of her temporary strength. She paused and pulled the broken slats out of the wooden shutter frame, one by one, until she had achieved a narrow opening. Then she gathered her strength once more and swung the shovel again, using it to break through each of the slats until she had a hole the size of her body. Dulcey wedged herself through the opening and turned on the dangling light bulb. She was shaking, weak—and outraged. Through hot tears, she saw that the buttons and knobs on the console had Turkish words above them. She didn't know the word for *on* or the word for *microphone,* so she flipped each switch in the opposite direction all the way down the console.

The microphone crackled to life.

What do I say? Who can hear me? There was no way to tell who
would be summoned by her voice spreading through the night sky.

"Hello? . . . Does anyone out there speak English?" Her throaty
voice shot up the wires and out through the four loudspeakers high in
the minaret. She could hear the strange sound of it bouncing back off
the curved walls of her towering prison.

Although speaking into a microphone had been her job for most of
her adult life, this was an entirely different experience. She leaned toward
the microphone again. "My name is Dulcey Moore . . . I need help."

Nothing.

"I'm hurt. Someone has locked me in the minaret at the new
mosque."

* * *

As the sound of Dulcey's voice wafted over the Euphrates toward
Zeugma, her friends, her coworkers, and her father cheered wildly.
Frank cupped his hands around his mouth and called encouragement
across the river, even though he knew Dulcey couldn't hear him.

Cantwell contacted one of his agents who had been searching
Tilmusa. "This is Cantwell. Do you read?"

"We hear her, sir," came the response. "We're a bit north of Tilmusa,
but we're on our way to the new mosque."

"I'll be there as soon as I can," Cantwell said, already heading
toward his jeep.

The group was quiet again as they listened to Dulcey's raspy voice
ring out in the night, from across the quiet river.

"I need help!"

Frank could tell Dulcey was choking back tears as she spoke. "I'm
hurt, and I need to get to a hospital."

Tanju bit into her thumb knuckle in sympathy for Dulcey.
"*Chabuk, chabuk!*" she yelled at Cantwell. "Hurry, hurry!"

"We're going as fast as we can, ma'am. We'll have Dulcey here
soon. No two ways about it."

* * *

Dulcey's voice was stronger now, and she continued her plea. "I have a family back home in America who is worried about me. Please, please, help me get out of here so I can tell them I'm all right. They need me, and . . . and . . . I need them."

There was no sound anywhere, and so Dulcey plunged on. "If someone has the keys to this mosque, please unlock the minaret. And if anyone finds my cell phone, I need it so I can call my family. This is an emergency."

Silence.

"Can anyone hear me?" Suddenly, Dulcey remembered that she had been able to clearly hear the calls to prayer from Zeugma, so anyone at the camp would be able to hear her now. "Frank! Frank, can you hear me?"

* * *

On the beach across the river, Frank sobbed, waved his arms, and stumbled back and forth on the rocky beach. He continued to yell across the water. "I'm here, Dulcey! I'm right here. Someone's coming for you. Hold on! Just hold on."

Nash watched as Frank wept and shouted on the river bank. He reached out for Asena and pulled her toward him. "I'm watching one of the men who has stood in for me in Dulcey's life. And I *envy* him. Frank knows my daughter in a way that I may never know her."

Asena sighed. "Yes, Frank loves Dulcey like a daughter. But you will have your chance to know her too . . . after you clear things up with her."

Nash looked thoughtful, then said, "It's odd. I can't understand why Frank would feel such fatherly protectiveness toward Dulcey, since she isn't his daughter—isn't carrying his genetic code."

Asena drew back and stared at Nash. "By that logic, Lee, you must be surprised that Dulcey adores her adopted children as much as any mother would love her natural children. Dulcey would do anything for Izzy and Mikey."

When Nash made no response, Asena continued. "You know, for a smart man, you are so . . . ignorant." Her eyes were bright, and she wiped the moisture away with the tips of her fingers. "You know the entire history of the world, but you don't understand much about the most important thing on earth." Asena stuck her hand into one of Nash's jacket pockets. She found the clean handkerchief exactly where she remembered putting it an entire year before. She dabbed at her eyes with it and put it back into his pocket.

"I'm an old fool, aren't I? But maybe it's not too late for me with Dulcey. And maybe it's not too late for *us*," he said. He moved to kiss her, but she buried her head against his chest instead. Nash wrapped her in his open jacket and rested his chin on the top of her head. "With all the horror of this night, I believe I've learned something about love."

She smiled up at him. "Are you sure you want to use that word? It is so . . . unscientific."

Nash stood on the shore, his arms wrapped around Asena, listening to Dulcey's eerie monologue echo across the Euphrates.

"You have a remarkable daughter," Asena whispered. "And you will have an amazing future with her and your grandchildren."

"Yes, yes," Nash said quietly. Then he added, "Fatma and Ali had a remarkable daughter too."

CHAPTER THIRTY

Dulcey heard a commotion outside the mosque. After a moment, she heard a female voice speaking loudly and other female voices murmuring in response.

"If someone is there, please let me know," Dulcey said into the microphone.

A woman shouted something in Turkish, and immediately several other hands slapped and pounded on the door and on the side of the minaret.

"Dulcey, we hear you," a Turkish woman said in English. "Can you hear me?"

"Yes. Can you get me out of here?" Dulcey called, nearly fainting with relief.

The woman's voice came again. "Stay away from the door so we can break it down."

Something or someone flew against the door. The thick door bulged inward but held. There was more shouting, then a crash, and Dulcey saw the door splinter in the middle. Then she saw the head of an ax rip through the door, followed by a woman's face. "Dulcey? Stay back. We will get you out."

"Thank you—*arkadash*—my friend."

After a few more whacks with the ax, a young woman in a long cotton nightgown stepped through the jagged hole in the door. A small group of women also wearing nightgowns and robes climbed through the door into the room. Several wore head scarves and pajamas, one had grabbed a dish towel and thrown it over her hair, and two were bareheaded. An older woman with a facial tattoo carried a sleeping baby in her arms.

The young woman holding the ax said, "Dulcey? My name is Turkan. Remember me? I am a school teacher here in Tilmusa, the one who brought the books to Aysha. I have been standing outside translating your words for the others. We tried to find the key, but we got . . . impatient. Many of us hurried here because a woman's voice from the minaret is very . . . *forbidden* . . . in Islam. You might be first in history." She grinned, and the other women swarmed toward Dulcey, arms outstretched.

Dulcey stood up from the chair, wobbled for a moment, and the women rushed to support her. They kissed her cheeks and patted her. "Thanks, *arkadash*," Dulcey said, patting back. From the sounds outside the minaret, Dulcey knew a crowd was gathering near the mosque. She heard a man shout something. He sounded angry.

"We will take care of you," Turkan said.

At that moment, a Turkish policeman burst into the room, gun drawn, shouting orders. Turkan and a tattooed woman holding a baby stood steadfastly by Dulcey's side, but the other women backed away at the sight of the gun, huddling together in the main part of the mosque. A few moments later, Commander Cantwell stepped into the room. As soon as he determined the other man was a Turkish policeman from Tilmusa, he put his gun back into his holster. "Ms. Moore? Are you all right? We found blood near the boat, and we thought—"

"Find my cell phone, and I'll be fine," Dulcey said, scowling at the policeman's gun, which was still pointed at her. "I need to talk to my family. They'll be worried about me."

A Turkish soldier stepped into the room and handed Dulcey a cell phone. "*Bu cep telephone sandal'dan*, Dulcey Hanim."

Turkan translated. "He found your cell phone in the boat."

Dulcey didn't waste a second. She grabbed her phone and redialed Matt's number. It rang once, twice . . . Dulcey had to sit down again on the chair in the alcove to keep from fainting.

"Matt? I'm so happy to hear your voice. Yes, it's really me—my voice is just scratchy. Everything is . . . is fine now. I had a bit of a fall earlier and lost my phone." She didn't want to worry him more than he already was. "I'll tell you what happened later. Is that Izzy wanting to talk to me?" Dulcey's tears came freely now. "Yes, put her on so I can hear about Galveston."

As the cheerful voice of nine-year-old Isabel chattered on and on, Dulcey cried and laughed at the same time. Baffled by all the emotion, the police and soldiers stepped out of the minaret, and the group of women made their way back in.

Taking the baby from the arms of the tattooed woman, Turkan asked Dulcey, "Is your family well?"

Dulcey nodded her head and laughed through her tears as she listened to her daughter describe every day of her vacation. Izzy's story was too confusing to understand, but Dulcey clung to every word from her daughter's precious, babbling mouth. Then Izzy put Michael on the phone, and she heard all about the sand castles he had built and the boogie board he'd learned to ride and how Poppie Joe and GramMaria were so funny.

As Dulcey repeated snatches of Izzy's story, Turkan translated for the others. The woman wearing the dish towel grinned, covering her mouth in the modest way of Turkish women. The women surrounded Dulcey, chattering in Turkish with a few English words thrown in.

Dulcey stayed on the phone with Izzy, who had thought of more things she wanted to tell her mother. As Izzy was talking, the CIA agents led Dulcey to a military vehicle. She walked past the men of the village, noticing their stern expressions and the way their voices rose and fell with anger and confusion. The men grumbled and pointed to the nightclothes and robes their wives were wearing in public. They pointed to the heads of the women who had neglected their headcoverings. The women smiled and waved back at Dulcey as their men herded them toward their homes.

An American agent offered to help Dulcey climb up into the military jeep. Dulcey said into the cell phone, "Slow down, Izzy, tell Mom again about the—"

But Dulcey didn't hear any more of Izzy's story. Cantwell and his driver rushed to catch her as she hurtled into unconsciousness, then laid her gently on the back seat of the jeep and sped toward the dam.

From the passenger seat, Cantwell picked up the cell phone that had fallen on the floor of the jeep. "Izzy? Your mom wants to hear your stories again later. Is your dad there?" As they drove toward the hospital, Cantwell waited for Matt to come back on the line. "Mr. Moore? I want you to know your wife's . . . had an accident, but she'll be just fine. She uh . . . she got cut, and we need to get her to a hospital. Oh, yes, don't you worry . . . Gaziantep Hospital . . . yes, very modern. What's that? Well, at the moment, you can't. Yes, sir. I'll have her call you when she feels better."

* * *

In the dark house next to the mosque, Kerim—the old muezzin— and his wife, Zeynep, stood looking out of their open bedroom window. They had been wakened when Dulcey's voice had pierced the silence of their sleeping village. Zeynep had put on her head scarf and found the keys to the minaret door.

But Kerim had kept his wife from taking the keys to open the door of the minaret. "No, wife, we will let Allah and the women of Tilmusa sort this out. You and I are caught between the old ways and the new ways—and we must stay in the middle."

The old couple had stood in their dark bedroom, watching the group of women from Tilmusa rescue the American woman. Then they had seen the soldiers put the woman into the back of a jeep and speed toward the dam. They had listened to the spirited discussions, arguments, and explanations as the villagers stood talking outside the darkened mosque. The men seemed sleepy and upset; the women wide awake and excited. Several men had thrown accusations toward the two women who had forgotten their head scarves. To the surprise of the muezzin, one older woman shouted back that the head scarf rule could be ignored because someone was in trouble. Then the villagers walked back to their homes, two by two, in families, in groups—babies fast asleep on strong shoulders.

The muezzin checked his watch and said, "It is only one hour until I call the morning prayers. I will stay awake and have my breakfast now, wife."

Zeynep closed their bedroom window and went to the kitchen to prepare her husband's breakfast. As she chopped the cucumbers and tomatoes and sliced off hunks of the white goat cheese her mother had taught her to make, she remembered the fear in the young Yildirim boy's eyes as he told her where the wounded woman lay near the river. She remembered how she had carefully avoided asking him how the woman had come to have her throat cut, so that she would not have to testify against a fellow Muslim. But Zeynep had known as she stitched the gaping neck wound that yet another woman had become a victim of tradition.

CHAPTER THIRTY-ONE

Early Sunday morning, while Dulcey drifted in and out of consciousness at the Gaziantep Hospital, a small group of people gathered at Asena's house to pay their last respects to Grandmother Yildiz, who had lived a full life, and to young Aysha, who had barely lived at all. An imam intoned the words of the Koran. Asena held Lee Nash's hand and glanced back at Selene, grateful her daughter had been there to share Yildiz's final days. Frank, Mehmet, and Tanju stood silently behind them. Turkan stood at the back of the group, crying softly for the student she had lost forever.

Two women from the town of Diyarbakir had come as well. They were members of a group called *Hayat*—the Turkish word for *life*—an organization devoted to ending honor killings. The group members had come to the funeral to fill the place left vacant by Aysha's family. They were also there to pay respects to the thirty-sixth female to die that year because of the old ways.

On the ground next to the open graves, there were two wooden caskets. The imam offered words of comfort about a paradise that was filled with flowing streams, delicious fruits, and beautiful flowers. "Paradise is a lovely place to wait for *Kiyamat Günü*—Judgment Day—when Isa will return to judge all the souls of the earth according to their deeds and to proclaim Islam the true and final religion of the earth. On that day, Aysha Yildirim and Grandmother Yildiz and all the dead of the world will rise from their graves. Peace be upon these two souls who have gone on before us to paradise to await that day."

* * *

Across the Euphrates, the air above Tilmusa rang with raging debates. The news of Aysha's death and the attempted murder of the American woman had torn the village into two factions. Some said that a case of mistaken identity was the reason that Dulcey had been hurt. Others, having heard rumors that Dulcey had tempted young Aysha into acting in the shameless ways of the West, said the American woman deserved to die.

Arguments in homes spilled out into the streets. Conflict in the streets marched into the mosque. On both sides, fires of outrage burned in the hearts of the people of Tilmusa. Although Sunday was not a holy day, the town's two imams had called special meetings at their respective mosques.

After the young imam led his congregation in prayer at the old mosque, the discussion began. Ignoring the emergency pronouncements from the Department of Religious Affairs in Ankara, the imam quickly identified his own position on the matter. "Our traditions ensure order in our village. If these traditions were good enough for Father Abraham, they are good enough for us now." The imam pounded his pulpit to emphasize his point. The men seated before him murmured and nodded their heads vigorously in support of their leader. Behind the screen in the back of the room, the women spoke in low, worried whispers.

The town grocer, who had two children at a university in Istanbul, spoke up from the congregation. "If we allow our women to shame us, where will it stop? My children are already rebellious. At the university, they listen to the music and ideas of the West every day, and it makes them forget the teachings of the Koran. If we do not stop this behavior, we will lose the next generation to the corrupting influence of the West."

The imam agreed. "We will resist the West and those apostates in Ankara who have become puppets of the Great Satan. We must fight this battle on the side of Allah. No civil law is higher than Allah's law, my brothers. And Allah's law never changes."

Then a man who owned an appliance store stood and addressed the crowd. "Let us start by ridding our town of this woman from America. I heard that Aysha Yildirim and the woman from the television were shamelessly bathing in the sacred Euphrates wearing nothing at all. Later, the television woman—naked, and in broad daylight—swam with a man in the river. It was this same American woman who influenced Aysha Yildirim to be alone with the soldier. Aysha would still be alive if the American had not cast her evil spell upon the girl. As a lesson to all our people, we should act now. And if we do not, that woman will testify against one of the families of this mosque who took proper action to restore their honor."

"Better yet, my brothers," the imam said in low tones so the women behind the screen could not overhear, "Let us join the holy warriors who seek to destroy the West. We have been called into jihad by the bravest, most obedient of all Muslims. Let us do battle with the West right here, where our traditions and our ways have been attacked on our own soil. This is the will of Allah."

* * *

In the new mosque on the other side of the village, Muezzin Kerim called his congregation to prayer. Then the imam stood to offer his opinion on the matter at hand. Behind the screen, the women listened, holding their breath, leaning forward to hear what the imam would say.

"The Koran speaks against the killing of one's own," the imam said. "The prophet Mohammed, peace be upon him, would be displeased with our traditions. And Allah does not approve of the murder of Aysha Yildirim or any other person—the American included. We have courts of law for the purpose of deciding guilt or innocence. The Koran speaks against acting without the agreement of a consulting council. Anyone who kills a daughter or a son to save face is in danger of Allah's wrath. Hell is too good for someone who kills his own family member or a guest who is visiting this country."

The men sitting in the mosque shifted uncomfortably and spoke to one another, throwing glances toward the back of the mosque where their wives sat. Behind the screen, the women murmured hopefully among themselves. Zeynep sat among them, calming them with her warmth and reassurances. "*Yavash, yavash,* my sisters," she whispered.

Turkan rocked her baby and shushed the frightened women, her own heart roiling with grief for her student who had shown such promise. "We must be strong, sisters. My sweet Aysha must be the last death in the name of honor."

The imam read a statement from the Turkish prime minister: "Honor killings are not the will of Allah. They are against the law of the land *and* against the law of Allah. They are wrong and they must stop."

"But surely the prime minister is under the influence of Western infidels," objected a man who sold shoes in Tilmusa. "Our leaders in Ankara never questioned this tradition until Turkey began to curry the favor of the West."

A carpet seller stood and addressed the group. "I was taught that each family is like a tree. A woman who shames her family is like a dead branch that should be cut away. We must sacrifice the dead part to keep the rest of the family alive. Our society depends on it."

"No. You are wrong," the imam said, piercing the man with an unwavering gaze. "I have told you many times before that the tradition of our ancestors is not the same as the law of Islam. We must stop these acts that are displeasing to Allah."

The men in the mosque bent their heads together and talked with passion, their hands gesturing, fists slapping palms, heads wagging back and forth. Suddenly, one of the angry men stood, went behind the screen, and pulled his wife to her feet. They left the mosque, the door slamming shut behind them. In one corner of the mosque, two men shouted at each other. A woman began to cry softly. Turkan comforted her, rocking her and her baby with the same soothing motion. Zeynep patted and smoothed and squeezed whatever hands found their way into her lap.

The muezzin stood in front of the men until the commotion died down. Then he spread his hands wide over the group and said, "Brothers and sisters, let us pray and ask Allah to speak peace to our souls on this matter."

The men knelt shoulder to shoulder in an effort to understand the will of Allah. Behind the screen, the women knelt as well, hands cupped, ready to receive direction from their Maker.

CHAPTER THIRTY-TWO

Dulcey woke up in a hospital bed. She fingered the starched sheets and called out in a groggy voice, "Where am I?"

"You are in the Gaziantep Hospital. Your husband called several times while you were asleep. And your daughter called—and your son—and your father-in-law and mother-in-law," a smiling Turkish nurse reported as she arranged a clean blanket over Dulcey's thin body. "You lost a lot of blood, Dulcey Hanim. We gave you several transfusions, and you are getting fluids to rehydrate your body."

"I feel a lot better now," Dulcey said, smiling back at the nurse. "And I'm hungry."

"Maybe you are feeling the effects of that good Turkish blood flowing in your veins," the nurse said with a wink. She went out of the room and came back with a cup of broth for Dulcey. "Dr. Kirdar will be in to see you soon."

"Who sent these flowers? And cards? My goodness, the whole room is full of them," Dulcey exclaimed as she sipped the warm broth and looked at the banners and handmade get-well cards taped all over the walls. There were three rolling trays at the side of her hospital room laden with fruit and flower arrangements. Balloons bobbed in the sunlight that streamed through the window.

"You are something of a hero, Ms. Moore," a young doctor said as he walked into her room. He took Dulcey's chart from the nurse and began to make notes on it. "And it is said that the wives and daughters of southeast Turkey are unfit to live with these days."

"What? What did I do?" she asked.

The nurse fluffed Dulcey's pillows and settled her against them. "*Yavash, yavash,* Dulcey Hanim."

Dr. Kirdar shined a small flashlight into Dulcey's eyes and then listened to her heart with his stethoscope. "You are the first woman in Turkish history to highjack a minaret." He rubbed his jaw, then shook his finger at her. "Some people admire you for the way you saved yourself. Others . . . well . . ."

Dulcey rubbed her eyes and shivered as she remembered what had happened in Tilmusa. "Who attacked me? Why would someone want to hurt me?"

"Mistaken identity, Ms. Moore. Someone thought you were Aysha Yildirim."

Dulcey looked at the doctor in horror. "Why would anyone want to hurt Aysha?"

The nurse adjusted the fluid drip on Dulcey's IV and said softly to the doctor, "She has only been fully awake for a little while. Should we be talking about this?"

"Is Aysha all right?" Dulcey asked, wincing as her IV needle got caught in the weave of the blanket. The nurse repositioned the needle in the back of Dulcey's hand and put more tape over it to keep it in place.

The doctor sat on the edge of her bed and fiddled with Dulcey's chart, avoiding her eyes. He scribbled some more notes and then turned to face her. "I guess there is no good way to tell you. According to police, Aysha Yildirim was killed just an hour or so after you were attacked."

Dulcey thought of the laughing, splashing girl with shampoo suds on her hands. "But why?" she asked, her brow furrowing, her mind racing to supply a reason why someone would want to hurt lovely Aysha.

"Aysha's mother saw that one of the soldiers seemed attracted to her daughter."

"Yes, I remember Aysha dancing with us and the soldier watching her. Then Fatma seemed angry and sent the girl away," Dulcey said.

The nurse nodded, seeming to know the story as well as the doctor did. She sat down on the side of the bed and took Dulcey's hand in hers. "Aysha left the women's tent late that night and met the soldier. He had been assigned to check the women's tent every hour, so it was easy for him to meet her without anyone knowing about it."

"What are you saying? Did the soldier do something to her?" Dulcey said, struggling to understand what could have happened to the girl.

The doctor said, "No. There was no sexual contact according to the soldier. It was an innocent courtship—by most standards. Her father found the two of them talking near the inlet, holding hands, looking at the moonlight over the river."

Dulcey stared at him, unable to grasp the connection. "But who killed her?"

"No one has confessed, but the police have pieced it together well enough." The doctor drew a deep breath and carried on. "Police think that in order to restore the family's honor, Ali Yildirim asked one of his sons to kill Aysha. This is the usual pattern. The police don't know which son yet—no one in Tilmusa and, of course, none of the Yildirim boys, will identify the murderer. However, generally it is the youngest son who commits an honor killing because the courts are likely to be more lenient on the youngest if he is caught."

"Right now, the police don't know who to arrest," the nurse added. "But they are reasonably sure that whoever attacked you also killed Aysha less than an hour later."

Dulcey had no words. There was nothing in her experience to help her understand. "But you said it was an *innocent* courtship between Aysha and the soldier. Why would her family . . ."

The doctor explained. "Innocent, that is, in the Western sense. What Aysha did is grounds for death in this culture. The honor of an entire family rests on the reputation of its women. It has been like this for thousands of years in this part of the world—like what you read about in your Bible."

"My Bible?" Dulcey snorted, shaking her head. Then she thought of the stonings and the beheadings and the crucifixions recorded in the Bible. She knew that in Old Testament times, a child could be stoned for even being disrespectful to his parents. Muslims had not made this up. They were simply carrying on the cultural traditions that had begun here in the Middle East. Dulcey said weakly, "But we don't do those terrible things anymore . . ."

The doctor shook his head. "People in this part of the world say that God's laws never change."

Dulcey's open mouth felt frozen in place, and her stomach clenched at what she was hearing. "What happened to the soldier?"

"The soldier was immediately transferred to Ankara, and the Turkish military will discipline him. Luckily, his parents are modern—they will not want him dead along with her."

"Dead along *with* her?" Dulcey suddenly felt woozy. The nurse brought a cold cloth and held it against the back of her neck. "Doctor Kirdar? Are we Westerners being blamed for this?"

The doctor answered by opening the door of her room and motioning a uniformed guard into the room. "The hospital put a guard outside your door, Dulcey. You are a hero among some of the people around here, but many others want you out of the country— or worse."

* * *

For the next two days, Dulcey was allowed no visitors as she recovered from her ordeal. She talked briefly and often to her family back home, and Frank called her with updates on the investigation of Aysha's murder. He and Tanju were assisting police as they pieced together who her attacker might have been.

On Dulcey's third day in the hospital, she awakened with the attacker's face clearly in her mind. She remembered seeing him on the hill when Asena had given her the tour of Zeugma. He was Rifat, the youngest of the Yildirims' four sons. The nurse called the police, and Dulcey gave them her statement. Although Rifat had attacked Dulcey, there was still no proof he had killed his sister.

The police had explained to Dulcey what to expect. "Even if we do find evidence that Rifat was Aysha's killer, the judge could say the young man was provoked into committing his crime by Aysha's sinful actions."

"Provoked? Now Aysha is to blame for her own murder?" Dulcey had no words for what she felt. She thought of Asena's declaration. *It won't make sense to the Western mind.* And she remembered her asking, *Do you have the will and the patience to try to understand?*

"No!" Dulcey railed. "I will never understand. This is evil, no matter whose tradition it is."

Dulcey spent the rest of the day and the next morning struggling with her emotions. More bouquets of flowers arrived, and the wall of good wishes could not hold another card or message. Many messages had come from women Dulcey had never even met, including some of the members of *Hayat*.

Preoccupied with thoughts of her family and the news about Aysha, Dulcey had barely thought about Nash. It was as though she had shelved her anger toward him and had returned to a state of not knowing he was her own father. It was her only defense against all that was happening around her. Nash had called her several times, and Dulcey had refused to speak to him each time. She changed the subject as quickly as she could when others brought up his name. Dulcey was not ready to figure out how Lee Nash fit into her life.

Dulcey knew that no matter how many get well cards adorned her wall, her hospital door was locked, and a man with a gun stood outside, protecting her. He occasionally peered into her room and checked her windows. He even examined her food and every gift and bouquet before they were allowed into her room.

Not thinking about Nash allowed Dulcey room to grieve for Aysha. Along with her anguish about the death of the dimpled, dancing girl, she also thought about the young soldier far from home—a student or a baker or perhaps a romantic boy who sold flowers in a bazaar—who had been doing his required two years of army service. She pictured him sitting on the bank of the Euphrates River, gazing at the stars— holding the trembling hand of a girl from the past.

CHAPTER THIRTY-THREE

Nayif al Aboud pressed his thin fingers into the chiseled inscription on the granite pedestal. He traced the Latin words as he listened to his father lecture him on the strategies of jihad. By a prior arrangement with Saif bin Rabeh, the pedestal was theirs, and they could keep whatever money they could get for it. They needed that money to get home to Riyadh.

"We need to be smarter than the enemy," his father was saying. "If we are to be victorious, we must use all our wits when we make our plans. And, if necessary, we must give our lives to carry them out."

Nayif was exhausted. After delivering the golden goddess to the training compound in the Syrian mountains, they had been given the ancient pedestal. Without resting, his father had driven to Damascus to have his treasure appraised by experts.

As they waited in the back of the truck for the experts to arrive, Nayif ran his fingers across the grooves of each carved letter and let his thoughts drift. An only child, Nayif had grown up in London with his father and mother. He had spent the last year of his life in Saudi Arabia and Syria, preparing for jihad. Although he had never attended public school, he had attended a Muslim school in London, a madrassa, and had grown up speaking English and Arabic. The madrassa had not taught him much in the way of math, computer skills, or history, but Nayif had been able to recite the entire Koran from memory by the time he left.

While they had lived in London, his mother had worked at the British Museum. Nayif had seen statues from all over the world—plundered by the imperial British Empire—displayed in the museum as souvenirs of their once-vast power. He had spent hours reading the inscriptions, studying the artifacts, and endlessly questioning his mother's coworkers about the details of the museum exhibits. She had always referred to him as her "budding archeologist."

Peace be upon her, thought Nayif, as he remembered the vibrant little woman who had been everything to him: mother, teacher—his best and only friend.

Even his father had not known her as well as Nayif had. His parents had grown apart after Nayif's birth had left his mother unable to bear more children. His father often talked of taking another wife to make up for his wife's "incompetence in childbearing." However, despite the tension between them—or perhaps because of it—the woman with the quick mind and the dry sense of humor had willingly sacrificed her life at her husband's request. The strike that had killed her was aimed at the Western employees of a Saudi-American oil company. In their greed for oil workers and oil customers, the king and his thousands of Saudi princes had allowed American workers and soldiers to trample the land that was home to the holy cities of Mecca and Medina. To Nayif's family and many others in the kingdom, this made the royals the worst kind of infidels, since they were, with full knowledge, shirking their sacred duty to keep the kingdom pure.

Nayif's family had been influenced by a fiery imam with the same convictions who ran a branch of Victorious Islam in Riyadh. He had needed someone who had an identification pass and worked regularly inside a compound where Western workers lived. Nayif's mother had been teaching Arabic to a family from Alabama who lived in the compound. She had been going there twice a week for several months.

At first his mother had refused to do it. She told the imam she was fond of the family and could not bear to take their lives. She pointed out that they were making an attempt to learn the Arabic language, and that although they were Southern Baptists, perhaps the family would convert to Islam someday. But the imam and Nayif's father had gradually worn her down, finally using dire threats against her if she failed to do her duty. They told her she was the only one who could breech the security check-point to allow the others through.

Nayif remembered his mother cutting up one of the large, man-sized vests and making it into a smaller one that would fit her slender body. She had designed the vests herself, claiming the traditional belts were too bulky and easily detected during a body search. Her special trademark was the small pocket between the shoulder blades that could be used for timers or remote control devices. Even in matters of death and war, his mother had used her intellect to solve problems. Nayif had been so proud of her.

As she was making her own vest, Nayif had watched her take a needle and thread and sew the little back pocket closed with a row of small, perfect stitches along its top. "This pocket is an insult to my honor," she had explained to him. "It's used only for jihadis who can't be trusted to detonate their bombs."

At the time, watching his mother sew her own vest had not affected Nayif very much. He'd watched her sew many vests just like it for the men his father knew. But Nayif had sobbed for days after he watched the videotape she had made as she had dressed herself in the vest and prepared herself for battle. Each of her vest's seven pockets now contained a C-4 plastic explosive pack. She had expressed her undying love for him as she had slid the billowy burqa over her head and said good-bye to him forever.

The videotape had been addressed to him in her fine, small handwriting—*To Nayif, my budding archeologist.* Then she had gone to the compound, walked past the checkpoint, and detonated her explosives—allowing the others to drive their vehicles toward the apartment complex with their own deadly bombs. Together, the six warriors had killed twenty-three infidels from the West that day.

As he thought about her, Nayif's breath became labored, his vision blurred. No matter how hard he tried to forget her, the memory of his mother brought only pain. He knew he should glory in her honorable martyrdom. But he was not a good son. A single thought condemned him every time her face appeared in his memory: *I will never forgive my father for asking my mother to die.* Nayif glared at the man who had to be appeased and worshipped like a Roman emperor, respected and obeyed like a military commander. *Father should attach himself to the top of this pedestal so he will finally have his proper place.*

As Nayif's thoughts wandered, his fingers continued to trace the inscription on the pedestal. He looked down now, carefully scrutinizing the words on the pedestal. "There is something wrong, Father."

Nayif's father stroked his mustache and smiled at him, ignoring his son's appraisal of the inscription. He prodded again, "Come now, let me see how good you are. Was this inscription carved in Zeugma during the early Hellenic period or the later Roman period? We shall see how close you are to the opinions of the experts."

Nayif looked again at the Latin letters, running his thumb over the indented shapes he was quite certain had been carved by a modern chisel. Several of the words were even misspelled. He repeated his assessment: "I think we've been fooled, Father."

"Fooled, you say? No one fools the warrior Aboud," his father growled, moving toward his son. Before Nayif even realized he had been disrespectful, he felt his father's fist smash into his jaw. "*You* are the fool, boy! You let them take my photograph in Baghdad." He caught Nayif up by his collar and threw him against the wall of the truck. "In all my years as a warrior, no one has ever taken a photograph of me."

Nayif fell to his knees, sobbing, shielding his head from his father's blows. "I have apologized. What more can I do?" He raised his face, his eyes begging for mercy. But the fist came again.

"The enemy has my photograph because of you. Your only job in Baghdad was to see that I was not photographed. I handled the bombs. I cleared the space in the traffic for the attack. All *you* had to do was run away with a camera."

"I also attached the explosives under CNN's van," Nayif reminded him, wiping saliva and blood from his mouth.

"The van was empty when the explosives detonated, so what good came of it?" Aboud raised his fist again, but Nayif slid away from him, crouching in the corner of the truck.

"I am young. I will learn from you as I grow older," the boy moaned and rocked himself. He wiped his eyes dry and straightened himself as he heard the voices of strangers and the sound of a forklift.

Aboud raised the rolling tailgate of the truck and welcomed two men wearing lab coats and carrying a box of tools. He helped each of them climb up into the bed of the truck. "Thank you for coming at this time of night," Aboud said, throwing a warning look at his son.

The men said little and immediately began to examine the granite pedestal with a strong flashlight and magnifying glasses.

After a whispered consultation, one of the experts turned to Aboud and said, "The lettering and words of this inscription are indeed similar to the ones already found at Zeugma."

Aboud shot his son a look of triumph and grinned proudly. "And how old do you think it is? How much is it worth?"

"Even though the words are similar to inscriptions at Zeugma, this inscription is not ancient. The person who carved it probably sandblasted the letters a bit to make them appear worn. But they are still too crisply defined, and the stonework is sloppy—as though it were finished in a great hurry."

Aboud's expression fell. He paced back and forth, clearly trying to grasp the meaning of the expert's pronouncement. He peered at the inscription again. "Are you sure? One of the best archeologists in the world has proclaimed the genuineness of this artifact."

The experts exchanged glances again. The older one said, "Yes, Dr. Lee Edward Nash made these claims on international television. We watched the CNN report as the goddess was excavated. It was very impressive. The goddess and the pedestal certainly *looked* authentic."

The younger expert said, "The people of Zeugma were wealthy. They could afford the best craftsmen in the world. So why would this inscription on the pedestal of their city's deity be so poorly carved? And look, two of the words are misspelled."

"But we can still sell this," offered the older expert, when he saw the expression on Aboud's face. "We can sandblast the inscription to age it even more, and we can smooth over the words that are not correct. But as it stands, even a layperson can see it is not two thousand years old."

"And you are sure of your assessment?" Aboud asked, running his thumb under his mustache.

"I will stake my reputation on the fact that this inscription was carved fairly recently," the older man said.

Aboud paced the length of the truck again, pounding his fist into the palm of his hand. Nayif winced at the sound. His father walked around and around the granite pedestal, murmuring to himself in an angry, low voice. Nayif knew that particular tone of voice was more dangerous than any fist. "They didn't think I would know what I was looking at. They considered me a stupid man who would not know enough to hire experts," he muttered.

"We can put acid on the metal scrollwork that held the statue in place. That will make the metal appear to be corroded with age," the younger expert said.

Aboud seemed to have come to a decision. Nayif's stomach balled up even tighter as his father's tone returned to normal. This meant his father knew precisely how to proceed against his enemy, and he had become relaxed and confident again. "Well, do whatever you people do," Aboud said with aristocratic impatience. He flicked his gloved hands at them like a diner in an expensive restaurant rejecting badly presented food. "Your percentage from the sale will ensure that you do your best work. I am sure you can fix it so we will all benefit from the highest possible bid. There are plenty of people out there with more money than discernment."

"We will be happy to find a good home for this very *ancient* artifact . . . and you will find a decent enough payment in your bank account," the older expert said.

Aboud and the men from Damascus laughed. Then, at his father's signal, Nayif helped them slide the pedestal onto the waiting forklift. Then the experts bade them good-bye and transported the pedestal into their warehouse.

Nayif and his father drove out of Damascus. After an hour or so of silence, Nayif realized with alarm where they were headed. "Are we returning to Turkey?" he asked, trying to decipher the determined expression on his father's face.

"So, not only will you allow yourself to be fooled twice, Nayif, but you will slink away into the night like a beaten dog? Of course we are returning to Turkey. Do you not realize that if the pedestal is a fraud, it means the goddess is a fraud as well?"

"I was thinking about that. But even if she is not ancient, the goddess is made of real gold. I'm sure of that. After it is melted, new gold is worth as much as old gold," Nayif said, smiling, frantic for his father to accept his logic.

"There may have been a thin layer of real gold on the outside, but our people will soon find out that she is not solid gold. I see that now. There will not be enough gold to make the mountain, so the goddess will be useless to the jihad. Because of what we have done, we cannot face the warriors in Damascus until we have set things right."

"But we are alone now," Nayif said, touching his father's sleeve with as much deference as he could manage. "What can two of us do to set this right?"

"You have much to learn about honor, my cowardly son," Aboud hissed, gripping the steering wheel of the truck, his face burning with fresh hatred. "Even if we fail, we will have died in the struggle—we will not have *run* from it."

Nayif touched the aching bruises on his cheek. He knew his father was preparing to teach him another lesson about saving face.

CHAPTER THIRTY-FOUR

From her hospital bed, Dulcey smiled as she cradled the phone against her pillow. It had been such a relief to hear Matt's voice again, to set things right between them. He had been prepared to come to Turkey to make sure she got home safely. But taking Matt away from the children was more than she could bear. "Let me picture all of you safe, darling. I want to picture you humming away at work, knowing that your family's all right. Do that for me, will you?"

"I just want you home . . . I miss you like I never have before," Matt said. "We nearly lost you. It was as though I had a dress rehearsal of what life would be like . . . without you."

Dulcey heard Matt cover the phone with his hand. She was touched by the tearful catch in his voice. She tried to keep her own voice level—to sound strong for him. "I'll be home as soon as I can travel. Wild horses couldn't—"

"Just come home," Matt said with such urgency, it seemed to surprise even him. "Right now I hate your job and CNN. I can't stop thinking about everything we almost lost."

Before she could catch herself, Dulcey felt herself bristle slightly. "Remember, we wouldn't have our two children if it weren't for my work." She recalled Michael's dirty, sweet, frightened face when she found him under that pile of clothes at the crack house. Dulcey had known since high school that she couldn't have children. She had prepared herself for a career and a single life. But there he was, holding his little arms out to her. And then came Izzy. And then came Matt to love them all. As the saying went—life happens while you're making other plans.

Dulcey said softly, "Matt, I know now . . ."

"You know what?"

She paused and then said, "I know there are a lot of people who could do this job for CNN—but I'm the whole world to Izzy and Mikey."

"And me."

Dulcey choked back her tears. "Put your hand over Izzy's face before she sleeps tonight. Tell her you'll hold back the world and make sure she's safe. And tell her I'm sending her the stars after I'm finished with them."

"I will." Matt's voice was thick as he replied. After a few moments of silence, he said, "Listen, one last thing. Nash called me again. You really need to talk to him before you leave Turkey. I believe his story about why he sold the goddess. You need to hear it from him."

Dulcey heaved a sigh and kicked back the covers on the hospital bed. "Frank and Asena and Tanju are all saying the same thing. Selene too. But Lee Nash is used to getting his own way. I barely know the guy—why should I trust him?"

"Asena has known him a long time. And she believes Nash's story about the statue and the money."

"Yeah, well, Asena isn't exactly objective these days. I can tell by the way she talks about Nash that she's falling for him again. And you know what they say about people's vision when they're in love."

"Okay, so you're not ready to listen right now. But try not to be so harsh on Nash in case you change your mind later. That's logical, isn't it? This man is your father—how can you keep fending him off?"

"The only thing keeping me going is the fact that we're all safe and that I'll be home soon," Dulcey said, allowing a sweet cascade of denial to wash over her. "I doubt very much if Nash and I will be able to salvage any sort of relationship anyway."

"Okay," Matt said, resignation in his voice. "Well, the bad stuff is all over now. We still have everything we love."

"The doctor says that in a few more days, I'll be well enough to travel. My blood count's almost back to normal. I love you, Matthew Moore. The way you kept everything together while I was getting into all kinds of trouble on the other side of the world . . . you're my hero."

"Wow. As long as I've known you, I don't think you ever had a guy for a hero before," Matt said teasingly.

"Well, you can be my first."

CHAPTER THIRTY-FIVE

Minutes before midnight, under a star-splattered sky, Frank and Tanju sat on the tailgate of the truck, dangling their feet over the water of the inlet. Around them were shovels of various sizes, buckets of sand and water, a roll of heavy, clear plastic, and Tanju's box of tools. It was an unusually warm night. The air and water were calm except for the ripples caused by the three fully clothed women standing in the middle of the inlet. From the photographs Frank had taken, Asena had identified the mosaic at the bottom of the inlet as hers. And Turkan and Selene were now helping Asena retrieve it from the river.

"What if Nash had found Asena's mosaic before we had? Would he have given it to her?" Frank asked Tanju.

Tanju drew back and smiled. "You have located the problem exactly. Now you know why we are all out here at midnight, rushing to find the mosaic before Dr. Nash and Mehmet get back from the museum. Dr. Nash would be *required* to turn it over to the Ministry of Culture, just as he would any other Zeugma artifact."

"But Asena has a photograph of the mosaic. Doesn't that count for something?" Frank asked.

"It does with me. I believe her. But Nash might say she cannot prove this mosaic is hers with that crackly old photograph of hers. Besides, Asena's home is a Pandora's Box of its own. That mosaic is, as Americans say, just the tip of the iceberg. Her photograph shows several rows of mosaics. It would make the government want to examine everything else that is in her home."

Frank looked at the three women wading around in the inlet of water. Turkan held Frank's halogen dive light just under the surface of the water, and Selene and Asena dove again and again, searching for the mosaic.

"Ever since I arrived in Zeugma, I have seen these women search for this mosaic," Tanju explained. "They do it each time Nash and Mehmet are away from camp. But until now, they have always searched in the wrong place."

"What if Mehmet and Dr. Nash come back before we find it?"

"If Asena does not find it tonight, she may not get another chance. It will be winter soon, and CNN's story about the goddess might bring a great deal of attention to this area by the springtime. And that is good—for everyone but Asena. Yildiz's last wish was that Asena find the family's precious mosaic and keep it safe. Even Selene is convinced there is nothing more important."

"I'm surprised the guards haven't become suspicious," Frank said.

"I told Cantwell and the Turkish soldiers that we Muslim women are bathing this evening and do not wish to be watched under any circumstances. And they think you are in your tent."

Frank checked his watch again. "We don't have much time."

"We will have it out of the water tonight, *inshallah*," Tanju said. She grew quiet and looked over the finger of water that extended from the Euphrates. "This cove will always be very important to me. So much has happened here."

"You're thinking about Aysha," Frank said, putting his arm around her shoulder, and then quickly removing it. "Now, you see? I was just trying to comfort you—but a man doesn't dare touch a woman in this part of the world." He shook his head and looked embarrassed. "And it was nothing more than what I just did that got Aysha killed."

"Even though I am Turkish, and I have heard stories about honor killings all my life, I cannot understand or accept it either," Tanju said. "This part of Turkey is nothing like the rest of my country. It is a foreign country to me, too."

A cry went up from the women. Selene shouted and motioned them into the water. Frank and Tanju picked up their shovels and waded toward them. Selene pointed to a carved Roman column on its side. "Right next to this pillar. Do you see it?"

Carefully, they took turns shoveling the sand and rocks out from under the mosaic. However, when they tried to lift it, they found that it was too heavy in its waterlogged condition. Frank went back to the truck and brought them the end of a chain that was attached to the conveyor belt on the other end. Tanju started the belt with her key, and the entire group shepherded the mosaic out of the water. With the help of the truck's winch, they finally got it up into the bed of the Mack truck.

"Is this your family's mosaic, Asena?" Tanju asked.

Asena beamed. "Yes, this is it. I thank you all for returning my family treasure to me."

Selene wrung out her soaked clothing. "Finally, we can stop obsessing about our precious mosaic. Ever since I was fifteen years old, we've been looking for that thing."

Asena laughed. "No, Hasan and Yildiz and I did all the searching and digging. Mostly you did not care about another old thing buried in the dirt—no matter how hard we tried to explain how important it was."

Selene sighed and put a dripping arm around her mother's wet shoulders. "I'm sorry, Mother. I'm less patient than you are. Really, I'm glad we found your precious mosaic. It was Grandmother's last wish. Now she can rest peacefully in her grave."

* * *

Frank was surprised to see that instead of examining the mosaic further, Tanju immediately poured a bucket of wet sand over it. She patted a thick layer over the woman's face and the hill in the background.

"What are you doing?" Frank asked, bending to help her.

"We do this with all artifacts that have been submerged in water. The water and wet sand keep the mortar between the tesserae from breaking down." After covering the mosaic with the sand, Tanju poured another bucket of river water over it to make sure the sand was wet enough. Then she began wrapping the mosaic in sheet after sheet of clear plastic. "We will have to examine the mosaic later. Asena has a special climate-controlled room in her house where she keeps some of her more fragile family heirlooms. We can unwrap it there."

"How long do you think the mosaic has been in the water?" Turkan asked, helping Tanju smooth the plastic around the mosaic.

"Asena's husband probably buried it on dry land, so it has likely only been in the water since the new dam was built." Tanju turned toward Asena. "You are very lucky Dulcey and Frank found your mosaic in all that water."

"Yes, and I am so grateful Turkan realized the mosaic was mine." Asena glanced at her watch. "We need to hurry. Lee and Mehmet will be here soon. There will not be time to drive the mosaic to my house tonight. We can leave it in the truck until we have a chance to move it."

Tanju and Frank drove the truck to the crosscut road and parked it in its usual spot. As she and Frank were walking back to camp, she said, "There is something unusual about the mosaic. Did you notice the hill behind the woman's face?"

Frank thought for a moment. "No. You were pouring sand and water over it so quickly, I didn't get a good look at it."

"I could be wrong about this—and I am not even sure Asena noticed this herself—but I think every tessera in that hill was made of some sort of metal. Not stones from the river, but metal. I think it could be gold."

CHAPTER THIRTY SIX

Around noon, Nayif al Aboud walked behind a group of Turkish high school students as they entered the Gaziantep Museum. The students carried sack lunches and cans of Cola Turka. Nayif carried his bag of *Çokonat* candy bars left over from his disguise as an Ülker delivery man.

Nayif stood quietly at the back of the group as the museum guide talked about the mosaic that told the story of Achilles. Here in the museum, Nayif was in his element. The low lights and smudged display cases made him wistful for the days he'd spent at the museum where his mother had worked. He knew all the Greek myths pictured on the artifacts. He'd seen them on the ancient pottery and in the famous paintings and sculptures at the British Museum and the National Gallery.

His mother had taught him that Western civilization and most of its literature had come from the philosophy and myths of ancient Greece. Nayif reviewed his mother's lessons. *This is why Islam is superior. Islam rejected these pagan gods. Islam reminded the world there was only one God, not hundreds of them. Not a trinity of Gods as some mistakenly believed, but only one God, the maker of the whole world.*

He followed the group of students from room to room through the museum, pretending to be engrossed by the Turkish guide's explanations of the mosaics and artifacts that had come from the Zeugma excavation.

After a while, it became clear to Nayif that the golden goddess was not at the museum; however, he saw a large glass case in the center of the main exhibition room that had to have been designed especially for her. Even the inscription was already there. The laser alarms and motion detectors were similar to the ones he had seen at the British Museum.

His assignment was to find the goddess, using whatever tactics were necessary. And Nayif could not afford to disappoint his father again. Incompetence was the enemy now.

As the students sat in the museum's courtyard eating their lunches, Nayif wandered casually behind the main building, munching one of his candy bars. He quickly found a large work area where several conservators labored over a mosaic. "Excuse me, does anyone here speak English?" he asked.

A deeply tanned man about his father's age laid his tool aside and lifted his goggles. He spoke with an Italian accent. "I speak English. But, my young friend, you should not be in here. This workshop is a private work area."

"I apologize, sir. But I am looking for the golden goddess. On television, I saw her come out of the ground on CNN, and I begged my mother to bring me here to Turkey so I could see the beautiful statue. We came all the way from London, sir."

The conservator smiled at him. "All the way from London? And you did not find out whether the goddess was on display before you came?"

"My mother believes in following my interests, sir. I'm going to be an archeologist when I grow up. We spend many days every year traveling to see the great things of the past that have been discovered in the ground."

The conservator showed the boy the mosaic he had been working on, as well as the bronze statue of Mars, the god of war, that was being cleaned by his colleague. "I was like you when I was a boy. It is strange—none of my seven children is the least bit interested in the things of the past."

The man who was cleaning the statue of Mars asked, "What happened to your face?"

Nayif's hand shot to the deep purple bruise on his face. "Rugby, sir. My mother says I'm a budding archeologist. That is, if I'd ever stop getting my brains bashed in on the rugby field."

The conservator laughed and leaned down, hands on his knees. "You are an amazing young man. I believe someday you will be someone great. Since you came from so far away, I will tell you something about the goddess no one else knows. And then maybe you can forgive us for not having our golden lady ready to display yet."

Nayif leaned forward and whispered, "Yes, sir. I would like to know where she is."

"The Goddess Fortuna is not here at the museum yet," the conservator whispered back. "What you saw on CNN was a trick to keep the goddess safe. They brought a decoy to the museum the evening the goddess was excavated."

Nayif looked puzzled. "But where is the real goddess, sir?"

The man chuckled. "Ahh. I cannot tell you *where* she is. Even I don't know that. But I have been told she will be here in three days."

"Three days? I'll tell my mother we must stay in Gaziantep until then."

The conservator smiled at him. "Yes, there is much to see in this part of Turkey for a boy like you. When you come back in three days, ask for Marco. I will tell you all about how we will make her gold shine like new again, and I will tell you what we are doing to keep the iron at her feet from corroding. I will also read for you the Latin inscription on the pedestal of the goddess. Will that do?"

Nayif beamed. "I'll be here in three days, sir. You are very kind. I will tell my mother of your most generous offer. She will know then that we did not make a mistake by coming so far."

The conservator laughed. "See you in three days."

Before walking out of the workshop, Nayif turned and watched Dr. Marco Cappoletti kneel near the mosaic he'd been working on. He watched as the conservator gently scraped the dirt away from a delicate wing feather belonging to Eros, the god of love.

CHAPTER THIRTY-SEVEN

Lee Nash went to his tent halfway up Belkis Tepe. On the other side of his cot, he threw back the woven kilim that covered the entrance to his private work space. He lowered his body into a narrow, rock-cut opening and, within seconds, was fifteen feet underground. Zeugma's underground water system had been a marvel of Roman ingenuity. Even with the tons and tons of hillwash that had covered the ancient city, almost the entire grid of tunnels was still intact. From the position of the vertical pipes, it was possible to tell where every latrine and sink and fountain were located throughout all of Zeugma. Though the tunnels were narrow, they were tall, much higher than Nash's head. They snaked around under the city, branching and dividing every fifty feet.

As he walked through the labyrinth of tunnels, Nash turned on the battery-powered lanterns he had placed every few feet all along the stone walls. The terra-cotta water pipes above his head, many of them still in pristine condition, had brought water to Zeugma from the spring that still ran along Asena's property behind the hill. As the water flowed quickly downhill toward the Euphrates, the water pressure became sufficient to cause the myriad fountains of the city to shoot high in the air. Nash smiled as he always did when he imagined Zeugma at the height of her glory.

After a few minutes of walking and turning on the lanterns, he approached the glorious fourth-century cathedral he had found the year before. It was here, in the spacious cathedral, that Nash was keeping the real golden Fortuna until he could deliver her safely to the museum.

Once inside the large underground cathedral, Nash turned on the klieg lights illuminating the Goddess Fortuna in the middle of the room. No matter how many times he saw her, he always gasped in sheer adoration. She gazed down at him with her ball of fate held high above her head. She was the most magnificent find of his entire life.

When Nash had written his article for the archeology journal about the likelihood of unearthing a solid gold statue, and when he had been interviewed by *Newsweek* magazine, he had not revealed that the goddess had already been excavated. The CIA had gotten into the act because they had needed a lure to draw out members of al Qaeda. Feeling patriotic and duty-bound after the terrible events of September 11, Nash had agreed to help set up the sting.

It had been a nerve-wracking venture, and one he was still not sure had been successful. Helping the CIA with the sting had also cost him the trust of a daughter he barely knew.

Nash walked around the cathedral, enjoying the frescoes and mosaics that told the Christian story. The painting on the domed ceiling showed an ascending Christ, angels lifting Him toward a starry heaven. A bearded God, already in heaven, looked delighted at the arrival of His Son. On the towering walls were twelve panels that showed the life of Jesus. At the front of the cathedral, behind an ornately carved marble dais and altar, was a twelve-foot crucifix in the pose favored by Helena, mother of the Emperor Constantine.

The history that could be learned from this one cathedral was astounding. Constantine had seen the need for a common religion to unify his empire. The bishops and priests from this cathedral had attended the Emperor's Council of Nicaea and had sought to resolve the debates raging throughout the Empire about the nature of God and Jesus. Some said Jesus was God incarnate. Others said He was the Son of God and not God Himself. The priests from this cathedral and those from all over the Roman Empire had created the creeds still chanted in Christian churches today.

Nash knew his discovery of a fourth-century cathedral would bring on a storm of controversy. From the horror stories told by his colleagues who had worked on the Dead Sea Scrolls, Nash knew better than to open the cathedral up to the theologians and biblical archeologists of the various religions. Any discovery that might cast doubt on their own precious dogmas was sure to bring trouble. He knew the scholars would go to any lengths to bury or discredit whatever went against their own religious biases.

Nash ran his hand along the carved marble of the altar and stood where the priest had intoned some of the earliest masses of the Christian world. *Yes. Yes,* he thought. *After the goddess is safely at the museum, I'll hire a team of very discreet archeologists to excavate this entire cathedral. We will not tell anyone about our discoveries until we have documented every artifact, document, statue, and wall painting of this magnificent structure.* Mentally, he ticked off the names of academic archeologists and field specialists who could be trusted.

Though Nash's secret cathedral was in disarray from having been burnt and smashed by Parthian invaders in the fifth century, modern looters had never found it. No archeologist had ever come across it before he had. Until he divulged its existence to the Turkish authorities and to the world, this magnificent cathedral and the golden Goddess standing there in the domed sanctuary belonged only to Dr. Lee Edward Nash.

CHAPTER THIRTY-EIGHT

At the American base in Incirlik, Turkey, Major Thurman and General Manheim examined the live satellite picture on the computer screen in front of them. The image showed the scattered ruins of an old Parthian fortress in the mountains above Damascus, Syria. Inside the walls of the fortress, an assortment of vehicles was parked. Three modern structures stood in the center of the compound.

Manheim pointed to one of the images with his pen. "I'd say this one is an airplane hangar. You can see the shape of a small plane outside it next to a long airstrip there. This structure here, I believe, is a large training and meeting room. And this structure is probably a barracks and mess hall."

"We've charted the operatives' movements for three days and find that most of them are in the compound from sundown on," Thurman said.

"Evening prayers and dinner," Manheim said. "Disciplined lot, aren't they?"

Thurman chuckled. "We owe our thanks to Fortuna, the goddess of destiny, who led us to three hundred of the most dangerous terrorists in the world. If we hadn't acted, these men would've moved on to form al Qaeda cells all over the world, and they'd have been nearly impossible to find."

"So the goddess was a Trojan horse from Turkey—where that military trick was invented," Manheim said appreciatively. He bent closer to the monitor. "Do you think al Qaeda intends to melt the goddess right there at the compound?"

"That we don't know," Thurman said, looking at his watch. "But in exactly forty-five minutes, it'll be a moot point. It doesn't even matter if she was moved somewhere else. We've gotten what we came for."

"And the pedestal?"

Thurman handed him a report. "The pedestal's tracking device led us to old Damascus, where it netted us an entire warehouse of looted artifacts. Mahmoud al-Imam, the curator of the Iraqi National Museum in Baghdad, loves us right now. Our agents found more than a hundred of Iraq's most prized national treasures in that warehouse."

"Wonders never cease," Manheim said. "My congratulations to your team."

"The Americans could use a success story where Iraq is concerned," Thurman said.

"Did the antiquities experts know who sold them the pedestal from Zeugma?"

"No. The art mafia and their experts are smart enough never to ask questions of either their suppliers or their buyers—they're all crooks."

Manheim shook his head and stood up from the computer screen. "But Aboud and his son have vanished . . . that's a rock in my jaw. Aboud's the one I really wanted."

"The top guys are always the hardest. They move quickly and know how to cover their tracks."

The general whistled through his teeth. "The antiquities experts told Aboud the pedestal was a fake—right? So that means Aboud and his son know Nash set them up."

"That's right. And now they can't return to the al Qaeda compound because they've dishonored themselves," Thurman said.

Manheim considered the possibilities. "Aboud has family in Saudi Arabia. Even if all his al Qaeda contacts are lost to him, he could still go home to Riyadh."

"We're making sure Aboud and his son Nayif have very few places to run," Thurman said, sitting on the edge of his desk and running a thumb over the crease of his trousers. "Pretty soon the whole world will know that Aboud *and* al Qaeda were duped. We're broadcasting the details of the raid, as well as Aboud's photograph, on all the major networks—even

Al Jazeera." Major Thurman walked across the room and looked at a map of Turkey, Syria, and Iraq. "If you were Aboud, and you had just unwittingly destroyed an entire training compound and three hundred fighters in your own organization, what would you do to restore your honor?"

Manheim thought a minute and drew a calculator from his desk drawer. "Assuming Aboud doesn't stop to rest and drives the speed limit, what's the earliest he and his son could be back in Zeugma?"

Thurman nodded slightly at first, then bobbed his head more vigorously as he saw where Manheim was going. "Would Aboud believe the real goddess is at the Gaziantep Museum or at Zeugma?"

"He might start with the museum," Manheim said, looking at the map, figuring up driving time on his calculator.

"The museum is open again. Anyone could call or go there and find out if the goddess is there," Thurman said.

"And if she's not at the museum, two things would look possible: one, that she never existed," Manheim said, hooking his index fingers together.

"Not likely," Thurman objected. "Six months ago, when Nash found what he was sure was a solid gold goddess, he documented the find at the Turkish Ministry of Culture. After his article came out and the media buzzed about it, the whole archeology world knew about it right away. And that was the reason we let the world see the goddess being excavated. We could have sold Aboud a fake without going to all the trouble of putting it on CNN. But the sting worked because al Qaeda correctly believed the goddess was the real deal."

"That leaves Aboud only one way to restore his honor. He has to steal the real goddess," Manheim said. "Zeugma may become a target again in the next few hours." He looked at his watch again. "We need to warn our agents in Gaziantep that Aboud may be heading back to Zeugma."

"Call in all the reinforcements you've got," Thurman said, sighing deeply as he considered this new possibility. "Make sure everyone understands that Ahmed al Aboud and his son have nothing left to lose."

CHAPTER THIRTY-NINE

"But I *am* feeling well enough," said a fully dressed and packed Dulcey Moore to Dr. Kirdar.

Dr. Kirdar frowned at her. "The wound on your neck has not healed well enough. And your blood count is not what it should be."

"Getting on with my life will do me a world of good, Doctor. I want to go home to see my family," Dulcey said, flashing him her most charming smile. "How about if I stay at Asena's house tonight, and, if I do well, I'll buy my plane ticket tomorrow. If I have any trouble, I'll come back to the hospital and let you stick me full of needles to your heart's content."

Dr. Kirdar finally relented. "I suppose that is a reasonable course of action." He examined the wound on Dulcey's neck, which now sported a neat formation of butterfly bandages. "When you get home to the United States, you may want to have the scarring on your neck smoothed over. The muezzin's wife is a pretty good seamstress—but she is no plastic surgeon."

"Nah. I'm not touching this scar. I'm going to think of it as a souvenir from Turkey. Pretty soon all the American girls will want one just like it."

"Well, if your sense of humor is any indication, I guess you are well enough to be released. Shall I have someone call you a cab?"

Dulcey looked toward the door and motioned Frank, Asena, Selene, and Tanju inside. "No need. My friends are here. They were going to bust me out if you didn't see things my way."

Frank came in, gave Dulcey a gentle bear hug, and showed her two airline tickets. "Our plane leaves tomorrow at noon. I already called Matt, and he's going to have half of Dallas there to meet you."

Feigning anger, Dr. Kirdar shook his finger at Dulcey and waved them all out of the hospital room. "You Americans. So bossy. Go. Get out of my sight. You pay me no respect. Go, all of you!" he said, smiling.

Selene stepped into the room and gave Dulcey a kiss on each cheek. "Come on. The cooks have prepared a welcome-home lunch for you at Mom's house."

Tanju bestowed cheek kisses, plus a hug for good measure. "Let's get out of here," she said, grabbing Dulcey's bag.

Asena stood near the door, smiling and waving the keys to her Land Rover.

* * *

A half hour later, they were seated in the courtyard of Asena's house, faces held toward the warm sun. The cook and the housekeeper rolled a cart toward them and served a first course of *mezes*. Dulcey loved the cold salads and tasty vegetable delicacies Turks ate before and during their multicourse meals.

Dulcey helped herself to several rolled pastries the cook called "*cigar borek.*" Then she spooned onto her plate a green pepper filled with rice and raisins and settled down on the daybed where she had first seen Asena's grandmother. "I wish I had known your grandmother," she said to Asena. Asena smiled and blinked her eyes in appreciation.

The cook poured a thick white liquid into a glass, and Asena held her drink up in the air. "*Ayran,* anyone? This is liquid yogurt. My grandmother swore it was what kept her going until she was ninety-two. Please have some."

Frank declined, but Dulcey and Selene each took a glass. "After what I've been through, I'm game to live a hundred years," Dulcey murmured into her drink.

Selene held up a plate of rolled grape leaves stuffed with rice. "We will have to save some of these *dolma* for Dr. Nash. He loves these. That man has become a real Turk."

"And there's no higher compliment than that," Asena said, intent on her cold eggplant salad.

Dulcey's foot began to bounce at the mention of Nash. She looked steadily at Selene and Asena, wary of any public relations efforts on his behalf.

Tanju finished the food on her plate and bent to examine the mosaic on the courtyard floor. After a minute, she said, "Asena, imagine how hard it must be for Dr. Nash to feel that he is the expert on Zeugma when you have lived and breathed the history of this place your entire life. I wonder how—"

At that moment, Hasan rushed into the courtyard and spoke in rapid Turkish. Asena and Selene quickly set their dishes down and hurried to the front door.

Asena spoke to the soldiers at the door, gesturing wildly. She returned to her English-speaking guests and announced, "We are under house arrest again. We are to go nowhere until the danger is passed. Does anyone know where Nash is?"

Tanju said, "Mehmet and I ate breakfast with him this morning. He seemed moody—lost in his own thoughts. Mehmet borrowed Dr. Nash's Humvee and went to the museum. I think Dr. Nash went to his tent. You know how he is when he's in there, Asena. We all have orders not to bother him. He says he is working on an excavation near his tent."

"Can you show the soldiers where the excavation might be, Tanju?" Asena asked, worry in her voice.

Tanju thought a moment. "No, he has never shown it to me, but I think the entrance must be somewhere above the crosscut road." Tanju explained this to the soldiers. They jumped back into their military vehicle and sped off toward Zeugma.

"The soldiers say the American CIA will be returning soon. We will be getting more guards here at the house, and we are not to go out this door," Asena said as she closed and locked her front door.

"No way," Dulcey said, shaking her head violently. "Frank and I have tickets to go home to America tomorrow. We *will* be on that plane."

Asena looked at her houseguests—fellow prisoners now. "Well, you had better take that up with the CIA when they arrive. We Turks would not even think of trying to negotiate with our military."

Dulcey unlocked the door and opened it, her frustration bubbling over. "But I'm an American."

Tanju quickly shut the door again and stood in front of it. Dulcey saw a defiance and pride in Tanju's eyes she had not seen before. "You might be an American, but you are still a guest in this country. Turkish people will go a long way to be tolerant of their guests, but while you are here, Ms. Moore, you are going to obey the orders of our military."

A little taken aback, Dulcey felt her jaw twitch as she stared at the usually well-mannered Tanju. "Wow. They've really got you under their thumb."

Tanju stared angrily back at her. Before she could respond, Frank stepped between the two women. "Now, listen. Dulcey, calm yourself. You're not even supposed to be out of the hospital. And Tanju is right. We're staying right here until it's safe to leave." Dulcey tried walking around Frank to continue her argument with Tanju, but he put his arms between the women and blocked her. "We've both caused enough trouble by not following orders. I'm to blame there too."

"Orders?" Dulcey said between clenched teeth. "There's no one on this earth who can stop me from being on that plane tomorrow. I need to see my husband and my children, and they need to see me."

Tanju's face flushed. "Ever since you have been here, we have been concerned about *your* needs, *your* wants, *your* comfort. Do you never think of things from anyone else's point of view?"

Dulcey felt as though Tanju had slapped her. "You're talking to the mother of two small children who has a demanding career and a husband. I never stop thinking about their needs and their wants. You think I want to go home so I can take a bubble bath or lie by my swimming pool?"

"You are so blind," Tanju muttered. "My culture may be imperfect in many ways, but at least I can see this. You do not even realize how corrupt the Western culture is. You push other people around, yell at people to get your way, and if that fails—you take out your wallets."

Dulcey's mouth dropped open. "Is that what you really think?"

Asena stood on her tiptoes, whispering into Tanju's ear, trying to calm her. But Tanju would not be calmed. "You are like big giants marching around the world stomping on all of us little ants. I can imagine your shock when finally one of those little ants found a way to throw an ember into the giant's eye on September 11 in the year 2001."

"An ember?" Dulcey echoed. "You call taking down the World Trade Center and crashing two other planes into American targets throwing an ember?"

"You have no idea how many ants you squish as you go running around doing your giant's business and taking care of your so-called *national interests.*"

Dulcey tested to see how far Tanju was willing to take this. "So the truth comes out. Is there some part of you that admires that turbaned man who hides in a cave and wants to destroy my country?"

Maybe it was because Tanju was hurt by Dulcey's question. Or maybe she didn't want to dignify the accusation with a response. But whatever the reason, Tanju's choice to stay silent was enough to stir Dulcey's frustration into a slow, simmering anger.

CHAPTER FORTY

House arrest was not as bad as Dulcey had imagined, and Asena's house was big enough to accommodate the warring factions of the group. Dulcey and Tanju avoided one another when possible, refusing to make eye contact when they were forced to interact. Turkish soldiers strolled up and down the road in front of the house. Their posture and the brisk way they walked made it clear they would not tolerate any attempt to circumvent their orders.

Hasan for one seemed happy about the situation. The soldiers had let him borrow a shortwave radio so he could call the dam or the police if anything went wrong.

"That's their way of getting Hasan to watch us," Asena said, miffed at having her own security guard promoted to being her jailer.

Meltem had brought the little goat inside the house because it had been bawling and seemed frightened by the soldiers. She had taken to calling him Ibo after her favorite singer from Urfa. The goat lay primly next to Dulcey on a folded kilim in front of the library fireplace. Dulcey stroked its wiry hair, lost in her thoughts, mulling over the words Tanju had said so angrily. Several times, Meltem brought Dulcey a tiny glass of freshly squeezed orange juice containing a concoction of Turkish herbs. At first Dulcey looked askance at the odd-colored drink, but Asena insisted that Dulcey drink each glass. "Meltem is famous in the villages for her knowledge of medicinal herbs. She kept my family very healthy for many years by serving us her secret potions."

Frank snoozed on a cushy lounger in a shady corner of the court-yard. Asena read the newspaper in the library with Dulcey. Tanju rummaged around at the back of the house, exploring the dusty warren of rooms that even Asena herself rarely entered. And Selene stayed busy in the climate-controlled room down the hall.

At about six o'clock in the evening, Tanju burst into the library. "Asena, you must come see this," she said, holding a lantern in her hand. Her jeans were dirty, and her hair was powdered with a layer of limestone dust.

"Where have you been?" Asena asked.

"Selene told me she wondered why a house of this magnificence did not have its own hamam. Well, it *does* have one."

"A bath house? Where?" Asena asked, putting down her newspaper and removing her reading glasses.

"Down those stairs at the back of the kitchen."

Selene came into the room as Tanju was describing her discovery. "You always said those stairs led to a storage room, Mama."

"I moved some boxes," Tanju said, "And I found a door to a narrow passageway that leads to a completely intact Roman bath."

To everyone's surprise, Selene, who normally paid little attention to talk of artifacts, oozed enthusiasm over the find. "Come on, everyone. Let's go see it."

Tanju led the way through the kitchen. "It has a cold room, then a hot room with baths, and a steam room with terra-cotta water pipes that run through a big stone oven."

* * *

As exciting as the find was, Asena found she was reluctant to follow the women into the mysterious rooms below her house. The first floor alone had always been too large for her, and it had never occurred to her that the house might have an underground area as well. She found her flashlight. "Please come with us, Frank," Asena urged. "You too, Dulcey. You and Tanju should put your quarrel behind you. This is a good chance to mend fences."

Frank yawned. "I'll come if you'll let me bring my camera."

Fear pricked Asena's heart. She hesitated a moment, conflicted, then nodded slowly. "All right. But only on the condition that I have complete control over that film footage." Asena took a handkerchief and soaked it with water so she wouldn't have to breathe the dust. The others did the same with whatever towels or scarves they could find. While Frank unpacked his camcorder and Dulcey found her notebook and pen, Asena stood staring at the door, looking hesitant about going down the stairs.

"Mother? What's taking you so long?" Selene called from the storage room at the bottom of the stairs.

"*Yavash, yavash,* Selene. I am coming," Asena said, walking slowly down the stairs, holding her wet handkerchief over her nose and mouth.

As she descended farther and farther, Asena turned around to go back several times. "You all go. I will wait upstairs."

"What's wrong? Aren't you anxious to see the baths? They belong to you," Dulcey said as Asena tried to push past her on the stairs.

"At least go see what Tanju is talking about. Then you can lock the door on it if you want," Frank said.

"Mom, why are you being so slow?" Selene complained from somewhere along the narrow stone passageway.

"I am coming," Asena said as she walked along the passageway. "We must be somewhere under Belkis Tepe. Look at all these water pipes." Warily, she followed Selene and Tanju with Dulcey and Frank bringing up the rear. After several minutes, they entered a dusty, cavelike room.

"What do you think?" Tanju asked, holding her lantern so she could see Asena's face.

"Amazing," Asena said, feeling her heart race. She used her wet handkerchief to rub a clean spot on a section of the smooth marble. It had rivulets of sparkling quartz running through it. Then she placed the flat of her hand on the wall and ran it over the smooth stone walls. In the light of Selene's lantern, the walls of the hamam seemed to glow with a soft, eerie light.

Sunk into the floor of the next spacious room was a magnificent bathing pool, now embroidered with layers of frothy cobwebs. From the center of the pool all the way to the ceiling, a vertical cloud of fat marble cherubs hovered in a happy chaos. The baby angels seemed to beat their wings vigorously as they tipped their basins over the pool, their arms and bodies and the billowy cloud formation encasing the clay pipes that brought the water to the pool.

Despite the chill inside her, Asena gasped at the beauty of the baths. All at once, she knew without doubt that these underground passageways would lead her to her destiny. She murmured a quick prayer.

Finding one's destiny was not always a good thing.

CHAPTER FORTY-ONE

Dulcey brushed away the cobwebs as she and the others explored the old Roman baths under Asena's house. Frank carried his big camcorder high on his shoulder, and Dulcey carried her notebook and the microphone attached to his camera.

"It feels so good to do something normal," Dulcey said, clearing her throat and transforming herself back into a reporter. She held the microphone under Asena's chin. "So, even you, the owner of this house, had no idea these magnificent baths were under your home?"

"No, this is my first time to see these rooms under the house." Frank went in close on Asena, covering the camera's red light with a finger so it wouldn't make her nervous. "My family always said that our home was nearly two thousand years old. Each generation of my ancestors repaired or built new structures, and the older parts were often forgotten or fell into disrepair."

"Who do you think might have built the original house?" Dulcey asked, smiling her encouragement at Asena. She knew Asena was struggling—weighing her need to share her burden against her decision to carry it alone.

Asena looked at the camera a long moment before responding. "I always heard it was once the palace where the governor of Zeugma lived. If this is true, it would not be surprising that it has its own baths. The governor of Zeugma would not have bathed with the commoners of the city."

Dulcey and Frank followed Asena to the cherub fountain to get her reaction to it. Dulcey pointed to the marble statuary. "This fountain is a wonderful group of marble carvings. Look at that little cherub holding his basin upside down over his head. He's trying not to get splashed by the water coming from above."

With awe in her voice, Asena said, "I simply cannot fathom that this has been here all along. There is still so much to learn about the place where I live."

"Coolest hot tub in the history of the world," Frank said, focusing his camera, circling the empty round pool and panning over the delicately carved marble.

They heard voices echoing in the room beyond. A minute later, Selene and Tanju appeared, their clothing and hair covered in even more layers of limestone dust.

Tanju had her excavation map in her hand and a look of triumph on her face. "Selene and I just found the entrance to Zeugma's underground water system. There's an iron door that leads out of the baths and directly into the tunnels."

Asena looked at the map. "So we know the water for my house comes from those springs nearby and is carried in these water pipes we see attached to the ceiling. So the waste water would have emptied into the sewer trenches, traveled under Belkis Tepe, then down the hill, and finally emptied into the river."

Tanju said, "The water for the whole town came from your springs."

Asena fixed them all with a stern expression. She walked around the fountain several times, and everyone fell respectfully quiet. "Frank, could you stop filming?" Asena took a place on the side of the pool next to Selene. She rested her feet on the marble ledge where bathers from thousands of years ago had once sat in steaming hot water. "I feel so exposed right now. You are making a film of all my secrets. Whenever anything about my house is revealed, it is one more thing that can be taken from us."

"This is difficult for my mother," Selene explained. "Generations of our family have lived here in this ruined palace. There are probably still many more rooms to be found. My grandfather used to ask, 'Where is the ballroom? Where are the stables and the enormous kitchens where hundreds of meals were cooked each day?' I guess those rooms are somewhere under this hill."

"Every time we find something, it's just one more thing we have to hide again," Asena said. "If people knew what was here, I would lose my home and everything in it. My ancestors entrusted these things to me. My good friend Tanju understands what we are facing. She has been so good not to report us to the Ministry."

Tanju spoke up. "The Turkish government would pay Asena and Selene for their home, of course, but the price would be a pittance of its worth."

"This place and everything in it is all I have left of my family," Asena said.

"What can we do to help you keep your house?" Dulcey asked.

"You will be home with your families soon; there is little you can do." Asena took a deep breath and took Selene's hand in hers. "I had always hoped Selene would live here someday when she inherits the home."

Selene looked at her mother and shook her head vigorously. "I have told Mother time and time again that my life is in Ankara. My friends are there. My work is there. But the cemetery next to this house contains all my people, and this home contains the history of my family. I will do what I can to protect it. But, I have to say, if it were entirely up to me, I would ask Dr. Nash to open its secrets to the world. Those secrets have cost my family everything. They even cost my mother the only man she ever loved since my father died."

Asena's face fell. "No, Selene. You cannot mean that."

Dulcey was on her feet. "Asena's right. Lee Nash can't be trusted with this house. He sold the goddess to terrorists."

Frank put his arm around Dulcey's shoulders. "Listen to me. It's time you caught up with things. You're a little like Rip Van Winkle waking up after a very long nap."

Dulcey looked at each person sitting around the marble bath. Just as she was, they were all covered in the eerie white dust of Zeugma and, in the dim lantern light, they looked like a circle of statues. Only their blinking eyes told her they were alive. And only their eyes told her she was the only one who still didn't believe Nash was telling the truth.

"Lee Nash is innocent," Asena said softly. "And he is your father. It is time you began to understand what that means."

Sitting there in the dim light among the strange, blinking statues, Dulcey felt small and alone. "You're all telling me you're convinced that Nash didn't sell the goddess to Aboud. Is that right?"

"He is a dedicated archaeologist and, more importantly, a good man," Asena said tenderly.

"Goddesses come in threes," Tanju explained. "There was the fake one that went to museum on the first night, the replica that was dug up and sold to Aboud, and the third one that is the real goddess."

Asena nodded. "Your father was working with the American CIA. They gave Dr. Nash and Mehmet Demirel the gold and the materials to create a replica in order to fool Aboud. And after you discovered the money, while the two of us were out there yelling in the storm, the CIA agents took the money Aboud paid to your father. But the *real* golden goddess is still right here in Zeugma . . . somewhere."

"So my father isn't a traitor who sold a golden goddess to terrorists?" Dulcey asked in a small voice, wiping her nose with her sleeve.

The blinking statues nodded.

CHAPTER FORTY-TWO

At about four in the morning, Hasan knocked loudly on Asena's door. Dulcey heard the commotion and followed Asena and Hasan to the front door, belting her robe as she went. On the doorstep stood Dr. Marco Capoletti, the Italian conservator who worked at the Gaziantep Museum. He removed his hat and stepped into the house. His face was ashen and drawn. "Mehmet and I were working late at the museum," he began. "Mehmet went out to Dr. Nash's Humvee to get a tool. I heard shouting so I went to the door that leads to the parking lot. I saw a man with a gun shove Mehmet into the Humvee, and the two of them drove away. I told the police, but I could not explain to them about the goddess or where she might be."

"Where is Dr. Nash?" Asena asked.

"He was not at the museum today. Mehmet told me he was working around the clock to get the goddess ready for the museum," Marco said, nervously fingering the brim of his hat. "I guess you heard about the raid in Syria."

"What raid in Syria?" Frank asked, emerging from his room, sleep rumpled and whiskery.

"You must not have television—everyone is talking about it," Marco said. "The Americans destroyed a training compound run by al Qaeda in the hills above Damascus. Most of the terrorists were killed, and many prisoners were taken."

Dulcey and Asena looked at one another. Dulcey asked, "Did anyone mention a man named Ahmed al Aboud?"

"Yes. They put his photograph on the news. They say he and his son got away and they are wanted criminals. This is why I came here. I am very worried, and I must speak to Tanju," Marco said.

Asena woke Tanju, and she joined them near the front door. "*Merhaba,* Marco. Asena says Mehmet was taken by a man with a gun?"

"Yes. Do you know where the goddess is hidden? Dr. Nash may be working on her, and we must warn him."

"I have no idea. Mehmet is the only person besides Dr. Nash who knows where she is," Tanju said.

Marco twisted the hat in his hands. "I believe I may have told the wrong person that the goddess had not been delivered to the museum yet. Today, a boy—you know, high school age—wandered back into the workshop wanting to see the goddess. He spoke excellent English. Then, later, I saw the photo of Aboud on the news. The man on television said Aboud had a son—about fourteen or fifteen years old. There was no photo of the boy, but I realized that the boy—who was full of questions about the goddess—could have been Aboud's son."

Tanju's eyes widened. She looked at the rest of the group in horror. "We must find Dr. Nash. Aboud could be coming here now."

"There's one last thing," Marco added. "Near closing time, before I saw the news report about the raid in Syria, a woman called the museum and asked if a young boy had been asking about the goddess. She said she was calling from London and that her son was missing. The museum receptionist sent the call back to me."

"The Abouds lived in London," Frank said. "But Cantwell said Aboud's wife is dead. She was a suicide bomber in Riyadh."

"I realize now the boy lied to me. He must have been with his father, not his mother."

"So who was the woman who called the museum?" Dulcey asked. "And did you tell her about the boy full of questions?"

"Yes, I told her he called himself a budding archeologist. Right away she said she knew I had spoken to her son because that is what she always called him. She asked me where he was, but I did not know."

"So, if his mother is dead, who was that woman?" Asena asked.

Tanju said, "That woman could have been anyone. She could even be an al Qaeda operative trying to track down Aboud and the boy."

"I should have been more cautious, but, at the time, I thought he might have run away to Turkey to see the goddess. He was an intelligent boy—he could have done that. Then I saw the news about the raid, and I realized I could have given information to Aboud's son."

Dulcey caught Frank's eye and nodded her head, finally convinced of her father's innocence. "We need to find Nash."

"But where is he? Even the CIA doesn't know where the goddess is," Marco said. "Of course, we all suspect she is still right here in Zeugma."

"Since Mehmet had the Humvee, Lee must still be here in Zeugma," Asena said. "With the goddess, I imagine."

Marco passed the brim of his hat through his nervous hands again. "Dr. Tanju, I feel so awful about this."

"This is not your fault," Tanju said. "How could you know the boy might have been the son of a terrorist?"

"Where is that map of yours?" Asena asked Tanju. "If I were Lee Nash, I would hide the goddess in that wonderful tunnel system underneath Zeugma." The group watched Asena as she flew into action. She spoke to Hasan, who went out the door and came back with two soldiers. Turkish words flew between Asena, Hasan, and the soldiers.

Red-faced, Asena turned to her houseguests. "They will not allow us to go to the Zeugma camp. They are under strict orders to keep us in the house."

Marco said, "I'm not part of your group. I can leave."

Asena grabbed Marco's arm. "Yes. Go to the dam and tell them Nash is in danger. They will know what to do." Marco put his crumpled hat back on his head and went out the door. Asena and her houseguests stood there helplessly, staring through the window, as Marco climbed into his car and drove away.

"We're like sitting ducks," Dulcey said, shooting a withering glance at Tanju.

"We may be." Tanju nodded, then pointed to the snaking trails on her excavation map. "But now we know how to get into the tunnel system from Asena's house."

CHAPTER FORTY-THREE

Dr. Lee Nash gazed up at the golden goddess looming over his head. He had waited for days to be alone with her. Every time he had walked over the metal sheeting that covered the domed ceiling of his secret cathedral, he had felt her shimmering beauty beneath his feet. He knew all too well what was coming when his goddess and his cathedral were finally exposed to the jaded glare of the world's scientists and theologians. The pushing and pulling, bidding and bargaining would begin as soon as he opened the lid of his underground treasure box.

Holding the bottom edge of his sketchbook tightly against his chest, Nash stepped over the chains and straps that had been attached under her heavy granite pedestal. He circled the goddess and sketched what he saw from below. He began with a page for her beautiful face, attempting to capture Fortuna's full lips, finely arched eyebrows, and downcast eyes. He tried to decide if she was blind, since some myths depicted Fortuna as "blind fate." *No, this goddess can see.* The sculptor had nicked both pupils in identical spots with his chisel as though there were a light source reflecting off her eyes. *No need for light if the goddess were blind.*

Nash positioned a tall step ladder next to the statue, climbed most of the way up, and drew the graceful curve of her throat. Then he sketched the place where her neck met her shoulders. Using the side of his pencil, he rapidly shaded the outline of Fortuna's curving, upstretched arms, holding aloft her golden ball. Everything about the goddess filled him with awe. The gold she was made of had stood the test of time. Every detail of her form fascinated him. He climbed down the ladder and used the top of the granite pedestal to steady his sketchbook. He flipped to a new sheet of paper to sketch the details of her feet and the flowing hem of her golden robe. Then he grabbed his camera and took photos of the goddess from every angle. *Fortuna is the kind of woman I can relate to,* he thought as he chuckled to himself.

For two more days, she belonged only to him.

Just as Nash finished shooting the photos, he heard footsteps in the tunnel leading up from the river. Nash checked his watch—nearly five in the morning. "Mehmet? Why are you coming from the river?"

"Dr. Nash?" the familiar voice called out.

"What are you doing here so early in the morning?" Nash answered, setting his camera down next to his tools.

"I am not alone, Dr. Nash," Mehmet said, his voice breaking. When the light fell on the young man, Nash saw that Mehmet's hands were bound together in front of him with a rope.

"What—" Nash gasped as a teenaged boy stepped into the cathedral from the tunnel, followed by Ahmed al Aboud carrying a gun.

"Dr. Nash, we meet again," Aboud said.

Nash stared at the boy, who gazed steadily back at him. There was no doubt the boy's sagging canvas vest contained explosives. "You would do this to your own son?" Nash asked, revolted by the sight of a child wearing the emblem of a fanatic.

"I am teaching my son the meaning of honor, Dr. Nash," Aboud said.

The boy's expression was calm, unreadable, as though a veil covered his awareness. Then he spoke. "I have failed my father, and I wished to show him I am a brave fighter. The vest was my own idea."

Nash stared at the boy and the adult-sized vest that extended below his thighs. Then he glared at Aboud.

Mehmet exiled himself to a dark corner, sobbing now, doubled over in agony. "I begged him to shoot me so I would not have endangered you, Dr Nash. But this man got my family's address from my university. He threatened to kill them . . . if I did not do what he tells me." Mehmet's voice broke, and he sobbed pitifully.

"How did you get past the guards?" Nash asked.

"I told them we had hired this man and his son to work for us," Mehmet said. "Forgive me!"

"Mehmet, be still . . . I forgive you. Aboud is a madman. Look what he has done to his own child," Nash said, his voice slathered with contempt. "Even animals try to protect their young, Aboud. Only insanity can account for why you and your kind don't obey the basic laws of nature."

"According to Western rules, I suppose jihadi warriors *are* insane," Aboud said, stroking his mustache and squinting in the bright light. "But I can assure you, what you call insanity is actually steadfast belief in our glorious religion. We will conquer the earth for Allah, just as the Prophet Mohammed—"

Nash seethed. "What do you want?"

"I have come for what is rightfully mine, Dr. Nash. Even in the corrupt West, a person is owed what he has already paid for."

"You'll never get away with this, Aboud. Do you think you and your son will just drive over the border with the goddess? Do you think you can get away with melting her into a mountain of gold so you can restore the caliphate all on your own? Your plan has failed!"

Aboud smiled. "You know our holy scriptures. I am impressed that a man of science also knows the words of Allah through his messenger, Mohammed, peace be upon him."

"The Prophet would condemn a man like you." Nash spat onto the rocks in front of Aboud. Aboud stepped back, holding his gun higher. Nash could see the boy's fists tightening, his face and body straining with anger. Nash said to the boy, "Calm down, young man. This is between your father and me."

"I want what I already paid for," repeated the terrorist.

Nash straightened, face-to-face with his worst fears. "How about if I refund your money and you and your son use it to get away from here? Go somewhere and raise your son to respect human life, Aboud. Otherwise the two of you don't stand a chance in this life or the next."

A hideous laugh burst from Aboud. "Money? Westerners always think it is about money. With us, Dr. Nash, it is *rarely* about money."

"No, it's about power—you were going to use the goddess to get power over the Muslims of the world. But even your own people despise you now. How much power would they share with a man like you?"

"Delivering the real goddess will quickly restore my faltering public image, Dr. Nash."

"In the end, that's all that counts—who gets to be the big man. Who gets to be the *last* man standing on top of a mountain of dead bodies. It's about who gets to gloat," Nash said, his words smoldering like hot coals as they spun out into the dusty air of the cathedral.

"No, it is about who did the one thing that will restore the Islamic caliphate. I intend to be the warrior who does that," Aboud said. "In the imagination of Islamists, Dr. Nash, the man on top is not necessarily alive. But we who *give* our lives in this fight will stand forever as honored martyrs at the very *top* of the heap—in Paradise. Just as you Americans revere your founding fathers, people everywhere will remember the martyrs who made it possible for Islam to rule the world," Aboud said. He wandered back into the shadows to check on the suffering Mehmet. Then he came back and stood in front of Nash. "You have made me into a very dangerous man, because you have shamed me in front of my people with your trickery."

"You shamed yourself," Nash said. "And you couldn't have shamed yourself any more than when you put your son in that vest full of explosives."

Nayif puffed out his thin chest. "I put this vest on myself."

"Then your father put the ideas into your head that made you put on that vest!" Nash yelled, his fists clenching and unclenching at his sides.

The boy stood defiantly, his fist firmly grasping the wire that protruded from the series of explosives. Aboud whispered in his son's ear, and the boy went to stand near Mehmet.

Just then, Nash heard voices calling from the tunnel.

"Lee? Are you there?"

Asena! Sweat sprang to the surface of Nash's skin; his stomach seized into a tortuous knot.

"Lee? Answer me!"

Aboud pointed his gun toward Nash's head and hissed, "How nice. You have a visitor."

Nash yelled, "Asena, go back! Aboud has a—" Aboud punched Nash in the stomach, and he doubled over. After he regained his breath, Nash tried to warn Asena again. "Don't come—"

"Lee?" Asena stepped into the cathedral, her hand warding off the glare of the bright lights. Aboud grabbed her by her hair and forced her to her knees. He held the gun to her temple and glared at Nash. Nash's heart dropped. After seeing what Aboud had done to his own son, Nash had no trouble imagining him killing Asena.

More voices. "Dr. Nash? Are you all right?" Tanju called, gasping as she came face-to-face with Aboud. Aboud pressed his gun harder against Asena's temple and motioned Tanju into the room. Seeing Mehmet, Tanju ran to him.

A moment later, Frank's flashlight bounced along the walls of the tunnel and both Frank and Dulcey stepped into the room.

"Oh no," Frank said as he saw the scene in front of him.

"Ms. Moore," Aboud said, leering into Dulcey's face. "How nice to finally be introduced."

CHAPTER FORTY-FOUR

Nash made his way to Dulcey and stood between her and Aboud. "You want the goddess?" He leaned close to the man with the gun. "Take her. We'll even help you load her up."

"And how will we lift the statue up out of the ground? Even with all of us working together, it is too heavy," Aboud said, leaving Asena in order to examine the statue, gesturing at it with his gun.

"It isn't hard with the proper equipment. Mehmet and I got her down here by ourselves. It only takes a few more people to get her back through the dome up there," Nash said, pulling out his set of keys, dangling them toward Aboud. "The crane is parked on the crosscut road. These chains and straps around the pedestal here can be pulled back up to attach to its cable. We could load her into a truck, and you could drive away right now."

"You would do this?" Aboud said warily.

"Yes," Nash said. "But if you hurt any of us, there'll be no one to help you."

"What about the soldiers?"

"I already told them I'd be transporting the last of the artifacts to the museum. If Mehmet told them you're working with us, they won't stand in your way," Nash said in an authoritative voice.

"Forgive me if I have trouble trusting you."Aboud took out his pocketknife and tried to plunge it into the golden statue. Nash winced as the knifepoint glanced off the solid gold. Aboud turned his knife around and used its handle to hammer various parts of the statue, assuring himself that it was the real thing this time. Nash looked away as Aboud climbed up on the ladder and hammered his knife against Fortuna's arms, torso, and face.

* * *

While Aboud was distracted with the goddess, Dulcey felt herself go calm. *Showtime,* she thought. She walked over to the teenaged boy wearing the vest. "Is this man your father?"

Nayif looked steadily at Dulcey without blinking, holding the wire away from himself. "If I pull this wire, you will all be dead," he said evenly.

"And how does killing us help your holy war? Exploding that vest of yours would be one more failure in a long line of failures. Most Muslims will detest the sound of your name," Dulcey said. "Right now, they probably spit on the ground when they hear it."

Nayif set his mouth and glared at her. "Not true. Killing Americans is my sacred duty."

Dulcey moved toward Aboud. "It is against the laws of Allah to kill or hurt women, children, or innocent people. You will never see Paradise at this rate, Mr. Aboud."

"Take the goddess!" Nash yelled. He leaned toward Dulcey and whispered into her ear. "What are you doing?" Sweat was pouring off Nash's forehead. While Aboud silently mulled over the offer, Nash turned toward the group of unfortunate interlopers. "How did you get into the tunnels? What possessed you to—"

"The soldiers would not allow us to leave Asena's house," Tanju said, holding up the excavation map. "We were looking for you—to warn you. We headed through the tunnels toward the spot where you pitched your tent. Then we heard voices farther along the tunnel."

Dulcey again felt the calmness she had trained herself to feel a split second before the cameras rolled—right after the stage fright ebbed away. "Everyone knows you escaped the bombing raid in Syria, Mr. Aboud. It's on all the news channels. Everyone in Turkey's looking for you and your son. And they've got photographs of you. You know— the ones John Barrows took."

Aboud waved his gun threateningly at her. "Close your evil mouth, woman. You are the devil's daughter—"

"Then that makes me the devil," Nash growled, going for Aboud's neck and shoving the heel of his hand into the man's throat. The gun in Aboud's hand went off, and the bullet exploded off the rock ceiling of the cathedral. It bounced back and hit the torso of the goddess before dropping to the floor and spinning like a coin.

Nayif's eyes were wide as he screamed, "Father! Shall I pull it now?"

"No, Nayif! Not now. I will tell you when to pull it," Aboud shouted, aiming his gun at Nash.

"Okay, calm down, everyone," Nash said, heaving, holding his hands up to calm Aboud. Dulcey closed her eyes and prayed fervently that the man from the museum had alerted the soldiers by now.

Aboud walked behind the group and tried to herd them all back against the wall. "As you can see, even if you were able to get my gun, my son stands ready to die. There is no way out of this for any of you. You help us lift this statue out of here, or we all die together."

Just then, Mehmet reared up out of the darkness behind Aboud with a rock held between his bound hands, his mouth contorted. But before he could smash the rock down on the terrorist's head, Aboud spun around and fired his gun. Mehmet screamed in agony and collapsed into the shadows. Frank went for Aboud, but Nash held him back.

Tanju and Dulcey went to Mehmet and quickly saw that the bullet had shattered his collar bone. "Monster!" Tanju shouted. The women set about staunching the flow of blood from Mehmet's wound.

Nash stepped up to Aboud. "Just say what you want. I'll make it happen."

Aboud glanced at his watch. "All right, all of you will help load the statue, and you will tell the soldiers I am the driver you hired. If anything goes wrong, Nayif will be instructed to pull that wire."

Nash sprang into action. "Tanju, show everyone how to prepare the goddess for the lift. Aboud and I will open the cover to the excavation from above."

"How long will this take, Nash?" Aboud said. "I want my son to know exactly how long."

"It depends," Nash said uncertainly.

"How long?" Aboud shouted.

"Twenty," Nash said. "Twenty minutes once she clears the hole."

"Did you hear that, Nayif? After the statue is above ground, you will look at your watch. It should take twenty minutes. If it takes longer and I don't come back for you, pull your wire!" Aboud went to his son and hugged him fiercely, kissing him on both cheeks. The boy seemed startled by his father's affection. Then Aboud checked the too-large vest his son wore and adjusted something in the single pocket between the boy's shoulder blades.

As his father walked away, Nayif's face became rigid with determination. His eyes were glazed as he shouted orders at the adults. "You heard my father. Once the statue is out of the hole, you have twenty minutes. *Get moving!*"

* * *

Aboud tugged on his gloves, bundled his leather coat around himself, and followed Nash into the passageway that led to Nash's tent. Once inside the tent, Aboud took a silencer from his pocket and screwed it onto the muzzle of his gun.

Summoned by the noises from the archeologist's tent, the guard from the covered trenches held back the flap and poked his head in. Nash spoke to him in Turkish. Aboud watched Nash tensely. When the guard turned to go back to his post, Aboud abruptly shot the man in the back.

"No!" Nash shouted, kneeling next to the guard, feeling for a pulse.

"Go get the crane," Aboud ordered, dragging the guard's body into Nash's tent. A light rain was falling now, keeping a steady beat on the woven fibers of the tent. In the faint morning light made dimmer by black rain clouds, Aboud followed Nash out of the tent toward the cab of the crane.

Nash seethed as he gripped the steering wheel and drove the crane over the crosscut road as close as he could to the cathedral.

* * *

In the cathedral below, Tanju's motions were trancelike as she unraveled the chains from around the granite pedestal. Frank positioned the stepladder next to the goddess. Murmuring in Turkish, Tanju sorted the tangled chains, giving one to Dulcey and another to Asena. Soon the chains and straps under the pedestal were laid out on the cathedral floor, ready to be used.

"Steady, Tanju. Show us what to do," Dulcey whispered. "We'll just let this guy have the goddess, and then we can go for help."

"No talking!" Nayif shouted.

"He will never let us live," Tanju whispered to Dulcey through clenched teeth. "Aboud is a madman."

"Have faith. We'll figure this out," Dulcey whispered back. "And Tanju, whatever happens, I'm—well—I'm sorry we had that falling out. And for what I said."

"I too am sorry—especially for what I said about September 11." Tanju offered a small smile. "Nothing like a common enemy to bring two friends back together."

CHAPTER FORTY-FIVE

The early morning wind was brisk, and Nash had a difficult time dragging the sheet metal away from the hole in the cathedral's ceiling. The rain had only been drizzling, but now it fell more steadily. He pulled his hat down over his forehead and shielded his eyes from the bits of gravel picked up by the wind. Lightning cut through the gray sky. Once he had shoved the metal to one side, bright light shot up from the kliegs as though he had excavated the sun. Nash looked down at his daughter, his coworkers, the love of his life—and the boy attached to a bomb. "Is the goddess ready?" Nash called.

"She is ready," Tanju shouted up to him.

"Hurry!" Frank urged.

Nash ran over the crosscut road, got into one of the Birecik Dam trucks, and backed it up until it was parked next to the crane.

Aboud had already climbed into the cab of the crane. Nash leaned into the open window of the cab and instructed him how to use the crane. "This switch here moves the outrigger to stabilize the crane. Then you slowly pull the lever under your left hand toward you, and I'll guide the cable into the excavation hole. Don't touch the other lever or it'll swing the cab out of position," Nash growled. "When I give you a hand signal like this, stop pulling it. Then when I give you a thumb in the air, push the lever away from you to raise the arm of the crane."

* * *

Rain poured through the wide opening in the cathedral ceiling, sizzling as it hit the hot lights. Aboud lowered the arm of the crane until the hook attached to the cable passed through the ground-level opening. Together, Frank, Dulcey, and Tanju wrapped the goddess with yards and yards of canvas sheeting and slipped the chains up over her head. Then they used the straps to snug the chains tightly around the swaddled goddess.

Nash stood above them, signaling Aboud in the truck. Lightning electrified the sky, and the rain came harder now. Heavy black rain clouds with thunder in their bellies crawled over the rising sun. Daybreak had been canceled.

"Now!" Nash gave the signal for the crane to pull the goddess upward.

"Get off the ladder, Frank!" Tanju yelled. "Keep her from swinging from below. She has to go straight up through that opening!"

Frank, Asena, and Dulcey surrounded the goddess, steadying her in her ascent. The chains clanged against each other and then went taut. The crane's cable strained and protested as it pulled its heavy load a few inches off the ground. Rain dripped into the cathedral, darkening the canvas that shrouded the statue.

"Steady!" Tanju yelled to Nash from her perch on the ladder.

"Is she off the ground yet?" Nash shouted back.

"She's clear!" Frank called from his place next to the pedestal.

"Once her arms and her head are above ground, she'll come up easily," Nash told Aboud. "But I need Tanju and Frank up here to load the goddess. You and I will be operating the truck and the crane."

"I do not care as long as it works," Aboud yelled back.

As the goddess rose, Tanju guided the ball in Fortuna's hands through the hole, then her arms, and then her flowing sleeves. Rain washed over Tanju's face and into her mouth, and angry tears streamed from her eyes. Finally, the bottom of the pedestal was above their heads and out of the hole above her.

Nayif stood as close as he could to the group, staring at the hands on his watch, wiping away the raindrops with his thumb, listening for his father's command from above.

Nash looked into the cab and saw a triumphant Aboud gazing at the statue as she floated higher and higher. Lightning illuminated the dangling goddess like a huge marlin caught on a fishing line. "Tanju will help you with the truck. I'll take the crane from here. She'll show you and Frank how to load the goddess onto the truck's conveyor belt."

As Aboud jumped down from the cab, he waved his gun at Nash and leered at him. "No tricks now. The lives of your people are at stake. All I have to do is say the word to my very well-trained son."

Nash swallowed and looked away, unwilling to gaze into the face of evil any more than he already had. Despite the chill of the rain, sweat dripped down the back of his shirt. He yelled into the hole, "Frank, Tanju, use the extension ladder and climb up here. We need you to help load."

Nash's heart clenched as he watched Frank and Tanju emerge from the hole. He didn't know whether the man with the gun or the boy with the bomb was more dangerous. Tanju used her key, and Nash saw the truck's tailgate roll up. Aboud jumped up into the truck bed, and Tanju followed him. Soon, the conveyor belt jerked to a start, its teeth ready to catch the canvas-swathed goddess and feed her into the belly of the truck.

Nash directed Frank into the cargo hold of the truck. "You and Tanju have to steady the goddess and make sure the belt grabs that canvas."

* * *

As soon as Frank got into the truck, he noticed an expression of alarm on Tanju's face. Frank's heart stammered in his chest as he saw Aboud kneeling next to Asena's precious mosaic, using his pocket knife to slit open the plastic wrappings.

"Help us load the goddess!" Frank yelled to Aboud.

Aboud whirled around and pointed his gun at Tanju and Frank. "Come here . . . both of you."

Frank looked behind him. Nash was absorbed in lowering the boom of the crane slowly toward the truck. The hill was so steep that only one of its two outrigger arms had been effective in stabilizing it. The crane listed downhill as the statue dangled near the truck. Lightning continued to flash, and the shrouded goddess lit up again and again.

Aboud motioned to Asena's precious mosaic with his gun. "What is this?"

Frank glanced at his watch. "We do not have much time left to load the goddess, sir. Please, help us get her into the truck so you can go."

"You people constantly underestimate me," Aboud said. He pressed his gun into Tanju's temple. "*What is this mosaic?*"

Tanju swallowed and answered. "It is nothing. It belongs to a local family. It is a poor piece of art that is not worth much."

Aboud brushed the wet sand off the mosaic revealing the woman's beautiful face and haunting eyes. "Strange. Her mouth is missing," he said. Aboud took his gloves off and ran his fingers over the tesserae. With his pocket knife, he scraped away the dark, tarry substance covering the tesserae that made up the hill. Slowly, as Aboud scraped, each tessera began to shine. Soon it was clear that the entire hill in the background of the mosaic was made of gold. "I have found it," he said reverently. "I am blessed above all other servants of Allah," he murmured to himself. "This surely is the mountain of gold . . ."

Tanju's knees buckled, and Frank steadied her before she could fall. "I was right . . ." she whispered into Frank's ear. "We cannot let him have this mosaic."

Frank looked at his watch. "Call off your son. We have eleven minutes left. Take the goddess and go."

Aboud began to breathe heavily, his eyes mesmerized as he scraped more and more of the sticky black substance off the mosaic. "Gold," Aboud muttered. "A *mountain* of gold. Allah has favored me above all others . . ."

Tanju regained herself and stood over the mosaic now. She put her hands on her hips and lied as though her life depended on it. "We found this mosaic in one of the trenches on the hill. It's of such poor quality, we didn't even bother taking it to the museum."

Aboud's breath gusted from him as he bent toward the wet sand he'd scraped away. He grinned as he held up a tiny fish. "Did you also find this *fish* swimming in that sandy trench on the hill?"

Aboud's laughter made Frank feel like retching. Tanju pressed her lips together and turned away from Aboud, holding her stomach in disgust.

"*Always* underestimating me," Aboud said as he threw the fish back into the wet sand and dusted off his hands.

"Take the goddess. There's far more gold in the goddess," Frank said. "We have only seven minutes left."

Aboud took his time contemplating. "Get Nash. Tell him I have decided not to take the goddess. I have what I want right here. It is smaller, more easily carried, and—above all—it is the real thing. The prophecy of Mohammed, peace be upon him, has come true. I have been blessed by Allah for my unwavering devotion." Aboud stood still, eyes half closed. One of his hands held the gun, the other was cupped at shoulder level. His lips moved in silent prayer.

Frank jumped off the back of the truck and ran toward Nash. The goddess hung in the air directly above the truck, ready to be loaded. Frank flung open the door of the crane. "Nash! Aboud wants you. No matter what, you can't let him take the mosaic that's in that truck."

"What mosaic?" Nash got out and looked at his watch. "Six minutes to go before the kid pulls that wire. What mosaic, Frank?"

Frank knew there was no time to explain. "A small mosaic belonging to Asena's family was in the back of that truck. Aboud wants it instead of the goddess. The mosaic has a mountain of real gold in it."

"He's leaving a solid gold statue for a mosaic?" Nash ran toward the truck, holding his watch in front of his face. "Aboud! Call off your kid!"

Aboud yelled back. "I am leaving the goddess behind. Get in this truck and drive me out of here!" He gave Tanju a rough shove away from the mosaic.

Tanju jumped out of the truck and ran to Nash. "He cannot take that mosaic. You've never seen the mosaic before—but it is the mountain of gold! At least he thinks it is. Do you understand what I am saying to you—the prophecy from the Hadith? Do you understand how he will use it?"

Tanju held Nash's eyes for a moment until it hit him what she was talking about. "The prophecy Asena's always worried about?" he asked.

Tanju nodded in obvious relief that Nash knew its importance.

"*Nash!*" yelled Aboud, closing the truck's tailgate. "No time for the goddess. Get in the truck. You are going to drive me out of here."

"Aboud, our agreement was that I would tell the guards you have my permission to drive out of here with the goddess. Now take her and go," Nash said, pointing to his watch. "Four minutes left!"

"I have decided not to tell Nayif when to pull the wire," Aboud announced. "Making his own decision will help him feel like a man," Aboud said, aiming his gun at Nash's face. "Now, get in the truck. I will sit in the back directly behind your seat as you talk to the guard at the gate. If they inspect the back of the truck, you are to say we are taking the mosaic to the museum. My gun will be pointed at you the whole time."

Nash turned the big truck around on the narrow, muddy, crosscut road. Sick to his stomach, Frank watched him drive away toward the main gate. Then he rushed to the hole in the cathedral ceiling. "Your father said not to pull your wire!" he yelled, falling to his knees near the opening. "There's no one in there, Tanju. They're gone."

Tanju dropped to her knees beside him, shouting above the sound of the thunder. "Mehmet? Asena? Where are you?"

"Dulcey?" Frank called into the empty cathedral, his words echoing off the cavernous walls.

No answer. No sound but the staccato beat of the rain.

Suddenly, a deafening explosion, which seemed to originate near the river, rocked the ground. Frank was thrown back from the hole. Tanju fell beside him on the rocks, her breath knocked out of her. The ground around them shook and cracked. A cloud of limestone dust rushed out of the hole, enveloping Frank and Tanju as they lay there, stunned. The dust rose and hovered above them as the sound of the blast echoed over the Euphrates. It bounced off the wall of the distant dam, reporting back to them like a sonic boom. The sound dissipated over the valley, mingling with the thunder from above.

The tarpaulins on the covered trenches collapsed, and the rain and wind blew them away like tissue paper, exposing artifacts and a few mosaic floors. The wall with the fresco of Ariadne and Theseus and the Minotaur toppled in a heap of rubble. The crane tilted crazily on its side, pulled downhill by the weight of the goddess. Farther up the hill, Nash's tent billowed for a moment, then collapsed in a heap, shrouding the dead guard inside it.

"Tanju?" Frank called, choking and groping in the stinging limestone dust. The gritty silt had blown into his mouth and down his throat, turning into a slurry of mud as it mixed with saliva and rain. He choked and spat, rolling over onto his hands and knees to spit the dirt out of his mouth. "Tanju!" he called again.

"Here . . ." Tanju rasped, gasping and choking in the swirling dust. Frank could hear Tanju but could not see her. "He pulled the wire," she choked in anguish.

Frank crawled toward the sound of her voice, then put his arms around her and held her.

They sat there for several minutes, faces upturned. The rain beat back the dust and rinsed their faces as they tried to recover their senses. Frank looked into Tanju's terror-stricken eyes as she huddled next to him. Neither of them could speak. They stared at each other, their faces filthy—frozen in agony and disbelief.

Tanju raised her face to the sky, her lips moving in prayer, her cupped hands held shoulder high, filling with rain water. "Dear Allah! Receive them into your Paradise."

Frank crossed himself and allowed his grief to engulf him. "Dear Father, please don't let them suffer down there. Let them die quickly and go to their rest."

Frank scanned the landscape of Zeugma. Nash's big Mack truck had gotten bogged down in the mud on the steep side of Belkis Tepe. Its tires spun in the ooze, trying to get some traction on the hill. He saw Aboud and Nash open the tailgate and carry the heavy mosaic to a big, battered step van Nash used to transport his backhoe. Nash looked toward Frank, then back at Aboud. Then, without warning, Nash took off at a dead run across Belkis Tepe toward them. Aboud fired twice. Nash stopped abruptly, raising his hands.

"No!" Tanju whimpered, watching in horror as Aboud took aim again. Frank willed Nash to turn around and get back in the step van. Lee Nash's death would not bring anyone back from the slaughter below ground. Reluctantly, Nash turned, walked slowly back, and got under the steering wheel of the step van. Once again, the two men were hurtling toward the camp's main gate.

After the truck was out of sight, Frank saw Selene running down the hill toward them from the main gate. "Where's my mother?" she cried.

Tanju responded by shaking her head and pointing to the gaping hole that still belched dust.

"*Annnaaaah! Annnaaaah! Annnaaaah!*" Selene collapsed on the wet ground beside them, wailing the Turkish word for "mother."

Tanju sobbed, talking to herself in Turkish. She pulled off the scarf she had been wearing around her neck and held it to the rain, screaming into the wind as she did so. She mopped Selene's face, then leaned toward Frank and wiped his as well, weeping and keening as she did it. Frank put his arms around both Tanju and Selene and rocked back and forth in anguish.

Nearby, the goddess swung madly in the rain and wind. The crane and its hundred-and-thirty-foot-long boom teetered downhill, and the front door of the cab swung open and shut, keeping time with the swinging goddess.

From the main gate, four Turkish soldiers ran toward them, their machine guns in firing position. When the soldiers were close enough to identify Selene, Frank, and Tanju, they put down their guns. Then they fanned out, trying to piece together what had happened.

* * *

According to her watch, Dulcey had reached the iron door that led to Asena's house eighteen minutes after the goddess had cleared the hole. She had half dragged the wounded Mehmet with her.

"Selene!" she screamed as she ran through the empty house. "Asena might still be alive in that tunnel. We need to get help!" Dulcey ran out the front door and saw Hasan and two soldiers talking to Nash at the wheel of the big step van he used at the camp. Two jeeps blocked his way . . . and he was alone. The big Mack truck was nowhere to be seen. *That means Aboud is well on his way with the golden goddess. The monster never thought once about saving his own son,* she thought.

"Nash, we need you," Dulcey cried, approaching the step van. "Mehmet is—"

"Dulcey! Thank heaven you're safe." Relief washed over his face. "What about the others?"

"Mehmet and I are fine—but we need your help," Dulcey said, heading for the passenger door of the big van.

"Dulcey, get back in the house. Now!" Nash said urgently. He turned to the soldiers and spoke loudly in Turkish, trying to convince them to move their vehicles and let him go through the checkpoint in front of Asena's house. Finally, the soldiers drove their jeeps away and waved him through.

"Go back!" Nash shouted, stepping on the gas. But Dulcey had already pulled open the passenger door and climbed into the step van as it picked up speed.

"Where are you going? We need you. I got Mehmet to the house, but we need to get him an ambulance. And Asena's still down there in the tunnels, Nash. She got the boy to go with her toward the river—but she could still be alive down there."

"Dulcey, get out," Nash said through clenched teeth. "I told Hasan to send help for everyone. Go see what you can do for Mehmet until the ambulance gets here, but get out of the van *now!*"

Dulcey stared at him. "Didn't you hear me? Asena might still be—"

"Drive," said a voice from the space behind the driver's seat. A gloved hand came over the seat and clamped onto Dulcey's forearm. "Nice that you could join us, Ms. Moore." The acid voice burned into her senses. Gripping Dulcey's arm hard, Aboud commanded, "Quickly, Dr. Nash, we haven't much time."

Dulcey looked from Nash to Aboud in panic and confusion. *What's going on? Where's the goddess?*

Nash sped toward the highway, muttering and growling at his daughter. "You never listen to anyone."

After a moment, Dulcey asked, "Where's the goddess?"

Aboud ignored her question. "Is my son dead?" he asked.

"I don't know. Asena convinced him to run toward the river—told him he didn't have to die. She told him to make his own choice."

"Fool! Worthless son of mine," Aboud muttered.

"You don't care about him at all, do you?" Dulcey asked angrily.

Nash drove through the wet trees toward the highway. "Save your breath. I don't think Aboud ever intended for his son to live through this." He turned to her as they bounced over potholes in the unpaved road. "And you. When someone tells you to do something, don't you ever consider the fact that it might be for your own good?" Nash slapped the steering wheel as he sped faster toward the highway. "You're impossible."

"You will drive on Highway 90 toward the Syrian border," Aboud said, holding his gun against Dulcey's neck. "And if you try anything, I would be most happy to end the life of your very disobedient daughter."

CHAPTER FORTY-SIX

As soon as he heard the explosion, Atila Tuzman, the foreman of the Birecik Dam, immediately activated an earthquake response plan. Twenty of his men raced through the bowels of the dam, using X-ray equipment to examine the bolts and connections of the long wall that held back the entire Euphrates River. Tuzman's workers ticked off checklists as they ran to each point of the dam that could be damaged by an earthquake. Tuzman stood in his front office with its panoramic view of the dam and the river, smiling with relief as the checklists came back one by one. The dam was in good shape.

Tuzman picked up the phone on his desk and called his boss to report the explosion. As he waited with the phone against his ear, he noticed a teenaged boy on a motorbike riding over the dam. He remembered that Commander Cantwell had asked him to watch for a kid on a motorbike. The American agents had put the bike back in the abandoned shepherd's tent in case the boy came for it. Tuzman hung up the phone and tried to reach Cantwell's satellite phone instead.

After Tuzman had hung up the phone, a call came over the shortwave radio from Hasan at Asena's house. Tuzman felt his relief turn to dread as Hasan asked him to send earthmoving machines, men, and every ambulance he could find to Asena's house and to Zeugma. Some of the tunnels at Zeugma had collapsed, and a rescue effort had been mounted to reach anyone who might still be alive.

* * *

Frank, Tanju, and Selene felt the ground vibrate as workers from the Birecik Dam used earthmovers to dig a hole near the blast site.

Selene continued to wail as the teeth of the workers' shovels bit into the ground until they had exposed the cut stones that had been fitted neatly together by Roman engineers. The stones had withstood earthquakes, floods, Parthian and Persian raiders, and a hundred years of looters only to finally be displaced by a modern-day terrorist. The soldiers and dam workers used shovels and metal tools to pry out a few sections of the passage, and soon there was a hole big enough to climb through.

The men in the tunnel coughed and spit dirt as they shoveled the debris into plastic bags. They passed the bags of rocks and dirt from hand to hand out of the tunnel. Within an hour, there was a sizeable pile on the ground above.

Selene's wail grew louder when a soldier called out that they had found a body. A paramedic with a dirt-smeared face finally climbed out of the hole. *"Üzgünüm."* He handed Selene a silver bracelet with a design of interlocking spirals.

"Annnaaaaaaaah," she moaned, kissing her mother's bracelet and holding it against her cheek.

Covered almost entirely with the gray dust and dirt, Asena looked like an ancient artifact being excavated from the ground as her stretcher emerged from the tunnels. It was clear she had been crushed by the falling stones in the tunnel rather than killed by the bomb itself. Selene covered her mother's body with her own and cried until she was spent. Tanju and Frank sat near her, helping her grieve, wondering how long it would be before Dulcey and Mehmet would be found.

An ambulance picked its way down the hillside toward them. Still weeping, Selene got in and asked that the paramedics take her mother to the house near the gate. Before the ambulance driver left, he informed Frank and Tanju that Dulcey had gotten Mehmet back to the house before the blast and that another ambulance was taking him to the hospital.

"So where's Dulcey?" Frank asked.

"When we got to the house by the gate, the other ambulance driver asked if someone could accompany Mehmet to the hospital. But the old security guard told us there was no one around. He said Ms. Moore left with her father a little while ago."

Frank closed his eyes, shook his head in disbelief, and put his face into his big hands.

* * *

Commander Cantwell set up an impromptu command center at the Birecik Dam, and Tanju offered to act as a translator. The American pilots of three Apache helicopters from Incirlik sat in the administrative offices, waiting for their orders as rain drizzled down the panoramic windows.

Cantwell had one team of soldiers on the highways tracking the transponder locator the Turkish soldier had attached to the boy's motorbike several days before. He had another team working on a plan to stop the step van. "I don't get it. Why didn't Aboud take the goddess?" he muttered.

Dr. Tanju Boyraz quickly convinced Cantwell that the little mosaic of a golden mountain that Aboud now possessed could do far more harm than the goddess ever could.

A short time later, Hasan radioed the dam to report that an ambulance had taken Mehmet to the hospital; Hasan was relatively sure the archeologist would live, and he'd sent another ambulance to the camp. Then, almost as an afterthought, he added that Dulcey Moore had climbed into Nash's step van when the soldiers had stopped Nash at the checkpoint in front of Asena's house.

Cantwell slammed his fist on the desk in front of him. "Dulcey again! Now Aboud's got her too."

* * *

After more than two hours on the highway, Dulcey broke her brooding silence and spoke to Aboud. "How can you not care that your son may be dead?"

"If he is, he is a martyr. You Westerners are afraid of death because you do not understand eternal life. I feel sorry for you. You live only for what is on this paltry planet."

"But he was your son . . . and you allowed him to die," Dulcey said.

"Nayif is in Paradise with his mother. A child belongs with his mother. Even you might agree with that," he said.

Dulcey felt woozy and thirsty. As she listened to Aboud ranting about his noble warrior son and his glorious martyred wife, she felt as though she were about to pass out. The wipers swished through the

rain on the windshield, making Dulcey even thirstier. She remembered
Dr. Kirdar's warning about getting enough fluids. "Nash, I need water."

Nash turned to Aboud. "We need to stop for petrol anyway. Any
objection to that?"

Aboud was silent for a minute, calculating. "How much petrol do
we have right now?"

"Less than a quarter tank," Nash said. "There's a TurkPetrol at
Kiziltepe just ahead."

"Fine. Stop there. Let the attendant fill the tank. You will tip him
and ask him to bring us some food and water from the service station.
Do you have cash?"

"Not much. I have a credit card," Nash said.

"I gave you five hundred thousand dollars in twenty dollar bills
for the goddess, and you have no cash?" Aboud sneered.

Nash dug out his wallet. "I have . . . sixty million lira." He looked
at Dulcey. "That's about forty bucks—won't even fill the tank."

"I don't have anything. I'm sorry, Nash," Dulcey said, leaning
against the window as her head started to spin again.

Aboud impatiently threw some money at Nash. "Use your money
for food. I will buy the gas," he hissed.

As they pulled into the busy TurkPetrol station, Dulcey looked
around at the other cars, wondering if anyone might guess what was
going on. With the way everyone seemed to be feeling about Americans
lately, it was a toss-up whether the people in those cars would consider
her an enemy or a friend. *What would happen if Nash and I jumped out
and ran in two different directions? Would Aboud try to kill one or both of
us? Or would he just drive away with his priceless cargo?*

Nash asked the attendant for a fill-up and an assortment of snacks
and waited, drumming his fingers on the steering wheel, avoiding
Dulcey's gaze.

Dulcey felt terrible for Nash. And terrible for herself. She had
made things worse again. She thought of Matt and Izzy and Michael
and half of Dallas going to the airport and finding out she was not on
that plane. She looked at Nash's rugged profile and pictured her
mother falling in love with him all those years ago.

After what seemed like an eon of time, the attendant brought six
bottles of water and a bag of snacks to the driver's window. As Nash
paid him, the attendant cleared his throat and pointed inside the

bag. Nash tried to take the bag, but the attendant wouldn't release it until Nash looked at the receipt inside.

"*Fis,*" the attendant said, pointing to some handwriting on the receipt.

"Yes, the receipt. Thank you. Where's my change?"

The attendant counted out some cash and then once again pointed to the note written on the receipt.

Dulcey grabbed a bottle of water from the bag and gulped it down, trying to feel normal.

"Better?" Nash asked as they pulled away from the gas pumps and waited to get back on Highway 90.

"A little," she said, looking out the window.

"Here, this might make you feel even better," Nash said, handing her the bag of snacks, tapping his finger on the receipt until she noticed the message written on it.

Uncle Sam is with you. We will rescue you near the border.

Dulcey felt relief wash over her as she emptied the bag of snacks onto the seat and selected the Magnum ice cream bar for herself. "Yes, I am feeling *much* better." She wadded up the bag with the message attached to it and stuffed it under the seat.

Aboud seemed content with his roll of Biskrim cookies. Using the hand that held his gun, he opened the package and delicately conveyed each chocolate-filled cookie into his mouth.

Buoyed by the nearness of rescue, Dulcey felt suddenly reckless. "Mr. Aboud, do you really expect we'll be allowed to cross the Syrian border with no papers of any kind?"

Aboud's voice was oily and confident. "I may leave you two on the side of the road somewhere. I have what I want. But then again, my boss could use a couple of high-profile hostages to exchange for some of our operatives."

"So you decided the goddess wasn't worth the trouble after all?" she continued, unable to understand why, after everything that had happened, Aboud seemed content to drive away without the goddess.

"The mountain of gold is the mosaic in the back of the truck," Nash blurted out. "Aboud wants to—"

"*Silence!*" Aboud commanded. "Not another word!" He waved the gun back toward Dulcey's face.

Dulcey stared straight ahead. Her brain screamed inside her head. *The mountain of gold—a mosaic? How could this have happened?* Had Nash tricked Aboud into thinking one of his mosaics was the prize of all prizes? Or had Tanju perhaps offered Asena's precious mosaic to him and convinced him it was worth more than the goddess? She looked at Nash out of the corner of her eye. He put his hand on hers and squeezed. Dulcey squeezed back.

Aboud settled down and said smugly, "I have resources of which you are unaware. I have a friend who will escort us over the border of Iraq. He has a house on the border."

"The border of Iraq?" Nash said, glancing at Dulcey. "I thought we were heading for Syria."

Aboud smiled and took another cookie. "As soon as I am safely in Iraq with the mosaic, you will become the property of my sheik." Aboud gestured with his gun. "Keep your eyes on the road, Dr. Nash, I'd hate to have an accident with my destiny so close at hand."

As Nash continued driving down the highway, Dulcey noticed perspiration beading on his temples.

"You'll never get away with this," Nash said.

"Don't try anything. I could dump both of your bodies and drive this van into Iraq myself."

"You wouldn't stand a chance. If you don't have us, the military will drop a bomb on this van without giving it a thought," Nash seethed. "And your mountain of gold mosaic would be destroyed along with you."

Dulcey's eyes widened. She wondered if, for the sake of the world, the military should bomb the truck—no matter what happened to her and Nash.

Aboud became agitated. "Enough talk," he said, grabbing Dulcey by the hair. "You! Get in the back!"

Aboud crawled over the seat, holding his gun against Dulcey's head. Her heart hammered as she crawled the other way and sat in the corner behind Nash's seat. She watched Nash's face in the truck's side mirror. Nash changed lanes and made eye contact with her. He winked, and Dulcey sent back a halfhearted smile.

CHAPTER FORTY-SEVEN

After rumbling for an hour over a potholed highway, Nash saw a sign for the town of Nusaybin, Turkey. That meant they were now driving parallel to the Syrian border. The steering wheel under Nash's hands grew slick with perspiration. The note promising rescue had indicated the rescue would occur at the border. But which border? Did the CIA know Aboud was taking them to Iraq rather than Syria?

Aboud's cell phone rang, setting Nash's teeth on edge. As he listened to the Arabic language being spoken from beside him, his skin crawled. He had learned a few words over his years of working in the Middle East, but when they were all coming at him at once, he couldn't distinguish one from the other. He heard the word *mosaic* with the last syllable emphasized instead of the middle one. To Nash, the lilting language of the Koran had suddenly become the language of death. Nash listened as Aboud's tone turned obstinate. He heard his own name and Dulcey's, as well as the Arabic word for *hostage*. Aboud said it over and over as though he were trying to convince his listener to accept his plan.

They drove another few hours on Highway 90 along the Syrian border through tiny villages and a desolate, muddy landscape. When they passed through Cizre, Nash saw a sign for Silopi, Turkey—and Zakho, Iraq.

"Go through Cizre, then on to Silopi," Aboud ordered. "We will cross the border at Zakho."

Nash reached behind the driver's seat and Dulcey squeezed his hand. He looked in his sideview mirror and caught her eye. She nodded and tried to smile, but her expression seemed frozen, and her eyes were wide with terror.

When he had driven a few miles past the village of Cizre, Nash saw a roadblock of vehicles ahead. He slowed the step van to a crawl as he surveyed the row of six or seven vehicles parked side by side across the road, their headlights forming a string of bright pearls in the mist. There were tall, rocky hills on both sides of the road—a perfect place for an ambush. As Nash stopped his vehicle, adrenaline and fear pumped through his body. His heart began to thud as he noticed that none of the cars were police or military or CIA. *No friends here,* he thought.

Aboud leaned forward, his gun pointed toward Nash. "Roadblocks are normal this close to the border. Do you have your passport?" Aboud asked, his eyes searching the crowd of men who stood next to their vehicles. Aboud too seemed to be seeking a comrade of his own.

"I carry a photocopy of my passport in my wallet," Nash said, rolling down his window.

As four people, none of whom wore uniforms, approached the van, Aboud said, "It is possible they are bandits. If so, they will want money. Here is a hundred million. See if they will take that." Aboud handed over a fold of Turkish lira and held his gun below the seat, still pointed at Nash.

A big Turk walked up to the van, pointing a Glock 9mm into Nash's window until the muzzle of the gun touched Nash's cheek. Nash thought he'd seen the man before, but couldn't place him. Three men stood behind the big Turk, also pointing their handguns toward Nash. With guns pointing at him from both sides, Nash's stomach lurched, then tightened into a knot.

The big Turk leaned into the window and smiled at Aboud, revealing a row of silver-edged teeth. "*Salom alikem,* Brother Ahmed al Aboud." He had been joined by several other Turks, and now a small crowd stood behind him, guns at their sides. "My friends and I will help you get across border of Iraq," the big Turk said in passable English. "We already make deal with Brother Saif bin Rabeh. You go Iraq; *we* take American man and daughter. Mohammed here will go with you. He help you cross border and take mosaic to Saif bin Rabeh."

"But I recently spoke to Brother Saif," Aboud said warily. "He said to bring these people to Iraq."

"No," the big Turk said. "We make better deal with Brother Saif."

Mohammed, a small man with a scar across his nose, stepped toward the passenger window, a small pistol in one hand, a cigarette in the other. He exhaled, blowing smoke into the open window, and grinned. "At Zakho, Brother Aboud, I take you to Brother Saif."

The big Turk turned on his silver smile again and cocked his pistol. "We have made good deal with your boss Saif. In return, you go—to safety house of Saif bin Rabeh."

Aboud appeared confused. "But I spoke to him just two hours ago. He said he would meet me himself at the border." Until this moment, Aboud had seemed to be in full control. Now he looked alarmed, unsure of what to do. "First, I will check your story with Saif bin Rabeh," he said to the men.

The big Turk and Mohammed nodded, gesturing that Aboud should feel free to check their story. A visibly shaken Aboud redialed bin Rabeh. As Aboud waited, Nash watched a rivulet of perspiration make its way down the terrorist's cheek and slide under his shirt collar. His cell phone beeped, and Nash could see the words *call failed.* Aboud slammed the phone onto the seat, breathing heavily.

"What does Brother Saif say?" the big Turk asked.

Aboud looked at the solid wall of vehicles in front of him. Men were standing between each vehicle, staring at him, their guns visible. He looked at the road behind him. Two more cars had pulled up, blocking the step van.

Nash slipped his hand between the door and his seat and brushed against Dulcey's knee. She took his hand and held onto it tightly.

"Brother Ahmed Aboud, we *arkadash.* We only want Dr. Nash and his daughter—not you. You go Iraq now. Saif bin Rabeh meet you at border. He take you to safety house."

"What will you do with the Americans?" Aboud asked.

The big Turk smiled. "We make sure Nash and daughter do not testify against Yildirim family. These Americans do not understand our ways—Aysha Yildirim was killed for family honor. "

Dulcey exhaled her breath as quietly as she could. Although she could not see the man who was speaking just inches away from her, she could hear the menace in his booming voice.

Nash repeated the big Turk's request. "So Aboud can go to Iraq if Ms. Moore and I go with you?"

What about the mosaic? thought Dulcey. Aboud would be free to take it to Iraq and drop it into the Euphrates River. At precisely the right time, al Qaeda would draw it out of the river before a great crowd of witnesses and be declared the legitimate leaders of the Islamic world—legitimate, at least, to radical Muslims. *Where are the U.S. agents?* Dulcey's mind screamed. *Are they at the wrong border?*

Dulcey's mind conjured the face of her husband and her children. She began to pray desperately that she would live through this—that she would see them and hold them again. In the side mirror, she saw that Nash's eyes were closed too, his lips moving. *Praying?* She squeezed her eyes shut again and prayed for their deliverance with every fiber of her body.

"Dr. Nash and his daughter will come with us now," the big Turk said, opening the van's door and motioning Nash out. Then the big Turk held the driver's seat back and took Dulcey firmly by the arm to usher her out of the van.

Gradually, Aboud relaxed. He slid under the steering wheel and said to Nash through the window, "It is ironic, is it not, that you and your daughter might have been safer with me after all. We had intended to trade you to the Turkish government in return for two of our own." Aboud put the truck in gear and leered at Dulcey. "I leave you to your fate, Ms. Moore. Today you will fully understand how important honor is to the people in this part of the world."

Dulcey glared at Aboud, squaring her shoulders. "I do believe your wife and son could be in Paradise. But I guarantee you'll never see them again."

Aboud's smile vanished, and he spat out the window in Dulcey's direction.

At that moment, three vehicles in the roadblock ahead backed up, then drove away, leaving a space big enough for the van to pass through.

Aboud called out to the big Turk. "Your man Mohammed will accompany me only if he is unarmed."

Grinning and shrugging, Mohammed passed his pistol to the big Turk who put it in his pocket. Then Aboud's new traveling companion climbed onto the passenger seat. Aboud ground through the gears trying to find the correct one. The step van jerked and finally went into a forward gear.

The entire core of Dulcey's body shook like a sapling in a strong wind. Nash put his arm around her and pulled her toward him. "Shhh," he whispered in her ear. Then he did the strangest thing—a gesture both Matt and Poppie Joe did instinctively whenever the children were afraid. As the big Turk came toward them, Lee Nash put his big calloused hand protectively over Dulcey's whole face.

CHAPTER FORTY-EIGHT

Though every nerve in her body quivered in terror, Dulcey raised her head. She took Nash's hand away from her face and held it tightly. *I will not give these people the satisfaction of seeing my fear,* she said over and over to herself until she thought she might actually look fearless. She saw that the gunmen had their backs turned and were watching Aboud in the van as it jerked along, grinding through its gears.

Then the big Turk gestured at them with his gun. "Follow me."

"What do you want with us?" Nash asked. "I don't know your name, but I know I've seen you in Tilmusa. People there have known me for twelve years."

The big Turk smiled at them, the silver of his teeth flashing, "No worries, Dr. Nash. Come." He motioned with his gun again toward the side of the road.

Suddenly, Nash shoved Dulcey to the ground in front of him and covered her body with his own. "This is my daughter! Please, I'll do whatever you ask, but don't harm her."

Dulcey closed her eyes and allowed the body of her father to surround her. Afraid that Nash had only succeeded in enraging the big Turk, she counted her breaths, trying to guess which of them would be her last. She closed her eyes and prayed fervently. *Father in Heaven, please protect us.* Then, like a last mantra, she whispered the names of everyone she loved. "Matt and Mikey and Isabel. Mom and Poppie Joe and GramMaria. All my cousins in Texas. Frank and Laney and the kids. Aysha and Asena and Tofer and John and Tanju. Gina and Jeanette. Nancy and Jim. Hank and Rob and Delia and Rhonda. Mehmet and Nash . . ." A drop of moisture fell on the crown of her bowed head.

Nash whispered, "I was wondering if I would make that list."

Dulcey looked up at him and watched him wipe a tear away from one of his weathered cheeks. "You're my father," she whispered.

They both looked up as they heard a shout and saw a man in a khaki uniform running toward them. "Nash! Dulcey! You're safe." It was Commander Cantwell. From behind one of the rocky outcroppings, a dozen men in fatigues and uniforms swarmed toward them, fanning out in all directions, their weapons drawn.

The big Turk grinned proudly and said to Cantwell, "Good success."

Still shielding Dulcey with his body, Nash stared at the big Turk. "What . . . I don't understand."

"You all right, Dr. Nash? Ms. Moore?" Cantwell asked, panting. He turned around and yelled to the men approaching them, "Stand down! All clear!" The men immediately stopped and holstered their pistols.

"Dulcey!" Frank yelled, running toward her, the sound of his huge shoes slapping against the wet pavement, the sound going soft on the grass.

"Frank? How'd you get here?" Dulcey asked, her mind swimming as she looked up into Frank's big, ruddy face. Then Tanju rushed toward them, her arms outstretched.

Frank knelt on the wet ground and gathered Dulcey in his arms. "We all came in military helicopters—and some folks from Tilmusa came with us to help. We had to get here before you did."

"Who . . . who organized all these people?" Nash asked.

"The Turkish military got the people from Cizre to help. The people never questioned the soldiers. They just acted right away. It was amazing how fast they put this rescue together."

"And the people from Tilmusa?" Dulcey asked, unconsciously rubbing her necklace of butterfly bandages.

"Yes, your friends from Tilmusa came too," Tanju said, tears streaming down her face. "You are safe now. Everything is all right." She looked toward the sky as the sound of several approaching helicopters grew louder.

"Nash," Dulcey said, looking up at the man who was still arched over her like a large umbrella. "You okay?"

"Never better," he replied. Big tears mingled with the drizzling rain and dripped down Nash's dirty face. He wiped them off with his sleeve.

For just a moment, as she got up off the ground, Dulcey found herself suspended between Nash and Frank. *Fathers,* she thought. She looked at the men who were her provenance—the two men who could vouch for her origins, and how she had come to be her very own self. She closed her eyes, relishing a feeling she had never felt before and could not name. Then she felt her knees give way, and both men reached toward her to keep her upright.

Now, everyone was talking at once. The men from Tilmusa gathered together, smiling, laughing, exchanging cheek kisses with the men from Cizre. Guns and car keys were returned to their rightful owners. There was hearty backslapping all around. Then all of their gazes turned skyward as three helicopters stood briefly in the air above them, then landed in a nearby field.

Tanju hoisted herself up on the bumper of a truck loaded with crates of tomatoes and yelled loudly so she could be heard above the sound of the helicopters. She spoke in Turkish, then translated for the Americans. "We thank you all for helping to rescue Dr. Nash and his daughter, Dulcey Moore. You all did a wonderful job. And to the people of Cizre, we thank you for lending us your vehicles and your guns, and for helping us with this roadblock. The helicopters that brought us all here will take us back home now. You have done a great thing here tonight, friends. It is a story you can tell your grandchildren someday, *inshallah.* Thank you, and may you go in peace."

Some of the locals laughed and drove away, waving, wishing the favor of Allah on Nash and Dulcey and their new friends from Tilmusa. Others waited in the light rain to see their visitors off in the helicopters.

An old man in a white tunic and crocheted skullcap broke through the crowd and spoke to Tanju. She led him toward Dulcey. "Do you remember Hajji Kerim, the muezzin from the new mosque in Tilmusa? I think you two have already met." Frank and Nash surrounded Dulcey protectively, watching every move the man made. "It was Hajji Kerim who got the people of his mosque to help in the rescue," Tanju added.

"Dulcey Hanim," the old man said, bowing slightly. Then the muezzin took Dulcey's chin in his gnarled hand and turned her face gently from side to side so he could examine her healing scar. He spoke quietly to Tanju in Turkish.

Tanju translated for him. "He wonders how you are feeling and whether his wife did a good job of sewing up your wound."

Dulcey touched her neck. "Oh, yes. Tell him she did a wonderful job. And thank him for saving my life—*two* times." As Tanju translated, Dulcey felt an overwhelming gratitude well up inside her. This culture—these people—had changed her life forever. Underneath the cultural differences, misunderstandings, and imperfections that stood between them, they truly were brothers and sisters.

The villagers from Tilmusa boarded the first two helicopters, talking and laughing as though they were in line for a ride at Disneyland. Dulcey could see that some of the women and older children from Tilmusa had gone along on the adventure. Tattooed faces and covered heads leaned out from the chopper. Hands waved at her. She recognized some of the women who had answered her call from the minaret on that awful, fateful night. Turkan held her baby up and called out, "Are you all right?"

"Never better!" Dulcey called back.

Hajji Kerim's wife, Zeynep, waved to get Dulcey's attention. Making a face, the old woman pinched the skin of her own wrinkled neck and pretended to sew with a big invisible needle.

Dulcey waved back, thanking her with a smile. Then she thought of Aboud and the mosaic in the back of Nash's step van. She ran to catch up with Cantwell. "How will you stop Aboud?" she shouted over the sound of the chopper blades. "He has the mountain of gold, and he's heading for Iraq. Do you understand what that means?"

"Relax, it's under control," Cantwell yelled back, leading her toward the last helicopter parked in the field. "You know how a Trojan horse works, don't you?" Cantwell asked, helping her on board. "Well, Mohammed is a Turkish soldier who speaks Arabic. He's wired for sound so we can hear exactly what's being said in Nash's van. When Aboud called Saif bin Rabeh on his cell phone, we listened in and triangulated the cellular signal so we could pinpoint the location of bin Rabeh's safe house in Zakho. We already picked him up at the Turkish border, where he was waiting there for Aboud."

"You were lucky Aboud didn't reach his boss on his cell phone to verify the new plan," Dulcey said.

"We knew Aboud would try to call bin Rabeh again, so we put the roadblock up in a place where we could jam his signal. That way

Aboud couldn't check the story of our friends from Tilmusa. We also had to make Aboud believe those men would kill the two of you as soon as you were out of his hands."

"But Aboud has the mosaic," Dulcey said again.

"*Yavash, yavash,* Dulcey Hanim," Cantwell said, gesturing downward with his palms in the Turkish way. "When Aboud opens the van's tailgate at the safe house to show off his mountain of gold mosaic, he'll find three American CIA agents and three Turkish soldiers in the back of that vehicle."

Dulcey's mouth dropped open. "How? When?"

Cantwell chuckled. "It's amazing how rattling a nozzle against the gas tank sounds just like the back doors of a step van opening and closing." Cantwell clapped his hand on the shoulder of a Turkish soldier. The man turned and saluted Dulcey—it was the attendant from the TurkPetrol station who had filled their tank with gas and had slipped them the note with their bag of snacks.

A few moments later, Cantwell helped Dulcey up into the Apache helicopter. Strapped securely against two of the seats was Asena's very precious mosaic. The three golden tesserae Aboud had scraped clean danced in the light. Dulcey knew that after restoration of the mosaic, hundreds more of those shining gold nuggets would form the shape of a mountain behind the beautiful woman's face. Her haunting dark eyes gazed out at Dulcey as though the two of them shared a secret.

CHAPTER FORTY-NINE

After the helicopters deposited the villagers in Tilmusa, they skipped across the Euphrates to Zeugma. One of them returned to the CIA base at the dam, another landed at the Zeugma camp, and the last one settled in the clearing beside Asena's house. On the flight back, Frank solemnly told Nash and Dulcey what had happened in the tunnels, and that Asena had been killed.

Dulcey held Nash in her arms as they both wept for Asena.

* * *

General Manheim wasn't taking any chances that the Americans would fall from their safety net yet again before the agents could get them on a commercial plane flight. He decided that, after Asena's funeral that evening, Frank and Dulcey would be flown to the base at Incirlik. From there they would board a military jet and go home to the United States. Until their departure, a ring of CIA agents and Turkish soldiers would be stationed around Asena's house.

* * *

At the Zeugma camp, Dr. Tanju Boyraz supervised as the soldiers loaded the goddess onto one of the helicopters to finally take the golden lady to the Gaziantep Museum where she belonged. Dr. Marco Cappoletti was also on hand to accompany the goddess and to secure her in her new glass case at the museum.

*　*　*

Later that evening, the local villagers, friends from Birecik and Nizip, and several people who had worked at Zeugma came to pay their last respects to the mysterious woman whose family had lived in Zeugma for hundreds of generations. Besides Meltem, Feyza, and Hasan, none of the mourners from the villages had ever visited Asena's home. Even Nash, the man who had loved Asena and had once wanted to marry her, had never been admitted to the private sanctuary she had guarded so well.

In her hands, Dulcey held three bunches of yellow field daisies she had picked from the orchard behind Asena's house. She stood with Selene, Frank, Tanju, Nash, and the others while Hajji Kerim intoned his prayers over the grave. Then the old imam gave everyone a chance to say something in Asena's honor.

Selene told everyone what she had learned about her mother's final moments: "Mother was a brave woman. She's been fiercely courageous all my life. Today, Marco Cappoletti took me to the jail to talk to Nayif al Aboud, the boy who wore the vest of explosives that killed her. The boy said my mother had convinced him that his own mother was alive. She told him his mother had called the museum looking for her son, referring to him as a 'budding archeologist.' Nayif said that he had known my mother was telling him the truth because his mother had always called him that. Then the boy told me something you all should know. He didn't pull the wire. With my mother's help, Nayif took off his vest and set it gently inside the tunnel that led to the river. He told my mother to go back the way she came. As he was running toward the dam to get to the shepherd's camp, Nayif heard the explosion. And then he realized the awful truth. When he had thought his father was checking his vest and hugging him, Aboud had actually set a timing device and slipped it into a little pocket between Nayif's shoulder blades. His father had not trusted him to pull the wire—and Aboud had never meant for his son to survive." Zeynep and Meltem embraced Selene when her emotions prevented her from continuing.

Commander Cantwell finished her story. "After Selene Hanim left the jail, Nayif's mother, Nala al Aboud, arrived to be with her son. She had flown to Turkey immediately after Marco had told her that

Nayif had been at the museum looking for the goddess. Nala went straight to the museum, found Marco, and he took her to the police station to see her son. Marco told the woman that many people thought she, too, had been a suicide bomber in Riyadh. But no, Nala al Aboud had escaped her terrible fate. She had imagined how her son's life would be ruined by her death. And she had realized that her husband would be free to command her son's death just as he had demanded her own. She told us that for the rest of her life she will denounce the terrorism her husband and other extremists embrace."

When it was her turn to say something, Dulcey said, "In a book that is very sacred to me, it says there is no greater love than when a person lays down his life for his friends. My friend Asena had that much love inside her. Rest in peace, sweet Asena. I will never forget you."

The other mourners watched as Dulcey placed one bouquet of daisies on Asena's wooden casket, another on the grave of Grandmother Yildiz, and yet another one on the mound of dirt over little Aysha. "Tanju told me that goddesses come in threes," Dulcey said, pointing at each grave in turn. "And here, in this cemetery, the innocent maiden, the unfinished mother, and the gentle, wise, and completed matriarch will rest together forever."

* * *

After the mourners from the villages had gone home, Dulcey saw Selene leading Tanju and Nash into the library. Selene motioned for her to join them.

"There are not going to be secrets in this house any longer," Selene said to them, holding up Asena's huge key ring, filled with old and new keys. "It's time for you all to see the things my mother has been hiding from the world."

Dulcey followed Selene and the others to the big aluminum door she'd seen the first night she had stayed at Asena's house. Selene unlocked the door and quickly pressed in the code to disarm the security system. Inside the huge room, the air was cool and dry, kept that way by a dehumidifier in the corner and a window air-conditioner attached to a humming generator. "Everything in this room is very old and fragile, so whenever Mother touched anything, she wore clean cotton gloves." Selene brought out a box of new white gloves and found a pair for each of them.

Along one wall of the room was a deep shelf that extended from the floor to the ceiling. There was a shelf of stone and iron boxes, followed by a shelf of copper and bronze boxes, a shelf of ornately carved wooden boxes, and finally a shelf of steel and tin boxes—all neatly labeled and securely locked with padlocks of varying ages. Selene led them to a long table, where several of the boxes lay open.

Selene said quietly, "All these boxes contain the history of Zeugma. There are journals and keepsakes and attempts at histories. They're written in Sumerian, Babylonian, Akkadian, Greek, Latin, Arabic, and both Ottoman and modern Turkish. All the women in my mother's family attempted to write the history of their lives and of this part of the world. Their words are priceless."

Tanju gasped at the number of boxes filled with artifacts and the historical documents of Zeugma. "Priceless," she echoed.

Then Selene opened a door at the far end of the temperature-controlled room and led everyone into a dark room that was long and wide like a hallway. The few pieces of furniture in the room were covered with dusty sheets and tarpaulins made of goat hair. "This wing of our house was just for its women. If this were a sultan's palace, which it may have been at one time, this room would be called the *harem*. But our home was here long before Ottoman times. All through the centuries, the women of this home enjoyed being together. And, it seems, they were never idle . . ."

Everyone gasped as Selene turned on a bank of overhead flood-lights. Every wall of the enormous hall was covered with small and large mosaics of female faces. "Each of the women who lived here—all of my female ancestors—made a mosaic of her own face. You might call it a family tradition. Think of it as a scrapbook of photographs before cameras were invented. You will notice that some are nicely done, while others are crude, as though they were created by a child. They all had varying degrees of skill and artistic talent," Selene said reverently.

Dulcey walked along the hall, looking up at the mosaics. "So Asena's precious mosaic of a woman's face with a golden mountain in the background was a portrait of one of your ancestors?"

Selene held a parchment document in her white-gloved hand. "Yes. That particular mosaic was made in the year 630 C.E., when the Prophet Mohammed was alive." Then she held up another document. "In 1732, one of my more recent ancestors calculated the modern equivalents of all the Roman, Islamic, and Ottoman dates and listed them along with the names of the women who made these mosaic portraits of themselves."

"There is provenance on all of these mosaics?" Tanju asked, looking at Nash, who was too overwhelmed to speak.

There was a catch in Selene's voice as she answered. "Yes. On the house too. These documents show the history of this house and when each of our ancestors lived here. If only my mother had lived to see all this." She held up Asena's key ring again. "Even Grandmother Yildiz had never opened those locked boxes. But when I was home this time, I suddenly realized these small rusty keys would open all those padlocks. It took some searching to find a document I could read, but I finally found some I could decipher."

Tanju put her arms around Selene and embraced her with all her strength. "Asena's destiny will be hard for you to bear."

Selene nodded her head, allowing Tanju to comfort her.

* * *

Dulcey walked along the wall, gazing up at the rows of mosaics. "Your precious mosaic was the only one made of gold, and so, of course, it was the one Yildiz feared would be stolen first if the mosaics were ever found by the outlaws. Of all the mosaics, the one with the golden mountain was her most precious one." Then Dulcey stopped short and let her shoulders fall as a perplexing thought occurred to her. "How did the Prophet Mohammed know the mountain of gold would end up being found in the Euphrates River? It had only been in the river since the new dam was built."

It was the first time Dulcey had heard Selene laugh. "Um, perhaps because he was a prophet?" she said, her own disbelief coloring her words. "I never thought I would hear myself say that," Selene murmured, busying her hands with her mother's key ring.

The group was silent as they returned to the tables where some of the safe boxes lay open. Nash carefully examined a document written on animal skins and another one written on silk. There were clay and metal tablets; there was a brass box full of papyri, parchment, and yellowed paper covered with flourishes of faded ink. "They're in no particular order, are they?" Nash asked.

"I guess organization was not in any of our genes," Selene said with a sigh. "When you live here, Nash, you can put them into some sort of order."

"Live here?" Nash said quietly. He turned around, and Dulcey watched as a tear trickled down his face.

"Will you live here too?" Tanju asked Selene.

"No. There is nothing for me here. I have a busy life in Ankara, and you know how much I hate this place after all it has cost my family." Selene smiled through her own tears. "My way of honoring the memory of my family is to let some light into this lonely house. Can you all understand that?"

Everyone nodded. They were silent, steeped in thoughts of irony and destiny.

Selene took a deep breath and handed Asena's big ring of keys to Dr. Nash. "And so, with Tanju and Dulcey as my witnesses, and in keeping with my desire to open this house up and let in the light, I'm asking Dr. Nash to live here and study Zeugma. Someday, he can turn the house into a museum if he chooses to do so."

Nash's expression was grim. He reached for the back of an old Ottoman-era chair to steady himself. "Why couldn't Asena have shared all this with me?"

"I have no answer to that," Selene said to the somber man before her.

"Sit here, Nash." Dulcey helped her father sit down in the old Ottoman chair and put her arm around his shoulders to comfort him.

Nash put his hands to his face and was silent for a long time. "Just when I thought I was beginning to understand some things . . ."

"What about the mountain of gold mosaic?" Dulcey asked Selene. "Anyone who acquires it could start a world war, right? What will become of it?"

Selene put her hand on Tanju's shoulder. "Tanju and I have already talked about what to do with this dangerous mosaic. We are going to make it our solemn duty never to let it fall into the wrong hands."

Tanju nodded in agreement. "There are some women in Tilmusa who can be trusted completely with the mosaic. Do you remember those exposed floorboards in the new minaret?"

Dulcey grinned, fingering the healing scar on her neck. "How could I forget them? Eighteen steps on plaster, eighteen on bare wood."

"Turkan and Zeynep already have those floorboards pried up, and a fresh bucket of plaster is waiting in the new minaret. We're going to bury the mosaic in the minaret tonight after everything settles down."

"But won't the imam or Hajji Kerim find it—or the men who pray there?" Dulcey asked.

Selene and Tanju gave one another a knowing look. Tanju said, "We have you to thank for that. The men say your voice desecrated the mosque, and all the men of Tilmusa have refused to pray there ever since. The women asked Hajji Kerim if they could turn it into a women's mosque and let the men share the old one. No one seemed to have a problem with that arrangement, so the new mosque has been turned over to the women of Tilmusa."

"My voice desecrated it?"

Tanju smiled at the American whose ways were so different from her own. "The voice of a woman is *haram,* or forbidden, in Islam—especially in a mosque. But you American women are so . . . so . . . uppity. You ruined that mosque for any self-respecting man when you spoke over the muezzin's microphone."

"Thank goodness for uppity Americans," Selene said, hooking one arm through Tanju's and putting her other arm around the shoulders of the bewildered Dulcey. "I believe it was your destiny, *arkadash.* It gave the women of Tilmusa a place of their own—and a safe place for the mosaic."

* * *

Dulcey's mind swam through a sea of emotions as she prepared to leave Zeugma that night. *Yavash, yavash,* she reminded herself as she packed the last of her belongings in her big rolling bag.

Nash stayed with her as she packed. "Need anything?"

"No, I didn't bring very much. I wish I could have found a souvenir for Izzy and Michael though." There was an uncomfortable silence between them. A soldier came in to take Dulcey's bag to the helicopter. When he left, Dulcey asked, "How do you feel about staying here in Asena's house?"

"I'd have been happier if Asena were here with me," Nash said sadly. "This house is what kept us apart—she couldn't trust me with her secrets. She never truly believed I loved her for herself."

"Maybe it's a place you can still feel close to her," Dulcey said. "There's a lot that can be done here. And Selene will back you all the way. You can do it all in honor of Asena Özturk."

"It'll take years just to find all the rooms in this house. I had no idea, no idea, what was in this place. Like everyone else, I was fooled by the way it looked from the outside. I never once suspected what was in this house."

Dulcey walked with Nash toward the front door. "Cantwell told me the CIA donated the five hundred thousand dollars al Qaeda paid for the goddess to your work at Zeugma. That should get you started here," Dulcey said.

"Yeah, how about that? I get one of my largest donation ever from a bunch of bloodthirsty terrorists." He smiled and combed his fingers through his hair.

Despite the noise and commotion all around them, Dulcey looked steadily into Nash's face. His eyes looked tired, and she noticed for the first time that they were the same shade of green as her own. "You're coming to the States for a conference sometime this year, right?" Dulcey asked, her voice cracking around the edges. "I'd like you to come for longer than you normally do—to meet Matt and the kids, GramMaria and Poppie, and all our friends."

"I'd like that," Nash said softly.

The two of them stood there for a moment, as though they'd just been formally introduced. Dulcey had the feeling they were starting over again.

At that moment Ibo tottered through the front door, bleating for his bottle, and settled on the floor at Dulcey's feet. She picked him up and scratched behind his ears, grateful for something to do with her hands. "We're saying everything but the important things, aren't we, Nash? You're my father. I'm your daughter. What are we going to do about that?" She avoided his eyes.

Nash patted the goat instead of looking at her. "I don't know. I've never been in this situation before. I'll bet not too many people have been in our situation."

Meltem appeared then and handed Dulcey a warm bottle of milk for Ibo. Dulcey cuddled the goat in the crook of her arm and popped the bottle into its mouth. Without realizing it, she began to sway from side to side as she had done when Michael was a baby. Ibo's eyes drooped as he swallowed his milk.

"Let's take this slowly. I think we have a lot to learn from each other," Nash said. His face looked pained now. "May I ask you one last thing?"

"Sure, Nash. And I hope it's not the last thing you'll ever ask me," Dulcey said.

"What changed your mind about me? What made you stop hating me and begin to trust me?"

Dulcey thought for a second, squinting and looking inside herself, tracing the exact moment when Nash had changed in her eyes. "The others had convinced me that you were innocent of a crime, but that wasn't the same as trust. It was when you gave away the goddess. When you sacrificed her to save me . . . and the others. I watched you give away what you loved the most."

"That was an easy trade—a golden goddess for the life of my daughter and my friends."

"It was an act of *love*," Dulcey said. "For me, for Asena, and the others. And you made your decision without even hesitating."

Nash reached over and rubbed the belly of the little goat. "Hmm . . . Imagine me loving anyone enough that they would notice."

"You chose me over something I know you love. And I *dare* you to say you did it because I'm carrying your DNA. You also did it for Frank, Asena, Tanju—and for Mehmet, who had been forced to betray you."

Nash laughed. "Dulcey, love is something I know very little about. And you're right, what I felt about the goddess definitely had to be love, because she has no one's DNA inside her."

Dulcey smiled and whispered, "That's right. And neither of my children carry my genes either. But I don't doubt that I love them with every ounce of my being."

"It makes me believe there's hope for the world if people can love what's not their own. It means they can love people who aren't in their own tribes. And that means there's a chance for the world to live in peace."

Ibo opened his eyes and bleated for more milk. Dulcey popped the bottle back into his mouth, and he sucked hungrily. "This little goat's making me miss my kids."

Nash smiled as he watched Dulcey snuggling the goat. "You know, the way humans love animals is even *more* proof that we can learn to care about beings that aren't in our own tribe . . . or even in our own species," Nash said and smiled.

Dulcey looked at Nash, memorizing him. His hat was folded and crammed into the front pocket of his grungy, highwater chinos. His T-shirt was from a 1973 Rose Bowl game. And the tops of both his socks were unraveling. *The man really needs a woman in his life,* thought Dulcey. Then she patted the front pocket of his T-shirt. "No smokes?"

"Gave 'em up on the day we excavated the goddess—figured I had too much to live for to go on smoking," Nash said, his cheeks reddening.

"So that's why you were so snippy with me that day—*live,* on international television."

"Yeah, I suppose. That, and I was about to sell a fake goddess to an al Qaeda terrorist, accept a five-hundred-thousand-dollar payment for it, cut my own forehead open, and knock myself unconscious with an overdose of sleeping pills."

"You're a piece of work," Dulcey told him, grinning.

* * *

It was time to leave. The blades of the helicopter were in full rotation, and Frank was already on board. Dulcey could see him settling into his seat and strapping his seat belt on, a look of utter relief on his big, lovable face.

Dulcey drew Nash toward her and kissed him on each cheek in the Turkish way. They held each other for a minute, awkwardly, little Ibo bleating between them. "E-mail me from the museum or call me, and we'll find a good time to meet in the U.S.," Dulcey said.

"Okay," Nash said, shifting from one foot to another. "I'll be in touch, and we'll make plans."

As Dulcey boarded the helicopter, she noticed that Hasan stood a short distance away holding a big bucket of water by its handle. Meltem stood nearby, holding Ibo in her arms, struggling to put the bottle into the little goat's mouth. Turkish soldiers stood at attention in the clearing next to the cemetery, shielding their eyes from the spinning dust.

Suddenly Meltem rushed forward, bending under the blades, shouting something in Turkish. Selene leaned through the side door of the chopper and shouted above the roar, "Dulcey! Meltem wonders if you would like to take Ibo to America. She says Ibo thinks he belongs to you."

Dulcey quickly calculated Matt's reaction to the addition of a baby goat to their burgeoning menagerie of house pets. She pictured Ibo in their backyard, keeping the grass around the swimming pool trimmed. Then she imagined how Michael and Izzy would squeal with delight at the little animal. Ibo could be the souvenir from Turkey she hadn't had time to buy. "Yes, I'll take him," Dulcey said, reaching out for the goat, refusing to acknowledge the shocked look on Frank's face.

When Meltem handed Dulcey the little goat, he nestled into her arms and took his bottle.

"I sure hope the Pentagon doesn't have a rule against goats on military planes," Frank grumbled. "Of course, by now the entire military must know you never listen to anyone."

Dulcey ignored him, but felt the little bone in her jaw twitching just a little.

As the helicopter rose into the air, Hasan swung the bucket back, then dashed water on the ground where the helicopter had been, shouting something they couldn't hear.

"Old Turkish custom," the pilot explained. "It means they hope, *inshallah,* that God will allow you to see each other again."

As the helicopter rose above Asena's house, Dulcey looked down at the cemetery. She could see the three fresh mounds of dirt, bouquets of flowers marking each one. The helicopter flew on over Belkis Tepe and hung like a lantern for a moment above the Euphrates. Dulcey looked down at the new mosque in Tilmusa, where she had called for help into the night sky. As they flew over the mosque, she saw Tanju get out of Nash's Humvee and lead a group of women toward the minaret. Tanju turned and looked up, then waved at the helicopter. The other women waved too. Dulcey saw Turkan with her baby and Zeynep, the woman who had sewn up Dulcey's neck wound. She saw other women who had been at the funerals, and yet others who had helped her escape from the minaret. She wondered how Asena and Grandmother Yildiz and generations of Özturk women would regard the new hiding place of their very precious mosaic. Would the mountain of gold now be safe from those who would seize power and subjugate the rest of the world? She wondered too how Islam's prophet might regard its new female protectors.

The minaret of the little mosque had once stood as a witness to Dulcey's deepest fears, but now all she could picture of the round room was the new plaster on the floor and the fresh paint on its walls—walls that went up and up and up and pointed toward God. *Steeples and minarets,* she thought. *Did they both point to the same creator of their shared universe? Did they both point to a Supreme Being who sat at an equal distance from all the humans who lived on this tiny ball of mud?*

Dulcey did not know the answers. All she knew in that moment was that her tribe was much, much larger than it had been when she had first come to Zeugma. She had found some of its members—and had lost others, whom she would miss dearly. And she knew that her life had been altered forever in this place.

As the helicopter banked toward the west, Dulcey felt a sweet stirring in her heart, like a key turning in a rusted lock. At that moment, she felt loved, essential—*golden.* Like a goddess who had been buried for a thousand years, she ascended up and up and up into a glorious galaxy of shimmering stars.

Truth or Imagination in *Missing Pieces*

Several people have asked me to include a section describing which parts of this novel are true and which are a product of my imagination. (Italicized words indicate words, phrases, or ideas from the novel.)

Turkey

All information in my novel reflects conditions and facts as they were during *October of 2003* at the beginning of the *Iraq war* (the time period and location in which this novel is set). Among countries with a majority Muslim population, Turkey is the only one with a secular, democratically elected government. As such, Turkey has become a microcosm in which to observe the conflicts between Islam and the West and other global issues. Turkey will be a key country to watch in the coming years as its Muslims wrestle with the text of the Koran and religious, democratic, and secular thought.

Baghdad

The theft of many *priceless historical artifacts* from the *Iraqi National Museum* during the fall of Baghdad was indeed a huge loss for Iraq and the world. Happily, many of these irreplaceable treasures were recovered in the months and years after the fall. *Mahmoud al-Imam* was the actual curator of the museum during this time.

The *Palestine Hotel* on the banks of the *Tigris River (in the Green Zone)* has always been a gathering place for journalists and military spokespersons.

The Wonders of Zeugma

The ancient city of *Zeugma* on the *Silk Road* is in actuality being excavated near *Nizip* in southeast Turkey. Luckily, it was found underneath an immense *pistachio orchard* rather than under an existing town or village. I remember the awe I felt at my first viewing of some of the *two-thousand-year-old mosaics and artifacts* that were coming out of the ground.

Although Zeugma is well established in history, modern archeologists were assisted in *discovering its location* when the *Birecik Dam* was built in the 1990s. My account of Zeugma is the result of many trips to the *excavation site*, the *Gaziantep Museum*, and conversations with many of the *excavators* who worked on the rescue operation called ZAP 2000. This emergency dig was directed by the Gaziantep Museum, the Birecik Dam, and the government's GAP Administration. It was funded by the Packard Humanities Institute (the *Randower Humanities Institute* in the novel). Currently, the water behind the dam has covered one third of the site, but the *five-million-dollar donation* from PHI saved many of the treasures that would have otherwise been lost under the water.

The *Mountain of Gold Mosaic* is actually called the *"Gypsy Girl"* and depicts a woman with a missing mouth and mysterious gaze. The background of this mosaic is made up of *stone tesserae* and not *golden nuggets* as in the novel. The mosaic has become a very popular icon in Turkey and is now referred to as the Mother Goddess, "Gaia." Although Greeks called Turkey *"Anatolia"* (meaning "land to the East"), Turks call this area of their country *"Anadolu,"* which means *"full of mothers."*

Zeugma does in fact boast an amazing *underground water system*, *Roman baths*, and numerous *fountains*. However, *Asena's palace home* is a product of my imagination. Every archeologist working this dig would love for it to have been real!

Woven goat hair was (and still is) a thriving enterprise in this part of Turkey. The Apostle Paul of *Tarsus, Turkey,* was a tentmaker and most likely used this material to make his tents.

At least three Christian structures were actually found at Zeugma, but Nash's wonderful *cathedral* is from my imagination. The flat top of *Belkis Tepe* (the large hill in Zeugma) is in truth the top of *Fortuna's*

Temple. Although no *golden statue* of the goddess has yet been found, *ground-penetrating radar* has located a thirteen-foot statue broken in several large pieces that is likely to be Fortuna. It is still unexcavated at this writing.

An *agora* (market), a *Roman fortress and baths,* a *cemetery,* a hippodrome, and *large villas with mosaic floors and frescoed walls* overlooking the Euphrates have already been discovered. All information about *Roman dress, hairstyles, and footwear of the statues* is accurate.

Although many of the mosaics and artifacts from Zeugma are displayed at the Gaziantep Museum, hundreds more are still undiscovered or unexcavated. The site is actually *littered with artifacts, pottery shards, and pieces of statues.* Under the direction of the University of Ankara, teams of excavators are currently exposing the city with the vision of one day building an open-air museum. The site is *four times the size of Pompeii.* All my information about *mosaics, frescoes, the "lost wax" process,* and the problems of *finding archeology that sheds light on the world's religions* is all true.

Early Christian, Jewish, and Islamic History

I tried to stay as true as possible when describing the *three major world religions that claim Abraham as the father of their faiths.* All three have roots in Turkey.

The "Mountain of Gold Prophecy" is real and can be found in the Bukhari Collection of the Hadith (Sayings of the Prophet) in Volume 9, Book 88, Saying 235. The Prophet Mohammed indeed warns against touching the mountain of gold when it is found in the Euphrates River, because it will cause war and bloodshed.

Turkish Food, Culture, and Honor Killings

All information about *Kurdish culture, dress, customs,* and the recent *fifteen-year period of terrorist activities by the PKK* is true. With the unrest in Iraq, many PKK separatists are again active in trying to create an area called Kurdistan as a homeland for the thirty million Kurds scattered around the world.

Turkish dancing, customs, and food are accurately described. *Turkish coffee grounds* are used for predicting the future. Many Westerners love the Mediterranean cuisine of Turkey.

Many Turks have a negative view of America because of the war in Iraq. In addition, many conservative Turks object to the "loose morals" of our society, I have heard several Turks mention the television shows *Ally McBeal*, *Sex and the City*, and *Buffy the Vampire Slayer* as the source of their negative views of American women. However, many more Turks—especially those who have visited or lived in the United States—admire our culture.

Honor killings are still practiced in southeast Turkey, although they are against Turkish law. *Thirty-six honor killings* occurred in the southeast during the year I was doing my research for this novel. One boy killed his sister because her male admirer dedicated a song to her on a radio program. The activist group *Hayat* (meaning "life") who attended Aysha's funeral is actually called "Kemer"—a group of women in Diyarbakir trying to eradicate honor killings and violence against women.

Honor is in actuality a driving force in this area of the world. However, no one in the world should condone any of the extreme acts sometimes committed in the name of honor.

About the Author

Photo by: Mire Images Photography

Jeni Grossman lived in Turkey with her husband from 2002 to 2004, after he received a Fulbright Scholarship to conduct research there. While living in Ankara, Jeni worked for an agency of the Prime Ministry that was responsible for building dams and for encouraging sustainable development in rural Turkey. The two-thousand-year-old city of Zeugma was discovered during the digging of one of these dams. Jeni also worked as a guest reporter for the *Turkish Daily News* and covered the Zeugma excavation. She won an international journalism prize for her newspaper series about Zeugma. She was sent to Kyoto, Japan, to receive the prize and also to write about the world's water issues as well as preserving cultural heritage during the digging of dams. Jeni has been a creative writing teacher and a legislative and educational activist.

Upon their return from Turkey, she and her husband and other friends founded an organization called "Tiny Peaces" that, among other projects, promotes the education of girls in rural Turkey and elsewhere. Go to www.tinypeaces.com to learn more. Jeni loves to read, travel to unusual places, and hike with her dogs in the Superstition Mountains near her Arizona home. She also loves to design, make, and sell beaded jewelry with her friends to raise money for Tiny Peaces scholarships.

Jeni is the bestselling author of *Beneath the Surface* (2000, Covenant) and *Behind the Scenes* (2001, Covenant). She welcomes your comments and messages at wordscreate@hotmail.com.